OUT FROM UNDER

Mark Carignan

This book is dedicated to the husbands, wives, and children of the 700,000 serving police officers in the United States. Yours is a silent, seldom acknowledged sacrifice, and the country owes you a debt of gratitude.

CHAPTER 1

New Hampshire State Police Detective Betsaida Diaz had no idea how close she would come to dying in the next five minutes.

Frustrated, she twisted her palms against squint-shut eyes. For the third time in as many days she stood on the rickety third-floor porch of 135 Lincoln Street. She lowered her hands and peered at her partner of the past six months.

Detective David Guthman blurted the first thing that came to mind.

"Sometimes I hate this fucking job," he said.

Diaz raised a judgmental brow. "Thanks for sharing. Knock again, would you?"

The two troopers were perched on a narrow wooden landing outside the one-bedroom apartment of Vincent T. Underwood, forty-three years old, white male, brown hair, brown eyes, medium build. The description was printed on the suspect detail card Guthman had received from his sergeant four days prior. Underwood had failed to register as a sex offender for the second time in two years. That failure warranted a visit from troopers assigned to the state police sex offender registry, rather than the city police.

As Guthman knocked again, Diaz peered over

the fragile bannister that wrapped around the cliff-like porch, held up by far fewer fasteners than the city building code required. She glanced again at Guthman and silently hoped the exterior network of loose stairs and rickety porches would hold their collective weight.

135 Lincoln Street was a large, box-like triple-decker containing six apartment units. It was nestled among dozens like it in a rundown, largely forgotten neighborhood of Manchester, New Hampshire, each maintained by its absentee landlord at a level just above that which would see it condemned.

Betsaida Diaz was an athletic, five-foot four-inch brunette with a slight Boston accent. Dressed in a conservative suit and practical shoes, she was towered over by her partner. Guthman was an awkwardly lean, six-foot two-inch German with tightly cut blond hair and bright blue eyes.

It was a cold, autumn afternoon and when the wind kicked up, the haphazard grid of sticks groaned beneath them. Diaz white knuckled the railing. Guthman, oblivious to it, rubbed the bridge of his nose in frustration as he beat the door again.

"He's not going to answer, Bets."

"Would you?" Diaz asked sarcastically.

The name Betsaida had been a gift from Diaz's grandmother, meaning 'house of fruit,' and implying abundance and success. The young woman embraced her heritage, but had grown tired of correcting people's mispronunciation. She had gone by Betsy since elementary school, which had organically devolved to Bets for those most familiar to her.

Just entering his tenth year with the New Hampshire State Police, David Guthman had hoped to be further along in his career. Assignment to the sex offender registry squad was lousy work, but had earned him a detective's badge. After a few years working the registry, one could usually move to other investigative bureaus such as property or violent crime. During his six years on the unit, Guthman had been denied such a transfer four times. He'd had three different partners and each had come in, done their time, then moved on. Diaz was the latest.

The frustrated detective unzipped the top half of his North Face jacket and stuffed his hand into the inside pocket. He pulled out a tri-folded sheet of paper and needlessly read it again.

"135 Lincoln Street. It's not going to change," said Diaz. "I think you take this shit too seriously. He's either here or he's not."

"Rookie," muttered Guthman. He did not look up from reading to see Diaz's one-fingered response.

"Rookie my ass, Guthman."

"It says here," he said, pointing to the center of the paper, "that sometimes in the afternoon he'll..."

Guthman's words were blunted by Diaz's shoulder slamming into his chest and shoving him out of the way. She was halfway down the first flight of stairs before he heard her yell "Runner! Runner!"

With police-partner reflex, Guthman sprinted after her without yet knowing why. His awkward stride carried him down two flights of stairs before he fully considered what he was doing. On the first-floor landing he looked over and saw Vincent T. Underwood climbing a chain link fence on the other side of the parking lot. Diaz gave chase, sprinting across the lot and catching up fast.

Guthman yanked out his cell phone and yelled for Siri to dial the local police dispatch. He watched Diaz veer to the right, opting to go around the fence rather than over it. His call connected on the second ring.

"Manchester police, Dispatcher Franklin," came the speedy greeting at the other end of the line. After eight years of saying it 100-150 times per day, it came out more as *Manster Plees, Spatcher Franklin.*

"This is Detective Trooper David Guthman, NHSP, badge number 696. My partner and I are in foot pursuit of a sex offender suspect. We are headed north on Lincoln Street toward Valley. Both officers are in plain clothes."

Guthman had included the last comment as insurance against responding patrol officers accidentally detaining him or Diaz instead of the suspect.

"The suspect is in blue jeans and a light-colored sweatshirt," he concluded. Guthman didn't hang up, so the call could be tracked, and slipped the device back into his pocket.

As a former University of Massachusetts Division-One track star and alternate to the 2016 US summer Olympic team, Diaz knew she had Underwood in the bag before they were ten yards across the parking lot. The suspect deftly cleared another eight-foot fence with the skill of a man experienced at such things. He continued north on Lincoln until he realized his pursuer, despite having taken the longer route, was gaining steadily.

Diaz saw Underwood make a quick right through a yard toward Hayward Street and started making mental notes.

Hayward.

He darted right onto Wilson, cutting off a turning car that had to slam on its brakes and jump the curb to avoid hitting him.

South on Wilson.

Fifty yards after joining Wilson, Underwood cut left onto the narrow, one-way Prescott Street.

This guy isn't just running. He knows where he's going, thought Diaz.

Diaz pulled up short and slowed when she turned onto Prescott and could no longer see Underwood. She reached into her left pants pocket and found it empty. She patted herself down – front pockets and back, then the breast pockets of her coat. Her phone was gone. She glanced around the immediate area, hoping it had somehow dropped just the moment before. She knew it was futile.

"Shit!"

The sound of crashing metal interrupted Diaz's frustration. A hundred feet down the street an alley cut to the left. She rounded the corner and noted the dead end. Two steel dumpsters on the left stood guard at the alley's mouth. Each was filled with restaurant waste and surrounded by overstuffed black bags. Half-way down the right side was a five-foot pile of wooden boxes, mostly vegetable crates from the back of a pizza parlor. The alley itself was littered with beer cans, broken glass, and a few scattered hypodermic needles.

For no reason other than disbelief at her bad luck, Diaz reached into her pocket again. The sound of approaching sirens bounced off buildings, but the urban environment made it difficult to gauge their distance. Regardless of how far out they were, she knew backup was on the way.

Diaz drew her weapon, a Smith and Wesson compact .45. She stepped into the alley and moved forward, the light from the street's entrance fading behind her. The buildings growing out of the pavement were twenty feet across from one another and blocked the midday sun. It grew cooler as she progressed deeper into the cave-like passage. A chill crept through her as sweat from running glued her blouse against her uncomfortably.

Her weapon at the ready, Diaz had cleared one dumpster, the pile of wooden crates, and was halfway down the alley when the downward blow from a pipe barely missed her head and crushed her right shoulder. The attack tore off a portion of her ear and splintered her scapula, driving bone fragments into the muscles of her upper back. She collapsed to her knees, pistol clattering to the ground.

Shock delayed Diaz's response long enough for Vincent Underwood to raise the four-foot pipe for another blow. She fell to her left and rolled in that direction, hoping to avoid the worst of it. The pipe impacted squarely on her right ankle, shattering tiny bones and pushing fragments through the skin on the other side.

Diaz hollered in pain as she curled and scrambled blindly to the right, feeling the lump of her gun beneath her. The pipe landed again, this time on her torso, snapping two ribs.

There was a brief reprieve as the panting Underwood adjusted his grip. His last swing had been so forceful the greasy pipe had nearly slipped from his grasp. Diaz tried to move her right arm, but it did not respond. Breath came in short spasms as panic began to set in. Her left hand found the grip of her pistol and she turned onto her back to confront her attacker.

It was hard to focus, and Diaz waved the pistol back and forth, hesitant to fire at shapes and shadows. The sound of rusty hinges groaning under the weight of a metal door drew her attention to the right. Looking over, she noted a figure pulling it open. Diaz fired all nine rounds from her pistol at the figure, splintering a nearby wooden pallet and blasting chunks of brick from the building.

The weapon empty, she let its magazine drop to the ground, but was unable to reach the spare magazine on her belt. She hoped like hell Underwood had fled, or that some of her .45 caliber hollow-point rounds had struck him. She knew she didn't have much fight left.

No further blows came, and the alley grew quiet. Diaz allowed the empty gun to slip from her hand. The sirens faded, and she could feel her heartbeat in her ears and temples. Objects grew wooly around the edges.

Diaz forced her mind to slow as she tried to calm the panic. She took a deeper breath, but when her chest expanded, the jagged edge of a cracked rib scraped the soft tissue of her lung, pushing blood into her chest. She gasped, which generated a deep, guttural cough. She suppressed it, knowing the agony it would have brought.

Fear of drowning in her own blood generated another adrenaline dump, which temporarily dulled the pain and allowed her mind to wander. Cotton-white clouds in the sky began to fascinate her. One of them looked like a dragon. It was breathing down on her.

The pain continued to wane, and she grew warmer. It was a comfort, a welcome reprieve, but slowly grew terrifying as Diaz acknowledged its meaning. Forcing herself back into consciousness, she tried to move. When she bent her legs the ankle bones shifted, and searing pain melted through the joint. It was nearly intolerable, but served its purpose and sharpened her mind for a moment.

Diaz groped around for her gun and found it. The slide was locked back, emptied of bullets. She didn't recall firing the pistol.

The scene began to dissolve again as the pain ebbed. Diaz heard the squeal of braking tires and the crunch of gravel as they came to a sudden stop. Her head lolled to the side and looked up the alley, where she made out the black and white paint scheme of a Manchester police cruiser.

There was a man standing over her now, yelling. He moved her leg and Diaz tried to push him away. Her arm didn't move. She lifted her empty gun to him and he took it from her. She blinked the officer into focus. A second appeared, then a third. Diaz summoned the strength to point to the door through which Underwood had fled. It opened, and a stream of blue uniforms vanished inside.

Diaz decided she had done enough. Returning her gaze to the dragon in the sky, she allowed herself to pass out.

CHAPTER 2

Jessica Warner was an attractive and smart, if poorly educated, young woman of twenty-three. 'Smart' had gotten her through high school despite an absent mother and occasionally violent father. 'Attractive' had gotten her a new job as a bartender at Slice of Life Pizzeria with no experience beyond years of pouring drinks for her dad and his greasy, leering friends.

Jessica's second shift had started much better than her first. As she worked the lunch crowd the day before, one of the usual patrons had a heart attack in the middle of the rush. When he fell off his stool, he had knocked his half-full beer off the back of the bar and onto Jessica's white t-shirt. While the old man grasped his chest, clinging to life, some of the Neanderthals in the dive bar could not resist commenting on Jessica's now-damp shirt as it adhered to her chest. It had been hard to force herself back for a second day.

Yesterday's tragedy seemed to have cast a calming pall over the bar. Even the clods were keeping their hands to themselves. Jessica was in the process of pouring a shaken martini out of the tumbler when sharp cracking noises rose up from the alley.

"Goddamn kids and their Goddamn firecrackers!"

yelled the owner, Leon Stawicki, from the kitchen. Jessica had stopped mid-pour at the cracking, but put her head back down and resumed after the owner's comment. A muted chuckle came from the far end of the bar.

Jessica glanced down the bar to Steve, a hunched man who bore the weathered face of forty years despite his age of twenty-three. She did not yet know Steve, but according to Leon he usually came in at noon, drank steadily until three and left, drunk. He kept to himself, and had an odd habit of closing one eye and gently nibbling the rim of his glass before every sip. That much Jessica had noticed on her first day.

Leon had told her Steve was a veteran, and that he'd come back to the neighborhood for some reason after being in the army only two years.

"Not firecrackers, Ms. Warner," Steve said. She had no idea how he knew her last name. "I think you should get down behind that bar, and call 911."

Jessica looked at Steve in confusion. She cocked her head toward him and was about to reply when she heard Leon yell from the kitchen.

"Who the fuck are you? Get the hell out of my bar!"

There was the sound of flesh being struck and a body falling to the floor, then of metal pans clattering. The swinging door that led to the kitchen lurched violently open.

Vincent Underwood's wild eyes darted around the room. His gaze fell on Jessica and he lunged toward her, arms outstretched. Grabbing her hair with his left hand, he drove a fist into her face, chipping a tooth and bloodying her nose. She stood stunned and offered no resistance as his left arm slithered around her neck like a python. He cinched down hard, cutting off her airway as he scanned the counter for a weapon. He picked up a paring knife next to a pile of macerated limes.

Underwood stepped backward toward the end of the bar and kicked at the hinged counter top. An empty bottle and full shot glass clattered to the floor as the barrier bounced up twelve inches then crashed back down.

"Pick it up!" he hollered into Jessica's ear. She reached forward to lift the bar but her hand slipped and it slammed down again. Underwood slashed her ear with the knife, opening a vicious wound. Blood poured down her t-shirt like a spreading juice stain.

Jessica's shriek masked the sound of Steve dismounting his stool.

"Try it again, bitch," muttered Underwood into her dripping ear. She gripped the bar tightly this time and lifted. It rotated on the hinge to its apogee where a hold-stop clicked into place. Underwood dragged his victim out from behind the bar, kicked over a stool, and started moving toward the door.

Underwood had his hostage halfway to the exit when the heavy end of a pool cue struck him low, by the calf. Underwood's leg buckled and he let go of Jessica as he fell to one knee. Steve swung the weapon again. Underwood lifted his left arm and allowed the cue to hit the soft flesh between his ribs and hip. It hurt, but did no real damage.

Jessica stood, mouth agape at what occurred. Underwood wrapped his arm around the stick and yanked it toward him, off-balancing his assailant. He lunged forward with his right hand, the small blade in his grasp, and raked it hard across Steve's throat. His right arm was now extended past Steve's torso, and he moved it back, quickly slamming the knife in and out of the man's abdomen in quick succession. Two, three, four times.

Steve stumbled backward as blood leaked from his neck, but did not spurt. The slice had missed both the jugular and carotid arteries. The stab wounds in his diaphragm were a different story, and he struggled to draw breath with the shredded muscle below his lungs. A raspy gurgle erupted from his nose and mouth.

Underwood ran toward the door. He glanced at Jessica, but passed her by.

Manchester police officer Clarence Andrews knew that every cop in sector eight, upon hearing the 'shots fired' radio call in the same vicinity as a NHSP foot pursuit, would converge on the alley off Wilson street. Andrews instead went to the front of the building that backed up to the alley. Suspects didn't tend to stay in the same place for long.

As he slowed to a stop on Wilson Street, the officer saw a man stumble out the front door of Slice of Life Pizza. He was medium built with short hair and looked, for all intents and purposes, like any of the dozen working stiffs found in a mid-afternoon bar nursing drinks over lunch. Andrews gripped his pistol but kept it holstered as he walked toward the man.

"Lemme see the hands, Buddy."

Underwood held both hands out in front of him as he walked toward Officer Andrews. He was limping, and Andrews could make out what looked like fresh blood stains that had oozed, but not splattered, onto the collar of his shirt. The officer concluded incorrectly that it was the man's own blood, not someone else's. Andrews made a quick decision. Better to be safe.

"On the ground, now!" he yelled as he defeated the security features of his duty holster and drew his Glock. The man hesitated, then got down onto his knees. Andrews stepped forward.

"Officer, please," the man yelped weakly. "There's a friggin' lunatic in there with a knife. He already stabbed someone, I think. I tried to help! I, I, please! Get in there, Officer!"

"Where?" asked Andrews, looking beyond the man as he approached.

"In the pizza place. I don't know what he's doing. He just busted in from the back and started attacking people."

Andrews squinted his eyes. He scanned the area and saw no other black and whites around. Keying his radio mic, he said "812, are any other units on Wilson?"

A number of garbled responses came over the radio as several officers 'walked' on each other by keying their radios at the same time, effectively muting their transmissions. Andrews realized he was going to have to make this decision alone.

"Stay here," he ordered Underwood and walked quickly past. When he did, he pressed down hard on his shoulder. "Wait for another officer to show up. Tell him I went inside."

"Okay officer, I will. Hurry, please!"

Officer Andrews approached the glass door in front of The Slice of Life and peered inside. It was chaos. He heard screaming and saw a man on the floor with a woman over him, covered in blood. He burst into the room.

"Where is he?" Andrews demanded, ready to engage an attacker as he looked around the room.

Outside, Vincent Underwood jumped to his feet and jogged down Wilson Street, fighting through the pain Steve's pool cue had put in his calf. He cut through back yards, making sure to avoid any front doors and the chance of a doorbell camera. He ended up on Valley Street and slowed to a walk. Grabbing the bottom of his sweatshirt he pulled it over his head, flipping it inside out. The action turned the reversible shirt from light to dark, and Underwood slipped back into it.

He continued west to Pine Street and dodged into the Valley Cemetery. A panhandler asked him for money as he entered. Underwood ignored him, but plucked off the man's Red Sox cap and slapped it onto his own head. He was gone before the vagrant could get to his feet. Finding a path into the center of the grassy plots of the graveyard, Underwood disappeared into the city.

CHAPTER 3

Detective Jimmy Brennan of the Manchester police department had been an undercover cop for seven of his twelve years on the job. He sat slumped in the driver's seat of a black 2021 Dodge Charger. The New Jersey plates were registered to Enterprise Rentals under the name Doris McFadden of Portsmouth, NH. The rental was real. The name was not. If any of the suspects he was investigating tonight had a cop on the take who would run a license plate for them, he'd be covered.

Even though he worked in Manchester, tonight's investigation had brought Brennan to the back lot of a closed Burger King in Dover, New Hampshire. The city sat on the seacoast, sixty miles east of Manchester. Recent years had seen its population explode as educated technocrats fled Boston for lower housing costs and less traffic. The police department had grown as well, but still lacked the technical ability to mount undercover operations of the caliber Manchester police could. They had called for help, and Brennan's boss had obliged. Dover PD did, however, have a SWAT team and although not visible, they were present.

There were two targets of the late-night operation.

The first, Jorge Maria Lopez, sat in the passenger

seat of Brennan's car. He was a skinny, twenty-year-old mid-level drug runner for the Almighty Latin King Nation, west side Roxbury, Massachusetts. He'd started in the game as an awkward, knock-kneed ten-year-old. Daily, he had walked down Columbia Road in Dorchester from his grandmother's house to school. The matriarch had strict rules. No side streets, alleys, or cutting through yards. She'd seen enough boys gunned down in her neighborhood.

What she hadn't considered was that every day the route led young Jorge down Washington Street, and that brought him right up against the cracked asphalt and rusted basketball hoops of Jeremiah E. Burke High School. She didn't know that every day the Kings that played ball there taunted, gibed, and grilled the boy for the entirety of the 185 steps it took him to travel past the courts. Lopez knew. He had counted.

Jorge Lopez had managed to resist the recruitment efforts, even though the teasing, promises of money and girls, and commitment to protect him were endless. Like his grandmother, he had seen where that life would lead. That was until the boys in his sixth-grade class at the Bridge Boston Charter School learned that his middle name was Maria. It had been his mother's name. When she died during his birth, his grandmother had made him the young woman's namesake. She'd been raising him ever since.

Once it was out that the skinny kid that walked funny also had a girl's name, the bullying became relentless. Jorge held out for three weeks before finally walking onto the scarred courts near Jeremiah E. Burke and asking for help. The Kings had more than obliged.

The two worst bullies at Jorge's school were

beaten. One had an "M" for Maria branded on his forearm. The other's family had their front porch burned. No one from Bridge Boston Charter ever uttered the name Maria around Jorge again, and the Boston Almighty Latin King Nation had a loyal soldier for life.

The second target was State Corrections Officer Joshua Donner. Although the money from illegally selling guns was good, Donner was really there for the ego bump. He'd failed the physical fitness test to enlist in the Marine Corps three times and had yet to score high enough on any police exams to warrant an oral board interview. Working as a CO had been alright. At least he got to knock around the male inmates, and get away with patting the asses of females who were there on pre-trial bail.

That had gotten old quickly. Cons respected him because they had to. Donner spent a few months trading pills for oral sex from three female inmates before one of them told him her boyfriend on the outside was supposedly some big-time dealer. Donner had arranged a meet and started doing business with the man. After a year moving pills, he'd grown apathetic again and had moved into methamphetamine, then guns. Joshua Donner had built a respectable client base selling firearms to gang members from Boston and Hartford.

Detective Brennan took a final drag off his cigarette and flicked it out the window. He turned to Lopez, seated next to him, and said, "Your guy's an hour late."

"Yeah," Lopez replied as he tapped at his phone.

Five minutes later Brennan spoke again.

"I'm leaving." He put the running car into gear.

"C'mon now," Lopez muttered, shifting his weight in the seat. "He's coming."

"You know that how, Jefe?" Brennan asked. He had taken to calling Lopez 'Jefe,' or boss, soon after first buying heroin from him.

"Just relax. He'll be here. He's always late. Makes him feel in charge. Just let it go," Lopez answered.

The case had started a month ago, and Brennan had bought enough dope from Jorge Lopez to lock him up for ten years. The police were up on his phone, his girlfriend's phone, even his grandmother's. Boston PD had run surveillance on the gang member three times after Brennan purchased heroin from him. They had identified the ALKN stash house his supplier was using in Southie, Boston's now gentrified former Irish enclave. The case was a wrap.

Both agencies had been ready to pull the pin and lock up the players for conspiracy when, at the last planned buy, Lopez had mentioned guns. He said he'd been purchasing handguns and AR-15's from some 'fat-ass white boy' in Dover for the past four months. A couple of cell phone search warrants had allowed the police to identify that person as Joshua Donner. The arrests had been delayed and the case expanded.

Unlike drug cases, where suspects could buy or sell drugs and then be allowed to walk away until arrested later, gun cases were different. People who sold guns, who were willing to illegally deal tools of death to anyone that would pay, were too dangerous to allow to walk.

After tonight's buy, the entire case would come to a finale. Two Boston police SWAT teams were staged, one at Lopez's grandmother's house and the other at the Latin King stash house. A Dover SWAT team sat in a broken-down van on Route 16, which ran adjacent and right up against the Burger King parking lot. Only a two-foot guardrail and low shrub line separated the break-down lane and parking lot. The Dover team was ready to take down Lopez and Donner as soon as Brennan gave the signal. In Farmington, where Donner kept a small apartment, local police were ready to execute the final search warrant.

More than fifty police officers were collectively sitting by cell phones, tactical radios, and surveillance wires waiting for word from Brennan to act. It was his show. He was nervous, but steady. He'd been running UC operations long enough to know the final bust never went down exactly as planned. Tonight would prove no different.

CHAPTER 4

Brennan was about to give and leave up when a blacked-out Subaru WRX rolled into the parking lot. The gray car was slung low with slim-profile tires mounted on rims with weighted chrome covers. The covers didn't rotate, creating the illusion that the vehicle was scraping along the pavement. It was a mid-level sedan converted into a slick gangster car by someone who couldn't afford the real thing.

Every cop within a quarter mile knew Joshua Donner was behind the wheel. Three days earlier a Dover police sniper had crawled through the woods near his apartment complex and placed a court authorized GPS tracker under Donner's car. Earlier tonight, police had surveilled Donner as he went to a storage facility and loaded two large soft-sided suitcases into his trunk. Then the GPS had followed him here. There had been one stop, at a gas station, that wasn't witnessed by an eyes-on detective. It had lasted nine minutes forty-seven seconds. No one suspected a driver change.

The dark sedan pulled into the lot, made a loop, and slid back out. Joshua Donner was an amateur, but even beginners knew how to run an SDR – surveillance detection route. Brennan suspected the young man had no idea what he was actually looking for, but gave him credit for making the effort.

Five minutes later the WRX was back. It carved a slow arc through the lot, paused near a concrete light stanchion, and backed into a space fifty feet from Brennan. As soon as Donner killed his lights, Lopez reached for the door handle.

"Nah, man. Not yet," muttered Brennan. Lopez stunted his movement.

"S'up?" Lopez asked. Brennan did not respond, and Lopez assumed he was just being paranoid. That was fine with him. Despite his young age, the aspiring Latin King soldier had been in on dozens of deals, stabbed once, and arrested a half-dozen times. If the old man wanted to wait, they would wait.

What Detective Brennan was actually doing was awaiting confirmation Donner was in the car. It was impossible to see through the WRX's blacked out windows, but the police didn't need to see Donner to confirm it was him.

A civilian technician working for Manchester PD laid in the trunk of a specially converted sedan on the south side of the lot. The reverse lights had been removed, but their lenses kept in place and black-mirrored. This allowed him to see out, but did not make the lenses reflective in the dark night. Reflections attracted a second look, and that was something no surveillance technician wanted.

The technician held two devices, a FLIR GF335 self-cooled thermal imagery camera and a Spectra M-plus laser microphone. The heat-camera would detect the presence of a person in the vehicle. The cumulative outline it drew would be compared with other known profiles of Joshua Donner. He keyed his microphone and told the arrest team the data image was a match.

"And the breathing? Is it confirmed?" came the squelchy reply in his earpiece.

The technician had fired the laser microphone at the front window of the WRX. It detected vibrations of the window generated by even the most subtle sound, in this case Donner's breathing pattern. This data would be compared to the breathing profile on file from previous surveillance. That is, if it had worked.

"I got nothing," the technician muttered into the radio. "He's got music playing. That's all I'm picking up."

The sergeant in charge of the surveillance team hesitated five seconds, then made a decision.

"Scene command to all units, we're confirmed. The operation is a go."

A series of clicks came over a dozen radio headsets as the SWAT officers in the van and sniper on the roof all silently pressed their radio microphone buttons in acknowledgement. At the same time, a text was sent which caused Brennan's phone to silently vibrate in his pocket. He knew the signal.

"Okay," Brennan said to Lopez. "Let's go."

The two men got out and walked around the front of the Dodge. Sitting on the hood, Brennan lit a cigarette. Lopez stared at Donner's car while Brennan scanned the lot, feigning looking for a setup.

Joshua Donner's door popped open and the chubby, twenty-six year old corrections officer emerged. He wore too-tight jeans and a zipped-up jacket over a sweatshirt. His sneakers were loosely tied and splayed open in the style of teenagers ten years his junior.

Donner scanned the parking lot as he walked to Lopez. The men shook hands and pressed shoulders.

"Josh, this is Jimmy," Lopez said, gesturing to Brennan.

"What's up," said Donner. Brennan looked the man up and down.

"You ready?" Donner asked.

"Yeah man, we're good," replied Lopez.

"You?" Donner asked, nodding his head toward Brennan. The detective did not respond. He just continued staring. Donner shrugged and waved them toward his car, turning to lead the way.

Then Donner stopped midway through his second stride and turned back toward his prospective buyers. There was something he didn't like.

"You talk, Buddy?" he asked Brennan.

Brennan didn't break the gaze. It was a game, and he needed to play it right. "I'm not your Buddy, Son."

"Son?" Donner parroted with raised eyebrows. He took a step back, his hands at his side. He turned to the gang member who had set up the deal, then back at Brennan. "Did you call me son, old man?"

There was weight to the damp, cool night air, and it allowed the tension to float between them. Donner looked back at Lopez.

"Lopez, who is this old motherfucker you brought to me?" he asked.

Brennan didn't look away, and took his hands out of his pockets. Donner picked up on the gesture.

"You wanna step-to, old man?" Donner taunted as he took a step forward. When he did so he raised his arms to the side dramatically. This caused the front of his cropped jacket to raise slightly. Brennan caught sight of the butt of a pistol.

From day one, undercovers are taught to never

look at their surveillance team or backup officers. It causes other people to look as well, and that could draw the suspect's attention to them. Brennan knew this. He had been in countless undercover arrest situations, faced down real danger dozens of times. This time, he slipped.

After seeing the pistol, Brennan thumbed his nose like a boxer, and briefly glanced at the SWAT van parked on Route 16.

Donner's gaze followed.

"What the fuck was that?" he asked. When there was no response, Donner's eyes jackrabbited back and forth between Brennan and the van. He was wired.

Brennan noted how jumpy the kid was. He was on something.

Donner turned to Lopez. "You see that? Why's he looking at that van?"

Donner lifted his jacket, drew the pistol, and stared at Brennan. "Why'd you look at that van, old man?"

It took a moment for the initial adrenaline dump to dissipate into Brennan's blood stream. He caught his breath and focused on not reacting. It was imperative his face and body not betray the terror that flashed through his gut.

At the same time, a dozen hands gripped their rifles tighter. In the SWAT van, knees bounced as the members' muscles tensed in anticipation of the rescue order. Seventy yards away the sniper on the Burger King roof settled the reticle of his ATN Corp night vision scope onto Joshua Donner's right ear.

Knowing what was going through the mind of every officer on scene, the SWAT commander keyed his throat mic and said, "All units stand by. We have no rescue signal yet. Wait for my call."

Brennan mentally pulled up his plan of action. Donner was a low-speed gun runner trying to increase his street credibility. The young man's lack of experience and ground-level intellect made him all the more dangerous. If he didn't succeed, Brennan's only option would be to throw up the distress signal and hope like hell none of the bullets that started flying hit him. He spoke in a monotone voice, a little quieter than necessary.

"What're you gonna do with that, Son?" He gestured vaguely at the handgun.

Donner took another step forward. Tactically, it was foolish. He was well within 'grab range' for Brennan, who could have snatched the weapon and twisted it away. But the detective wasn't ready to do that yet.

"Don't fucking call me son," Donner growled. "You hear me, old man?"

Brennan squinted. This wasn't going well.

"Listen, Kid." Brennan hoped 'kid' would be less odious to Donner's ego. "Are you here to wave that thing around, or are you here to make some money?"

Donner glared at Brennan, then back at Lopez, who had taken a half-shuffle-step back. He'd done deals with Donner before and knew he was posturing. He had pulled the same shit the first time Lopez had bought from him.

Donner's face relaxing just perceptibly. "You know I'm no motherfuckin' joke, old man."

"I hear that. Respect," nodded Brennan. "I'm just here to take some hardware. Not making any friends today."

Donner sneered oddly, then his visage softened further. His mouth opened slightly, which provided a longer view of his front teeth. Brennan saw they were browning. One was chipped. The man's meth-mouth confirmed Brennan's suspicion. He was high on methamphetamine.

Donner unzipped his jacket, lifted the sweatshirt over his ample belly, and tucked the handgun back into his waistband. Brennan allowed his shoulders to go down a bit in relief, but it was too soon. Donner took an aggressive step forward and drove an index finger toward Brennan's face.

"We're not doing the deal here, *friend*," he said. "I don't like it. I don't know you, I don't know that van, or that fucking car over there." As he said the last, Donner gestured toward the vehicle from which the technician was conducting his electronic surveillance. Maybe this kid was sharper than his actions suggested, worried Brennan. If he had picked out the van and the electronics car, what else had he noticed?

There was no convincing Donner to stay. It wasn't a Netflix series where gun runners and drug dealers argued and convinced each other to change their minds. Once someone got spooked and a deal went bad, it was over. Brennan had one shot at saving it.

"I hear you, man," he said, lowering his gaze to feign submission. "You name the place. Gotta be tonight, though. I've got people on the other end." Brennan hoped referring to whoever he was selling the guns to would snap Donner out of the moment. He only partially succeeded.

Taking a step back and crossing his arms, the corpulent corrections officer jutted out his chin and squinted. He slapped at his pocket and felt his phone. Pulling it out he checked the time, then pointed to Lopez.

"IG in an hour," he muttered, referencing an Instagram message. Teenagers and movie stars weren't the only ones using the untraceable and anonymous platform. "I'll tell you where."

Looking at Brennan, Lopez raised an eyebrow, asking if that would work. Brennan considered his options, made a quick decision, then committed to it.

"Yeah, alright. But look, I gotta see something now. Show me a piece so I know you're not full of shit."

"This wasn't enough?" Donner growled, patting the front of his waistband. "You know I'm no punk."

"Any swinging-dick can get ahold of a handgun. I need to see something heavy." Brennan argued. He was there to buy AR-style assault rifles. If they were going to lock up Donner for the time he deserved, the prosecutor would demand automatic rifles, not handguns. "I gotta see some shit, or we walk."

In the eyes of the prosecutor and courts, possession of an illegal firearm with the intent to sell carried the same prison sentence as actually consummating the deal. All Brennan had to do was confirm Donner had transported the rifles to the lot. That overt act would be sufficient for an arrest.

It took Donner only a moment to decide. He turned and walked to his car, nodding his head toward it as he did. Brennan followed, the fluttering of adrenaline beginning to buzz again in his gut. As they walked, Donner slid a hand into his pocket and withdrew a small plastic device. He pressed buttons and the trunk of the WRX popped open.

The three men gathered behind the car. Donner lifted the trunk lid, reached in, and pushed a blanket aside. Beneath it were two large soft-sided suitcases. He unzipped one and peeled back its rough canvas cover, revealing the lower receiver of a Colt AR-15 rifle. Darkness prohibited a greater visual analysis, but Brennan could see there were several more beneath it. It was good enough.

"Good enough," Brennan said loudly and clearly as he took off the Boston Bruins ballcap he'd been wearing and ran his hand through his hair. He turned and walked at a steady pace back toward his car, leaving Jorge Lopez and Joshua Donner behind.

If Brennan had turned to look, he would have seen that his signal to the arrest team was not as subtle as he hoped. The suspects had noted something was off. Donner was lifting the front of his jacket and sweatshirt, revealing his handgun, when the first explosion detonated.

CHAPTER 5

Sierra-1, the call sign for the sniper on the Burger King roof, had radioed in as soon as Donner had lifted his trunk lid to show Brennan the rifles. Doing so had obscured all three men from his view.

"Sierra-1 is red. Say again, Sierra-1 has no shot."

As it turned out, that didn't matter. Once Brennan had given the signal, eight SWAT operators erupted from the back of the van and leaped over the short guardrail separating Route 16 from the Burger King lot. At the same time, two officers secreted in the shrubs adjacent to the drive-through tossed flashbangs into the lot on the opposite side of the emerging team.

Each explosion rocked the area with 170 decibel thunder, rolling across the pavement like a storm across the plains. The accompanying flashes shocked Donner's overexposed retinas. Brennan knew enough to close his eyes for the moment, and was unaffected.

Donner fumbled his pistol and it clattered to the pavement. Looking up through injured eyes, he made out eight heavily armed figures moving across the blacktop toward him. He ran for the car.

Once at the door, Donner tore it open and slammed his husky mass into the seat. He pressed the starter button and mashed his foot down on the accelerator. The front tires erupted in smoke as they gouged into the pavement, struggling for purchase.

When Donner had been arguing with Brennan, he had not seen a SWAT officer crawl up and place a miniature spike mat under his front right tire. As the wheel spun, it shredded itself and the vehicle lurched uncontrollably to the right. Donner tried hard to counter-steer but was too slow. The vehicle swept broadly across the parking lot and struck a concrete light stanchion twenty feet away. Steam poured from the mangled hood as metal steering components tore through radiator hoses. Donner sat for half-a-beat, stunned.

Outside the wrecked WRX, four SWAT officers converged. Two stood behind the vehicle, offset at forty-five-degree angles. With their M-4's at the ready, they could fire upon anyone that emerged from the vehicle without endangering other officers with a cross fire. A third officer was prepared to go hands-on should the suspect emerge unarmed. The fourth, carrying a twelve-gauge Remington 870 pump action shotgun, had an entirely different weapon at his disposal.

Donner only saw the contact officer and he appeared to have his rifle slung behind his left hip. His already muscular mass was enhanced by the bulky level III vest and a tactical helmet. And his hands were empty. The officer was heavily laden, and Donner concluded there was no way he would catch him in a foot chase.

As often happens to methamphetamine users under stress, Donner's body started acting before he fully realized what he had decided to do. He climbed from the car and lumbered off in a flat-out sprint. While forming the strings of a plan for his escape, Donner was struck with something that felt like it tore him in half.

The shotgun armed officer had fired an Axon Taser X-Rep shotgun shell. It left the barrel at 300 feet per second and flew with the accuracy of a BB gun, striking the fleeing suspect in the back of his left shoulder. Upon impact, the frontal probe penetrated and attached itself to Donner's jacket. Secondary electrodes ejected from the back of the projectile and fell downward, still attached by wires. When the falling electrodes contacted the back of Donner's churning legs it completed a circuit and the integrated battery unleashed a hell storm of electrical current. 50,000 volts tore through Donner's unsuspecting body. Waves of pain cascaded down his torso as every fiber locked in neuro-muscular incapacitation.

The current flowed for twenty seconds. When Donner's body stopped convulsing and cognition returned, he was in handcuffs.

Detective Brennan, upon hearing the first flash bang, had dropped to the ground. Donner was the priority, and he was confident SWAT had quickly taken him into custody. He looked across the pavement until he caught sight of Lopez. The gang-banger had wisely given up and submitted to arrest. He knew the deal. You don't resist SWAT unless you want to get hurt.

A SWAT operator with sergeant's stripes on his arm walked over to Brennan, who was still prone on the ground. He started handcuffing him as he spoke softly.

"I won't put 'em on too tight, Detective. Just enough to make it look good."

Brennan managed a grimace and snarl as he was hauled to his feet and dragged to a waiting cruiser. But he was smiling on the inside.

CHAPTER 6

Betsy Diaz's trip to the emergency department in the back of a Manchester police cruiser had been excruciating. The hard plastic seat was not built for comfort, particularly when occupied by a terribly injured trooper in a vehicle driven with erratic haste. But she had arrived at the hospital alive, was stabilized, and awaiting surgery.

The Special Care Unit of Elliot Hospital, located just off Tarrytown Road on Manchester's east side, was busier than usual when Detectives Charlie Wilcox and Donovan Mollie of the Manchester police department pressed the buzzer to be granted admittance. An inattentive nurse glanced casually at a surveillance monitor that showed who was at the door. She pressed a small button under the counter which activated a solenoid in the door frame, and a dull grinding noise inside the wall deactivated the lock.

Wilcox, an overweight black man in his late forties, was clad in a neatly pressed and well-tailored suit. He shouldered past the growing crowd of uniformed troopers and walked directly to the nurse's station. Mollie, a much younger and more daringly dressed Irishman, eased through the wake behind him. Once at the desk, they both smiled transparently at the woman who had toned them in.

"Diaz?" Wilcox asked.

The nurse looked up from her chart and saw the Manchester Police detective's badge twelve inches in front of her face.

"Over there," she replied with a head nod toward the troopers.

Wilcox leaned back and peered around Mollie to take a closer look at the throng of cops. Three-quarters of them were in uniform, the rest in suits. They were broken off further into smaller groups of three to four men. Each subset was chatting about the welfare of their fellow injured trooper, frustration with the wait, and what they would do to the suspect if *they* ever found him alone in an alley.

"Ma'am," Wilcox called quietly to the nurse. She did not look up. "Ma'am," he repeated, this time with a touch of authority. The only response was a raised index finger making the 'wait a moment' gesture as the woman continued writing on a chart. Wilcox raised his eyebrows and glanced at Mollie, who made an 'I dunno' look with his. They waited ten seconds. Twenty. The nurse's hand went down but she still didn't look up.

Wilcox adjusted his grip on the badge and rapped it hard against the fabricated plastic countertop.

"Ma'am," he said, louder than necessary given the clanking of the badge. The nurse adjusted her gaze upward, but not her head, and peered over her glasses.

"I told you," came her curt response. "Cops are waiting over there." She waved to her right with a pen, not averting her eyes from Wilcox. "This is a nurse's station, not a police department."

"Nurse," Wilcox tried again. "I'm Detective Wilcox with the police department. My purpose here today is to..."

"Yes, I know," the woman interrupted, putting her pen down loud enough for it to slap. Wilcox ignored the intrusion.

"No," he said. "I don't think you do." Wilcox extended his hand in a 'stop' fashion, still holding the badge between his thumb and index finger.

"Nurse..." he paused as he looked for her name tag, which was absent. He continued unabated. "I'm with the Manchester police, not the State police. We are here as the find-out-what-happened-and-arrest-the-bad-guy-who-did-it police. We are not the hang-around-and-wish-we-could-help-but-really-have-nothing-to-do police. I am here to speak to the victim in this assault. After that I intend to conduct an investigation and if that inquiry bears fruit, to charge the suspect with a crime. Now, can you please point me to Betsaida Diaz's room or should I ask someone else?"

The nurse held his gaze for five seconds before her face softened.

"Swanson," she said.

"Excuse me?"

"Nurse Swanson. I saw you looking for my tag." She held up the chart on which she was writing, which coincidentally was the medical chart of Detective Trooper Betsaida Diaz. She pointed to the name on the form, then moved her finger two inches across the top of the page to the box labelled 'Assigned Room.'

Charlie Wilcox grinned. "Thank you, Nurse Swanson."

"You're welcome Detective Wilcox," she replied.

Thirty seconds later the two men reached the end

of a long hallway and turned right.

"I detect another obstacle," muttered Wilcox as they approached the door to room 318. Mollie assumed he was referring to the uniformed trooper that stood next to the closed door, but Wilcox nodded subtly toward the man seated across the hall.

"That's David Grant. You know him?" Wilcox whispered as they approached. Mollie responded with a downturned mouth and head shake.

"He's an NHSP lieutenant, and if history holds, he's going to present a problem. We're going to have to deflate his ego a bit. Just follow my lead."

"You got it, Boss," Mollie replied. They took the last few steps and approached Grant, who was seated awkwardly in a plastic and chrome chair.

"Lieutenant," greeted Wilcox, his voice saccharin. "I'm glad you're here."

"Are you?" Lieutenant Grant replied as he shook hands with Wilcox.

"This is Detective Mollie. Don, this is State police Lieutenant Grant."

Grant ignored the introduction and continued to look at Wilcox. "Are you just here to say 'hi,' Charlie?"

"No. We caught this, actually," Wilcox responded as he nodded toward Diaz's room.

"Caught what?" Grant asked coldly.

Wilcox had no patience for the political aspects of police work, and he considered jurisdictional dick measuring to be the worst of it. A case should be assigned to the best qualified woman or man who could handle it, then obstacles removed while they investigated. It had become apparent that Lieutenant Grant was going to flex his muscles and put on a show about why NHSP should handle this case. Wilcox intended to put the man in his place.

Looking at his partner, Wilcox asked, "Don, are you sure you and Lieutenant Grant haven't met before?"

"Maybe," Mollie said, focusing his attention to Grant, an unnecessarily grandiose smile across his face. "Sir, I think we have met once. At 'death school' maybe? You taught the block on bugs."

Detective Mollie was referring to the New Hampshire Police Academy's introductory homicide investigator course, known colloquially as 'death school.' Grant had been a guest instructor.

"Entomology," Grant said flatly.

"Yeah, that's right. Entomology," Mollie repeated as he extended his hand to Grant. They shook perfunctorily.

"So, bugs," Mollie continued. "You still teaching that?"

"No."

Grant's annoyance with the conversation was apparent. He had no desire to talk about his career trajectory, particularly with some snot-nosed baby detective from a city police department. He thrust one hand into his pocket and held the other in front of his torso, gesturing toward Wilcox.

"Why is it again that the two of you are here?"

Mollie wasn't done yet.

"Not doing that anymore? How come? You still working homicides, Sir?"

Mollie's memory had since kicked in, and he knew full well that Lieutenant Grant had been transferred out of the elite major crimes unit six months earlier after the husband of one of his female subordinates had filed a complaint against him with the internal affairs bureau of the New Hampshire State Police. The complaint alleged that the father of the female detective's unborn child was in fact Grant, not the woman's husband.

A rapidly conducted internal investigation had resulted in no disciplinary action against Grant. However, he had been transferred to supervise the wildly unpopular sex offender registry unit. The unit, to which Betsy Diaz and David Guthman were assigned, did not investigate new crimes. They were widely considered to be babysitters, traversing the state checking on people who had already been caught by the 'real police.' If a detective from the SOR unit discovered a registrant had committed a new crime (other than not registering) they had to refer it to the proper bureau for investigation rather than doing it themselves.

"No," muttered Grant. "I'm running 'sex' now."

"Oh, good for you, Sir. That's important work. Rapes, child assaults, that sort of thing?" Mollie knew that was not what Grant had meant.

"I run the sex offender registry, Detective Mollie," said Grant.

"Oh." Mollie took on a look of feigned interest replacing the previously present smile. "Well hey, that's good too, I guess."

Silence fell over the three men as they stood uncomfortably. A few seconds passed, then Wilcox broke it.

"Did Burdeau call you?" he asked.

Grant struggled to summon the bravado and jurisdictional arrogance he had intended to show earlier. He just wanted to sit back down and wait for Diaz's family to arrive.

"Yeah, Wilcox," he muttered. "Burdeau called." Major Clinton Burdeau was the commander of the support services division of the NHSP. Beyond the captain who commanded the various divisions of state police detectives, Burdeau was Grant's boss.

"Good," replied Wilcox. "I was worried some of your guys might give us trouble on this." He paused long enough to glance over at the rows of troopers by the door. "I'm glad you're here to grease the skids."

Grant looked at Wilcox and Mollie in turn, indignant disgust on his face, but said nothing in response. The dick measuring was over, and good police work had won the day. Detective Mollie cut the tension.

"Where's Diaz's family coming in from?"

"Boston. They ought to be here in a few hours. You going to need Guthman, too?"

"You know we will," Wilcox stated, unwilling to cut the man any slack. "He around?"

Grant settled into his chair, communicating clearly that the conversation, and his willingness to help, had reached an end. As he picked up a magazine and flipped it open, he gestured toward the closed door of room 318.

Mollie and Wilcox looked at each other and turned to walk away.

"Poor bastard," Mollie muttered. "To end up on that shitty unit after twenty-five years on the job."

"He made his own bed," asserted Wilcox. "There are no victims on this job. But there sure as hell are a lot of dumb decisions."

"Vincent Underwood," Betsaida Diaz declared with authority.

"You're certain?" asked Wilcox.

"Positive."

Don Mollie was scribbling furiously in this notebook as his partner interviewed the trooper.

"To what do you attribute your certainty?" asked Wilcox.

Diaz was exhausted, and in pain, and under the influence of a cocktail of opioids that blunted the ache, but not her frustrated temper.

"Can we do this later?" she asked. "I hurt like hell."

"Yes, absolutely," Wilcox agreed. "The details can come later, but right now we require sufficient information from you to establish probable cause for the assault. That way I can seek an arrest warrant and we can cast a broad net for the man."

"Fine," she said. "I know what he looks like from the pictures we had, and I chased him into the alley. It was him."

"Did you see the person that struck you?"

"What?" she responded.

Wilcox repeated the question. "How can you be certain it was Underwood who actually assaulted you?"

Her stretched patience began to fray.

"Who the hell else would it have been? I saw the guy run into that alley, and I went after him. Fifteen seconds later I was unconscious on the ground."

"Fair enough," said Wilcox as he closed his notebook. He turned to Mollie. "I think we've got enough for now. You get some rest, Diaz."

"Was anyone else in the alley?" pressed Mollie, ignoring his partner.

Diaz shook her head and looked away.

"Something wrong with my question, Trooper?"

Mollie challenged. He didn't like the resistance they were getting from her.

"Yeah, there is. It's a stupid question. I would have told you if someone else was in the alley."

"How would we know that, Diaz?" Mollie asked. "You're also the woman who decided it was a good idea to go into that alley by yourself in the first place."

"What the hell is that supposed to mean?"

"You tell me. Maybe you weren't thinking straight," said Mollie.

"Not thinking because I was chasing a suspect? Or not thinking because I'm a woman?"

"Hey, you said it. I didn't," Mollie said smugly.

"What are you, in junior high?" she said.

"That's enough, Don. Let's go," said Wilcox.

"Did you have something to prove out there, Diaz?" Mollie continued. "Trying to show your partner how you could handle Underwood without waiting for his help?"

Diaz shook her head and looked at the wall, battling tears. She cleared her throat and spoke again.

"I'm done here. Come back another time."

The room was silent for a few seconds before Wilcox spoke. He looked at his partner.

"Don, would you excuse us for a few minutes."

"Why?" the younger detective asked.

Wilcox raised his eyebrows and gave Mollie a look that demanded compliance.

"Whatever," Mollie said as he folded his notebook, opened the door, and stepped out. There was a hissing sound from the pneumatic retractor as the heavy wooden door closed. It contacted the jamb, paused, then clicked secure.

Wilcox walked across the room and sat in a chair near Diaz's bed.

"He's not a bad kid," he said.

Diaz gave Wilcox a withering look. "Right. And I'm sure he jumped for fucking joy when he saw he was partnered with you," she said.

"Are you implying my partner is less than happy to be working with a black man?" Wilcox asked.

"I'm implying your partner is an asshole."

Wilcox smiled, but said nothing. He liked the trooper's spirit.

"Clearly he doesn't think women should be on the job," she continued. "Racism isn't usually far behind."

"I assure you, that's not the case with Detective Mollie," Wilcox said.

"Yeah, well maybe you just haven't noticed."

Wilcox adjusted in the chair as he stared unabashedly at Diaz.

"I've been on this job for twenty-seven years," he began, "And a detective for the past fourteen. I started out working financial crimes. All that were assigned to me were bad checks and small-scale embezzlements, most likely because the racist son-of-a-bitch who ran my unit at the time was not going to let some nigger detective work what he thought of as 'real cases' that actually mattered."

At the sound of the epithet, Diaz's eyes flashed to Wilcox before quickly returning to the ceiling.

"As I'm sure you have figured out, I now work major violent crimes. That progression was neither easy nor linear. Over the decades I have seen admirable performers ignored, and substandard workers promoted. That is not always the case, but it happens. So, allow me to disabuse you of the notion that this job is fair, or that I do not believe there is rampant racism within it. I clawed my way to this position, and do not assume for a moment that bigoted bosses didn't stand in my way. So, when I inform you Mollie is not a racist, I know what I'm talking about."

"Well," Diaz said. "He clearly thinks having women on the job is a mistake."

"All evidence to the contrary," Wilcox said.

Diaz gave him a questioning look.

"You've performed exceptionally well today, Diaz. You bravely pursued a suspect, survived a brutal attack, and provided a detailed description of him to the responding officers. Then when they tried to put you in a police cruiser to drive you here, you pushed them away and attempted to go into that restaurant and keep chasing Underwood, despite the fact that you couldn't even stand. It required several officers to convince you otherwise."

Diaz furrowed her brow. She did not remember doing that.

As if reading her mind, Wilcox said, "Severe physical trauma sometimes affects judgement. And memory."

Diaz grunted, but didn't respond.

"May I call you by your given name?" Wilcox asked.

"Betsy. Call me Betsy."

"Are you certain?" Wilcox asked. "Betsaida is a lovely name."

"Yeah, I'm certain. In a state full of white cops, it's just a lot easier," Diaz said. She then looked at the heavyset black detective before her and realized the awkwardness of her assertion.

"Sorry," she said lamely.

"Not at all, Betsy. Perhaps, as we work together, we will find that a fat black detective in the twilight of his career and an aggressive Puerto Rican trooper at the dawn of hers might in fact have much in common."

Diaz chuckled, which hurt her ribs. She winced, then said "Do you always talk like that? So formally?"

"Yes, why?" Wilcox said flatly as he reopened his notebook. "Now, can we move forward with your statement, so the docs here can get you squared away?"

"Sure," she said.

"And by way of advice," he added. "Don't think for a minute that your success in this case is going to magically end misogyny in police work. This job is a marathon, Betsy, not a sprint. Your work today was far beyond what I would expect of any of the simpletons milling about that hallway. I see no reason for you to allow self-pity to get in the way of you continuing that work. You have much to be proud of, and have to move past it."

"Maybe they should be the ones to get past it," Diaz said. "I'm not the one with the problem."

"Indeed."

Forty-minutes later Detectives Wilcox and Mollie walked through the sunny parking lot full of state police vehicles to their own unmarked car, parked in the back.

"Back to the house?" Mollie asked, referring to the police station as he pressed the button to unlock the car.

"Lunch," was the one-word reply from his partner.

"I brought something," said Mollie.

"Well, aren't you the pinnacle of health," Wilcox teased. "I'll grab something on the way. I want to head back and get with the registry on where Underwood's mother resides."

"Why mom? You don't want to see what the neighborhood canvass showed first?" asked Mollie.

"The canvass is going to give us nothing. Underwood has been running his entire life, and he's good at it. Too good to have let some grandmother out hanging laundry on Valley Street get a good look at him walking away from a crime scene."

"Okay, then. Mom, I guess?"

"Mom," Wilcox repeated decisively. "Everyone's got a mom."

CHAPTER 7

Detective Charlie Wilcox fully intended to conduct a comprehensive investigation into the assault of Detective Trooper Betsy Diaz. That in and of itself would take weeks. In addition to interviews of the troopers involved and every responding Manchester police officer, the detectives would conduct background checks on each person who'd been in the Slice of Life Pizzeria the moment Vincent Underwood had burst onto the scene.

They would retrace the route Underwood had fled, knocking on every door he had passed. There would be endless coordination with the state forensic laboratory and county prosecutor. An insatiable desire for information from the media would be matched only by relentless demands for updates from the Manchester police command staff. Without a doubt, they were going to be busy.

Wilcox knew that despite these pressures, developing a plenary case would have to occur in concert with efforts to locate Vincent Underwood. The litany of investigative tasks could be delayed a day or two, or delegated to other detectives. But the search for Vincent Underwood had to ascend to the top of the list. The violent sex offender would now be feverishly planning and stealing to set up his out. If he wasn't picked up soon, he'd be gone.

Mollie had conducted a search of prison records to discover who had previously visited Underwood when he was incarcerated, and found a name. The same woman had bailed him out when he was first arrested for a sex offense at age twenty-six. Even violent sex offenders had a mother.

Charlie Wilcox was car sick. They had been driving down River Road, a long, windy, poorly maintained macadam street that connected Route 114 to 149, just west of Concord. The neighborhood was dotted with poorly maintained ranch homes and trailers, the latter making up the majority of homesteads. Don Mollie estimated they were getting close to number fourteen-fifty-three and stomped on the brakes.

"I think this is it," Mollie said. "The last box with a number was thirteen-eighty and it was a half-mile ago." The younger detective turned his head to Wilcox for some kind of response, but received none. Wilcox's stomach-stabilizing stare out the front window prevented him from looking sideward.

The road narrowed severely and gave way to a dirt driveway on the left. A brand-new mailbox was nailed to a weather-worn four-by-four post that had been driven into the ground. A crushed and rusty mailbox lay nearby.

"No numbers," said Mollie. "And they didn't even bother to pick up the old one." He steered to the side of the road and stopped. Pulling a long, thin notebook from his breast pocket and flipping to a marked page, he checked to confirm the address.

"This is it," grumbled Wilcox as he opened the

door and stepped out.

"Lemme double check."

"This is it," Wilcox repeated. The monotony of his voice betrayed his frustration.

Mollie flipped the notebook closed and shut down the vehicle. He hopped out and followed Wilcox, struggling to find the opening of a breast pocket to reinsert the notebook as he jogged after his partner. Wilcox was halfway up the cratered driveway by the time Mollie reached him.

"You think he might be in there?" Mollie asked.

"Well, now that I no longer need to concern myself with becoming nauseous from your driving, I can focus on that very question."

"Is that what's bothering you?" Mollie asked with a chuckle.

"There's no reason to drive like a teenager showing off for your friends. You're a detective. You should be thinking about the case, how we're going to go at Underwood's mom, not driving like you're trying to impress your high school girlfriend."

"Whatever," said Mollie. "It's a car, okay? It's fun to drive."

"I understand. Perhaps it's a generational difference in our approach to the job." Wilcox said. "Let's just focus on the case, shall we?"

"Yes, we *shall*," Mollie said, mocking him. He broke into a smile. "I was starting to worry you were really mad. That we were going to break up or something." He patted his partner's shoulder tenderly.

Wilcox ignored the comment.

"To answer your initial inquiry, no. Underwood is not going to be in here."

A 2015 Ford Taurus, green, with bald tires and a duct-taped black trash bag for a rear window was parked haphazardly on the right side of the driveway. The transmission from a pickup truck and part of the rear axle had been swallowed by overgrown weeds. A lawnmower handle peeked out of the growth like an arm grasping for freedom.

They arrived at the trailer, and Wilcox placed his foot on the first step of the rickety landing that led to the front door. He added weight gradually, convincing himself the contraption was safe. Mollie stayed at the bottom, alternating his gaze between his partner and the front windows.

The banter was over. They were switched on.

The rusted-out screen door was designed to open outward, and there was a hole where the knob had been. Wilcox fingered the edge near the jamb in an effort to gain purchase and tug it open. Looking suspiciously at the knob hole, he considered inserting his finger and pulling, then decided against it. Finally, in frustration, he just rapped noisily on the metal door.

"What?" barked a woman's voice.

"Police, Ma'am," Wilcox replied. "May we come in, please?"

"He ain't here."

"I know that, Ma'am. That's not why we came. We're here for you."

Both detectives heard a soft flopping sound followed by a 'meow' as someone eased a cat onto the floor. Then came the groan of couch springs, and footsteps. Wilcox gestured with a head nod for Mollie to go around the back of the trailer.

"I ain't done nothing," the voice muttered. The

sound dynamic made it clear she had moved closer to the door.

"Yes, Ma'am. We know that. We just need to talk to you."

Wilcox heard a deadbolt, then the movement of a hotel-style privacy chain. Mollie had turned and started moving around the house. Wilcox snapped his fingers as a signal for him to return.

The front door opened and Lorraine Underwood pushed the screen door out, striking Wilcox's foot.

"What do you want?"

"May we come in?" he repeated. "We'd like to talk to you about your son."

"I told you, he's not here. You wanna search again?"

"As I said, we know that," Wilcox responded. "Another search is not necessary. I'm quite certain the state police did a fine job. But we do need to come in and talk to you."

Lorraine did not answer. Instead, she turned, left the doorway, and walked deeper into the trailer.

"At least you guys asked. Fucking troopers barged right in. Tore the place up good, too."

Wilcox stepped forward onto the worn red carpet as Mollie started up the stairs. Mrs. Underwood had stopped and turned by that point, and as he entered, Detective Mollie held up his badge in her general direction.

"You should ask for ID when someone comes to your house and claims to be the police, Lorraine," he said.

"Son, the only people that come out here dressed like you two are cops. Except for last week when some asshole from the bank came to tell me they're going to take that piece of shit back." Lorraine gestured toward the Ford in the driveway.

The woman pointed at a couch with broken supports. Its structure was collapsed, and the cushions nearly rested on the floor. The upholstery was a patchwork of bare fabric and cat hair. Mollie saw a wooden kitchen chair next to an end table and made for it. Wilcox beat him and smiled as he settled onto the hard, non-porous seat.

"Have a seat, Don," smiled Wilcox, waving at the couch as Lorraine flopped down and a cat leaped onto her lap. Mollie glowered at Wilcox and sat gingerly on the edge of the sofa.

"I'm Charlie Wilcox and this is Don Mollie. We're with Manchester PD."

Lorraine looked back and forth between them, confused.

"Why Manchester? Like I said, state police were out here a few days ago looking for Vincent. They said he hadn't been registering. That he had skipped out on his parole. What the hell does Manchester care about him? Don't you people talk to each other?"

Wilcox winked at Mollie, then turned back to Lorraine. "Actually, no. Not very much," he answered honestly. "But that's not why we're here."

"Lorraine, Vincent got himself into a lot of trouble," Mollie said. "And we need to find him. We need to find him soon before he hurts someone else or gets himself killed."

Lorraine made a doubtful face. "How's he gonna get himself killed, Detective..."

"Mollie," he provided.

"Yeah. Detective Mollie. How the hell's Vincent

gonna get himself killed? He's pretty smart."

"He hurt a trooper, Mrs. Underwood, very badly. Someone else, too, while he was escaping. We want to make sure your son gets brought in safely."

Lorraine grabbed a soft pack of cigarettes from the end table and stabbed two stubby fingers into it. She came out with a half-smoked butt and jammed it between her lips. Grabbing a lighter from the coffee table she lit up, inhaled deeply, and pushed out a cloud of blue-gray smoke onto the cat. She took another drag, clamped the cigarette between her fingers, and put her hand on her knee. She stared blankly at both men.

"Anything else, fellas?"

"We want him brought in safe," Mollie repeated.

Lorraine cocked her head and focused through pinched eyes.

"Yeah, I heard you say that," she said accusingly. "So, bring him in safe then. What do you need me for?"

Wilcox cleared his throat to get Lorraine's attention and leaned forward, placing his elbows on his knees, hands together in front of him.

"Lorraine, this is a different kind of situation, and perhaps one with which you are not familiar. We know that Vincent has gotten into his fair share of trouble over the years. And we know you have been there with him throughout most of it. In the past, police have been able to pick up Vincent without much fanfare. He has a few assault convictions, but rarely for fighting with the police. And I know you assisted in finding him once, a few years back."

"That was different," Lorraine interrupted. "He was drinking and high all the time and he needed rehab or he was gonna die. I convinced him to turn himself in for that reason. I didn't do shit to help you."

"Yes, Lorraine. That is my point. Vincent again finds himself in a situation where his life may be at risk. Vincent *is* going to be arrested, and we want to make sure he's not injured in the process."

Lorraine's unrefined id overpowered her super-ego, and disrespectful frustration erupted.

"So, go fucking arrest him! You keep talking about *not* hurting him. So, don't. What do you want from me?"

"Charlie, may I?" asked Mollie, prepared to try a different tack. Wilcox leaned back in his chair and gestured toward the woman.

"Of course. Please," he said.

"Lorraine, my partner here has a reputation for his eloquent articulation, but sometimes certain folks miss his point, so allow me to be a bit more blunt. After what your son did, each and every one of the five hundred-fifty men and women of the New Hampshire State Police wants nothing more than to add to their personnel files the fact that they were the brave and dedicated officer who shot and killed Vincent Underwood while he resisted arrest. Now, Detective Wilcox and I intend to locate your son, arrest him, and interrogate him for these crimes. We will then present our case to the prosecuting attorney who will charge Vincent in court.

"Frankly, I don't particularly care if Vincent catches some trooper's bullet between the eyes. But I do care about doing my job, and that is to arrest your son for beating a cop with a metal pipe and stabbing some poor bastard in a bar. Now, you can help us find him and perhaps visit your son once per month in prison, or you can wait until the NHSP does and attend his funeral."

Lorraine Underwood stared in silence. She had

dealt with a lot of cops over the years, but hadn't expected this one to enlighten her with such a clear picture of her son's potential death.

Wilcox took advantage of the pause. "Lorraine, what kind of things does Vincent like to do?"

The woman's vacant gaze was still focused on Mollie, but she was looking past him into space. Her thoughts were elsewhere, on her potentially dead son, and she couldn't decide after all these years which scenario would be better for her.

"Lorraine," Mollie said. "Lorraine," a little louder. Her eyes snapped back to him and focused, blinking rapidly in an effort to clear her hazy thoughts.

"Yeah, okay," she said.

Wilcox continued in the gentled, measured voice of a practiced detective using an old interview technique.

"Vincent, Lorraine. What kind of things does he like to do?" he asked again softly.

The exhausted woman let her eyes fall to him. "The state police already asked me all this."

It wasn't an objection. Simply a statement that betrayed that the good-cop-bad-cop tactic was breaking through.

"Sure, Lorraine. We have obtained their reports. But they didn't ask that. They asked where he drinks and who his associates are and what kinds of drugs he uses. They asked where he'd go if he was on the run and who would provide him refuge. That's not what I asked. I'd like to know what Vincent does for fun. What sports did he play in high school?"

"Are you kidding me? What do you care what he did in high school?"

"Humor me, Mrs. Underwood," said Wilcox.

She huffed in resignation. "Football. Well, he tried football at least before getting kicked off the team. Some bitch cheerleader said he slapped her ass."

"Yes, thank you. Things like that. What else?"

"He bowled."

"On a team?" Wilcox pressed. "Or on his own?"

"On his own, mostly. He wouldn't join any teams. He liked it a lot though. We used to go a couple times a week. It was a long time ago."

Something resembling a smile pulled at the edges of Lorraine Underwood's mouth. It hovered there for a moment before disappearing when she stuffed the cigarette between her teeth.

"Anything else, Lorraine?"

"Maybe, I dunno. Let me think."

The non-sequential conversation continued for twenty minutes. Wilcox spoke calmly and reasonably about Vincent Underwood. Mollie peppered in worst-case scenarios of Underwood's inevitable death while avoiding arrest.

Lorraine offered coffee, which Wilcox accepted and Mollie declined. The younger detective thought his partner a fool. Cops never took food nor drink from people in their homes. At least not people like Lorraine. Then again, cops also never sat on dirty, flea-infested furniture and that had not turned out in his favor.

When their conversation wore thin, Wilcox smiled kindly and thanked Lorraine for her time. She ushered them to the door under the premise that *The Price is Right* started at 11:00am.

After descending the driveway in silence, Wilcox looked up at Mollie, waiting for him to unlock the car.

He smiled at his partner and tugged the door open.

"Good-cop bad-cop, Don? Really?"

Mollie raised an eyebrow and shrugged before he slid into the front seat at the same time as Wilcox.

"I have no idea why that shit still works."

"Well, based on what she told us, I've got a pretty good idea where to look for our friend. Let me make a quick call to narcotics first. Then we'll hit it."

CHAPTER 8

Judge G. Robert Christiansen, prone on a leather couch, woke with a start to the grinding vibration between his ears. The pain continued even after he silenced his alarm clock. The chubby, partially dressed man rolled onto his side and used both arms to heave himself into a seated position. Decades of unrestrained abuse of food and alcohol hid his core muscles, and more lately his wits, beneath layers of strength-robbing fat.

The sixty-two-year-old jurist had spent the majority of his life in some aspect of the criminal justice system. After graduation from Northwestern University School of Law he had earned a highly sought-after clerkship with the Second Circuit Court of Appeals in New York City. Earned was a misnomer. Senator George Christiansen of New York, his father, had ensured that patronage resulted in the placement.

George junior, who early in life decided to go by his middle name Robert, was of course not told of the back-room dealings originating from the Hart Senate Office Building that landed him the gig. That said, he was no fool, and knew he was not the best candidate for the appointment. Since that day, Christiansen never failed to exploit an opportunity, or a weakness, to ensure success.

The clerkship led to a prosecutor's post in the US Attorney's Office, Southern District for New York. Christiansen put in time as a mediocre attorney avoiding difficult cases and dodging litigation. During his four years at DOJ, Christiansen was widely ignored, which was fine with him. Those doing the ignoring couldn't help his career, so their worth to him was minimal.

'Putting in time' in public service was considered a prerequisite for a lucrative career in the private sector and possible political appointment. After the brief stint at Justice, Christiansen's father arranged for his 'recruitment' into Clark, Merton, Vincent, and DuPaul, the eighth largest firm in the United States.

CMVD were tax lawyers, and tax lawyers needed politicians in their corner. It was necessary to lawyers that the tax code be written in a particular manner – a confusing manner. The attorneys wanted to ensure their help would be required by the super-rich when interpreting the thousands of pages of convoluted law. Further, the taxes that lawyers saved the elite one-percent through a proper interpretation of these laws had to be just perceptibly higher than the exorbitant fees firms like CMVD charged for their services. It was a delicate balancing act, and the laws had to be written just right.

Fortunately, the greased-up system provided for this. Sufficient donations had been made to the right congressional candidates to ensure the ballet could continue. It was a fraudulently graceful frolic among politically connected elites. A dance few knew existed, and even fewer were invited to attend.

Sometimes the pool of political donations became sufficiently slushy, and the names of lawyers and politicians adequately aligned to result in a nomination to the bench. Judge Christiansen had been the beneficiary of such a circumstance.

The jowly man finished hoisting himself up onto one elbow and pushed his feet off the edge of the couch. He let out a grunt as he forced himself into a seated position. The dull pain turned to a throb, and Christiansen massaged his temples in a failed effort to rub it away.

He had been spending too many nights in chambers. During the past five years it had worsened, and alone in chambers usually meant drunk in chambers. Too drunk to make it home. He managed to stand, gained his balance and a modicum of strength, and shuffled cautiously into his private bathroom.

There was a half inch rise between the carpeted chambers and marbled bathroom that almost proved fatal. Christiansen caught a toe and pulled his left leg forward to step and avoid a fall. Pain shot through his upper thigh and into his groin as old, atrophied ligaments stretched under the unexpected movement. He sat on the toilet, rubbing the strained muscle.

A new sound interrupted his thoughts. It was his office phone. He had never in the four years since it was installed been happier that there was a desk phone extension in the bathroom. Picking up the sleek black handset, he held it gingerly near his face. As was his custom, he offered no greeting.

"Judge Christiansen?"

"Mmm-hrmm, yeah," he muttered in reply.

"Davidson, Sir." Ron Davidson was his clerk. "You have the Malone sentencing this morning, Sir. I can bring in the case if you'd like. The hearing is at nine."

Christiansen removed the phone from his head in a concerted effort to sooth his desire to scream into it. He waited a full ten seconds before responding.

"Davidson, the hearing is at nine. It's seven. I'll be out to review the case shortly."

Christianson had grown to think of Davidson as an arrogant little shit. Who did the overachieving punk think he was, summoning a sitting judge to review a case?

It occurred to Christiansen that Davidson had not responded.

"Davidson, you there? What the fuck..." he muttered, moving the phone from his face as he prepared to hang up.

"Sir, the time is 8:45, not seven," Davidson said plainly.

Christianson's brow furrowed involuntarily and he snapped his head toward the grandfather clock visible through the open bathroom door. It had been a gift from the senior partners of CMVD upon his nomination to the bench. The sudden movement caused a lightning bolt to rocket from one side of his brain to the other with such intensity he actually dropped the phone. It rattled noisily off the side of the toilet and onto the tiled floor.

He squinted while the burst of pain subsided then eased his gaze back to the clock. When the hands came into focus, they confirmed what Davidson had told him. Christiansen was due to court in fifteen minutes for sentencing in a major case, and was not even certain he was sober.

For many years the judge had managed the world around him in order to allow his vices to continue unabated. He was adept at formulating plans on the fly in the face of potential professional disaster.

"Call the attorneys," the old judge began, his voice notably clearer, "and push the hearing off until eleven. Get coffee and two breakfast sandwiches from Nikki's. Bring them and the case file to my office in a half hour."

Nikki's was a breakfast counter across the street from the courthouse. They also sold lottery tickets and single cans of beer.

"Roger on the sandwiches and joe, Sir. But we've already delayed this case..."

Christiansen had hung up and begun the effort to stand before Davidson could finish his sentence. He yanked open a chest high cabinet, fumbled until his hand grasped the right bottle, and violently twisted off the cap. He dumped out three pills and slapped his palm against his gaping mouth, hoping that launching them further down his gullet would somehow make them work faster. He gulped aggressively, choking the capsules down his cigar-ravaged throat with no consideration of water.

He pushed the cabinet closed, then pressed his hands onto the sides of the sink and leaned deep into the mirror. What he saw was the waning career of a corrupt and broken man. A weakling who had hidden behind the strength of titles and other people's ambition to become part of a system nearly impossible to break into. It was rigged, he knew, and he had benefitted from it since birth.

Christiansen pushed the fragile seedling of morality from his mind before it had a chance to take root. He stepped into the shower and turned the cold lever full on. Bracing under the deluge as long as he could tolerate, he forced his mind to Brass Malone, the defendant he was about to sentence to prison for decades.

Malone and his attorney knew about Christiansen, and had tried to use their knowledge of his weakness to their advantage. They had tried to break into the system, one in which they didn't belong, and work it to their benefit. They might yet succeed, but it was going to take a hell of a lot more money than Malone had offered thus far.

Christiansen turned off the frigid water. He was glad for the mind-sharpening effect it had on him. He needed all of his somewhat clouded faculties for the fight he was about to pick with Malone, arguably the most dangerous man north of Boston.

CHAPTER 9

Hillsborough County Deputy Prosecutor Peter Hamlin, a tall, slender, somewhat pale man with a hawkish nose, was having a very good day. He knew, despite Judge Christiansen's last-minute postponement of the hearing, that Brass Malone was about to be sentenced to fifteen to twenty years in federal prison. And frankly, that was a gift.

Malone had pled guilty to trafficking cocaine and conspiracy to distribute illegally obtained firearms. Handguns, specifically, two of which had been traced and linked to three different murders. One had been recovered at the scene of a robbery that took the life of convenience store clerk. The same weapon had been used in the prior murder of a mid-level drug dealer who was considering talking to the police. The last had been a thirteen-year-old kid who flirted with the girlfriend of another seventh grader. That seventh grader had taken his drug dealing older brother's gun and killed the competing suitor.

Brass Malone was suspected of ordering more than ten murders in the past five years. A lack of evidence and living witnesses meant the indictment to which he would plead guilty included only cocaine trafficking and conspiracy. It said nothing about the murders.

Hamlin had built a rock-solid case. ATF had recorded conversations during which Malone personally mentioned 'doing' two gun stores in eastern Connecticut. Three days later, both stores were burglarized. One had been burned to the ground.

Two different confidential informants, CIs, were prepared to testify that each had distributed over fifteen kilograms of cocaine under the supervision of Malone. Hamlin had managed to scurry them both off to Florida with the US Marshals before Malone could shut them up.

Victor Portman, Esquire sat across the courtroom at the defendant's table. He was a stout Englishman of forty-five with slicked back hair and a thick but neatly trimmed mustache. He, too, was having a good day. As a defense attorney, he did not often know exactly how a contested sentencing hearing was going to end up. But today he knew exactly what was going to happen to his client, Brass Malone. It had all been arranged.

Even with a two-hour delay to prepare, Judge Christiansen had not made it to the bench until 11:15. Hamlin laid out the particulars of the case with the linear mind of an experienced litigator. The dangerous nature of the crimes, Malone's extensive prior record, and the public's demand for a harsh punishment were all noted. He ended with the government's request, fifteen to twenty years.

Portman's argument was brief. Malone was remorseful and fully intended to pay his debt to society. He wanted to volunteer at the Boy's and Girl's Club in order to steer youngsters away from the mistakes he had made. And of course, he had started attending church in prison. Portman ended the presentation with a request for leniency and a sentence of two to four years.

It was all standard fare, lawyers posturing for each other, their clients, and the public. Only ten minutes after breaking for lunch, the judge summoned the parties back to the courtroom for his decision. Following the perfunctory rising and sitting at the call of the bailiff, Judge Christiansen instructed Malone and his attorney to stand.

"As you know, I'm not one to pontificate on the merits of the decisions I make," he began. "The sentences I impose generally speak for themselves. I am inclined to agree with the government here. It is my intention to impose a sentence of fifteen to twenty years, with no parole prior to ten."

The easy smile that had rested on Malone's face throughout the morning melted. His expression washed white, only to pink-up, then darken to red. His jaw clenched as rage packed into him and balled his fists. The vigilant bailiff took note and stepped toward the defense table.

Portman's more practiced demeanor allowed him a measured response.

"Your honor! This is...frankly this is not what we expected. We were under the impression..."

"Under what impression, counselor?" interrupted Judge Christiansen.

"Well, that you...that we...that a more lenient sentence was likely to be imposed."

"And why would you think that, Mr. Portman? Your client has pled guilty to a very serious pattern of criminal conduct. This sentence seems appropriate given the circumstances."

Malone managed to gather himself during the brief exchange. He leaned toward his attorney, grabbed the nape of his neck with a vice grip, and pulled his ear so close to his mouth that they touched.

"That motherfucker wants more money!" It was barely a whisper, but Portman gawked at his client in disbelief that he would utter the statement in open court.

Hamlin, the prosecutor, spoke again.

"Your Honor, is there something going on here the government should be aware of? We've both presented our arguments and the court has imposed a sentence. The matter is closed now, is it not?"

The Judge fired a look of distain at Hamlin, then refocused on Portman. "Are we finished here, Counselor?"

There was a perceptible pause.

"Your Honor, my client wishes to withdraw his guilty plea," Portman stated.

"Well," the judge said. "He certainly has that right."

"Your Honor!" Hamlin said as he jumped back to his feet. "This is a completed plea agreement, signed just this morning by Mr. Malone and his attorney. And now the court has sentenced him. The defendant can not withdraw simply because he does not like the answer. He rolled the dice and they didn't come up for him."

This time Judge Christiansen's rebuke was verbal.

"Mr. Hamlin, I determine who may or may not plead guilty in my courtroom, as well as who may then withdraw that plea. Is that understood?"

Hamlin stood dumbfounded. Judge Christiansen looked to the stenographer.

"Well, I suppose we better set this case for trial," he commented casually. "Cheryl, find us a date, would you."

"Certainly, Judge." The clerk typed and clicked in order to open the proper scheduling application on the computer before her.

"I have an appointment, actually," the judge said, interrupting his own plan. "Cheryl, email the open dates to both parties and schedule it. Bail is continued pending trial." Christiansen banged his gavel once on the bench and stood up. "We're done." He walked from behind the bench to a door secreted in the rich wood paneling behind it.

Malone looked at his attorney in utter dismay. This time he was smart enough to wait until the judge had left the courtroom before blurting, "Jesus fucking Christ, Victor! What the fuck was that? It was supposed to be two years. You said it was arranged!"

Victor Portman looked at Hamlin and moved to shield his client from the prosecutor's view.

"Not now," he said.

The two men stalked out of the room. Hamlin, still unsure what the hell had just happened to his slam-dunk case, did not get up for five minutes.

CHAPTER 10

Sarah Brennan loved her husband beyond words, but the phone call they had just shared confirmed that sometimes he could be a real horse's ass. He had called to tell her that not only would he be unexpectedly home for dinner, but would be bringing his partner with him.

Over time, Sarah had learned that being married to a cop came with a lot of compromise, a lot of patience, and a lot of trust. Mostly, it had to come with acceptance. Acceptance of the fact that if Jimmy was going to succeed in his career and get the assignments he wanted, he'd have to volunteer for extra shifts, come in at a moment's notice, and stay late whenever needed. The job competed with his family, and there wasn't always time for both.

Acceptance often competed with disappointment. Special dinners cancelled, planned events postponed, and for Sarah, attending social events alone while hoping not to be perceived as the sad, single guest she felt like. Years had passed and Jimmy had arrived at a place in his career where they were doing well. First grade detective pay was better than patrol, and the undercover work came with a bonus. When he was around, Jimmy Brennan was a good husband. Their marriage was solid, and he was a wonderfully involved father to their twelve-year-old daughter, Maggie.

Notwithstanding all of this, sometimes Jimmy Brennan really missed the mark. He and his partner had been scheduled to work until nine that night assisting homicide detectives with the surveillance of a suspect. The suspect had snuck into his grandmother's house, written a confessional suicide note, and hanged himself. Case closed, and Brennan would be coming home early, with a guest.

Sarah was often frustrated by Jimmy's myopic view of such situations. Dinner for her and Maggie was going to have been cereal and carrot sticks. She was exhausted, and something quick and easy that made no dishes, no mess, and no cleanup was planned.

Now there would be a side dish to make, a table to set, and dishes to do. Maggie was in her pajamas already, and Sarah wanted to tidy up. Jimmy had been astute enough to interpret the brief pauses in their phone conversation as frustration.

"Don't clean up. Rey's been over a thousand times, Hon. He knows we don't live in a museum," he had said. That was the horse's ass part. It wasn't about him. Or about Rey. It was about Sarah, and how she wanted their home to look when someone came over.

By the time Jimmy and Rey arrived the kitchen was working. Steam rose from the sink where boiled potatoes were draining in a sieve. Maggie was making a rookie effort to chop celery. Both would go into potato salad.

When Jimmy walked in, he wisely made a beeline to his wife.

"Hey, Babe," he said, grinning. "Thanks for being cool with the change of plans."

"Mmm-hmm," Sarah said behind a strained smile, offering a cheek. Her hands were busy cutting carrots, the only survivor of the original dinner plan. She paused that work and walked to Rey Johnston, wrapping her arms around him in a hug. Rey's hung at his sides, one heavy with a bag of meat, the other beer.

"Hi, Sarah. Thanks for having me," he said.

"Anytime Rey. You're always welcome here." With that, she shot her husband a snarky glance. He missed it.

Turning his attention to Maggie, Rey reached for the refrigerator door to deposit his load.

"How's it going, kid?" he asked.

"Hi, Rey. Good."

"School good?"

"Yup."

"Eighth grade now, right? How's that?"

"Seventh. It's okay."

Jimmy walked over and gave his daughter a nudge. "Mags, this isn't the first time Rey's been over. You have anything to say other than one-word answers?"

The girl flushed.

"Leave her alone, Jimmy," Sarah laughed, but it was a rebuke, and Jimmy caught the look that time.

"Rey, grab us some beers and meet me on the deck. I'll start the grill."

An hour later they were eating. Jimmy had broiled the steaks perfectly, which was the exception when he drank beer at the same time. Sarah later learned Rey had manned the grill while Jimmy did most of the talking and drinking.

As soon as dinner was done, Maggie started angling to be dismissed. She liked spending time with her parents but knew when another adult was over and the beer and wine were flowing, the conversation became tedious for her. The adults would grow weary of guarding their language and while they fought hard not to, they'd make Maggie feel like an outsider. Ten minutes after dinner was over, she went upstairs.

They moved to the living room where Sarah snuggled into a loveseat, her long legs curled beneath her, and Jimmy and Rey sprawled on opposite ends of the couch. Both detectives held beer bottles. Rey's rested on his ample belly and Jimmy held his in a hand laid across the back of the couch. Sarah fingered the edge of a glass of merlot.

"How's Maria doing, Rey?" she asked. Maria was his eight-year-old daughter. Johnston had her every other weekend, rotated holidays, and other times arranged with his ex-wife.

"She's good. Smart. Really liking school," he replied.

"Gets that from Stephanie, clearly," Jimmy joked. Stephanie was Rey's ex-wife and Maria's mother.

"Don't be a dick, Jimmy," said his wife. Rey ignored the interaction.

"You still see her a lot then, it sounds like," she asked.

"Yeah, pretty regularly," Rey answered.

"That's nice. It's important. I'm glad for you."

They sipped their respective drinks and sat in silence, the contrast between their situations apparent. Jimmy and Sarah were partners, a matched set that complemented each other well. Rey was divorced, and while he and his ex-wife were civil, they were not friends. He was doing his best to be a decent parent, but he was doing it alone. So was Stephanie.

After freshening up her wine, Sarah decided to lighten the mood.

"Well Rey, young James here usually tells me exactly jack-shit about what's happening at work. So, I'll ask you. How're things going?"

"Ha!" Jimmy mumbled around the mouth of his beer bottle. Rey looked at him questioningly. "She's right, Rey. I don't tell her shit."

Rey's discomfort was visible. Sarah was having fun with them, and decided not to let him off the hook just yet.

"So, Rey. What is it? When he's undercover is my husband smoking weed with teenaged girls at the mall? Or is he soliciting street walkers on the low end of Elm Street?"

Rey had had three beers and was working through his fourth.

"Sometimes, if we're lucky, we do both!" he said.

"Jesus, Rey," Brennan muttered around a sip of beer. "You think that helps?"

Sarah rolled her eyes. "Relax, Romeo."

"Sorry Jimmy. I'm just screwing around," said Rey.

"No worries. She knows the weird shit we get into on the street sometimes," said Brennan.

"Nice talk, Dad," chimed in Maggie. They hadn't seen her make her way down the stairs. "Just grabbing a snack. You all keep going with the 'responsible grown-up talk.'"

"Hey, kiddo," said Jimmy in a weak attempt to mitigate his embarrassment.

"Hey, Dad," she said with a Cheshire cat smile. The young girl walked back upstairs humming her satisfaction.

The three adults were alone again.

"Are you still meeting with Soffit tomorrow?" Jimmy asked. Captain Edward Soffit was the commanding officer of the Manchester police department's detective division.

"Yeah, I think it's a good idea."

"What's a good idea?" Sarah inquired.

"Rey's looking to move undercover. He's sick of doing surveillance for me, of living in my shadow," Brennan teased.

"That's true!" agreed Rey. "But the fifteen percent pay bump is kind of nice, too."

"Will you two stay partnered-up if that happens?" asked Sarah.

"Depends," Jimmy said with a head wobble. "Technically no. When you're teamed up you've got one UC and one handler. Helps you keep each other sane. But maybe they'd let us switch off, right Rey?"

"Yeah, maybe," his partner said. They smiled at each other and allowed for a momentary overt display of their fondness for working together, and for each other.

"Would that work?" Sarah asked again. "I mean, practically, from an investigative standpoint?"

Both men smiled.

"No, not really," Brennan laughed.

"Probably not," agreed Rey.

The evening wound down, and at nine o'clock Rey stood up to leave.

"Get some rest, Jimmy. Tomorrow's a big day."

"You, too," Brennan replied.

Brennan finished the dishes while Sarah put on comfortable clothes and settled into a novel in the living room. His task complete, Brennan walked to her, toweling off his hands.

"Hey, sorry I was an idiot earlier."

"Oh, you weren't. It's fine," she lied. "I know you two were just screwing around."

"I don't mean Rey. I mean the last-minute dinner change. I saw the cereal box on the counter. I can put two and two together. You and Mags had plans."

"Yeah," she smiled, cocking her head. "We did. But it's fine."

"Just let me apologize, would you? I was an ass. I'm sorry."

"Thanks." She returned to her book then looked back up quickly. "What was Rey talking about, 'big day tomorrow?'"

"Nothing too crazy. I'm doing a meet with a guy for the first time. He's looking to hire someone to do a murder."

"And that's not a big deal?" Sarah challenged.

"No, it is. But it's not as high-risk as it sounds. I'm sure we'll move to make an arrest long before it gets dangerous. Tomorrow is just a meeting. That's all."

"Okay, well, be careful," Sarah said lamely.

"I always am," Brennan said. He bent over and kissed the top of her head. As he moved away, Sarah caught him by the neck and pulled him in. Their lips met, and he felt hers open. When their embrace broke, he stood up.

"I'm just about done in here," he said, gesturing toward the kitchen.

"Oh yeah?" Sarah replied with a grin, acknowledging the unspoken offer. "Maggie asleep?"

"Probably."

"You finish and make sure the house is locked up. I'll go check on her."

Jimmy bent down and kissed her again.

"I love you, Sarah Brennan."

"Yeah, yeah," she said. "Go finish and meet me upstairs."

Jimmy Brennan felt his wife swat his behind as he turned and walked back to the kitchen.

CHAPTER 11

Jimmy Brennan had not sipped a whiskey sour since doing it at Dirty Ray's Bar and Grill in Roanoke when he was eighteen years old. That had been an effort to appear cool in front of his friends. He did it now for much the same reason.

"Are you going to do it yourself?" Torren Carter asked. The leather-clad thug sat across a booth from Brennan.

Brennan eyed him suspiciously. "What the fuck do you care?" he muttered around the edge of the squat whiskey glass. "You writing a 'how-to' manual?"

Carter cut an intimidating figure, but to Brennan's practiced eye his weaknesses rose to the surface. He was fat and greasy, and three days of lazy growth painted a splotchy pattern across his face. His jet-black hair was medium length and pushed back from his forehead. Brennan had sized Carter up early as physically weak. But weak didn't mean not dangerous. Weak often just meant unpredictable.

"You killing this guy just can't come back on us," Carter said as he leaned across the table toward Brennan.

Visibly annoyed at the man moving closer, Brennan said nothing. He exhaled cigarette smoke into his face and set his drink down. He looked away from Carter dismissively and put his right arm over the back of the booth in order to twist and look over his shoulder toward the entrance behind him. Scanning the room, he worked to convey his disinterest in anything the sweaty low-rent thug had to say.

Turning back to the table, Brennan picked up his cell phone and glanced at it. He took another sip and without looking at Carter said "It's ten past. Where's your boss?"

"He'll be here."

"I hope so," replied Brennan. He drained his drink, then knocked the thick-bottomed glass against the table twice to summon the bartender. She glanced at him, jutted her chin toward the table, and reached for a whiskey bottle.

"You actually do this shit for a living?"

Brennan ignored the question and looked at his phone again as the underage waitress walked his drink to the table and slid it in front of him.

"Six bucks."

Brennan pointed silently across the table.

"Asshole," Carter grumbled as he leaned hard to his left and reached into his right pocket. He withdrew a wad, flipped a ten off the top, and tossed it onto the table in front of the young woman.

"Keep it, Sweetheart."

The girl was already turning to walk away as she picked up the bill and slid it into her apron.

Bars like Three Brother's Tavern where the two men sat were common to the reformed mill city of Manchester, New Hampshire. The early afternoon crowd consisted of unemployed drunks, grumpy old timers, and a few second-shifters getting their load on before work. No one wanted anything to do with anyone else's business. The six-hundred square foot dining area consisted of booths on the walls and two pool tables in the middle. The state's ban on smoking in restaurants had not yet filtered down.

Carter was taking a swig of his own drink when his gaze fell to the door behind Brennan. His eyes grew wider then settled back to their usual lazy squint. Quickly, but not without effort, he swallowed his sip and put the drink down with a jerky motion that betrayed his anxiety.

"Here he is."

Carter shuffled his bulk to the edge of the booth, stood, and walked toward the door. Brennan sucked a deep drag from the cigarette and stuffed it down hard into a black melamine ashtray. He heard hushed voices as the two men drew closer, came around, and sat across from him. The newcomer slid in first, followed by an almost giddy Torren Carter.

"This is Paul," announced Carter, motioning grandly to this left. "Pauly, this is the guy I told you about. The one Tricky wanted us to meet."

The two men nodded at each other. Brennan scanned the man's shoulders and torso as his gaze fell to the table. Paul carried himself differently than Carter. He may not be the ultimate boss, but he had power. It would take some conversation to determine where exactly he fell in the pecking order.

Brennan fingered the contents of the cigarette pack, feigning difficulty in retrieving one to buy himself time to think. A street-walker informant named Tricky had introduced him to Carter, who had said his boss was looking for someone to 'do' something for them. Carter and Brennan had already met once, and the detective had quickly assessed the sloppy thug as little more than an errand boy. He'd left that meeting knowing they wanted someone killed, but wasn't at all confident he'd hear from Carter again.

Two days later Carter had called him to set up this meet. Within that time, the intelligence unit had linked Carter to Paul Nessman, a mid-level lieutenant for Brass Malone. Malone was a serious target, and was already under indictment for multiple drug and gun offenses. After Brennan had briefed his boss on the case, it moved quickly up to the command level. When it came back down, Brennan had been informed that 'a lot of eyes' were on the case and he'd have anything he needed to make it stick.

Carter may have been low rent, but Paul Nessman and Brass Malone were the real deal and into drugs, guns, and extortion. Malone had recently been linked to several high-end financial crimes in Hartford, Connecticut, which was decidedly outside his area. He also had multiple homicides tied to him in Manchester as well as Lowell and Boston, Massachusetts.

Brennan had jumped to the top of the criminal food chain quickly and knew when that happened, and you operated at this level, things rarely went to plan. When they didn't, someone usually got killed.

CHAPTER 12

"What part of Detroit you from?" Paul Nessman asked after settling into his seat.

"You know Detroit?" asked Brennan.

"Some."

"Hazel Park."

"Ah, an Eight Mile boy. Lot of work out there?" asked Nessman.

Brennan took a sip of his drink and rubbed the side of his nose with the same hand. Thanks to the MPD intelligence unit, he knew a lot about Paul Nessman. He had been briefed on his criminal history at headquarters and looked at his license photo, booking photo, even his high school yearbook photo. But Nessman didn't know he knew, and Brennan needed to act accordingly.

"Is this some kind of job interview?"

"Yeah, sure," Nessman chuckled, glancing at Carter.

Brennan caught his gaze and pointed at him with the hand that held his cigarette. "Thing is, I don't really need a job," he said.

"No?"

"No. So really, the one getting interviewed here is you, friend. And you're not doing too good so far." Before looking away Brennan caught an upward twitch at the corner of the man's mouth.

Nessman glanced over at Carter. "Grab me a drink, T."

Carter immediately smiled at Nessman, pleased to satisfy a simple request, and got up to walk to the bar. Brennan said nothing, but looked down at his drink and struggled to restrain a condescending snicker. It was not lost on Nessman.

"Yeah, I know," he said, reading the detective's mind. "But in five years he has never questioned a single thing I told him to do. That's valuable."

He was right, and Brennan knew it. Loyalty among criminals was scarce. Brennan nodded silently, then saw his opportunity and took it.

"But you obviously don't trust him with every-thing."

Nessman frowned. "How's that?"

"If you did," Brennan continued, "I wouldn't be here, would I?"

Nessman leaned back in this booth and crossed his arms.

"Sometimes it's better to hire from the outside, if you take my meaning."

"Mm-hmm," Brennan grunted around his cigar-ette as he pinched it between his lips and inhaled. It allowed him a moment's pause. They were making pro-gress, and the next moments would be determinant.

Nessman pointed to the cigarette pack on the table and when Brennan nodded, picked it up and shook one out. He lit it, took a shallow drag, and blew the smoke out his nose.

"Your guy in Boston said forty-five."

No one met a potential killer for hire cold off the street. When setting up the first meeting with Carter, Brennan had told his hooker-CI to feed the low-level soldier the name of a Boston financier whose wife had been murdered the year before. The banker had been a suspect, but was cleared when his alibi checked out. Brennan's team of detectives had decided to use it as a cover.

It was an opportunity to provide a referral of sorts. The case was a legitimate unsolved murder they could spin to look like Brennan had been involved. Like all stories on the street regarding who committed a crime, it had some veracity, a cloudy explanation, and some outright lies.

In order to set the hook with Carter and Nessman, an undercover Boston cop had been set up with a Google phone number. He had played the part of the Southie ex-con who had supposedly put the banker together with Brennan to kill his wife. The detective wasn't surprised Nessman had followed up on it.

"Boston's a big city," Brennan replied. "Lots of places to get lost. It's a much more distracting environment."

"Distracting for who?"

"Cops, witnesses. People I generally like to keep, well, distracted." He smiled at his own joke. Nessman didn't.

"You don't like this city?"

"Small."

Nessman nodded softly and made a 'maybe so' gesture with his face. "I do alright here."

"Do you?"

Nessman broke the gaze and looked up as Carter

ambled back to the table with his drink. When he settled his bulk into the booth, Brennan made eye contact with Nessman then flicked his eyes toward Carter in question.

Nessman nodded. "Yeah, he's okay."

Brennan decided to push the conversation.

"It's fifty-grand, not forty-five, and I need a three-day window to do it."

Not surprising Brennan at all, Nessman didn't hesitate before responding.

"Forty-five. Thirty up front and I pick the day."

"Thirty-five up front..."

"Done," muttered Paul, interrupting.

"...but I need the window to do it right," continued Brennan. "Killing people takes planning, you know."

It was a risk, saying it out loud like that. But getting the statement on the body-wire recording would lock the case, and it seemed like a point in the conversation he could get away with it.

"No," Nessman stated authoritatively. "I pick the day."

"Then have him do it," Brennan said as he tossed his head toward Torren Carter and slid his drink across the table. It clanked into Nessman's and dark liquid spilled onto the sticky surface. Shifting his weight, Brennan slid across the booth, stood up, and dropped a ten-dollar bill on the table.

The detective made it as far as the door and placed his hand on the pull-handle when he felt someone uncomfortably close behind him.

"Hey," Carter said, almost at a whisper. "Back here the same time Friday. Thirty-five thousand up front and

you can have the window to do it."

Brennan looked over the shorter man's shoulder to Nessman. He hesitated a beat, then shouldered past him and walked aggressively toward his boss. Carter was caught off guard and struggled to catch up. By the time he arrived at the table, Brennan was already standing over Nessman.

"You have something to say to me?" Brennan asked, looking squarely at Nessman and ignoring Carter, whose hand fingered a trigger inside his pocket.

"You heard what he said," replied Nessman, looking at his helper.

"I don't take messages, *Paul*. I want to hear you say it." There was an intolerant undertone. Brennan was posturing. It was part of the game.

The two men stared at each other for ten seconds. Another patron picked up on the tension, decided he wanted none of it, and moved from a nearby booth to the bar.

"Thirty-five up front, ten more after, and you get your window," Nessman said clearly.

Standing erect, Brennan looked back at Carter and smiled. He patted the man's forearm where it entered his jacket pocket and said, "Don't hurt yourself, Son."

Carter tensed and took a sharp breath, but said nothing.

As he walked up the crumbling sidewalk outside the bar, Brennan texted the number 1 to a pre-programmed phone number. The reply was also a 1. He rounded a corner, pressed the car remote which generated a series of chirps, and yanked open the door of today's rental. Driving off, he told Siri to call Rey Johnston. It connected, but there was no greeting.

"You get all that?" Brennan asked.

"Yeah, we're good."

"Excellent, thanks."

"Do you think we need to keep surveillance up on Carter?" asked Johnston.

"No. He'll catch a conspiracy indictment for setting up this meeting, but we can forget him for now. Paul Nessman is the name to remember. He's the link to Brass Malone."

"You got it," Johnston replied, but there was something else in his voice.

"What's the problem, Rey?"

Two blocks away, Johnston was seated in the front half of the cargo section of a blacked-out van. Before him was a desk of electronic monitoring and recording equipment. Behind him were four uncomfortably cramped MPD SWAT officers, rifles standing on the floor between their knees. They were Brennan's unused rescue team.

"'Killing people takes planning?' Did you really say that?" Johnston asked, incredulous.

"Hey, you want a solid case or not?"

"Sure, but I'm not too interested in a dead partner."

"You don't think it was a good idea? Not worth the risk?" asked Brennan, feigning seriousness.

"No, I don't."

"Yeah, you're probably right. I'll go back and apologize."

"You're an asshole," said Johnston, smiling.

"That's probably true, Rey."

There was a pause.

"Nice work, Brennan."

"Thanks. You, too."

Both men grinned warmly as they hung up.

CHAPTER 13

Brass Malone was in jail, but business needed to carry on. Kyle Ostrowski, his most reliable asset and a loyal counselor, was there to make sure that happened.

Ostrowski was an overweight, bald on top, well-dressed man of forty-eight. 'Kyle', he had always thought, was a sissy name. Ostrowski was a mouthful, and betrayed more of his heritage than he wanted. For these reasons, and several others, he had been known as 'Ozzy' as long as he could remember.

Ozzy turned off Hayward Street and pulled into the employee parking lot of the Hillsborough County Jail. He was more often than not allowed to park wherever he desired without molestation. Over the course of seven very interesting years he had done enough work around the criminal justice system to almost elevate himself back to 'employee' status. The truth was he liked it better this way.

Former Police Officer Kyle "Ozzy" Ostrowski had worked for the Concord, New Hampshire police department for ten years, during which time he amassed enough informants and criminal co-conspirators to ensure himself significant financial gain. Regrettably, it had been one of those same co-conspirators who had reported to the Concord Police that Ozzy regularly enjoyed the company of several Center City prostitutes in the nearby city of Manchester. An exhaustive internal investigation and two suspensions later, Ozzy found himself on the unemployment line.

If they had discovered what he'd really been up to, he would have ended up in prison.

Ozzy found a parking space half-way down the third row and pulled his six-month-old Mercedes in nose-first. Walking around the front of the jail, New Hampshire's largest save the state prison, he proceeded to the front entrance. Abusing his familiarity with the jail staff got him an easy parking spot, but did not translate to having access to any doors but the front.

Visiting day was Saturday, at which time the lobby was generally lousy with disappointed children and the mothers who felt obliged to bring them. Lawyers came Mondays, Wednesdays, and Fridays. Today was Thursday, and the only people in the jail were crooks and guards. As he entered the surprisingly airy foyer, Ozzy proceeded to the bubble, a heavily fortified, glass enclosed office that housed the primary door controls and three duty officers.

When he rang the buzzer, the face that appeared to greet him was new.

"Help you?" the young man inquired over an intercom.

"I'm here to see Malone, Brass, number 35986," Ozzy said.

The guard was surprised, but not impressed, by Ozzy's familiarity with the proper way to identify an inmate at the Valley Street Jail. Valley Street was the sobriquet frequently assigned to the facility, simply enough, because it was located on Valley Street.

"You a lawyer?" the guard prodded.

"No, but I work for one. Malone's his client."

The young corrections officer struggling through his eleventh day on the job post-corrections academy graduation, gritted his teeth in frustration. He hoped his face did not betray the inner monologue.

Why cannot any of this shit ever be simple. It seems every jackass that comes in here has a different story, and I'm stuck trying to figure out which rule to apply to him. Visitors only on Saturdays. Lawyers anytime with reasonable notice, but usually Monday, Wednesday, and Friday. There is, of course, nothing in the rules about short, fat, bald men who claimed to work for attorneys.

"Just a minute please, Sir."

A massive inch-and-a-half thick laminated glass panel separated the stark tiled lobby from the dark and elevated control bubble. As a result, once the CO turned off the intercom and picked up a nearby telephone, Ozzy could hear not a word. The call ended, and the guard reached over and snapped the intercom back on.

"Apparently, I was supposed to get your name before calling my sergeant and bothering him."

Ozzy failed to hide his chuckle and said, "Ostrowski. Kyle Ostrowski."

He reached for a pen. "Can you spell that, Mr. Ostrowski."

"Who's your sergeant on-duty, Kid?"

The young CO was surprised that he didn't really mind this guy calling him 'Kid.'

"Sergeant Flannery."

"Well, you call him back and tell that lousy Irishman that Ozzy is here to see Brass Malone. He'll know."

Wisely skeptical, the CO asked again. "Can you

please just spell your name for me, Sir. I have to enter it into the log anyway."

"My visits don't go into the log."

"Sir," he stated with authority. "You must be mistaken. Not just all visitors, but even visit requests, must go into the log."

Ozzy didn't respond. Instead, he just pointed past the young man to the phone on the console next to him. He then extended the thumb and pinky finger of his right hand and held them to the side of his head, feigning a phone call. After a moment, the CO slapped the intercom button off and picked up the phone.

This time the conversation was much shorter, and when it was over, the CO did not reactivate the speaker. He pointed past Ozzy's shoulder to a door across the lobby. Ozzy smiled and gave him a thumbs up.

Across the lobby stood an imposing four foot wide steel gray door, cut into the cement wall. Laid into it at eye level was an eight-by-eight-inch wire reinforced window. There was the dull mechanical buzz of a solenoid deep in the cement wall. A well set-up, square jawed corrections officer shoved the door open, partially emerged, and held it ajar with his foot.

"Hey Oz," he said without smiling.

"Hey Peter. How's it going?"

"Good," he said, gesturing for Ozzy to come through. Then, as an afterthought, he asked, "Any reason for me to search your briefcase?"

"Nah, I think we're safe," Ozzy said, smiling.

They proceeded through the door into a small room, where a baffled door system stopped them. Once the door behind them closed, the next one could not be buzzed open until the prescribed time period had elapsed. The purpose was to retard the progress of prisoners attempting escape, and to thwart the efforts of someone forcing their way inside. Even officers in the main control bubble could not override it.

The tooth-rattling grind sounded again and Peter yanked the door open. Ozzy went through and walked down a short hallway that opened into a larger space. There were two rows of eight small tables, four chairs to each. All the furniture was metal, gray, and bolted to the floor.

"Something a bit more private, maybe?" inquired Ozzy.

Glancing around the obviously vacant room, the guard shook his head and walked to one of six open doors on the far-left side. He peered in, saw that it was empty, and waved to Ozzy.

Ozzy entered the room, another starkly cold setup measuring ten-by-ten, and saw that it had a table and two chairs of the same design. The table was bolted down, the chairs were not.

"This is fine, thanks."

The officer grunted a parting salutation and walked out. Placing his briefcase on the table, Ozzy sat and waited.

Five minutes later Brass Malone, dressed in pale green pants and a button-down shirt just a shade darker, walked into the room. A corrections officer, this time a woman, peered in behind him.

"Knock when you're done," she said pleasantly, then pulled her head back and closed the door.

Malone smiled at his friend, who rose from his seat. The two locked eyes, then embraced. It was brief, but heartfelt.

"How you holding up in here?"

"It's jail, Ozzy. How do you think?"

He nodded, acknowledging the foolish inquiry.

"You know what I mean. Since that bullshit in court the other day. How are you?"

"I'm not worried about it."

"Why the hell not?" asked Ozzy. He glanced vertically to the camera in the corner of the ceiling, remembered that attorney rooms had video feed but no audio, and looked back down to Malone. "A hundred thousand dollars should have bought you a lot of years off, Brass. The two-to-four deal took a long time for us to set up. What'd the lawyer say? Did Christiansen get spooked or something?"

"I guess it wasn't enough money," Malone replied smoothly.

"You gonna offer more?"

"Nope," Malone popped casually, accentuating the last sound of the word.

"Jesus, Brass. How can you be so damn cavalier? You're about to do twenty years if we can't figure out how to fix this."

Malone did not initially respond. Instead, he leaned back in his chair and put his hands behind his head. Then he smiled, and winked. Ozzy grew concerned.

"You alright?" he asked.

Malone glanced up at the camera over Ozzy's shoulder. He took his right hand from behind his head and slowly rubbed his neck. He extended his index finger across his throat, feigned itching a scratch, then subtly drew the finger across his Adam's apple horizontally.

Ozzy wasn't sure he had properly read the signal, but the man's expression confirmed it.

"Jesus Christ. A sitting judge?" he hushed. Malone did not respond. A moment later Ozzy continued. "You need me to do anything?"

"Nope," Malone said with another pop. "It's taken care of. And it's only costing me forty-five thousand. Killing the crooked bastard is going to be less than half what it cost to bribe him, turns out."

"Forty-five? Damn. Who?"

Malone's face darkened. "You've got a lot of questions today, Oz."

He let the veiled threat hang in the air. The two men were close, but Ozzy needed to remember his place in the order of things. After a few moments Malone let him off the hook.

"Pauly Nessman's taking care of it. He hooked up with some guy out of Boston."

"Okay, then what happens? You're still looking down the barrel of the same twenty years with whatever judge the case gets reassigned to, aren't you?"

"Portman said..."

"Who's Portman?" Ozzy interrupted.

"Victor Portman, the lawyer," he continued in annoyance. "He says he's got it worked out. Apparently, the next judge in the rotation likes to visit Asian massage parlors more than he likely wants the world to know about."

"This judge does that here?" Ozzy asked incredulously. "In the city? What is he, a fucking idiot?"

"No, Hartford."

"How do we know that?"

Malone looked at Ostrowski with disappointment. "C'mon, Ozzy. Think about it."

He did, initially without success. Malone waited until the man's face reflected that he had made the connection.

"Because it's our massage parlor," Ozzy said, nodding. "Of course."

"Well no, not our business. But we run the girls."

"Nice," Ozzy nodded. "Smart."

"Anyway," Malone continued. "It shouldn't take much to get this new judge to buy into the same deal Christiansen turned away from."

Breathing in deeply and letting out a sigh, Ozzy marked the end of that part of his visit.

"Down to it, then, shall we?" he asked. Malone waved his hand forward gesturing him to proceed. Ozzy took out three thick manila file folders from his briefcase and plopped them onto the table.

"The cash is all set," he began. The feds ain't gonna get a dime of it past whatever fines they impose."

"And the state?" interrupted Malone.

"I don't even think they know what you've got, Boss. You should be good on that end, too."

Malone nodded and waved him to go on.

"So, you...then you, um..." Ozzy stumbled until he found the right forms. He moved two pieces of paper to the back of a stack and read briefly. "Yup, here it is. Okay, you've got to decide what you're going to do with the houses before you start your sentence. They're going to take the one in the North End because that's in your name. There's nothing we can do about that. That leaves Aspen and Miami."

"Sell them?" Malone asked.

"Can't," Ozzy answered. "The Feds will screen real estate transactions for a few months before and after your sentencing. They'd find it, link it, and take the money. Probably charge you for not disclosing them during the PSI, too, just to be dicks."

The PSI, or pre-sentence investigation, was conducted before anyone was sentenced in a felony case. In addition to informing the judge as to the criminal record and general character of a defendant, the accused was required to disclose cash, investments, and real estate.

"Keep them then," Malone decided. "Empty them out and pay some local stiff to check in on them. Or have someone shack up there."

Ozzy stuck out his lower lip and nodded. "That might work. We have money in on a guy with the Colorado State Police, and two narco cops on the hook at Miami-Dade Metro. We could have them keep an eye on it, too, if you want."

"When did you set that up?"

"A couple-three years ago. Just after you bought them. I thought it'd be a good idea in case something came up down the road."

"Smart," Malone said as he considered the benefit of police protection of his property against the drawback of the local cops knowing his business.

"Set it up. We'll dump the properties after I get out."

Ozzy jotted a few notes, then looked up to continue. They discussed financial matters for another fifteen minutes. Then, when it was time to leave, he decided to express a nagging worry one more time.

"I have to say, Brass, I'm worried about us outsourcing to take care of this judge thing. What do we know about this guy from Boston that Nessman is talking to?"

"We know enough. Nessman's pretty sharp," said Malone.

"I know he is, but you want me to look into the guy, maybe? Just a little bit?" Ozzy pushed.

"Fine," Malone said, waving him off. "Get together with Nessman and check the guy out. Name's Jimmy, that's all I know."

"Jimmy, got it," Ozzy repeated to commit the name to memory. He finished stuffing his briefcase then sat silently. He raised his eyes to Malone's.

"Something else?" Malone asked. There was no response as Ozzy shifted his weight uncomfortably. "Spit it out, Oz."

"Your brother, Brass. He's on the lam again."

Malone's face tightened. "Half-brother," he said, because the detail was important to him. "Yeah, I heard. What kind of problems is that going to cause us?"

"None. We're way-insulated from him. I put layers in place the last time he was locked up."

Malone twisted his mouth into a scowl and shook his head. "I don't know what's wrong with that fucking kid. Beat a goddamned state trooper nearly to death, and a broad for Christ's sake."

"Vincent Underwood's no angel, Brass. He does what suits him in the moment, consequences be damned."

"I know. What about the cop. How bad is she?"

"Tough as nails, from what I hear. A nurse at Elliot Hospital that one of our guys sells dope to said she'll probably be discharged tomorrow. I tell you, the fact that Lorraine Underwood could give birth to both you and that undisciplined degenerate never ceases to amaze me."

"You can't pick family," Malone said.

"Sure, but that doesn't mean you have to snuggle up to him. He's been a real pain in the ass over the years. I say you leave him to rot."

"He's blood," Malone said plainly. There was a long pause, and Ozzy shrank in his chair.

"Sorry."

"Can we scrape together ten-grand for him? To get his ass out of town, at least?" Malone asked.

"Ten is too much. The government's watching your money pretty closely. You want to take a chance getting linked to Vincent, then eat an indictment for helping a fugitive that tried to kill a cop?"

"No, I guess not," Malone said.

Tipping his head back and closing his eyes, Malone held the pose a full fifteen seconds. Ozzy had seen it before, whenever the man was weighing what he wanted to do against the often diametrically opposed wiser choice.

"You still have a hook into that kid on the job? What's his name?" Malone asked.

"I never told you his name, Brass. You can't get jammed up for having a cop on the take if you don't even know his name. And yeah, I've still got him. He just gave up five thousand on the Sox-Yankees series, and I know he doesn't have it. The hook's set pretty deep with that one."

"Get some cash to Underwood through him. And let's do five thousand to attract a little less attention. If it starts to come back on us, we'll hear about it from the cop and can get in front of it."

"Good," Ozzy replied, jotting a note. "I'll set it up." He slipped his pen into a breast pocket and raised his eyebrows to Malone. "That's it then."

"That's it. Thanks Oz."

Ozzy stood up, shook the man's hand, and left the room.

CHAPTER 14

Betsy Diaz's discharge from the hospital had gone as she expected. Delayed, inconvenient, and slow. Nevertheless, as her mother pushed her wheelchair across the lobby of Elliot Hospital, Diaz was grateful to be free.

It had been a week and a half since the attack, and while the doctors said her recovery was progressing faster than expected, Diaz was frustrated with her limited mobility. Her right arm rested in a sling to relieve the broken shoulder of bearing weight. The early diagnosis of a punctured lung had been inaccurate, and further examination showed the fractured ribs had only bruised it. Her ankle was a different story. The first surgery had stabilized the joint and removed two pieces of splintered bone. During the second, an orthopedist had installed a small metal plate. Diaz would walk again, eventually even run, but the installed hardware was permanent.

Camila Diaz, a tall, elegant woman of sixty-one with smooth greying hair pulled discreetly into a bun, paused at the automatic doors long enough for the motion sensor to respond and pull them open. She eased the wheelchair out, secured the foot brake, and walked around to open the passenger door of her Toyota Highlander SUV. She had pulled it up to the pickup loop just before Betsy's discharge.

It was cold, more so than expected for a mid-autumn afternoon, but the sun shone down and warmed them. Camila bent to take her daughter's hand.

"Can I sit here for a minute first?" Betsy asked. "I want to try to do it myself."

"Sweetheart, no," cooed Camila as she swept an errant lock of hair from her daughter's forehead. "The doctor said no weight bearing for another day, and then only gradually."

"I can do it on the other foot," Betsy countered as she pressed down hard on the wheelchair's railing with one arm and rose to her feet. The awkward move required bracing her core, which shot bolts of pain through her torso. Wincing, she hesitated at the top to gauge her balance. When Camila took her by the elbow, Betsy didn't resist.

They negotiated the awkward five-foot shuffle to the car. Seated painfully on the front passenger side, Betsy tried unsuccessfully to fasten her seatbelt one-handed. Her effort failed two more times. Closing her eyes in frustration, she leaned her head back against the rest. Her bottom lip tightened as her eyes grew wet.

"I hate this," she said quietly.

"Let me get it," Camila said, pretending not to see the tears. She reached over her daughter and clicked the belt into place. After closing the door, she retrieved a bag hung on the back of the wheelchair, put it in the backseat, and got behind the wheel. Camila pulled through the lot, turned into traffic, and headed for the interstate. Five minutes later they were headed north toward Concord.

"Thanks for picking me up, Mom."

"Of course. I told your father we'd call as soon as you got out. You want to do it now or wait until we get to your place."

"He's working. I'll call later."

"He's off at five, but he's not driving today. He's working in the office so he can take your call."

Betsy's father, Guillermo Diaz, had worked for the Massachusetts Bay Transit Authority for twenty-seven years. He had risen to the position of supervisor, and was in charge of six stations on the Green Line section of Boston's train system, known simply as the T.

"I'll call him tonight," said Betsy.

After a pause, Camila said, "He wanted to come."

"I know."

"He came the day it happened, to meet with your lieutenant and make sure you were okay. He wanted to come today."

"I said I know, Mom."

"It's not that he didn't want to. He just...I think he thought it would be easier for you if only I came up. You know, to get you settled."

"Yeah, easier for me," Betsy said quietly as she looked out the window.

They rode in silence for five minutes.

"You're father's a proud man, Betsaida. It's hard for him to see what that man did to you."

"I understand."

"Don't be dismissive. He wants to try and protect you."

"I'm twenty-seven, Mom."

"That doesn't matter."

"Does he get into that same maudlin and worrisome mood when Billy gets hurt? Or Robert for that matter?"

"It's different. They're older."

"And they're men."

"That's not fair, Bets," Camila said defensively.

"Billy's an officer in the navy, Mom. And Bobby's a fireman. You're telling me that's not worth worrying about?"

Betsy cleared her throat, which caused her to cough, which hurt. She adjusted her posture and suppressed a groan.

"Are you okay?" Camila asked, resting a hand on her daughter's knee.

"Yeah," Betsy replied, carefully taking a painful breath. "Once I get settled in, I want to take another pill and go to bed."

"The doctor said you're not due for another one until six."

"It'll probably take me that damn long to get into my apartment," Betsy said with a chuckle. She smiled, and her mother returned it. Betsy took her mother's hand, and they rode silently until the exit. Back on surface streets, it was painful for Betsy to keep herself upright through the start-and-stop traffic.

The apartment was a third-floor walkup just off North Main Street, and the only elevator was a service lift accessible through the back. The landlord helped get them up, then gave Betsy a key to the elevator and a standing offer for help any time she needed it.

"He seemed nice," Camila said after getting Betsy settled onto the couch.

"He just likes having a cop live in the building."

"Or maybe he's just nice, Betsaida."

"Maybe."

Camila cooked them dinner, which pleased Betsy immensely. The hospital's food had taken a toll. After her mother cleaned up, Betsy struggled through a shower, with help, and got into bed.

"I'll stay tonight. And tomorrow until the home nurse comes."

"Thank you. I'm going to call a physical therapist tomorrow, too," Betsy said. "I want to see if they'll come to the house."

"Will your insurance cover that? Didn't the doctor say to wait a week before starting PT?"

"I don't know, but I want to do it anyway, even if I have to pay on my own. I want to get started."

"What's the rush?"

"The sooner I'm back, the sooner I can help find Underwood."

"Betsy, they'll catch him. Let the police do their jobs."

"I *am* the police, Mom."

"You know what I meant."

"Yeah, I do."

"Why are you trying to pick a fight with me, Honey?"

"Forget it."

Camila, who had been sitting on the edge of the bed, stood up and pulled the down blanket to her daughter's shoulders and tucked it around her. Betsy lifted her good arm and pushed it back down. Their eyes met in frustration. Camila sat back down, facing away. A minute passed.

"It happened on Olivia's birthday, you know. The day you got hurt." Camila said.

"Mom, please. I don't want to do this again."

Camila's voice broke when she spoke. She cleared her throat and tried again.

"She would have been thirty."

"That doesn't mean anything. Not as if it were some sort of sign," said Betsy.

"I know, it's just something your father and I were talking about last night."

Betsy didn't respond.

"Why do you insist it's such a bad thing, us worrying about you?"

"Because of the way you both do it, Mom. Like I'm made of glass. Babies get sick sometimes. Olivia died. It happened a long time ago."

"How can you be so cold, Betsaida. She was your sister."

"No, Mom, she wasn't. I wasn't even alive when she died."

"Betsaida Maria, don't you..."

"We've been over this, Mom," Betsy interrupted. "I don't want to rehash it every time. I'm the only one in our family who didn't know her. The only one who doesn't mourn her death every year. I just wish you all would stop holding it against me as if I had done something wrong. As if I was some kind of jerk."

"No one does that. It just colors what your father and I think when something bad happens to you, or you face a tough challenge. That's just the way it is. And I know you're upset right now and on medication..."

"That has nothing to do with it."

"...but you are being incredibly insensitive to me, and to your father."

They sat in heavy silence for a moment until

Betsy spoke again.

"I'm not going to quit my job."

"I don't want you to, Sweetheart."

"And Dad?" Betsy asked with a skeptical eye.

"That's a different story. It's more complicated for him. He feels helpless."

"That's my point, Mom. He *is* helpless. So are you. It's my life now."

"A point you're committed to proving every chance you get."

"You think I wanted this to happen?"

"I think you take too many chances."

Betsy opened her mouth to reply but stopped short when she realized she had no rebuttal. She laid her head back and allowed her eyes to rise to the ceiling before closing them. After a moment, she felt her mother raise the blanket to her neck again. This time she didn't resist.

"I'm going to make tea. Do you want any?"

"No," Betsy mumbled. She tried to roll onto her side, failed, and turned back.

"Rest then," Camila said, stroking her daughter's forehead. "I'll leave you alone for a little bit."

Betsy didn't respond. Five minutes later, when her mother noticed Betsy's breathing had slowed and become rhythmic, she stood silently and slipped out of the room.

CHAPTER 15

Officer Peter Shattuck was rotund, stretching his uniform shirt into broad, lateral creases, taut at the buttons. He was an avuncular man of fifty-two with thick shoulders and a full head of graying hair. Shattuck had been pushing a police cruiser through the streets of Manchester for thirty-one years and had never sought, nor received, promotion or reassignment. A cantankerous malcontent who never had to search for something to bemoan, he was also phenomenally good at his job. That is, when he actually found the motivation to do it.

For the past three weeks Shattuck had been partnered with Officer Jon Porter, a graduate of the police academy six months earlier and from Manchester PD's field-training program three months after that. He was a rookie, a career classification for which Shattuck had little patience.

The two officers stood outside their parked cruiser on Henriette Street, Shattuck's hip casually pressed against the fender and Porter focused intently on the task at hand. Before them stood Detectives Charlie Wilcox and Don Mollie, preparing to update them on the effort to locate and arrest Vincent Underwood.

"You think he's in there?" Porter asked of no one in particular.

"You think he's in there?" Shattuck repeated mockingly. Porter looked at him, frustrated, then at the ground in embarrassment.

"You about done, Pete?" asked Wilcox.

Shattuck took a sip of cold coffee and smiled at his fellow veteran officer.

"Sure Charlie. What've you guys got?"

Henriette Street was just east of Mast Road on Manchester's West Side. The ethnic makeup of the former French-Canadian enclave had changed, but its character had not. It was still dominated by working-class families living paycheck-to-paycheck, some day-to-day. A mixture of Puerto Rican, French-Canadian, and Portuguese families now lived in tight and loyal, but distinctly separate pockets. The one commonality was their Catholic faith, and much of the West Side attended one of the nine masses offered every weekend at Sainte Marie's Church.

"Like I told you on the phone, Vincent Underwood's mother said he loves to bowl," Wilcox began. Porter, the rookie, almost came to attention as the briefing started. "She seems to think he'd even try to get a few frames in while on the run."

"Moron," Shattuck interrupted, grousing around his coffee cop. "You guys ever catch the smart ones?"

Wilcox ignored him and continued.

"This guy has a lot to lose. He's looking at three-and-a-half to seven years for failing to register and another seven-and-a-half to fifteen for the assault on Diaz. Probably twenty-five or more for stabbing that kid in the bar. The prosecutor is expected to charge him with attempted murder on that one."

Wilcox paused for effect and looked back and

forth between the two uniformed officers before continuing.

"Add that up and he's looking at a life sentence.
And we've learned a few things about Underwood since
his flight from the state police."

Porter stood erect, his lithe frame tense with anticipation. Shattuck looked bored. He kicked at a loose
stone on the ground and continued to sip the same cup
of coffee that Porter noticed seemed to last all day.

"Underwood enlisted in the Army immediately
following high school, and was two months into a tour
in Afghanistan when they shipped him home with a
dishonorable discharge," continued Wilcox. "We're still
waiting for reports from the defense department, but at
this point all we know is he beat up his commanding
officer.

"When he returned, he moved back in with mom
for a month before she threw him out. He was in and
out of jail for a while, mostly small-time drug offenses,
until he caught a rape charge that was pleaded down to
sexual misconduct. He did four years for that, which is
why he's on the registry."

"You think he's going to fight, Detective?" asked
Porter.

"Or run. As I said, he's got a lot to lose. Sadly, it's
a fairly easy endeavor for a criminal to obtain a gun in
this town, and we know what he did to Diaz in that
alley. Don't take any chances with him."

Wilcox looked over at Mollie and nodded. "You
want to brief us on the rest of this, Don?"

"Sure thing. A buddy of mine in Narcotics has an
informant that does a lot of heroin cases for him. The
guy is working off a child porn charge and apparently

knows Underwood, or at least knew him before he was in the wind. This guy says Underwood's been hanging his hat on the West Side, laying low until he gets his out set up."

Officer Shattuck, who nobody thought was really paying attention said, "That make sense. They used to run whores out of the back of this place."

Both detectives looked over to Shattuck. "Which place is that?" asked Mollie, not very pleasantly. "I haven't said where we're going yet."

"Queen City Lanes," Shattuck replied. "Around the block on Mast Road. That's where we're headed, right? Why we're set up here?"

"What makes you think that?" asked Mollie.

Shattuck spit on the pavement and smiled at the detectives. He winked at Porter, which caught the rookie off guard.

"Well, *Detective,* it is true that I am a washed-up street cop that couldn't find a felony arrest if it walked up to me and confessed. But it's more for a lack of desire than a lack of ability."

Mollie looked at his partner, then at Porter, then back at Shattuck.

"What the fuck are you talking about, Shattuck?"

The old-timer feigned a thoughtful look and scratched his chin with the back of the hand holding the coffee cup. When he spoke, his voice dripped of condescension and sarcasm.

"Well, gee. Let's see. You are looking for a bad guy who likes to bowl. Loves it, according to his Mommy. You just said your buddy in Narcotics told you that this particular bad guy hangs out on the West Side. And here we are, less than one block from Queen City Lanes, a hole in the wall bowling alley with only three lanes, the rest of the space being reserved for the unlicensed 'massage tables' behind the office.

"Whores being whores, and sex offenders being sex offenders," Shattuck continued, "it stands to reason your guy might be interested in that sort of thing. If I were a bowling-loving horny sex offender who was hiding out on the West Side and wanted to kill two birds with one stone, Queen City Lanes would be right up my alley."

Shattuck lifted his cup to take a sip, but paused for a self-satisfied chuckle at his pun.

Wilcox stood grinning, his arms crossed. He'd known Peter Shattuck a long time. The man had been burned by the department early, and never clawed his way back. But he was a good, solid cop with excellent instincts. He would have been a very capable detective if things had gone a different way all those years ago.

"Yes, Peter," Wilcox continued. "We're going to Queen City Lanes. You both have had the benefit of examining pictures of the suspect, right? We've got a few more. Computer mark-ups that Mollie created for us show him with facial hair, bald, so on. Take a few of them and commit the face to memory."

Mollie pulled a series of eight-by-ten photographs out of a folder and handed them to the two uniformed officers. He flipped his notebook shut and jammed it into the breast pocket of his suit coat, then tossed the file folder in the back seat of the Charger. He confirmed the patrol officers were looking at Wilcox, not him, and typed rapidly into his phone.

"We're going to walk in. Me and Mollie in the front door," Wilcox said. "Shattuck, you cover the north side,

Porter around back." As he spoke Wilcox held up his portable police radio and wagged the antenna. "We're on channel two. Got it?"

Shattuck winked. Porter removed his radio from his belt and dutifully checked the frequency setting. Wilcox, aware as he walked that Mollie was not with him, looked back and saw him still leaning on the car.

"You going to join us, Detective?"

"Yeah, sorry Charlie. Knocking out a quick text. I'm with you."

"Okay fellas," Wilcox said as he turned to walk away with Mollie. "Look sharp. We already know what this guy will do to avoid getting arrested. He's not going to go easy."

Neither Detectives Donovan Mollie nor Charlie Wilcox actually believed what they had told Shattuck and Porter. It was exceptionally unlikely that Underwood was going to be at Queen City Lanes. Wanted felons tended to burrow deep, and no one burrowed deeper than a sex offender. It was a long shot, but it was a box that had to be checked.

Sex offenders were the scourge of society, the dingy castoff smeared along the bottom of society's undercarriage. Unlike what movies and media had done for some criminals, there was no over-romanticized connection between violence and sex, no visage of a reputable scoundrel representing honor among thieves. Sex offenders didn't even benefit from the pity afforded heroin addicts and the petty theft some committed in an effort to scrape together cash for their next hit. They were grotesque, soiled to the soul, hated.

Vincent T. Underwood was finishing his fourth

beer at a small table in the back corner of the bar, which was itself settled into the rear of the building. He had done a little coke with Daisy, or Dorothy, or whatever the hell her name was. She'd been a disappointment, and between that and the coke he needed something to mellow him out.

Underwood looked up from the drink and his gaze fell upon the bartender. As he polished a chipped-up glass, the man squinted toward the lobby. Underwood followed his eyes and saw two men in suits walking toward the concession counter, thirty feet away. He recognized their role immediately.

Cops.

Releasing the glass bottle, Underwood lowered his hand below the table and allowed his forearm to press against the outside of his jacket pocket. He noted the weight of the Colt .357 revolver and felt relief. His quickening pulse leveled off as he began to assess and plan.

The fat black one won't be able to run. The tall skinny one will, so he needs to go down first. If this happens, my best chance is a few shots to distract them, then bolt for the door.

Underwood slid the beer bottle across the table, making a scraping noise louder than he intended. Neither detective looked over. His right hand entered the jacket pocket and he wrapped all five fingers around the rubber grip of the weapon. His index finger touched the trigger, as if double checking it was there, and he slid the first pad of his digit up and down its length.

The three-hundred dollars Underwood's mother had given him hadn't lasted. He'd stolen the gun, but paid for the beer and cocaine, leaving sixty bucks for an oversized Patriots jacket and a bottle of hair dye. He'd shaved most of his face and blackened his hair and newly formed goatee. Hopefully it would be enough.

The fat one looked right at him, then turned back to the concession clerk they were bracing. She wasn't helping. The other one was looking around, seeming bored. The black one was the boss. He was thorough, putting the clerk through her paces.

They looked like they were wrapping up. The black cop pressed his card onto the counter and slid it across to the clerk, who didn't pick it up. Underwood's heartrate relaxed further.

Then the boss looked across the room and his eyes fell to Underwood. He touched his partner's arm, who was preparing to leave, and whispered something to him. They both turned their bodies square to Underwood and started walking. The lithe detective's jacket came open and his hand went inside.

Underwood took a deep breath, held it, and exhaled hard. As he firmed up the grip on his gun he started to stand. It was on.

CHAPTER 16

The front sight of Underwood's gun barrel snagged on his pocket as he pulled it out and as a result, he lost much in the way of time advantage. Action was always quicker than reaction and if he had gotten a clean draw, he likely could have put one of the cops down right out of the gate. Now, he'd be lucky to start shooting the same time they did.

Underwood's first two shots went high and struck the ceiling above Mollie's head, causing puffy bits of ceiling tile to rain down. Mollie moved behind the edge of the counter and fired back. Two bullets smashed into a pool table that stood between them, sending wood splinters into the air. A third punched a tidy hole in the side of Underwood's unzipped jacket, leaving the intended target unscathed.

"Delta-thirty-two reporting shots fired, our location!" Wilcox bellowed into his portable radio as he ducked for cover. The transmission was immediately followed by an intense exchange of squelchy chatter, none of which the detective heard.

Squatting behind a rack of bowling balls, Wilcox looked over at Mollie, confirmed he was uninjured, then focused back on Underwood. The suspect was running toward the back of the building along a thin strip of carpet that ran the length of the lanes. Wilcox jumped to his feet and sprinted across two bowling lanes to cut him off. The moment his leather-soled shoes contacted the highly waxed hardwood planks, he lost his footing. Wilcox slapped down hard as he landed painfully on his back. Mollie saw what happened to his partner and elected to stay on the carpet.

"You alright?" he yelled. Wilcox didn't reply, but Mollie saw he was rolling onto his side and starting to sit up. That was a good enough answer.

"Delta-three-two," Mollie called into his radio during a break in the transmissions. "Suspect is in a red Patriots jacket with black hair, headed out the back." If there was a response, he didn't hear it.

Underwood made it to the back of the room and located a dirty steel door. Above it hung a dimly lit exit sign, dangling by one screw. He kicked at the bar across the door's midsection and popped it open. Sunlight burst into the darkened space and temporarily blinded him. He continued to run unabated, tripped over the raised threshold, and painfully ground his elbows into the pavement. The revolver went skittering across the macadam.

Underwood put his hands under his chest to push upward when a flash of black appeared a few feet to his right. Glancing over, he saw leather boots. He didn't need to look up further.

"Freeze, Police! Show me your hands!" screamed Officer Jon Porter, an octave higher than his usual tone.

Underwood noticed the officer's timbre and recognized its significance. Anxiety. Fear. A rookie. Rising to his knees, he put his hands over his head. The officer was fifteen feet away, his gun grasped in both hands in standard police fashion. Underwood began to stand up.

"Stay on your knees or I'll shoot you!"

The officer stayed where he was. Not too close and not too far. Good police tactics. Underwood needed him to get closer.

Underwood rocked back onto his feet, as if he were going to try and stand, but didn't. This time the threatening gesture worked, and Porter took three steps forward and repeated his threat.

"I said stay on your knees or..."

Porter's sentence was cut in half when Underwood lunged. He gripped the barrel of the officer's pistol with both hands, twisting hard to the right while moving to the left. A shot rang out and burrowed into the pavement next to Underwood's foot. Pushing up and backward on the pistol, the weapon slipped from the officer's sweaty palms.

It was a classic disarming move, practiced a thousand times in prison, and Underwood now held the officer's gun.

The young man's shock was still evident on his face when Underwood crushed the .40 caliber Glock directly into his nose. He struck again, viciously, and the officer went down, blood gushing from a fractured eye socket. The assault had leveled Porter to a seated position, and Underwood stepped forward and delivered a devastating blow with his knee to the officer's head, knocking him out.

Underwood ran north onto Pinard Street. He turned right, his head on a swivel. He needed a place to hide, hostage to take, or car to steal. Another lot opened up on the left and he ran toward it, dodging a passing car and hopping a waist high fence.

Sprinting through two parking lots and one backyard, Underwood found himself on Edmond Street. He looked behind him but saw no one in pursuit. There was a distant wail of sirens, but he ignored them. On a 'shots fired' call all the responding officers would collapse onto the scene, especially with an officer down. That would leave him space to run. It would be five minutes before they even set up a perimeter, let alone started to search.

Underwood slowed his pace to relieve his burning lungs. His tunnel vision started to widen as he recognized the neighborhood. It was Edmond Street, about a block, maybe two, down from Roosevelt. Tully's was on Roosevelt.

The thin strands of an idea began to knit together into a plan. Dave Ester, the bartender at Tully's, sold crack as well as booze and used to do burglaries before serving two-to-four in prison a decade earlier. He had no love for cops, and Underwood could hide there.

Rounding the block, Underwood saw a small sign on the corner of the building that housed Tully's Road House. He slowed to a walk and checked again behind him for pursuers. In doing so, he didn't see the man emerge from an alley just before the entrance to Tully's until he felt an oversized fist smash into his face.

Underwood's legs went out from under him. Officer Peter Shattuck grabbed him by the hair, lifted him unceremoniously, and delivered another driving blow to his nose. It burst like a tomato and Underwood collapsed to the pavement, dazed. Shattuck stood erect to catch his breath. He had stationed himself in a nearby alley and when he'd heard the radio transmission of the shootout and escape, had suspected where Underwood would flee. He himself had jogged the two blocks to arrive at Tully's in time, and was badly winded.

His breath returning, Shattuck reached to the small of his back and unsnapped a handcuff case. Holding the first cuff, he bent, then knelt as he reached for Underwood's right arm.

As Shattuck had caught his breath, Underwood retrieved a small blade from inside his belt. When the officer reached for him, Underwood's left hand erupted from beneath his torso and slashed across Shattuck's forearm. As the officer recoiled from the attack, Underwood sat up onto his hip, repeatedly driving the four-inch blade through Shattuck's calf, into his knee, then his thigh. He grasped the front of the officer's duty belt and pulled him closer as he struck again and again, working his way up the soft inside of Shattuck's upper leg in search of the femoral artery. Each stab was accompanied by a twist and pull, tearing and cutting through fat and muscle.

Shattuck lost his balance and sat backward as Underwood found his footing and stood. When he did, he drove an upper-cutting elbow into the cop's chin. The attacker was on the move again before Shattuck hit the ground. He ran to the entrance of Tully's and was met with a scowling Dave Ester, visible through the glass window. Ester quickly reached down and deadbolted the door.

Underwood's face registered rage as he slapped at the glass menacingly, smearing it with Shattuck's blood. Sprinting away, he slipped into an alley and saw Shattuck's cruiser, parked a block away. He continued north, and saw the road ended at a tree line a hundred feet deep before opening into a park of unused sports fields. There was a small structure, and Underwood made for it. He'd rest, clean up, and make a plan.

Back on Edmond Street, Wilcox pulled his cruiser up to Tully's in response to Shattuck's panicked radio transmission. Four additional 911 calls had come in for an officer being attacked. Wilcox slammed the column shifter into park before the car was fully stopped, then leapt from the vehicle and ran to the old cop.

Shattuck was slumped against the brick wall outside Tully's. Blood pooled thickly around him and continued to erupt from his leg. It pumped at a slow pace, revealing how little remained in his body. His face was gray, his skin sweaty but cool. Wilcox grabbed Shattuck's neck violently in search of a pulse, which caused him to stir. He was alive.

A uniform pulled up, then another, braking too hard and too late and bumping the back of Wilcox's car. The detective yelled for a tourniquet and the second officer to arrive tore one from his duty belt and extended it. He wrapped it quickly around Shattuck's upper thigh and yanked it taut. The five-inch windlass popped free, and the officer began to twist. Two turns in, Shattuck moaned.

"It's alright, Brother," Wilcox said, pushing hair out of the cop's face with a bloody hand. "It's gonna hurt, but it's good for you. Trust me."

Shattuck moaned again as they continued to twist, painfully constricting the nylon band around his leg. One eye opened, and he raised a hand to his thigh and weakly tried to brush the tourniquet away. Wilcox pushed his arm back down, and turned his attention to the other officer.

"Crank it down hard," he said unnecessarily. Then, looking up the street, "Where's the fucking ambulance?"

Having staunched the blood flow, the uniformed officer locked the windlass under a Velcro strap. He produced a pen, checked his watch, and wrote the time on a plastic tab attached to the tourniquet. Wilcox smothered his index finger into the pooling blood and drew a large 'T' on Shattuck's forehead so that overworked and harried ER staff would know to look for it. He looked at the two officers, then back up the street for the absent ambulance.

"We're not waiting. You each grab an arm. I'll get his feet. We're bringing him to the hospital ourselves."

CHAPTER 17

Charlie Wilcox sat at his desk, pushed front-to-front with his partner's. The file drawer on the left was slung open, and Wilcox's feet rested on it. A short divider rose between the workstations, providing a modicum of privacy. It had also been pressed into service as a coat rack.

Wilcox had removed his suit jacket, revealing a neatly ironed and spotless shirt. It was far better than he usually looked when a case carried him into the wee morning hours. After getting Shattuck to the hospital and briefing the brass who responded there, he had gone back to the bowling alley to provide a statement to the internal affairs unit that would be investigating the officer-involved shooting.

The IA interview had taken longer than he'd hoped, and Wilcox had not arrived home until ten that night. He had quickly showered and put on a fresh suit, the previous one having been covered in dried blood. It wasn't salvageable. Wilcox had made a sandwich, kissed his wife, Charlene, and gone back to work.

"We'll get him, Charlie. He's bound to slip up. It's only a matter of time."

Donovan Mollie sat across from his partner. He knew his words of encouragement rang hollow.

"And how exactly will we accomplish that?" Wilcox challenged. "He's unlikely to patronize another bowling alley any time soon."

"Ah, Christ. I don't know. But we sure as hell aren't going to find him in the squad room at one in the morning." Mollie replied. He leaned back and ran his fingers through crew cut hair. He looked around the empty detective squad and let his hands slap down onto his thighs. "How's Shattuck doing?"

"He's going to pull through," Wilcox said, happy to change the subject. "Old and slow, but a tough sonofabitch, that guy."

"How about the kid, Porter. He okay?" Mollie added.

"Yes, him too. His face was smashed up quite badly. They're going to take him up to Dartmouth tomorrow morning. They have a rather accomplished surgeon who specializes in facial reconstruction."

"Jesus."

"Indeed," Wilcox said. "Shattered eye socket, detached retina, and a lot of damage to the optical nerve. He probably won't lose the eye, but is unlikely to see out of it again."

"He's young, at least. How long does Shattuck have on the job?"

"I don't know, twenty-five, thirty years at least. His bitterness was already imbedded when I came on, and I'm considered one of the Old Guard."

"Think he'll cash it in now?" Mollie asked.

"If he's smart, yes. I suspect he was holding out a few additional years to add some percentile to his retirement multiplier. That said, with a medical drop he'll be awarded a fifteen percent bump on it. That, plus a worker's compensation settlement, and he should be in pretty good shape. Financially, at least."

"He married?"

"Yes," Wilcox said with a smile. "Betty. Sweet woman. You wouldn't think so, him being such an ornery bastard, but they enjoy what is likely the happiest marriage in the department."

"You know him pretty well? I picked up on it when we briefed in the parking lot before going into Queen City Lanes," Mollie asked.

"We did a couple years together on the overnight tour before I transferred into investigations."

"Lot of stories I bet," Mollie prompted. Wilcox looked down at a file folder before him and shuffled a few sheets of paper. "Well?" Mollie pushed.

"Well what, Don?"

"Stories! There have to be some doozies. The guy's a legend. He's been in patrol longer than half the force has been alive. What the hell else is there to talk about at one AM while we wait for something to break in this case."

"Another time," Wilcox said dismissively.

"C'mon, Man. What's wrong with now?"

"No, I mean it *was* another time. It was a different city, with different bosses."

"And?"

"I said leave it alone, Mollie. Let's just work the case before us, shall we?"

Mollie sighed and shifted his weight in the chair, refocusing on the computer in front of him. "Do you want to go at the mother again?"

"Perhaps," said Wilcox. "Someone gave him money to buy that gun. And the girl at Queen City Lanes said he paid her, too. It had to come from somewhere, and the mom is as likely a candidate as any."

"You want to go out there tonight? A visit from the cops in the middle of the night might rattle something loose."

"We could. But there has to be something else. I'd rather shake a different tree and see what falls out."

"What have you got in mind?" Mollie asked.

"When was Underwood last arrested?"

There was the sound of rapid key-tapping as Mollie checked the department of correction internal database.

"DOC has him doing six months on a parole violation in 2019."

"Is his visitor log listed?" Wilcox asked.

"Yeah, sure. Hang on." More typing, followed by a long pause. "Okay, here. Got it. Nothing, no visitors."

"No visitors for six months?" Wilcox asked. "That's significant."

"You going to visit a guy like that?"

"No, but his mom would, I should think." Wilcox paused to rub the mental dust from behind his eyes. "How about his canteen. Who put money in there?"

Because Mollie was already into Underwood's online DOC profile, the information did not take as long to load.

"Looks like Mom did. Two hundred dollars during the first week."

"Lorraine?"

"Yeah."

"Did anyone else give him money?" Wilcox asked. "No."

"How about during other tours, other times he's

been locked up?"

More banging of keys, then "Nope, just her. Anywhere between fifty and three hundred dollars, usually in the first week of his sentence. That's it," Mollie said.

Wilcox pulled his feet off the drawer and planted them on the floor. Leaning back, he crossed his arms and pinched in his lips together. He looked right, then down, and held it.

"What have you got?" Mollie asked after fifteen seconds. Wilcox remained in silent thought another ten before speaking.

"Instead of looking up who else has donated money to Underwood's canteen, can you look up if there are any other prisoners that Lorraine has given money to?" Wilcox asked.

"What do you mean?"

"Look up Lorraine's profile, and tell me if there are other prisoners to whom she has given money over the years."

"Gotcha," muttered Mollie as he typed. "Online records only back to 2005, but it'll give me anyone else she has contributed to since then." He continued typing. "Got it!"

"What?" Wilcox asked, getting to his feet and walking around to peer over Mollie's shoulder.

"She never gave anyone else money, but in 2006 she visited someone in Strafford County Jail."

"Who?"

"Doesn't say. Just gives the inmate number, 35986. Let me see what I can do with that." A moment later, the prisoner file for inmate 35986, Brass Malone, appeared on the screen. Mollie removed his fingers from the keyboard and leaned back in his chair. Wilcox stood up erect.

"Well, shit," Mollie muttered. "*That's* a lead."

"Is that the same Malone I'm thinking of?" Wilcox asked.

"DOB looks right," Mollie said. "Says here he was locked up on a robbery charge that eventually got dismissed."

"That sounds like him. Bring up a photo."

Mollie did, and they both looked at the most recent booking photo of Brass Malone, currently lodged in the Valley Street Jail in Manchester, New Hampshire.

"Now tell me, Detective Mollie," Wilcox said in a sonorous investigative tone. "Why would Lorraine Underwood have visited Brass Malone in jail in 2006 when he was locked up for a robbery?"

"The visitor log says she wrote 'mother' as the relationship."

"Is that credible?" Wilcox asked.

"It'll be easy enough to confirm. Just nail down Malone's birthplace and we can get his birth certificate from vital records."

"Do that tomorrow, first thing," Wilcox said. "In the meantime, get out of the DOC database and log back into our local files. What is Malone into nowadays? I thought he was locked up again."

"According to this he is," Mollie said. "Pretrial confinement for a gun charge. But he's also got an open UCX file." UCX was the designator for a clandestine investigation, and the reports within it were not visible to other members of the department.

"Does he really?" Wilcox asked curiously.

"That's what it says. But of course, we can't access sealed UCX files, and you know how undercover guys are. We'll get exactly jack-shit from them. Vice, narcos, the whole special investigation unit is squirrely as shit. They won't tell us a damn thing about why they're looking into Malone."

"Don't be so negative, Don. I know a guy over there I can reach out to. He might be willing to shed some light on our as yet darkened case."

"Another one of your 'back in a different time' partners?"

"Yes, something like that."

CHAPTER 18

The ride from Manchester to Alton was only an hour, but the slow-moving traffic of autumn leaf-peepers added monotony and anxiety to Wilcox's impatient mind. When he had called, Jimmy Brennan had agreed to meet, but insisted they do so far from the city. It was a common demand of undercover detectives. That was, if they agreed to meet with you at all.

Wilcox had a decade of departmental seniority over Brennan, but they had briefly worked side-by-side on several cases when Brennan first became a detective. They shared a common outlook on police work. Both were aggressive, hard chargers with little tolerance for the internal political bureaucracy which sometimes obstructed investigations. They recognized the value of chasing down obscure leads and a focused analysis of facts. Wilcox had transferred to a different unit after six months, but they had become friends and stayed in touch.

Wilcox turned off Main Street into the dirt lot of Aroma Joe's Coffee. Brennan's car was already backed into a space near the rear. Wilcox decided against checking the parking area, knowing Brennan already would have. He nosed in next to his old partner.

As both windows descended, Brennan extended a

paper cup of black coffee, nearly saturated with sugar, out the window. Wilcox smiled as he wordlessly took it, popped the sip hole, and sampled a taste.

"I'm touched. You remembered," Wilcox said. "How've you been?"

"Good, Charlie. You?"

"Same. Quite busy, to be sure. How's Sarah doing? And your daughter, I'm sorry I can't recall, Molly?"

"Maggie. No problem. It's been a minute, hasn't it?" said Brennan.

"Indeed."

"How was the drive up?" Brennan asked after taking a sip of his own coffee. "You want to get out, stretch your legs a bit?"

"I appreciate the offer, but no. It's probably better for you not to be seen going for an afternoon constitutional with the police."

Brennan chuckled. "Good point."

"How's that going? You've been under what, six years now?"

"Seven. It's good. The extra pay is nice and as you know, the nature of the job tends to insulate us from a lot of the political bullshit you guys have to deal with."

"Of this I know for sure. I came up through financial crimes, remember? Now *there's* politics. Nothing like arresting the mayor's brother for embezzlement to shorten one's police career."

"You came out of that all right, though."

"Yes, but certainly not for a lack of trying by Mayor Phillips and his cronies. See how much better you've got it working UC?"

"Better in some ways. At least when working financial cases, you don't have to drive an hour north to a sleepy little hamlet just to get a cup of coffee with an old friend."

"Touché," Wilcox said, gesturing toward Brennan with his cup. "Are you planning to stick with it?"

"Funny you should ask."

"Funny how?" Wilcox asked cocking his head.

"I've been thinking, and talking to Sarah a lot, about coming in."

"Not back on the road."

"Oh, God no. Investigations, I mean. Major crimes, if there was room."

"I bet there is. You talk to Soffit yet?" Wilcox asked. Captain Edward Soffit commanded the detective division of the Manchester Police Department.

"Not yet. We're getting together in a couple of days. He won't travel like this." Brennan gestured toward the coffee shop. "So it takes a few days to set up a safe meeting in the city somewhere."

"You think he'll go for it?" Wilcox asked.

"I don't plan on giving him a choice. UC is voluntary duty, or so I'm told. I think I can convince him."

"Fair enough. Well, I hope it works out. We could definitely use you. There's no shortage of work."

"How is Lieutenant Dawson to work for?" Brennan asked.

"You've heard the adage. Promote someone to lieutenant and all they think about is when they're going to make captain. But he's fair, and sharp as a tack. You won't sneak much past him, so I don't recommend attempting any of your usual independent-undercover-cop tomfoolery."

Brennan slapped both hands to his checks in feigned shock. "Charles! Whatever do you mean by that?"

Wilcox didn't bite the hook. "I'm serious, Jimmy. I've seen some of your work-arounds. Dawson will give you a lot of leeway, let you do your job, as long as you're straight with him."

"Fair enough," Brennan agreed.

Wilcox looked down at his cup, not entirely sure how the conversation between two old salts had grown awkward. Brennan broke the silence.

"What've you guys got going, case wise. Anything good?"

"That's actually why I wanted to meet," Wilcox said.

"I figured, maybe," Brennan said with a wry smile.

"Have you anything going with Brass Malone? He's organized, linked to Boston and Hartford."

Brennan's face hardened. "I know who he is. Brass Malone's in jail, Charlie."

"Yes, I'm aware. But there's an open UCX file on him."

"Who told you that?" asked Brennan.

"It's in the system. Anyone can see it."

"Anyone who goes looking can see it. Why are you looking?"

Wilcox was not surprised by the reticence. In fact, he respected it. Undercovers put their lives squarely in the hands of fate every time they worked a case, and secrecy was one of the few ways they could exercise some modicum of control.

"You know the name Vincent Underwood?" Wilcox asked.

"Sure. He's the sex offender who beat that trooper half to death. Then the shooting at the bowling alley yesterday. I was surprised when you called, frankly. That you had time for a coffee social with that case so active."

"Underwood and Malone are brothers."

"Bullshit," Brennan said. "That would have shown when we did our background on him."

"So, you are working him then," said Wilcox.

"That was cheap," Brennan acknowledged, shaking his head. "You walked me right into that, didn't you?"

"Yes, I did. And quite easily, too. You're getting sloppy. Perhaps it is time to give up undercover work."

"Fuck you, Charlie," Brennan said, laughing. "Talk to me about this brother business."

"Half-brothers, actually. Take a look at this." Wilcox manipulated his cell phone, brought up the proper screen, then handed it through the window to Brennan's outstretched hand.

"The first one is Underwood's birth certificate. Listed mother is Lorraine P. Underwood. Father is blank."

"Shocker," Brennan muttered.

"Scroll over. The next screen is Brass Malone's birth certificate. Same thing. Lorraine P. Underwood."

"No shit," Brennan said under his breath. "How did we miss this?" he asked himself.

"Look at the date of birth. For Lorraine, I mean. It's July 8th on Underwood's and July 3rd on Malone's."

"Gotta be the same woman. That's too similar."

"I'm sure it is, Jimmy. 'Three' and 'eight' look an awful lot alike if you write them too quickly, or if you make a copy-of-a-copy a half-dozen times."

"That also explains why it didn't pop on our

background of Malone. I'm sure the analysts only did a database search, using typed numbers," Brennan said. He pinched and scrolled around the documents before asking, "where did you get these?"

"Mollie called me on the way up here. I had him text them to me," Wilcox said, taking his phone back from Brennan.

"Mollie?"

"You've yet to meet. We've been partnered about eight months. Sharp kid. He came over from property."

"So, he's another person that knows about this Underwood-Malone connection. Are you going to tell him I'm working UC on Malone?" Brennan asked.

"I'd prefer not to, but you can be certain he'll inquire. He noted the UCX designation and is aware of our meeting today. Not with whom, of course. He's sure to ask how it went when I get back."

"It's a murder-for-hire case, Charlie. You can't tell him. My ass is really hanging out there on this one."

"Who's he looking to murder?"

"Don't know yet," Brennan said. "We've only met a few times. I'll probably find out at our next parley."

"I'm disappointed," Wilcox said. "I was hoping you were working him for something inconsequential. That would have allowed that we could help each other and get a lead on Underwood. Obviously, the murder case you're working is a priority."

"Ordinarily I'd agree, but that animal almost killed Shattuck. I can't jeopardize my case, but I'll certainly keep my ear to the ground. If anything comes up about a crazy brother, or if I get a chance to poke, I will."

"Don't do anything foolish. Enough cops have gotten hurt already," Wilcox warned.

"I won't."

Brennan took a final sip, crushed his paper cup, and tossed it on the floor of his car, symbolically ending that conversation.

"How's the trooper doing?" he asked.

"Her name's Diaz, and she's quite resilient. She's already been discharged from hospital and my understanding is she's hoping to return to light duty as soon as an appropriate assignment is available. She knows she can't work the street but wants to be a part of running Underwood to ground."

"I thought he smashed her up pretty good," Brennan said.

"He did. Fractured ribs as well as her shoulder, which is in a sling. The original diagnosis had a rib puncturing her lung, but it turns out the organ was bruised, but not torn. Her ankle was badly damaged as well. There is enough metal in there now that it'll take her an extra ten minutes to negotiate airport security."

"All that, and she's already itching to come back? She should take a break. God knows she earned it."

"Would you?" asked Wilcox. Brennan just looked at him. "I didn't think so."

"Back to this Malone-Underwood thing," Brennan said. "The court is pretty deep into Malone's financials regarding his upcoming sentencing. I'll ask them to look for any movement or transfers that look funny. Bus tickets, flights, that sort of thing. Usually, they only flag transactions over ten-thousand dollars but if Malone is helping his little brother it would probably be less than that. I think we could do that without spooking anything."

"I'd appreciate it. Anything would help."

"What's the background on Underwood, any-way?" asked Brennan. "When I first heard about him running from the state police, I figured he was just another shit-bird sex offender who got lucky in the alley with Diaz. Then I hear about yesterday with Shattuck. That guy's a friggin' legend. How did Underwood get the drop on him?"

"I've got Mollie looking into that," said Wilcox. "There is certainly much more to him than just being a sex offender. So far, we know he was discharged from the army for punching out his commanding officer. He came home and was in and out of the system for some low-end drug offenses. Then he raped a woman and did four years."

"Okay, that's all bad news, but hardly the stuff of a hardened street criminal, which is what he's acting like," challenged Brennan.

"I'm not done," said Wilcox. "When he was in for the rape, he got assaulted. Nothing serious, but he told the guards what happened. Two days later he was beaten so badly he spent four days in the infirmary. It took him weeks to recover."

"Well, I'm sure he learned his lesson about ratting out other prisoners."

"More than you realize. A few years later he went inside again, this time for a robbery. He got beat up again, although nowhere near as badly. He didn't say a word to the guards. When he got out, *two years later*, the ex-wife and teenaged son of the prisoner that assaulted him turned up dead."

"And they didn't link it to Underwood?"

"He wasn't even a suspect. No one made the connection," said Wilcox.

"You did."

"Not enough to prove anything. We spent much of last night going through prison records. There is an amazing amount of information in there. For instance, the corrections officer assigned to Underwood's cell-block during his last stint was arrested for sexually assaulting male prisoners. This, three years after Underwood got out. He turned up dead, too."

"Here? In the city?"

"No. The ex-wife of the prisoner was in a small town in Vermont. The CO was killed in Keene, New Hampshire."

"And no one connected the dots," said Brennan, picking things up. "How is that?"

"Because no one was looking. Underwood is small time."

"Apparently not."

"Indeed," said Wilcox. "Something happened to him, or continued happening to him, while he was on the inside. He was already damaged, but prison broke him. Holding a grudge for two years and then killing someone's family over it? That requires some serious psychological injury."

"Why is it Diaz and Guthman didn't have any of this information when they knocked on Underwood's door two weeks ago?"

"Because no one had made any of these connections. For all they knew, he was just another sex offender out of bounds on his registration," said Wilcox.

"So, Diaz walked into the lion's mouth, like a lamb to the slaughter."

"As did Shattuck yesterday," added Wilcox. "And he's no lamb."

"Fair enough," said Brennan. "You know what I meant."

"Yes, I do."

"Okay," Brennan said after a moment. "Let's keep in touch on both these cases. There's not much of a chance Brass Malone is going to help out his little brother, especially if he's so out of control, but a little information sharing between us might help. As long as you can promise me you'll keep the UCX part of it close to the vest."

"Of course. I remember UC work. I'll keep it tight," said Wilcox.

"And if you need another set of hands working the Underwood case, let me know. Rey Johnston, too."

"I always liked him. Are you two still partnered up?" asked Wilcox.

"Yeah, and he's a whiz on surveillance. Let me know if we can help."

"Of course, Jimmy. Thank you."

"Good to see you, Charlie," Brennan said as he slid the car into drive.

"You too. Be safe."

CHAPTER 19

As Wilcox was pulling out of Aroma Joe's, his partner, Don Mollie, was backing between two newly painted parking lines on the campus of Southern New Hampshire University. The school was on the northern border of Manchester, tucked between the Merrimack River and the city limits.

Commuter parking was at the western terminus of Martin's Ferry Road, and on Saturday it was nearly vacant. Five minutes after he had run a surveillance detection route and parked, Mollie saw Ozzy Ostrowski pull into the lot. The former Concord police officer and Brass Malone's fixer drove straight in and parked next to Mollie. Their windows slid down.

"Morning, Ozzy," he began.

"Jesus, Mollie," Ozzy said, dispensing with the pleasantries. "You sure took a fucking bath on the Red Sox last week, didn't you? Are you good for it?"

Mollie winced internally at the biting comment. He was into Malone for thousands.

"Roll it over. Put it on New England Monday night," he said.

Ozzy chuckled. "Two things. First, I'm not a bookie. If you want to place a bet, call the right people. Second, the Patriots haven't covered a spread all year, and you know they won't until they find someone decent to replace Brady. You're wasting your money."

"After you hear the information I'm giving you today, you'll post it for me. I don't have the time to be making calls to every goddamned criminal in your organization just to place a bet."

"Criminals?" Ozzy said. "That's rich, especially coming from a police detective who's into Malone for what," Ozzy took a moment to scroll through a list in his phone. "Eighty-thousand dollars?"

"Just post the bet for me, would you?" Mollie asked.

"What have you got for me?" Ozzy asked, ignoring the comment. He glanced at his watch.

"They made the connection," Mollie said. "Malone and Underwood. The cops know they're half-brothers."

"Were you there when that happened?" Ozzy asked, but it was an accusation.

"Yeah."

"And what did you do to prevent it? To steer them away?"

"Nothing. I couldn't. One, it would have been obvious and two, they'd figure it out eventually anyway."

"What are they doing with it? How are they going after him?" Ozzy asked.

"I think it's getting used to hunt down Underwood, not jam up Malone. We're going to look closer at his financials. I know that much for sure."

"'We,' Don? You work for me, remember? Not the police."

"Fuck you, Ozzy. I work for Malone. You're a washed-up cop acting as a low-rent middle man."

"A washed-up cop who had the common sense to

get off the job *before* jumping in bed with Malone. And I don't owe him shit. You on the other hand..." Ozzy smiled and held up the Microsoft spreadsheet displayed on his phone that accurately documented Don Mollie's debts.

"Jesus. I cannot believe you people keep that shit online," Mollie said. "That's how you're going to get caught, you know. Do you have any idea how easy it is to get a search warrant for a Google account? The financial crime unit does it all the damn time."

Ozzy knew better. The server on which the cloud-document sat was in North Korea, completely inaccessible to American government agencies. The Dark Web had been a gift to organized crime.

"Get on with it," Ozzy instructed.

"*They* are going to look into Malone's financials, deeper than they already did with the pre-sentence investigation. They are searching for any money he might have steered toward his brother."

"Are they keeping to the ten-thousand limit?"

"No. They're going deeper than that. And not just cash. They're going to look into other transactions that could be converted to assets, or travel. Buying a charter flight with stocks, renting an RV but paying with bonds through an investment firm, crypto-currency, all of it."

Ozzy pinched the bridge of his nose in frustration. The police investigation into Malone's finances was deepening, and it would take a lot more work to cover them up. The money they were going to give Underwood wasn't the only problem. In culling through Malone's affairs with a finer toothed comb, the police would turn up things he assumed had been adequately concealed.

"There's more," Mollie said.

"What?"

"Not so fast. This one has value, and I'm betraying a trust giving it to you."

"Are you shitting me?" Ozzy laughed. "You're a dirty cop and a degenerate gambler and you're going to deal me down based on an assertion that all this violates some higher moral code you've got?"

"No, I just figured..."

"Forget it," Ozzy said as he hit the automatic roll-up feature on his window and smacked the column shifter into drive.

"They've got a UC going on Malone," blurted Mollie. Ozzy stopped the window's ascent, but didn't roll it back down. He eased the car into park, and peered through the five-inch gap that remained at the top of the glass.

"And?"

"That's it. That's all I know. They keep those files pinched down hard. Wilcox is meeting with an old buddy of his to try and find out what the case is about."

Ozzy stared at Mollie for ten seconds, then made a decision. He rolled the window back into the door.

"We've taken on a couple of new people in recent weeks. I need you to keep up on this UC file, so I can make connections on our end and be certain no one has gotten inside."

"I get it, Ozzy. I'm worried, too. The last thing we need is our little arrangement here getting out." Mollie gestured between the two of them.

"There is no 'we', Mollie. Our arrangement is that you give me information, and I make sure you don't get a dislocated finger for every five grand you owe us. You know that's the going rate for someone as delinquent as you, right? You don't have enough fingers to cover your eighty thousand."

"How do I know these extra people you're taking on aren't looking for me? How do I know that isn't what the UC file is really about?" Mollie asked.

"Relax," Ozzy said. "The only two people that know about you are Malone and me. He compartmentalizes. You know that. You're good."

"So, that info ought to be good enough to knock a few grand off, right?" Mollie asked lamely.

"I tell you what. You find out what the UC file is all about and bring me that, and I'll have them clear the five-thousand you lost on the Sox last week, and cover you for the Pats Monday night."

Mollie's eyebrows went up, along with his pulse. An anxious smile broke. "Maybe I should bet ten on the game Monday then, huh? What do you think?"

"Jesus fucking Christ, Mollie. You've got to get control over yourself," Ozzy said as he hit the window button and drove away.

CHAPTER 20

Charlie Wilcox's plan for Monday morning had not included peering into the drooping, ceramic eyes of a strangled hooker. He had been in his boxers, halfway through a cup of coffee and the front page of the Union Leader, when the phone rang. It had been his hope to have another cup, finish the comics, and maybe even be a little late for work. Instead, he had caught a murder to add to his already unmanageable case load.

Wilcox was headed for an alley off Gold Street, tucked between Hannaford Grocery Store and an AAMCO Transmission Center. Two dumpsters sat adjacent to the back wall of the auto shop, angry green boxes standing as sentries to guard the space between the buildings. The steel corner of one was rusted thin, opening a rat hole. Maggots and filth spilled onto the concrete footing beneath.

When the containers had last been slammed to the pavement by a garbage truck, they slid sideward, causing the corners to dig in and leave barely eight inches between them. The space had been more than sufficient to stuff in a twenty-two-year-old prostitute.

Wilcox turned off John Devine Drive into the Hannaford lot and snaked around to the delivery docks. The dispatcher who had called him passed the message that CSU set up their vehicles and equipment on the south side of the scene, blocking access to it. He would be unable to arrive from that direction. Once they settled and set themselves in motion, getting the Manchester police crime scene unit to redeploy, or even to move one of their vehicles, required monumental effort. That was as it should be. You only got one chance to examine and document a crime scene unmolested.

An overnight shift officer manned the outer perimeter where a small clutch of print reporters had begun to congregate. His face registered no response at Wilcox's arrival. He did not recognize the detective, but also didn't doubt his bona fides. There was little chance an intrepid reporter had obtained a new Ford Taurus with blacked out windows and donned a Brooks Brother's suit merely to get close enough for a few lurid scene photos.

The uniform lifted a long strand of yellow tape and allowed Wilcox access without so much as a wave. The detective drove past a throng of vehicles, but stopped short of CSU's processing van. Ahead of him, in the hundred feet between the vehicle and the body, lay a field of small yellow cones, littered about like leaves.

Numbered evidence markers had been placed next to anything possibly relevant. Even under close field observation, it was difficult to tell the difference between a small white rock and a tooth fragment. A drip of oil from a passing vehicle looked the same as DNA-filled spit from a tobacco-chewing murderer. Dozens of cigarettes had littered the alley, likely left over the course of days by lunch breaking employees of both businesses. Conversely, the obscure European brand of one of them might lead investigators to a specialty shop, where video surveillance would offer a timeline for the victim's pre-mortem activities. It would all be photographed and collected for further analysis in the lab.

A lone technician, a tall, lean, black man, methodically shuffled and bent, picking up each marker and returning it to its proper place in a large, black case. He was likely the newest member of the team enduring some sort of hazing ritual. The monotonous clean-up effort indicated the necessary photos had already been taken and evidence collected. The team was preparing to examine the body. For that, they usually waited for the assigned investigator.

A middle-aged white man wearing khakis and a long-sleeved polo emblazoned 'Senior CSU Analyst' descended the stairs from the CSU van and approached Wilcox. He held a soggy paper cup of coffee in one hand, and a freshly poured one in the other.

"Let me get my notes and I'll run this for you, Detective."

Briefing the assigned detective and walking him through the scene was not quite an honor, but bore enough significance to usually be reserved for the most experienced analyst on scene. There was ceremony to it, a recognition of the importance of CSU's role in solving murders. It was the maddeningly detailed minutia of their work, combined with investigative follow up, that most often cleared cases.

Wilcox, in recognition of the fact that some old-time CSU techs arrogantly considered themselves infallible, took the coffee, but not the briefing.

"Thanks for this, I desperately need it. But I'm good on the run-down for now," Wilcox said. He turned on his heel and walked directly to the young technician, arriving by his side just as he bent to retrieve a yellow wedge of plastic. When he stood, Wilcox was extending the paper cup.

The lead tech Wilcox had left behind huffed and turned back to the van muttering under his breath. "Figures."

"Oh, no thank you, Sir," the young man said to Wilcox. "I've got to finish collecting these markers."

"Are you familiar with this scene?"

"Yes, Sir. I've been here all morning. Since dark."

"Name?"

"I don't know, Detective. I don't think anyone has ID'd her yet."

"No," Wilcox chuckled. "What's your name?"

"Oh," he smiled awkwardly. "Stanley, Sir. Dave Stanley."

"Well, Dave Stanley, I'm Charlie Wilcox. I was hoping you could run this case for me."

"Me?" Stanley asked, eyeing the CSU van his boss had disappeared into.

Wilcox tipped his head to the side, interrupting Stanley's view. "Yeah, you."

"I can try. I've done several dead-body scenes, but this will be my first time briefing one."

"Just take me through it, same as they taught you," Wilcox said encouragingly.

"I actually have a cheat sheet," Stanley said, withdrawing a laminated eight-by-ten piece of paper that indicated the necessary facts, and in what order, to be relayed to the primary detective.

Of course you do, Wilcox thought, not unkindly. A crime scene analyst's hyper-vigilance for consistency and details was second to none.

"Good idea," Wilcox said. "Take me through it."

"Yes, Sir. Early this morning the produce manager of Hannaford came out back here for a quick smoke before his shift. He claims to have gone over to the dumpster to toss in his butt when he saw the body. That doesn't seem credible, since there were burnt cigarettes all over the ground. Why would he walk over to the dumpster to do it? My guess is he saw something and was curious."

"Facts, please, Mr. Stanley. Not opinions or theories," Wilcox cautioned.

"Right. Sorry. He made a 911 call at 0455 and the first uniform arrived at 0501. The uniform claims she was clearly dead, so he didn't call EMS. The sergeant arrived at 0515. That's all I have on that. The rest you should be able to get from the officers."

"Good. And the scene?"

"Right. Should I run it outside-in?" Stanley asked unnecessarily.

"Yes, if that's what your 'cheat sheet' says."

Crime scenes were examined and documented from the outer edges inward, unless there was perishable evidence deeper inside that would be lost if not immediately seized, such as blood spatter in the rain. Otherwise, it was wise to document things first, taking photos, drawing sketches, and collecting each item before stepping over it to repeat the process with the next. It was a painfully tedious but necessary endeavor.

"There were cigarette butts and broken glass all over the place, each marked and seized. Closer in we found a bunch of empty heroin bags. The stamp was 'Rock 'N Roll' with a music note in the middle. Those were about eight feet in front and two feet to the side of the left dumpster."

"How many is 'a bunch'?" Charlie asked, taking notes.

Stanley looked at his phone, on which his notes resided. "Twelve."

"All Rock 'N Roll?"

"Yes."

"No others? Anywhere at the scene, I mean?"

"No."

Wilcox made a note. He would need to have someone get with narcotics and find out who was selling the particular branded stamp. It was unusual that it was the only one found in the alley.

"Needles?"

"Yes," Stanley said. "Three. Two by the front corner of the left box and one way over there." He gestured toward the back door of the transmission shop. "Bottles, cans, and an empty Skoal chewing tobacco canister. That is all documented and will go to the lab. Nothing overtly obvious."

Stanley paused his narrative to allow Wilcox to catch up his notes. He noticed the detective was writing with a pencil, the kind you sharpened, and smiled.

"Can I take you up to the body?"

Wilcox did not respond, but smiled and gestured forward. The two men carefully picked their way through the remaining number cones to the center of the scene.

"We haven't moved the body yet, obviously, but if you look closely there are some pretty dark ligature marks on the neck," Stanley began. "My guess is that's what killed her."

"Your 'guess,' Mr. Stanley?" Wilcox said with a frown. This was why he liked to force new technicians to stretch from the comfort of the shadow of their betters. Stanley would learn more from fifteen minutes of corrected misstatements with Wilcox than he would in fifteen hours of watching someone else explain a crime scene.

"No, not a guess. I have no idea what killed her."

"Better. Go on."

The body of the skinny woman had been wedged in sideways between the metal containers. One leg was pulled tight to her side, the knee to her armpit, twisted like a frog. The other was extended from the hip, pointing outward. Both arms were haphazardly tucked in above the head, extended toward the sky. One bicep touched her ear, the other jammed between her skull and the wall.

The torso was clad in a loose-knit bright red sweater through which a black bra was visible. A leather micro-skirt, probably fake, was twisted high enough to reveal a lack of underwear. There was no other clothing.

"Look at the face, Detective."

The left side of the face was visible. A cold eye stared out from a half open lid. The lid itself was puffy and swollen with blood. Together, they looked like a white marble tucked inside a burst tomato. The entire side of the face was pinkish purple, with a pattern of lighter lines crossing diagonally.

"Paradoxical lividity," Stanley said. "You know what that means."

When blood stops circulating in a body, gravity begins to act within seconds. Over the course of a few hours, it drains to the lowest point, resulting in lividity, dark red or purple skin at lower places and white, even translucent skin higher up. If the body is moved during this time, blood will drain again and find a new low point in which to pool.

Six to twelve hours into the post-mortem process, the blood begins to jell, not unlike its behavior outside a body. This 'fixed' lividity will not drain and pool again if the body is moved. It will stay where it congealed, fixed in place.

In the case before them, fixed lividity had settled into the victim's face and neck, the obvious low point in the hours following her death. The white lines were caused by dermal pressure, something akin to wrinkles in the sheet on which her face was pressed. The wrinkles created pressure points, which prevented the settling of blood. She had lay for hours after her death, pressed face down onto something, while her blood pooled and jelled inside her body.

"Yes, I know what it means," said Wilcox. "She was probably killed somewhere else, left there for at least six hours depending on temperature, then moved and dumped here. That one I'll let you get away with, Stanley. It is supported by facts, at least."

"I know the autopsy will confirm or dispel all that, but I like to take note of it," Stanley said. "It helps me consider what I'm looking for at the scene. For example, if she was alive and fighting when he jammed her in there, I look for scuffs on the pavement, disturbances in the debris, maybe blood spatter. If she was already dead, as it seems she was, I'm looking for drag marks, maybe places he touched or knelt as he stuffed her in."

Sharp kid, noted Wilcox.

"Tell me about that," Wilcox prodded.

"Well, she's tiny, maybe runs a hundred pounds."

"If that," Wilcox added.

"Still," Stanley continued. "It's not easy moving a hundred pounds of dead weight, so to speak. And there were no drag marks, which means your suspect is strong enough to lift her completely off the ground and haul her over here."

"Unless he pulled a car right up to this spot," Wilcox challenged.

"I checked. No tire marks, and there was a thin layer of dust around here from some roof work next door, so it would have shown."

"That's convenient. What else have you got?"

"Well, if you look closely, she has some fairly deep lateral abrasions on her cheek and forehead. You can see some subcutaneous tissue under the torn skin, but it is white. There was no bleeding, so it was post mortem."

"Meaning she got it after she was deceased, maybe when he jammed her in there," Wilcox followed.

"Exactly. And since they are horizontal, not vertical, I'm guessing he set her down on the pavement, then slid her in, as opposed to dropping her down between the dumpsters from the top."

"More guessing?"

"Let's call it conjecture," Stanley said, his confidence growing. He stood up to demonstrate.

"Follow me through this. Your suspect carries her over and sets her down in preparation of pushing her in." He bent down to simulate dropping the body, then squatted down. "It's somewhat unnatural, mechanically, to push like this." Stanley stayed there, on his feet with bent knees like a baseball catcher, his hands extended in front of him. "You can't get enough leverage to push forward like this."

"You'd have to put your knee down," Wilcox said.

"Exactly. Right here," Stanley said, pointing to the ground.

"I don't see it."

"Here, try this," Stanley offered. He withdrew a small flashlight from a cargo pocket and held it near the ground, pointing oblique light across the surface of the pavement. Previously invisible detail appeared as shadows were cast across the pavement. A small oval impression, two inches by three, was barely apparent in the dust. A knee print.

"Good show, Stanley!" Wilcox said proudly. "Tell me something was there."

"Well, it would have been nice if he was wearing shorts and scraped off some DNA for us, but I think I got the next best thing. There were two items, a fiber and a hair. We bagged them both."

Wilcox's eyes popped. "A hair?"

"Not quite what you're thinking, Detective. I think it's an animal hair."

"A pet, perhaps?

"Maybe. I don't know. I wouldn't want to *guess* about something like that."

Age and weight stiffened Wilcox's legs in their squatted position. He stood slowly. His knees made a pepper grinder noise.

"Cute," he said.

"Those are the high points," Stanley said. "As of now we're just waiting for the medical examiner to arrive, do a quick check of the body, then she'll go to Concord for a full autopsy. We'll be getting all the evidence to the lab this afternoon."

"I'm curious about that hair. How certain are you it's a..."

Wilcox was interrupted by a distracting vibration in his breast pocket. Pulling out his phone, he saw it was a number assigned to a Manchester police duty phone. He knew it would be work related, but had no idea who was actually calling. He slid the green circle.

"Wilcox."

"Wilcox, it's Soloman."

Wilcox searched his memory without success. He remained silent.

"You still there, Detective?" Sergeant Adam Solo-man asked.

"Yes. What do you need? I'm a bit preoccupied at the moment," Wilcox replied.

"Yeah, I know. A dead hooker. By any chance is your girl in a red top and black skirt?"

Recognition finally came, and Wilcox pictured the short, stoutly muscular sergeant.

"Why do you ask, Sergeant?"

"I'm out on Sagamore, just off Elm Street. We got a rescue assist call for a woman passed out. She's a dancer, if you take my meaning. Bad mix of booze and Oxy's is what the EMT's are guessing. She's coming out of it okay now, though."

Wilcox rubbed and squeezed his temples to prevent himself from barking his impatience into the phone.

"And?"

"Well, we got her talking. You know how these girls like to talk once they get started. It's all I can do to get her to..."

"Sarge, I'm going to have to ask you to get the point," Wilcox said.

"The point is she's worried about a friend of hers. The name is Daphne Something."

A fleeting image of a silver necklace around the victim's neck flashed into Wilcox's mind. He stepped forward and squatted again to confirm it. A small heart with the letter 'D' engraved hung delicately below her chin, juxtaposed with the gore of the scene.

"Said she goes by D, if that helps you," Soloman continued.

"Why is she worried about her?" Wilcox asked.

Hooker who-dunnits, as some detectives irreverently called them, usually cleared with an arrest in short order. But Wilcox had not expected a lead to call him on the phone and offer itself up so quickly.

"She said a guy that picked D up last night felt like bad news, but she couldn't figure out why. He looked the part of a straight-up-john, average height, average weight, middle aged white guy. But something seemed off to her. Then this morning she's been texting D and there's been no response. She said they always text each other first thing in the morning, to make sure they got out okay. Some sort of street walker safety program, I guess."

"Tell the girl to call her again," Wilcox instructed. There was mumbling in the background Wilcox could not understand.

"She said they never call. Just texts," Soloman offered when he returned to the line.

"Yes, I understand that, but I'm not interested in what they usually do. Have her call the phone." Wilcox felt his patience waning again.

"Sure. Hang on."

Ten seconds later, Wilcox heard a dull humming noise mumble from beneath the victim's thigh.

"Tell her she's going to have to come into the station," Wilcox said. "Get her a coffee and some breakfast, and allow her to clean up. Then bring her in. Go ahead and tell her it's going to be a long day."

"Got it. So, you think her friend is your victim?"

"Just bring her in," Wilcox said, prepared to hang up.

"One more thing," Soloman offered. "She said she knows who it is. The guy that picked her up, I mean."

"Is that right?" Wilcox asked, skeptical.

"Yeah, she says it's that guy who beat up the trooper a few weeks ago."

"Underwood?" Wilcox asked, then before Soloman could answer, quickly added, "put her on the phone."

There was a sound of muffled scraping as the phone was passed from one person to another.

"Yeah?" said a meek voice.

"Ma'am, how do you know Vincent Underwood?"

"I don't. Who the fuck is Vincent Underwood?" she said.

Wilcox's hope for a quick clearance of two major cases evaporated. "Never mind. Just put the sergeant back on."

The woman didn't comply. "Listen, I don't know why y'all don't talk to each other much, but the freak that picked up D last night is the same asshole you guys posted a wanted photo of this morning on your department Instagram feed."

"You read our Instagram?" Wilcox asked.

"Sure, doesn't everybody? I don't know what the hell his name is, but the photo you guys posted of the guy who beat that trooper is the same john that D hooked last night."

"Young lady, the sergeant is going to set you up. Get you some food, a shower if you'd like. We're going to have to talk some more in person," Wilcox said.

"Yeah, okay," she said, surrender in her voice. "I just wish you guys had posted that photo yesterday."

"Yes, Ma'am. I do, too."

CHAPTER 21

Jimmy Brennan was already ten minutes late when he backed into the bumper of a pickup truck as he tried to parallel park on Amherst Street, half a block east of the Manchester City Library.

Brennan exited his car, then casually looked and concluded that the scratch he caused was indistinguishable from the plethora of dents and dings already present on the decades-old truck. After waiting for a lull in the relentless one-way traffic, he dashed across the street and rounded the corner to the imposing building.

Libraries were seldom visited by active felons, which made them among the best places for Brennan to meet his boss. He was about to request reassignment, something he had never done before. Advancement and specialized duties had always been offered to him. Despite more than a decade of service and his comfort with the man he was meeting, Brennan felt uncharacteristically anxious.

At age twenty-eight, James Brennan had started his law enforcement career later than most. After graduating from Pennsylvania State University, he had been commissioned a second lieutenant in the Marine Corps and was sent through Officer Candidate School. Following OCS was The Basic School, a six-month education unique to marines, where officers learn to lead soldiers in combat. Every officer, from pilots to infantry to financiers, attended the course.

At TBS, Brennan's commanding officer had noticed the young man's penchant for bending the rules. Never a cheat or a liar, Brennan reframed problems and twisted resources in ways not thought of before. He innovated, thought on his feet, and took risks. They were calculated risks, but risks none the less.

After graduating third in a company of two-hundred marines, Second Lieutenant James Brennan applied for the elite Special Operations Command. MARSOC was a highly disciplined, fast-paced group assigned the most challenging military tasks in the world. They worked in hostile areas, committed to both direct action and training local forces to defend their own interests. It was arduous and complicated work, and Brennan thrived.

He was promoted to first lieutenant in twelve months rather than the conventional eighteen, then put on the double-bars of a captain two short years later. Five years in, he learned he was on the top of the list to make major. No MARSOC officer had ever made major at the age of twenty-seven.

Two days after the promotional list came out Brennan's colonel, a tight chested, leathery southerner out of Texas A&M, told him if he played his cards right, he'd make major within months and lieutenant colonel by his early thirties.

"Brennan," the man had said, dragging out the first syllable with his southern drawl. "Y'all have a fightin' chance 'a making general before you're forty. That ain't been done since World War II."

It turned out that 'playing your cards right' meant leaving the special forces community for a staff job at the Pentagon.

"You'll still be with MARSOC," a personnel officer had reassured him. "You'll be an aide to Lieutenant Colonel Gerard. He's the MARSOC rep for Colonel Randolph. She is the corps' overall liaison to the senate foreign relations committee. You'll meet a lot of important people over there."

Captain (major designate) Brennan had been around the block enough to know that majors and lieutenant colonels were a dime a dozen at the Pentagon. In order to 'meet a lot of important people' he would have to endure years of getting coffee and making copies as the assistant to an assistant. After years in special forces, oak leaves on his shoulders would be a minor salve to that wound.

Then Brennan's father died. His mother started drinking again. Eight months later, sitting on a swinging bench on his mother's porch, one of the most promising young officers in the United States Marine Corps wrote a letter resigning his commission.

Brennan transitioned well to his new profession. The same kind of outside-the-box thinking that had attracted the attention of MARSOC quickly had the Manchester police command staff examining him for promotion. He came to the attention of Captain Edward Soffit, commander of the Investigative Bureau, and after a brief recruitment campaign James Brennan was promoted to detective and transferred to narcotics.

He initially worked street-level crack cocaine buys and ran prostitution stings to learn his trade. Gradually, Brennan moved up, building a cadre of reliable informants and street contacts. Three years ago, he had infiltrated a fledgling motorcycle gang planning a bank robbery that likely would have resulted in several deaths. A year later, he'd worked as the Manchester distribution head for the Rinaldi crime family out of Providence, Rhode Island, a feat the FBI had failed to accomplish for decades. That case had resulted in the federal indictment of more than fifteen family members. Following the high-profile case, he was promoted to detective first class while working undercover, something that had never happened before.

Brennan walked into the Manchester city library, past a half-dozen rows of public-use computers, and into the stacks. The back of the ground floor housed several small reading areas set up like living rooms. Brennan went to the left and located Captain Edward Soffit seated in a worn but serviceable leather chair in the corner of that room.

Soffit was a man of average height and build, indistinguishable from any other well-dressed bureaucrat. He kept his salt and pepper hair slicked back and wore a superbly tailored suit. Possessed of a deep, gravelly voice and slow mannerisms, he carried an air of powerfully quiet authority. When Soffit spoke, people listened.

"Morning Cap'," Brennan announced as he flopped down hard into the chair next to his boss. "Of all the gin mills..."

Soffit's head snapped up from the magazine he'd been perusing as his eyes came to rest on Brennan. His elbow reflexively tapped his hip, then relaxed. His look of surprise melted into an eye roll.

"Is that how they teach you to make undercover

meetings with your handler in 'How-To-Be-An-Under-cover-Cop' school?" Soffit asked.

"Actually Boss, I'm more interested in what they teach at 'How-To-Be-A-Straight-Detective-After-Work-ing-Undercover' school," Brennan replied. His eyes met Soffit's and held them.

"I gather you're serious this time?"

"I was serious *last* time, Captain. I seem to recall you weren't too serious about letting me transfer out."

Flipping the magazine closed and tossing it onto a low table between them, Soffit pivoted in his seat toward Brennan.

"UC work is voluntary. You know that."

Brennan's eyebrows went up and he tipped his head down skeptically.

"Really, Cap'?" he said, dragging out the 'r'. "I think you know there's voluntary and then there's *voluntary.* The last time we had this conversation both you and the deputy chief made it pretty clear you wanted me to stay on the street. To stay under. *Voluntarily*, of course."

"Fawcett had nothing to do with it, Jimmy. Keeping you out and under was my call."

Deputy Chief Lewis Fawcett was the commander of the Support Services Division of the Manchester Police Department. Serving under him were three bureaus, each headed by a captain. The Tactical Support Bureau included K-9, SWAT, and Fugitive Apprehension. The Professional Standards Bureau included training, accreditation, and internal affairs. Last was the Investigative Bureau, headed by Captain Edward Soffit.

"If keeping me 'out and under' as you so elo-quently put it was your call and not Fawcett's, how was that voluntary for me?" Brennan asked.

Soffit held his hands up a chest level and released a sigh.

"Okay, Jimmy. I get it. You want out. Am I allowed to ask why?"

There was hesitation, then Brennan said, "I'm not entirely sure you want to know why, Captain."

"Yeah," the older man said chuckling. "That's probably true."

"Let's just say my priest is making me do it."

The chuckle turned into an outright laugh. "I doubt that!" Soffit joked. When the moment had passed, he asked again. "Is Sarah behind it? Too many late nights?"

"Nah, she doesn't even know yet."

Soffit's eye's widened. "Really? You might want to run a decision like that by your wife, don't you think?"

"Don't get me wrong," said Brennan, correcting him. "We've talked about it. I just haven't told her I made a final decision."

Brennan smiled. Soffit was a decent boss, but he'd never been much of a family man. Brennan thanked God for his wife and marriage every day, but understood it was the exception, rather than the norm for his profession.

"What's funny?" Soffit asked, picking up on Brennan's hesitation.

"Nothing. Sarah will be good with it. She'll be happy."

As if he had read Brennan's mind, Soffit held his left hand to eye level and wiggled his ring finger. "Wife number three, remember? I wouldn't dream of giving anyone marriage advice."

There was an awkward pause before Soffit continued speaking.

"So, we're back to 'why?' You have a reason, or just sick of the work?"

"No, not sick of the work. Sick of not knowing why I'm doing it." Brennan didn't think his boss would understand, but Soffit surprised him by nodding.

"I get it."

"Yeah?"

Soffit smiled. "You know what I did for my last two years as a detective before I was promoted to sergeant?"

"No, what?"

"Undercover. Now this was back in the day when we used to buy marijuana and arrest hookers. Can you imagine?" he asked. "When was the last time Narcotics did a weed case? I don't even think patrol officers arrest people for weed anymore. It's all but legal now anyway."

"True. It's been a while, for sure."

"And hookers," Soffit laughed, warming to his jaunt down memory lane. "We used to drive around and solicit them, then patrol units would roll up and arrest them. What a waste of time that was. As if the girls had any choice in the matter. At least now we know they're the actual victims and just go after their johns and pimps."

Brennan was pleased, and a little surprised, to hear such progressive talk from his veteran boss.

"Anyway," Soffit concluded. "I get it. UC work can make you feel like a salmon swimming upstream to spawn. You're fighting as hard as you can to get somewhere, and when you arrive you realize you're just going to die there."

The two men looked at each other silently.

"Where do you want to go?" Soffit asked after a moment.

"Major crimes, if I could."

"They might have a spot for you. I'll talk to Lieutenant Dawson and see what we can do. In the meantime, do a –219 and send it up. I'll sign it and bounce it to personnel."

The MPD-219 was an employee action request form. It was used to ask for vacation, sick leave, or reassignment and transfer.

"Really?" Brennan asked. "You're going to make me do a –219? It's not like I'm some two-year patrol cop asking for a transfer to the traffic unit."

"Yes, *Detective*, you need to do a –219. You may think you're some hot-shit untouchable undercover investigator, but you're also a civil servant in the employ of the City of Manchester."

"You got it, Boss."

"One more thing. Besides this murder contract thing you have going with Paul Nessman and Brass Malone, what have you got on the burner right now?" Soffit asked.

"Nothing, that's it. Although we've found some links between Malone and Vincent Underwood."

"Who's Underwood?" Soffit asked.

"He's the guy Major Crimes is looking for after tuning up that trooper."

"And the shooting at the bowling alley?" Soffit asked to confirm his recollection.

"That's him. Charlie Wilcox is on it and some new kid, Don Mollie."

"Wilcox is sharp. Are you two comparing notes?"

"Yeah, more or less. We're getting together again tomorrow."

"Good," Soffit said, standing up and securing the top button of his suit. "Forgive me for not shaking your hand. You look like a felon, and there might be people I know watching."

"Oh, I understand completely. You look like a cop, and who the hell wants to be seen with one of those nowadays?"

Brennan smiled and reached over to pick up the magazine Soffit had set down on the chair. He flipped it open and pretended to read, ignoring his boss as he walked out the door.

CHAPTER 22

Bridget Patterson, a tall, slender, redheaded twenty-year old dabbed her right eye gingerly with a crumpled-up piece of toilet paper. She smeared a tear out of the way and leaned far over the bathroom sink, easing closer to the mirror. Placing one finger from her right hand above the injury and one from her left below, she gently pulled the lids apart.

The bruise wouldn't set until morning. Bridget was off work tomorrow, so no one would see it and ask. She texted to cancel a lunch date with her mother, and lamented the fact it was growing easier to lie. Putting ice on the injury tonight, and again in the morning, would calm the ruptured capillaries that caused minor contusions. Then tomorrow she'd alternate a warm face cloth with gentle massage to increase circulation to the area. A few hours of that would wash away the blood that had leaked into her skin. It wouldn't go away, but it would lighten enough to say it was caused by bumping into something.

Bridget was pretty good at this sort of thing. Experience counted.

She heard the electronic chirping noise that the over-amplified video game in the next room made when it was paused. That meant her boyfriend, Frank Doran, was either getting another beer or coming to see where she was. She prayed for the former.

Creeping from the bathroom as quietly as possible, Bridget heard a muffled wooden 'clap' from the living room. It was a well-known sound. Doran had flipped shut the small wooden box where he kept marijuana. If he smoked, he'd be distracted, and it tended to mellow out the alcohol.

Bridget knew that Frank smoking weed this early, it was six o'clock in the evening, meant that his friend Mike Thompson was coming over. Frank would want to get high before Mike arrived so he could pretend he was out of weed and not have to share.

More importantly, if Mike came over, Frank would ignore her.

"You're going to have to stay in the bedroom with your face looking like that," Frank offered helpfully.

Bridget had been walking down the short hallway of their apartment toward the kitchen. When she looked up, he was standing in the opening to the living room, staring at her.

"I know," she replied.

"I'm really sorry it came to that, Bridge," he said gently, approaching her. Her mind flinched but her body didn't move. Better to wait. His arms opened slightly to allow her smaller body in and he embraced her, pulling her head to his chest. Her arms hung limply at her sides.

"You don't have a hug for me?" he asked, his voice up just a bit. Silently, Bridget put her arms around his waist and touched his lower back. It counted.

"You know I'm sorry?" he asked again, but it was a statement. When she remained mute, he pulled his head away and moved his hands up to her neck. Her chest still pressed to his stomach, he put his hands softly around her throat, fingers in back and thumbs in front. He did not squeeze, but pressed the thumbs up gently, causing her face to rise. She looked up at him.

"Did you hear what I said?" he asked.

"I did, Frank. I know. I'm sorry, too," she replied. He smiled at her, put his hands behind her back again, and pulled her close.

Their embrace ended and he walked to the couch. Flopping down with a huff, he began packing a small glass pipe.

"You get food today?" he asked absentmindedly.

"I came straight here from work. You followed me, remember?" She regretted saying it immediately.

His head snapped and he glared at her.

"C'mere!" he ordered. She walked quickly to him. Still seated, he gripped her upper arm, hard. "Can I just have a simple goddamn answer to a simple friggin' question? Are we going to go through this every time?"

"I'm sorry. No, I didn't get food. I meant to but forgot," she lied. He let go of her arm casually, as if they'd been holding hands.

"Well I guess you're lucky Bristol Market is only one block away, huh? Chips and beer, please, and not those nasty cheese flavored things you got last time."

"You need butts, too?" she asked.

Frank ignored the attempt at civility and went back to packing the bowl.

"Fifteen minutes, Bridge. There and back. And a receipt."

Bridget Patterson rushed to the kitchen and put on her jacket. As she passed the counter, she snatched a pair of sunglasses and pulled them over her ears. It was dusk, but no one would really pay attention.

"Going on fourteen minutes now," Frank called out.

Ducking out the door and pulling it shut, Bridget went through the ritual of reminding herself of the intangible benefits of being with Frank Doran. He loved her, he had a job, he paid half the rent, sometimes. Eventually, maybe as early as tonight, he would apologize for real. By the time she'd descended the stairs and hit the sidewalk, Bridget was reinvested in the relationship. Sure, it needed some work, but she was committed to helping Frank be a better man.

CHAPTER 23

The hair that Evidence Technician Dave Stanley had recovered at the murder scene two days prior turned out to be that of a cat. The lab report indicated 'felis catus,' because nothing from the crime lab could ever be easy. That, combined with a statement from D's friend that identified Vincent Underwood as her last known customer had led to a new search warrant at his Lincoln Street apartment. Marvin the cat, now in the custody of the Merrimack County Animal Humane Society, had been taken weeks earlier when Underwood's apartment was searched after his initial escape. The new warrant had resulted in the seizure of, among other items, several samples of cat fur.

A rush request for DNA analysis had been granted, and Marvin's mange had been positively matched to that seized next to the dumpster. As soon as Wilcox could write up his reports, Underwood would be wanted for murder.

"So, Charlie," Jimmy Brennan said to Wilcox as they sat side by side in the back seat of a blacked-out SUV. "Explain to us how Marvin the cat is going to get you promoted."

"Must your sarcasm always be presented in a manner that paints you an ignorant ass, Jimmy?" Wilcox replied.

Laughter came from the front seats, where Wilcox's partner, Don Mollie, sat in the driver's seat with Brennan's partner, Rey Johnston, to his right. The four men were in a Chevrolet Tahoe, tucked into the crowded parking lot of the Concord Greyhound bus terminal, twenty miles north of Manchester. They had deployed near the center of a pack of SUV's and trucks, just off Higgins Place, in an effort to secrete their presence. The terminal itself, a long, single level T-shaped structure, sat in the middle.

Lorraine Underwood, Vincent's mother, had been under twenty-four-seven surveillance by the fugitive apprehension unit. That had produced no leads, but in the twenty-first century digital surveillance often bore more fruit than the physical variety. That morning Lorraine's credit card had purchased a bus ticket from Concord to Virginia Beach, due to depart at seven that evening. The name she had used was Victor Wood.

It stood to reason the purchase was for Lorraine's son, and that her hope was that an accommodating terminal operator would recognize that, perhaps in the haste of purchasing the ticket online, the man who would eventually appear to claim it had mis-typed his own name. It was also possible Vincent Underwood had a fraudulent ID in that name. The ticket purchase and analogous names were more than sufficient to justify the presence of the four detectives.

Wilcox and Mollie were trained in surveillance, but Brennan and Johnston were far more skilled and practiced. When Wilcox had asked them to assist, they had gladly obliged.

They weren't alone. A six-person SWAT unit sat in

a van behind the adjacent U-Haul building, and a sniper and observer were on top of the same structure. State troopers were standing by to deploy road blocks on both Interstates 93 and 393. Concord PD had marked cruisers in the area. The net was loose, but ready to snap shut.

"I'm serious here," Brennan continued, anything but. "You stand to be the first detective to clear a murder that way."

"What kind of case are we talking here?" Johnston asked, picking up the taunts. "Feline-o-cide? Feline-y level assault?"

Wilcox remained silent, shaking his head.

"I'm kind of worried about that cat," Brennan said. "Underwood is a dangerous guy."

"Hmm, good point," Mollie agreed. "Witness purr-tection, maybe?'

There were boos and hisses.

"Will it have to testify? The cat, I mean?"

"I sincerely hope not," Brennan said. "A *dogged* defense attorney will tear him apart."

"Charlie," Mollie asked. "If we arrest Underwood tonight and interrogate him on the murder, are you going to go at him with the cat-hair angle."

"Might as well," Brennan added seriously. "Just let the cat out of the bag."

"Enough!" bellowed Wilcox as the vehicle erupted in laughter. Once it calmed, Brennan shuffled across the bench seat so his hip touched Wilcox. He beckoned the man closer, feigning a desire to whisper.

"Does Charlene know you're getting this kind of pussy at work?"

"Sierra-1 to Delta," crackled the Tahoe's in-car radio transmitter. The radio call sign for a group of detectives, when their individual call signs were unknown to the caller, was 'Delta.'

The laughter came to a stop, and faces turned hard.

"That's the sniper unit," Brennan said. "Where are they set up?"

"On top of the U-Haul."

Mollie picked up the radio mic and pressed the transmit button. "Go ahead for Delta."

"I've got a green Ford Taurus that just pulled into the lot off of Stickney Avenue. That make and model is on the watch list for this operation. It's listed as belonging to Lorraine Underwood."

"What time is it," Mollie asked out loud.

Brennan picked up his phone. "Six-fifteen. She's early, but it fits."

Mollie keyed the radio transmit button again. "Sierra-1, go ahead and call it for us."

"Copy, stand by. Logging this as Vehicle-1"

There were no further transmissions for ten seconds. Brennan pressed a pair of binoculars against the inside of the blacked-out glass of the Tahoe. A 2015 green Ford Taurus turned left into a row of cars and continued its slow progression toward the terminal.

Brennan was about to open his mouth when the radio cracked again.

"Sierra-1, all units. Vehicle-1 is occupied by one white female. Loose visual ID has her as Lorraine Underwood."

Brennan, who had looked through a fair number of high-powered rifle scopes during his years as a marine, pictured in his mind's eye what the sniper team was seeing. Razor thin cross-hairs were superimposed on the head of Lorraine Underwood. The electronic scope was wired to a computer, which displayed the image and recorded it on a solid-state drive. The observer had likely set up a split screen with Lorraine's DMV photo on one side, and the scope-view on the other. It wasn't fool proof, but was a fairly reliable identification.

"Any sign of the target?" Mollie asked over the radio.

Both Brennan and Wilcox gave him a disap-pointed scowl. If Sierra-1 had seen something, he would have said it. They both imagined the eyerolling sniper team having the same thought.

"Ahh, no, Delta. Just the female driver."

Lorraine Underwood cruised slowly down the row of cars, headed directly toward the bus terminal. As she got closer to it, she traveled laterally across the sniper team's field-of-fire, thereby reducing the angle of their shot and increasing visibility of the vehicle's inter-ior.

"Sierra-1, Delta. Interior view is going green in about ten seconds."

Thick silence enveloped the interior of the Tahoe. They could hear Wilcox breathe. Mollie shifted his weight, causing his shoes to squeak. They waited.

"Sierra-1, Delta. The floor of both the front and back are empty. Rear seat unoccupied."

"Shit," Mollie mumbled.

The vehicle arrived at the terminal and stopped. The rifle element of the two-man sniper unit fingered the safety of his Remington 700 rifle, but didn't turn it off.

"Don, tell all units to hold. Let's see what she does," Wilcox decided.

"Delta to all units. We're going to hold. Stand-by," Mollie said into the mic.

"Sierra-1 all units, she's looking around. Vehicle is still running."

As soon as the sniper observer stopped talking, Lorraine began to roll forward. She eased past the building and stopped again before turning sharply to the left, into a marked space. A small sedan was in front of her, allowing the sniper team a nearly unobstructed view through the windshield. Unfortunately, a minivan was parked just to her right, interfering with the view of the detectives.

Five minutes later, the observer spoke again.

"She turned the car off. Still just her in it. Looks like she's texting."

Rey Johnston had an idea, and took the microphone from Mollie's hand. "Delta, Sierra-1. You have a laser mic up there?"

"Affirmative, but we're at about four-hundred-fifty feet. The A-of-A is too much at this range. We won't hear anything."

"Try it out," Johnston said. Three confused faces inside the Tahoe looked at him with anticipation.

"A-of-A is angle of attack," he said. "The interior sound makes the windows vibrate, and when you hit the glass with the laser it picks up the vibration and feeds it into a computer, which interprets it into sound. The problem is at that distance, and with the angle of the windshield, it's going to screw up the laser."

"Can they get closer?" Brennan asked.

"Sure, they can redeploy. That will either get them closer, or they could keep the same distance but move to the side and hit a vertical side window. Either might work."

Wilcox nodded his head toward the radio, signaling consent.

"Delta, Sierra-1. How long for you to redeploy?" Johnston asked. Thirty seconds passed.

"Undetected, it'll take us thirty to forty minutes. Hasty, we could do it in five."

Johnston set down the radio mic and looked into the back seat at Wilcox. "It's your case. What do you want to do, Boss?"

Wilcox looked over at Brennan and raised his eyebrows in question. Brennan spoke quietly.

"Sure, that would get us sound, but then we lose the sniper overwatch while they move. This guy already shot at you and just about killed Shattuck. I wouldn't give up having Big Brother out there ready to pop Underwood's head off if it came to that."

Wilcox nodded subtly and looked at the floor, gears turning. He looked up at Johnston. "Tell them to hold in place."

Seconds slogged into minutes as the team waited. Sierra-1 continued providing updates if Lorraine reached to tune the radio or typed into her phone. If no change was observed for five minutes, they gave a negative report. That happened five times, with a sixth due soon.

"Sierra-1, Delta. No change."

"How long are we going to wait?" Mollie asked. No one answered the rookie question.

Brennan leaned forward and tapped Johnston on the shoulder. "If we call her credit card company again, will they update us based on the last search warrant, or do they need a new one? Maybe there's been more activity."

"The old one would probably be fine, but they only do it during business hours unless it's an emergency."

"This doesn't qualify?" Brennan challenged.

"Not really, no. Emergency in their book means it is needed to prevent serious injury or death. We're just looking to get intel to make an arrest. It'll have to wait."

"C'mon, Rey. They don't know that. If we call and tell them it's needed to locate a potential victim, they'll give it to us."

"Sure, but they'll want to see a follow up warrant supporting that."

"And by then maybe we'll have Underwood in custody, so it won't matter. Stretch it a bit, Man. I'll explain it to..."

Brennan felt Wilcox's hand on his thigh. He looked over and saw the large detective softly shaking his head side to side.

"Let it go, Jimmy. He's either going to show, or he's not. We wait."

Brennan heaved back into the seat and sighed before gazing out the window. He let his mind wander to pass the time.

"Do you guys remember Ross Patterson?" Brennan asked. Wilcox looked at him strangely, confused by the non sequitur.

"Patrol lieutenant, right?" Johnston said helpfully.

"Yes," Wilcox added. "I think that's correct. Currently on day shift, I believe."

"Yeah, that's him," said Brennan. "He asked me for a sit-down. Doesn't want to meet in town."

"What's it about?" asked Wilcox.

"I don't know, but I got the feeling it wasn't work related."

"His daughter has been giving them fits, he and the wife, from what I understand," Johnston said. "A couple petty shoplifting arrests, got busted with a little bit of coke."

"And a DUI," Mollie chimed in. "Last week."

"Hadn't heard about that one," said Johnston. "How old is she?"

"Early twenties, I'd guess. She was a little kid when he went through the academy."

"That seems to fit, then. Well, I'll find out tomorrow, I guess," said Brennan.

"Why did he reach out to you? You guys have history?"

"Nothing heavy. He was my patrol sergeant on the overnight shift when I first started on the job. He's a good boss."

The radio crackled. "Sierra-1, Delta. I've got a blue Honda Pilot with a roof rack that just stopped a few cars down from Vehicle-1."

Heads snapped to attention in the Tahoe.

"Copy," Mollie said over the mic. "Is it on your list?" There was silence as the sniper-observer team checked if the vehicle was on the list of cars potentially involved in this case.

"Negative. This will be designated Vehicle-2. Stand by. I've got movement." Ten long seconds passed. "Single occupant is exiting. Hispanic female. Stand by. We're attempting a match to photos in the case file now."

After sixty seconds, which was thirty painful

ticks longer than the process should have taken, Johnston grumbled "Jesus Christ," and grabbed the radio mic from Mollie. He spoke with authority.

"Sierra-1, this is Delta. We've got to make some decisions here based on who that is, or if it's a new player. Can you get us some intel, please? We're running blind right now." His frustration leaked heavily into the transmission.

There was no response, because no one was listening. The Sierra-1 observer had turned his attention to his partner.

"Unplug that thing," he ordered.

"What?" the sniper asked.

"I said unplug it. Do you see who that facial image matches to? Disconnect the digital link between your rifle scope to the computer. Whatever is about to happen, there is no way we're recording this."

After he had broken the data feed, Sierra-1 looked through the scope again and watched Trooper Betsy Diaz get out of her Honda and approach Lorraine Underwood's car.

CHAPTER 24

Detective Trooper Betsy Diaz eased from the driver seat of her Honda Pilot with considerable effort. The air cast that rendered her ankle immobile scraped noisily on the edge of the door frame, then clunked onto the pavement. Her right arm in a sling, Diaz awkwardly eased the door shut with her left. It had taken a long time to get here.

Diaz's surveillance of Lorraine Underwood had started at noon. The rural road that led to the old woman's house was not conducive to clandestine observation by the police, so Diaz had taken up position on its north end, where it intersected with Route 77. Still far from urban, the intersection offered a few places for her to sit and watch, including a small convenience store and farm stand.

At around four that afternoon, Lorraine had finally emerged. Identification had been easy, as she pulled into the very convenience store in which Diaz had hidden her car. Lorraine had gone in for a cup of coffee and had not seemed to notice Diaz. That was not surprising. If she was hip to the surveillance, Lorraine would be looking for a sedan full of middle-aged men, not an SUV with a kayak rack driven by a woman.

Her head down and mind elsewhere, Lorraine

had turned on 77 and headed east toward Concord. Once in the city, she'd gotten directly onto an Interstate spur and swung round to the far side of town. As the woman turned on to Loudon Road, Diaz had begun to suspect her final destination.

The Steeplegate Mall was a small complex on the eastern border of the city. Notwithstanding its size, it fit the standard shopping mall model, a beefy structure planted in a sea of a thousand parking spaces. A few out-buildings, including an Applebee's and Toronto Domin-ion Bank, anchored the corners of the lot.

Lorraine had parked on the north side of the building, near the main Sears entrance, and got out of her car. Diaz picked a spot four rows away, and had to struggle to get out of her car before losing sight of Mrs. Underwood. The woman was surprisingly quick given her sixty-eight years of hard living.

Lorraine pulled open the doors and walked into Sears with purpose. Diaz had been lingering by the edge of a row of cars, and had to scurry across the open pave-ment to catch up. Her plastic boot was not an asset.

Diaz had to admit she had no idea what she was doing. The young trooper had worked four years on patrol before transferring into the sex offender regis-try. That move had come with additional investigative training, and a school on conducting proper interroga-tions, but she had no training or experience conducting surveillance. She was flying by the seat of her pants, and hoped her common sense and Lorraine's obliviousness would combine to generate success.

Diaz had spilled into Sears just in time to see Lorraine walk from power tools into men's clothing, then make a beeline to the entrance of the mall itself.

She gave chase, shuffle-clunking her plastic anchor as quietly as she could.

Once in the mall, Lorraine ducked into CVS drug store. Diaz took a wide path around the gaping entrance, hoping to spot her target. She picked up the woman in a center aisle, standing in front of a display rack. She walked past the store to the adjacent Dunkin' Donuts and bought a coffee. Diaz took her foam cup to a bench near a tacky garden display in the center of the broad, bricked corridor of the mall.

Five minutes later Lorraine had emerged, made a hard-left turn, and headed back to Sears. Diaz had almost missed her. She had, however, gotten a look at the single item Lorraine appeared to have purchased. The plastic blister-pack that held a throwaway Tracfone was easy to identify.

Lorraine quickened her pace as she backtracked through Sears. She showed no signs of suspicion. Diaz's inexperience in tradecraft seemed commensurate to that of her target.

Back outside, Lorraine had spent a half-hour in her parked car activating the burner phone. She texted for another thirty minutes. Diaz couldn't see the content, but the hunched-back head-down posture of a texter was unmistakable.

While Diaz weighed her options, Lorraine started moving again. She had pulled out of the lot, turned west, and headed back into the city.

Loudon Road was the spine that supported the east side of Concord, running from downtown to the eastern stretch of its border. Dotted with strip-malls and chain stores it was a straight shot for Lorraine to get where she was going. Three miles later, she turned right onto Stickney Road, then into the bus terminal lot.

Diaz had watched from across the parking lot for forty-five minutes, grew impatient, then convinced herself that her interrogation skills were stronger than her surveillance. She pulled a few car lengths past Lorraine Underwood's Ford, dragged her own sore body from the Honda Pilot, and walked to her target.

"How damn long is the sniper team going to make us wait before we get an update?" Mollie asked the group in the Tahoe.

"What the fuck are they doing?" Johnston asked, expressing the same frustration.

In the back seat, the two senior detectives waited. They knew an answer would come eventually, and getting frustrated served only to cloud their decision making with emotion.

Wilcox felt his pocket vibrate. The others heard it, causing heads to turn. He looked at the screen, recognized the number, and narrowed his eyes just enough for Brennan to pick up on it, but not the others. He answered.

"Who?" was all he said. Then, "What?" Followed by "Why?"

"What is this, a fucking junior high English class?" Mollie muttered. The comment was ignored.

Wilcox hung up, slipped the phone back into his suit, then said "It seems events have come full circle. Our mystery woman is Detective Trooper Betsaida Diaz."

"You're shitting me," said Johnston. Mollie's eyes widened as he mouthed a vulgarity as well. Brennan, for his part, smiled approvingly at Wilcox.

"Tough kid," he said.

"Indeed."

"Okay then," Mollie announced, making an assumption. "Who's contact and who's cover?" He reached for the door handle. Wilcox placed a firm hand on his shoulder from the back seat.

"We're going to wait, Don," he said.

Mollie's head spun between the front seats to look at Wilcox. "Why the hell would we do that? She just got out of the damn hospital. Is she even cleared for duty yet? I thought she was driving a desk until she fully recovered and we picked up Underwood. She can't be out in front on this."

There was no response, and Mollie's frustration grew.

"This surveillance is going to be blown if we leave her out there. Besides, she can't handle this on her own. She's liable to get hurt again."

"First of all, this surveillance is already blown," Wilcox started. "Lorraine's going to know, and if Underwood isn't already watching to see if the coast is clear, his mother is surely going to tell him when this is over. We're going to let it play out a bit. See what Diaz can squeeze out of her."

There was silence in the Tahoe.

"And yes, I'm confident *she* can handle this, Don," Wilcox added, calling him out for what they all knew he meant.

Mollie, reddened, turned forward in his seat. Johnston keyed the radio again. "Delta, Sierra-1. We're going to let this play out. But we're blind so call it out for us, please."

So began an open-microphone monologue from the sniper-observer team, dotted with brief breaks in the transmission in case someone else had emergency transmissions to make.

"Female-1 is still seated in Vehicle-1. Female-2 approaching from the driver side."

"One must be Lorraine, two is Diaz," Mollie said.

"Shut the fuck up, Don. I can't hear them," Johnston chastised.

"F-2 knocked on the glass. Window is rolling down. They're talking. Stand-by," continued Sierra-1.

"You think they could pick something up if they used the laser mic now?" Mollie offered. His question was met with glares that all but threatened physical violence if he didn't stop talking.

"F-2 has her arms crossed. She's leaning against the car. Okay, it looks like they're just talking." There was a fifteen second pause, then "Still just talking. F-1 just lit a cigarette."

Brennan allowed his eyes to soften as he nodded gently at Wilcox, silently communicating that maybe Diaz was getting somewhere, and that they should let her continue.

Thirty painfully silent seconds passed, then a full minute.

"Stand by. Something is going on down there," reported the sniper team. There was another pause. "Okay, F-2 has her back up. Hard finger pointing into the window now. Yelling. It looks a little heated."

Johnston looked behind him at Brennan with a question on his face, who in turn looked at Wilcox, who just perceptibly shook his head. They would keep waiting.

"She reached in," Sierra-1 said. "F-2 has her arm in the window, grabbing F-1's shirt collar. She's shaking her around. It's getting physical."

"Good thing the other arm is in a sling," Brennan whispered with a smile, "or Diaz would probably slap her with it."

"Okay she let her go," the observer said. "Wait, F-2 is moving. She's walking around the other side of the suspect vehicle."

Concerned faces filled the Tahoe.

"F-2 just opened the passenger door. She's getting in," Sierra-1 said.

"Jesus, you don't think Diaz would take a ride with her, do you?" Johnston asked. "Try to get the old lady to take her to Underwood?"

Taking a ride with a suspect gave up all control, and was tactically dangerous. Especially in this case, when Diaz had no cover.

"The car is backing up, now. They're moving," Sierra-1 advised.

Wilcox let out a resigned sigh. The hope had been for them to take Underwood into custody when he tried to board the bus, or failing that, to follow Lorraine to him. Any hope of that plan coming to fruition was now gone.

"Okay, we go now," said Wilcox. He lay a calming hand on Brennan's leg and caught his gaze. "You run it, Jimmy. Let her save face, at least. It's got to be tough on her."

Brennan nodded assent, then began issuing orders.

"Mollie, block them in," he said.

The junior detective immediately dropped the column shifter into reverse and squealed out of the space. He popped it into drive and spun the wheel hand over hand as Brennan continued.

"I'm contact and will take Lorraine on her side. Johnston, you get Diaz out of that car. Mollie, be ready to roll out."

Silence in the vehicle indicated everyone knew their role as they sprang into action.

Lorraine was backed halfway out of her space when a large vehicle appeared behind her. Slamming on her brakes, her head snapped toward Diaz seated next to her, wondering if there was a connection. When she looked back at her side window, there was a scruffy looking man with a police badge tapping against the glass. Confused, she rolled it down.

"Good evening, Ma'am. Could I have your license and registration, please?"

"What the fuck is going on here?" Lorraine protested. She looked at Diaz, who bore the same confused expression she did. Her eyes moved back to Brennan.

"I think there has been a mistake, Mrs. Underwood. You of course know we're looking for your son, Vincent," Brennan said.

"Yeah, no shit. That's what this one has been jacking me up about for the past five minutes," Lorraine complained, jerking a thumb toward Diaz.

"Yes, I know. That's my point, exactly," Brennan said reasonably. "It seems Detective Diaz wasn't aware of the current status of the search for your son, so she may have said some things that were not entirely accurate."

"Yeah, like that if I didn't take her to Vincent, she'd jam her fist down my throat and pull the truth out of me," Lorraine protested.

While Brennan dealt with Lorraine, Rey Johnston had moved to the passenger side of the vehicle and tapped his badge against the window. When Diaz looked, he was moving his index finger in a small circle, signaling her to roll down the window. Compliance had come slowly, and when it did, Johnston saw that Diaz had her hand on her holstered pistol.

"Good evening, Betsy. I'm Detective Johnston. Would you mind terribly coming with me?"

Diaz looked over at Lorraine, who was talking to a street thug holding a badge, then back at Johnston. She realized, suddenly and with concern, that she was now in well over her head.

Johnston tugged the handle and the door opened. Diaz stepped out, awkwardly, then stood staring at him. He took her by the arm and led her to the Tahoe.

"Let go of my arm," she complained, jerking it away.

"Diaz, you need to come with us," Johnston said, nodding toward the Tahoe.

"The fuck I do," she objected. "I don't even know you."

Johnston looked at the Tahoe, which caused Diaz to do the same. The blacked-out rear window rolled down to reveal the pleasant yet firm face of Charlie Wilcox.

"Do you remember Detective Wilcox, Betsy?" Johnston asked. There was no response. Wilcox waived a hand and beckoned Diaz over. Not knowing why, she complied.

"Please walk around the other side with Rey, Betsy, and get in. Then maybe we can sort out this whole affair," said Wilcox.

"I'll take my own car," she objected.

"Do you think it is wise to confirm for Lorraine which vehicle is yours?" Wilcox asked reasonably.

Diaz hesitated, then shrugged and walked around the other side of the car. As she climbed into the Tahoe, Brennan was wrapping up with Lorraine.

"So, as you can see by what I just said, Mrs. Underwood, Trooper Diaz was merely acting on old information. She did not know how cooperative you have been up to this point. As a result, she could hardly be held responsible for the aggressive nature of some of the things she said."

"That bitch threatened me, and you're only saying all this so I don't go complain about her and get her ass fired," Lorraine said.

Brennan smiled.

"As a matter of fact, that is exactly right. You're a smart woman, and I think we both know what is going on here. You've got a few options, but you should recognize that I do as well. For example, one option would be for me to drag you out of this car, handcuff you, and have a Concord patrol officer take you to the station. You'll sit in a cell there for hours until I can get all the necessary bosses to approve transporting you to Manchester. Once there, you'll be interrogated about why you are trying to help your fugitive son get out of town. After that you'll at best be released with continued surveillance, at worst arrested and charged for aiding a fugitive."

Brennan let the explanation hang in the air for five seconds.

"Option two is that you accept my apology for this miscommunication between government agencies, and you can drive home right now. There would, of course, be no reason to complain about any of this since it was all settled right here between us."

Lorraine looked Brennan up and down, assessing whether the way he appeared was the way he was, then said, "If I had another hundred dollars in my purse, all that bullshit would wash down a lot easier."

Brennan removed a pair of handcuffs from behind his back and began to tug on the door handle.

"Alright! Hey, you can't fault me for trying," Lorraine said. "Just get that big piece of shit behind me out of the way."

Brennan silently walked to the Tahoe and slid into the back seat next to Diaz. Mollie pulled forward ten feet to allow Lorraine Underwood to back out and pull away.

"Where to," asked Mollie.

"Manchester," Brennan said.

"The PD?" he asked again.

"Just drive, Don."

There were a few minutes of clunky silence inside the vehicle. Once they were safely on Interstate 93, headed south at eighty miles-per-hour, Wilcox turned on his hip to face Diaz.

"So, Betsy. How has *your* day been?"

"Shit."

CHAPTER 25

Following awkward introductions to the team of detectives that had rescued her from a career ending mistake, Betsy Diaz had decided her best option was to just come clean. Ten minutes into the ride from Concord to Manchester, she had finished telling Wilcox and the rest of them how she had followed Lorraine Underwood.

She did not confess it was the fourth time she had done it.

"So, how bad am I jammed up," Diaz asked, turning to Wilcox.

"Jimmy?" Wilcox asked, passing the question on.

"As far as Lorraine is concerned, I don't think you have anything to worry about," said Brennan. "She's been around the block, and knows what kind of heat she'll take if she makes a stink over what happened."

"Lorraine Underwood is only part of our problem," Wilcox offered. "What remains are the bosses from three different police agencies I now have to call and explain this to."

"Shit, Detective. I'm sorry for that. Is it something I can take care of myself?" asked Diaz. "I made this mess."

Brennan and Wilcox exchanged glances.

"I don't think that would be wise, Trooper Diaz. You're too invested in the outcome of this, which is part of why you should not have been there in the first place. I suspect you'd get yourself into more trouble trying to explain it away."

"Call me Betsy. And if I'm jammed up, then I'm jammed up. I'll take the medicine for it. I'd rather not add 'coward' to the list by having other cops cover for me."

"Betsy," Brennan said. "There's a difference between being a coward and letting us do you a favor. Yeah, you fucked up bad here, but it doesn't mean you should lose your job. That you're not cut out for this."

A muted huff came from the front of the Tahoe. Diaz's picked up on it, and her eyes narrowed.

"You all right up there?" she inquired, but it was an accusation.

"Oh yeah, I'm just fucking great," Mollie said sarcastically.

"You have something to say?" she challenged.

There was a pause, then "Yeah, I guess I do. I was wondering if you hadn't tried to play Wonder Woman out there today if we might have Vincent Underwood in handcuffs in the back of our car right now instead of you."

"Easy, Mollie," Johnston cautioned.

"No," Diaz said, holding up a hand. "Let him go."

"That's all I've got, Diaz. Just wondering how this would have played out if you hadn't shown up trying to play hero," Mollie said.

"I didn't know you guys were on her, okay? If I had, I would have backed off."

"What did you think we were doing with our

time, waiting around the office drinking coffee until Underwood turned himself in?"

Diaz shook her head. She was determined not to let anger at herself reflect out onto the others, but she was infuriated at her own rash behavior, and it needed an outlet. Mollie was setting himself up as the best candidate.

"Listen," Johnston said, trying to reduce the temperature. "It's over, all right. We'll figure out where to go from here. It's just good you didn't get hurt."

"I already got hurt," Diaz barked, angrier than she intended. Johnston put his hands up in surrender.

"And a lot you learned from that," Mollie said, pushing again.

"What was Lorraine going to do, shoot me?" Diaz said. "Let's not forget I was getting somewhere with her until you four showed up."

"If you weren't there, and Vincent had never shown up, we would have picked up the mother and brought her in for interrogation," Mollie said. "And you can be damned sure we would have gotten a hell of a lot more out of her than you did."

"What does that mean?" Diaz accused.

"It means...look at you. Your foot in a cast, right arm in a sling. Dainty little pants on with a tiny belt that barely holds up your gun. Can you even shoot that thing left-handed?"

That was enough.

"You have a fucking problem with women on the job, Mollie?" Diaz erupted. "Because I seem to remember you sitting in the cozy-warm Tahoe while I was out bracing the mother of the asshole that jacked up my shoulder in the first place."

"Oh, no. Of course not. I have no problem with women on the job. Look how well all those fucking emotions of yours helped us today," Mollie said.

"You think you could've gotten somewhere with her I didn't?"

"Yes, because I bring something to this job that you'll never have."

"What's that, Mollie? A big dick and a tiny brain? Pull this fucking car over. I'll find my own ride back."

The vehicle was not stopped, and fell silent as they slowed for an exit. Back on surface streets, the heat of the conversation reduced with the pace of traffic. Johnston spoke first, and turned to face Diaz.

"You said Lorraine was texting on that phone non-stop since she bought it." He looked next at Brennan. "You didn't grab it by any chance, did you, Jimmy?"

"No. My priority was trying to get...no, I didn't," said Brennan.

"Shit, no warrant then," Johnston said.

"And now we'll never get it, will we," Mollie said, shaking his head as if the fact proved some larger point.

"Shut up," Johnston said.

As the men focused their collective gazes forward, counting the moments until the trip was over, Diaz withdrew something from her pocket.

"You guys mean this phone?" she asked, holding it up in front of her chest. She allowed Johnston to snatch it out of her hand.

"Is this the one Lorraine was using?" he asked, smiling.

"When did you have time to grab that?" added Brennan.

"Somewhere between you asking for her driver's

license and Johnston here yanking me out of the car. I thought we might need it."

"Nice job remembering to take the phone, Rey," Wilcox said.

"What?" Johnston asked, confused. "I didn't grab it. Diaz did."

"Listen up everyone," Wilcox said with authority. "I'm going to be making the calls to the brass to explain how this operation ended, and I'm going to write up the reports. This is how it went. After Diaz got out of the car, Detective Johnston grabbed that phone from Lorraine. We're not going to get into the weeds about why Diaz, who is on light duty, would have been there seizing evidence. Everyone got it."

There were nods around the car, with the exception of Mollie. Wilcox called him out on it.

"You have something to add, Don?"

"No, I get it. We're good," he said.

They pulled into the Manchester police department's rear parking area just as the conversation ended. Everyone entered the building save Wilcox and Diaz, who stood by the Tahoe under the guise of Wilcox needing to gather some equipment from the rear hatch.

"Thanks, Charlie."

"None needed," said Wilcox.

"You agree with Mollie, don't you? That women are emotional and shouldn't be doing this part of the job."

"I agree entirely with Detective Mollie that women are emotional, and it is for that very reason that you *should* be doing this part of the job. That's the part guys like Mollie don't understand yet."

"I just can't sit behind a damned desk all day,

knowing cops are out there taking risks to catch the son-of-a-bitch. I want to help."

"And you are, by keeping yourself healthy and your credibility intact so you can testify against this monster once we bring him in."

"You think he's coming in alive?"

"That's not for us to decide, Betsy. Certainly not for you to decide." Wilcox caught her eyes and held them for an uncomfortable moment.

"Okay, I get it. I'll back off."

"You're on light duty, is that correct?" asked Wilcox.

"Yeah, confined to the office. I took vacation today in order to do this."

"I'm sure you can find better ways to spend your leave time. Look, I'll see what I can do to keep you better informed about what we're doing on this case, as long as you promise not to get involved without my explicit knowledge."

"Are you going to involve me?"

"More than you have been. Let's leave it at that for now."

"Fair enough. Thanks again."

"Sure, now let's go inside and see if I can find a uniform to give you a ride back to your car."

CHAPTER 26

Lieutenant Ross Patterson of the Manchester Police Department, having been on the job for eighteen of his forty-six years, had come to believe that in all likelihood his daughter was being beaten. And after much thought he decided it was his responsibility to stop it.

The thumbprint bruises on the underside of Bridget's upper arm could not possibly have been caused by a falling shoebox as she removed it from a high closet shelf. Frank Doran, Bridget's boyfriend, was always inexplicably unavailable to come over to break bread with the family. Bridget Patterson, who for two decades had shared an exceptionally close relationship with her mother, had herself not found the time to visit in nearly a month.

Two weeks earlier, Ross Patterson had driven by Bridget's apartment and checked Doran's license plate, learning that the registration was expired and the man's driver's license suspended. For the rest of it, he'd had to call in favors.

Favor number one was asking a sex crimes detective from the state police, because no one ever audited record checks done by the state police, to run Doran's priors. He had two arrests for domestic assault and one conviction. He had also been arrested three years ago for possession of cocaine.

Favor two came from a Manchester PD overnight shift sergeant whom Patterson had helped through a particularly difficult officer-involved-shooting investigation a year earlier. He owed Patterson a favor, and this would be an easy way to pay it back.

The sergeant had followed Frank Doran home from a night of drinking and pulled him over for failing to signal a turn. Smelling the booze, he'd ordered Doran out of his car to submit to sobriety tests, which the young man summarily failed. Following that he was handcuffed, searched, and put in the back of a police car.

Out of Doran's view, the sergeant had quickly produced a Cellebrite UFED-19. The brick-sized extraction device had been borrowed from the financial crimes unit the day before. Plugging it into Doran's cell phone, the sergeant quickly transferred all of his contacts and text messages onto a thumb drive.

"Just don't arrest him, okay Sarge?" Ross Patterson had asked when cashing in the favor.

"Sure, no problem. But why not? Don't you want to jam the kid up? Isn't that the point of all this?"

"Yeah, but a DUI arrest is too petty. And he'll just take it out on...it'll just get worse. Trust me. Just get me the info off that phone," Patterson pleaded.

"You got it."

After extracting what he needed from the phone, the sergeant had pulled Frank Doran out of his cruiser and told him he had second thoughts.

"You seem like a decent kid, and I don't want to hem you up with a DUI arrest. You'd probably lose your job, insurance goes up, a bunch of fines. Just get home safe and I don't want to see you out here again, alright?"

As he had pulled away from the curb in a prudent and measured fashion, Frank Doran couldn't believe his luck. "Dumb-ass cop," he'd muttered.

Now, three days later, Ross Patterson sat in a red vinyl booth at the Roundabout Diner in Portsmouth, fingering the handle of his second cup of coffee. In the other, he toyed with the thumb drive from Doran's phone. The texts had substantiated his worst fears. After reading several hundred of them two nights ago, he had decided to get drunk. No father should read the intimate, personal, and disturbingly brutal text messages of his young adult daughter. But he had to know.

The texts had confirmed his suspicions, but also provided a solution. They revealed that Frank Doran was a drug dealer, selling cocaine, both crack and soft, all over the city. That was where Jimmy Brennan came in, and favor number three.

When Brennan walked into the diner, Patterson looked to make eye contact but was not surprised when the detective avoided it. He knew Brennan would check the room before coming to sit with him. The last thing the undercover detective needed was someone he was looking into seeing him meet with a police lieutenant. Patterson's face was known. Brennan's, by design, was not.

Brennan saw his old supervisor, but ignored him. He walked to the back of the restaurant, scanning tables casually, and entered the restroom. Coming out four minutes later, he walked to Patterson's booth and sat. The men shook hands.

"How are you, Jimmy?"

"I'm good, Boss," Brennan said. "You?"

"'Boss'," Patterson repeated back, smiling. "The

good old days, huh?" It had been ten years since to two worked the overnight shift together.

"Fights in the bars, drunks in the cars, right 'Sarge'?" Brennan acknowledged, joining in the memories. "A simpler time."

They were smiling when a waitress arrived at the table. She looked at Patterson, who raised his eyebrows and nodded her attention to Brennan.

"Just coffee for me, thanks," he said. The waitress glanced back at Patterson, who ignored her for the moment.

"Get something to eat. You drove all the way out here. My treat."

Brennan, awkwardly rushed, picked up the menu and glanced at it. "How about an egg sandwich."

"Bagel or English muffin?"

"Muffin."

The waitress, already bored with the back and forth indecisiveness during her breakfast rush, looked again at Patterson.

"A refill on this, and the same to eat," he said, tapping the mug with his wedding ring.

"Two egg sandwiches," the waitress said plainly as she collected the menus and walked toward the kitchen.

"Thanks for meeting me, Jimmy. I know it was last-minute."

"No problem, L-T. How's Janet, the kids?"

"Call me Ross, Jimmy. Drop the L-T stuff."

"Sure," Brennan responded. He waited for Patterson to answer the question about his wife and kids, but it didn't come.

Patterson took a sip of coffee as the waitress set a

full cup down in front of Brennan. He lowered his own mug so she could top it off.

"How's the family? Sarah and Maggie. What is she, ten now?" asked Patterson

"She's twelve. Just finished a big project in school about President Roosevelt."

"Which one?"

"Webster Elementary, down the far end of Elm Street."

Patterson chuckled. "No, Jimmy. Which Roosevelt?"

"Oh," smiled Brennan. "FDR. She's turning into quite the World War II buff."

The conversation paused as both men sipped from their heavy, china mugs. The pause dragged, then turned awkward.

"How's work?" Patterson started.

"Good. You know, busy."

"I hear you're coming back. Back into a suit."

Brennan knew the rumor mill of the Manchester Police Department, like most others, ground along nonstop. Still, he was surprised by the speed it had done so in this case. He'd only spoken to Soffit two days prior and had yet to file his −219. Someone had been talking.

"Yeah, that's the plan."

"Just had enough of it?" Patterson asked.

"Sure. Yeah, you could say that."

Patterson caught Brennan's eyes and held them.

"I did say it. I'm asking if you would." Even after the passage of nearly a decade, Brennan felt the man's authority.

The waitress arrived with their sandwiches and the topic dropped. Brennan was grateful.

"My daughter went to Webster, too. Did you know that?" asked Patterson.

"No, Ross. I didn't. Where'd she go after that? We're thinking Memorial for Maggie. Or Bishop Brady in Concord, if we can afford it."

"Memorial. It was a good fit for us."

Brennan wasn't surprised Patterson's only daughter had gone to Memorial High School. In a bustling city with a perennially overloaded public education system, it was the most reliable choice, and the place most city cops' kids attended if they could not afford private school.

"Good for her. What's she up to nowadays?"

Patterson broke eye contact with Brennan and took a bite of his sandwich, washing it down with a swig of coffee. He wiped his mouth deliberately with a napkin before folding it in half and placing it back on his lap. The entire process was unnecessarily prolonged.

That confirmed it, and Brennan decided to take a chance.

"What's her name, Ross?"

"What?" Patterson asked, his thoughts snapping back to the moment.

"Your daughter. I forgot her name."

"Bridget. It's Bridget." He looked back down. "She's been having a hard time."

"I heard," Brennan said, and when Patterson looked up, he added, "It's not that big of a city, and you know cops talk."

"Yeah, I know."

"You mentioned a favor when you called. What can I do?"

"I'm hesitant to ask. Especially with you transferring out of undercover and back to major crimes. I don't want to put you in a spot."

"Try me. If it's too much I'll let you know. Hey, worst case we enjoy our sandwiches and maybe I can try and give you some advice."

"I don't know," Patterson said weakly. "I'm having second thoughts about even asking."

The man seated before Brennan was not the strong, confident, barrel chested Irishman he had worked for ten years prior. He was a slouched, emotionally drained father, terrified for the future of his daughter and unsure where to go for help.

"You know," Brennan began after clearing his throat and adjusting his posture. "As cops we spend an awful lot of time and energy on other people's problems. You ever notice that?"

He didn't give the man a chance to answer.

"And generally, we do a damn good job at it. But sometimes we have to refocus on ourselves. Help each other out. You know what I mean?"

"Sure, but..."

"For example," Brennan drove on. "Last week a detective from the domestic violence unit called me up to ask if I would drop a case for her. It was a woman on Douglas Street I had bought a bunch of Oxy's from. A real piece of work. She was stealing them from her job as an LPN at Villa Crest Nursing Center. When we arrested her, she confessed to the whole thing."

"What a piece of shit, stealing pills from old people." Patterson interjected. "Why'd this detective want the case dumped?"

"It turns out my suspect was also consistently getting smacked around by her shit-head husband. He got locked up when she finally got brave enough to dial 911, and now she wants to skip town. She's going to take the kids to her aunt's place in New Jersey. Try to get a fresh start."

"Good for her."

"Well, she can't. Because the bail conditions from my pill case prevent her from leaving the county, let alone the state.

Brennan paused the story. He picked up his mug, sipped deeply, and cupped it in two hands beneath his nose, breathing in the steam. Patterson's face betrayed his desire to hear the rest of the story.

"And? So, what did you do?"

"You mean what did I do when a fellow cop asked me to drop a rock-solid pill case so some chronic domestic abuse victim could leave town?"

Patterson raised his eyebrows and nodded.

"I flushed the case like a day-old turd," Brennan announced.

"Jesus, Jimmy. Some nurse stealing pills from the elderly and you drop the case so she can just move somewhere else, get another job, and probably do the same thing all over again? What the hell for?"

Brennan leaned far forward over his plate and put both hands flat on the table. "Because another cop asked me to, and it was important to her, which means it was important to me."

Ross Patterson was about to speak again but pulled up short. He took a breath, mental gears clicking into place, and leaned back into the booth. Brennan sipped his coffee. When he spoke again, it was softer and less animated.

"What's going on with Bridget? What can I do to

help?"

Patterson waited to respond. His throat had grown thick and for the moment, he didn't trust his voice.

"Thanks, Jimmy."

"You're welcome, partner."

Patterson let out a sigh and waved off the waitress who happened by with more coffee. Brennan allowed her to fill his.

"Okay, this is what I need. How do you feel about setting up a low-level drug dealer to take the fall for heavier weight?" asked Patterson.

"I don't know. You recall that the goal of my job is generally to have *fewer* drug dealers in Manchester, not create new ones," Brennan said dryly.

"Yeah, well this one happens to also be beating my daughter."

"Oh," said Brennan. "Well, in that case my only question is when do you want to start?"

CHAPTER 27

Brennan stood outside the door of number four-fifteen Wellington Heights, on the east side of Manchester, trying to decide if he should kick down the door and storm in, or simply knock.

Once Patterson had opened up at the diner, his account of Bridget's struggles flowed like a river. He trusted Brennan, so confessing the called-in favors came easily. The hard part would be getting Bridget some help, back into the family fold, once her boyfriend was out of the picture. That was, assuming what they were going to do succeeded in extracting the man from her life.

With all the information they pulled from Frank Doran's phone, a plan had come together quickly. Doran had made no effort to conceal his drug dealing. He had made the same false assumption most people did, that information in their mobile phone was secure. There had been hundreds of contacts, but one in particular piqued Brennan's interest. Alan McBride.

From the age of seventeen, McBride had spent five years in prison for multiple burglaries. He had put every one of those years to use. As well as availing himself to an education on the basics of street crime from fellow inmates, he earned an online bachelor's degree in marketing with a minor in, of all things, criminal justice. Upon his release he'd satisfied his parole obligations, maxed out his time, and was free of government supervision.

Now twenty-eight, McBride had wasted no time setting up a mid-sized methamphetamine distribution ring. He had multiple supply chains in case one went down, a minimum of two layers between himself and every transaction, and never touched the drug himself. He dabbled with a little coke now and then to party, but was smart enough never to use his own product. McBride ran his business like an LLC, keeping the profits and avoiding the risk.

Brennan and his unit had been up on McBride twice in recent years. Each time they had missed. They made an arrest once, but three weeks later the informant they had used was found floating in the Merrimack River. McBride's previous reputation as a quiet and peaceful drug dealer who kept to himself had been tarnished, and his profile was lifted a notch.

According to texts on Doran's phone, Alan McBride bought a gram of cocaine from Frank Doran twice, sometimes three times a month. It was a misdemeanor at worst if McBride was caught, and he'd be looking at maybe a couple hundred dollars fine. Tonight, Brennan had other plans for him.

Brennan now stood outside McBride's condominium. The units on Wellington Heights were narrow and tall, two stories stacked on top of a wide single-car garage. Tactically, it was a nightmare, full of stairs, blind corners, and reflective angles. As he debated his options, Brennan absentmindedly fiddled with the door knob. It turned, and he decided to let that fact make the decision for him.

Entering the door adjacent to the garage, Brennan felt its weight. It had a steel core, reinforced. He was glad he had not tried to kick it.

The carpeted stairs afforded an easily silent climb. Brennan heard the muffled sound of explosions and rock music from McBride's amplified video game system and breathed in the familiar odor of marijuana. Stoned and preoccupied was how the detective wanted McBride. It would be that much simpler to rattle him. As Brennan mounted the final step a boisterous voice boomed.

"Good evening, Detective Brennan!"

Snapping his head to the left, Brennan saw the back of an ergonomic gaming chair occupied by Alan McBride. He sat fifteen feet from an eighty-inch flat screen television with a split screen. One half displayed the continuing carnage of a World War II Pacific Island first person shooter. The other revealed a high-definition 1080p surveillance video image of the stairwell Brennan had just ascended.

It took a few beats for Brennan's heart to descend back into his chest.

"Jesus, McBride! I almost shot you," Brennan said.

"That would have been a challenge for you to explain, wouldn't it? Now, I trust you have a warrant to enter my peaceful home without first having asked politely?"

Brennan walked further into the living room, passed McBride, and flopped down into an overstuffed leather couch. McBride picked up a smoldering marijuana cigarette from a nearby ashtray and pressed it between his lips. He paused, exhaled, and held it out toward Brennan, who shook his head and smiled.

"Suit yourself," McBride shrugged as he set the joint down.

"You the only one home, Alan?"

McBride failed to answer, then looked back at the television, prepared to deactivate the pause feature. The lack of response got Brennan's back up, and he let his right arm fall to his side so his elbow could feel the pistol beneath his coat. He adjusted his posture in order to note the backup gun pressed into the small of his back.

"You going to answer my question, Alan?"

"You going to answer mine, Detective?"

Brennan smirked. Verbal sparring with a criminal was usually a fight with an unarmed man, but McBride was a little shrewder than the average felon.

"No. No warrant."

Looking newly curious, McBride reached for a remote, snapped the television off, and looked at the trespasser. "Okay, then. I'm the only one here."

"I need a favor," said Brennan.

McBride's eyebrows went up. "Do you now? You in trouble with the cops or something?"

He snickered at his own joke and reached down for the cigarette again. Brennan's sober hand was faster and he stuffed it down hard into the ashtray. McBride looked up disapprovingly.

"I think you better leave."

When there was no reaction from Brennan, McBride tried to stand. Strong hands grasped his shoulders and pressed down hard. He looked behind in confusion and met the gaze of Lieutenant Ross Patterson.

"Who the fuck are you?" he exclaimed, trying to stand again. This time Patterson slapped his palm into the side of McBride's head, knocking him out of the chair. On the way down his foot hit the nearby end table upsetting three beer bottles, two empty and one full.

"You probably should have kept that camera on a little longer," Brennan said dryly.

Rubbing his ear gingerly, McBride crawled back into the chair. He was smart enough to know now was not the time to pick a fight.

"What do you and 'knuckles' here want, Brennan? Before I call the cops."

"Do you know a guy named Frank Doran?" Brennan asked.

"No."

Brennan looked up at Patterson, who again placed a hand on each of McBride's shoulders and applied pressure. Brennan said again, "You know a guy named Frank Doran." This time it was a statement, not an inquiry.

"I know a lot of people. How the hell am I supposed to remember some random idiot."

"Frank Doran is the low-rent coke dealer you and your girlfriend have been buying grams from for the past three months. He is best friends with Mike Thompson, your moron cousin, which is how you met him."

McBride opened his mouth to retort, but Brennan's threatening head tilt and piercing gaze shut him up. The dealer's face softened and he nodded subtly.

"Good. Why are you only buying grams from him?"

"Because that's all I want, just to party is all."

"And maybe," Brennan added, "because Doran is a drunk-driving cop magnet who's liable to get picked up for any number of foolishly planned crimes."

McBride picked up on the comment and raised an

eyebrow. "How do you know he drives drunk, Detective?"

"This is where the favor part comes in, Alan."

Looking over his shoulder at Patterson to gauge the safety of asking a question, McBride said, "So that's what this is about? You want to ask me questions about some coke dealer?"

"Close. I want you to jump in bed with him."

"Why?"

"Don't worry about the why," Brennan assured him. "Just start out making another buy from him. Talk to him about signing up."

"Sign up for what? Do I look like a fucking employment agency to you?" McBride reflexively winced, ready to be struck, then saw that the big man behind him had taken a step back and crossed his arms.

Brennan softened his tone, trying a different tack.

"Look, Alan. You need to focus. Don't worry about the details. Just get ahold of the guy and talk him up. Set up a deal for a few nights from now. And I want you to go heavier than last time. Maybe an ounce."

There was a pause, and a perceptible change to the energy in the room as McBride decided to consider the offer.

"He's going to know something's up if I call him and go from grams to ounces. You know that." When Brennan didn't reply, McBride continued. "Maybe I'll ramp it up slow, over a couple of weeks."

Brennan glanced beyond McBride to Patterson, who gently shook his head side to side.

"No, Alan. We're going to do it quicker than that. Get him on the phone and set it up. You've dealt with the guy. He's weak. Stroke him a little bit and he'll jump at the chance to do weight."

McBride stared at Brennan for ten seconds, then shook his head slowly as he reached down and picked up his cell phone. Patterson took a step forward then stunted his motion as the dealer held up his left hand and scrolled through messages with his right.

"You wanna keep your gorilla at bay, Brennan? I'm just checking something."

The silence continued until McBride found what he was looking for.

"Okay, so the last time I dealt with this guy was a week ago."

"Then it wouldn't be too far out of the realm of possibilities for you to be looking to score again," Brennan prompted. McBride glowered at him.

"You're assuming a lot here. Why would I help you? What am I getting on my end?"

"Six months."

McBride immediately misunderstood. "Six months? For what? You don't have shit on me. How do you suppose you're going to lock me up for six months?"

"No, Alan. Six months *off*. No heat on you for six months. MPD, state police, DEA, all off your back for six months."

McBride considered this briefly, then decided.

"No, thanks. Don't do me any favors. None of you have touched me yet, why should I worry now? Besides, you're done on the street anyway, aren't you? Getting back into a suit, I hear."

Brennan was really starting to wonder who at MPD was being so public with his duty assignments. He silently asked the same question of Patterson with a furrowed brow. The lieutenant replied with a shrug and an *it doesn't matter* head shake. Brennan refocused back on the problem before them.

"You're right. We don't *currently* have shit on you. But we know who you are, where you live, and what you drive. I'll put an MPD cruiser on you seven days a week. Every time you go for groceries, you'll get pulled over for something. DEA will park one of their painfully obvious blacked-out SUV's right out front here."

Brennan bent over and snatched McBride's phone from his hand, then tossed it to Patterson, who started scrolling through.

"And we'll pull every name out of that thing and hem them up, too. You won't be able to make a move for months. I'd be surprised if you could sell an Adderall to a middle-schooler, let alone meth to motorcycle clubs. You're done, *Alan*."

Brennan let the threat sit in the room before continuing.

"Or, you can make a five-minute phone call, and you'll never see me again. It's that simple."

"And when word gets out I'm a rat?" McBride complained. "What then?"

"You let me worry about that."

McBride stared at his captor, then pointed at the ashtray. Brennan nodded his assent and the man re-lit the joint and took a long pull.

"In writing," he said.

"Kiss my ass, McBride. Do I look like I offer a written guarantee? Take it or leave it."

"Then let me call someone as a witness. My girl, maybe," McBride retorted, thinking fast.

"You mean Chelsea Morris? Sure, dial her up."

Brennan glanced at Patterson who tossed McBride's phone back to him.

Visibly discomfited by the police knowing his girlfriend's name, McBride spun to her contact and waited for a connection. He pushed another button and set the phone on the arm of his chair.

"Babe, it's me. I got a favor."

"What Alan? I'm sleeping. Leave me alone."

"Shut up and listen," he replied then turned to Brennan. "Okay, say it."

"If you do what I ask with this Doran kid, you'll get a free pass for six months," Brennan recited.

"Who the hell was that?" Chelsea complained. "Where are you?"

"Jesus, woman. Did you hear it or not?"

"Yeah, sure. I heard it. Free pass for six months. What the fuck does that mean, anyway?"

"I'll call you later," he said and pressed the red button.

"Sweet girl," Brennan mocked. "Do you think she's the one, Big Al?"

"Kiss my ass," said McBride. "So now what?"

"Now you call, chat up Doran, and order that ounce."

"No way, Brennan. That's not gonna work. If I order up heavy and the first time we do a deal with weight the cops swoop in and arrest him, then word will be out in thirty-seconds I'm a rat."

"Relax, would you. You make the calls and set it up. We'll take him down on the other end, at his pickup. He'll think the informant is on the supply end, not demand."

"You know his supplier, then? Why not just go

after him? Move up the food chain and all that," McBride asked logically.

"Are you looking to apply for a job as a cop? Just make the goddamned call so we can get out of here."

McBride threw up his arms in resignation, picked up the phone, and started scrolling again.

As he made the call, Patterson walked over and leaned into Brennan.

"You think this is going to work?" he whispered.

"I have no idea, Ross. But we're going to give it a shot."

CHAPTER 28

Paul Nessman had met Ozzy Ostrowski twice, and owed both occasions to his association with Brass Malone. First had been an after-hours gathering of interested parties at The Ledo, a since closed cave-like Italian eatery on the west side of Springfield, Massachusetts. An effort was being made to maintain peace, if not establish partnerships, between Springfield's Pugliano Family and the Irish. Both were pushing northward, and there was talk of cooperation before inevitable conflict developed.

Heading into that meeting, Nessman had anticipated holding the honored position of counselor, akin to an Italian consigliere. When they arrived, he found that position filled by a former flat foot named Ozzy Ostrowski. Nessman had simply been brought along as muscle.

The second time was last year, when Malone's youngest son had been murdered following a night of drinking in Portland, Maine. It had been a drunken brawl gone awry, and the youthful Malone had been shot in the street like a dog. Worst still, the perpetrator had escaped.

Brass Malone had dispatched Nessman and Ozzy to the port city, each with a narrowly defined task. Ozzy had worked over the Portland police in an effort to identify the suspect, and he squeezed the name out of a patrol officer with a pill problem. He then fed the name to Nessman. Three days later the suspect was found hanging from a pier on the Old Port neighborhood, an eight-inch swordfish hook through his chest and his genitals in his mouth.

Both men worked nearly exclusively for Malone, but had occupied the same space only twice in eighteen months. It was a testament to their boss's commitment to compartmentalizing everything. Collusion between subordinates was less likely, and it was easier to smoke out a rat. Nessman did not like Ozzy, but had grown to respect his connections and capabilities. He got things from the cops no one else could.

It was based on this skeptical respect that Nessman had agreed to meet Ozzy at the Red Arrow Diner. The phone call had been cryptic. Ozzy had said he knew Nessman 'had something in the works' for Malone, and the ex-cop wanted to talk. Nessman suspected it was about the murder they were hiring out. It was exactly the kind of information sharing that lawbreakers generally, and Malone particularly, did not condone. Nevertheless, Nessman reluctantly accepted.

As he crossed the Notre Dame Bridge, Nessman organized his thoughts. He'd hear the man out, but reveal nothing. While it wasn't something Nessman admitted out loud, Ozzy was smarter than he was. He'd have to be on guard. The last thing Nessman wanted were problems with Malone.

After continuing on Bridge Street, Nessman turned right on Elm. He proceeded up one block, turned left, and eased past the diner. Parking on the street, ra-

216

ther than the lot, he briefly walked the neighborhood to check for a surveillance car before going in.

The lot was clean. Nessman mounted the few steps to the entrance and yanked open the glass door. The clubbers looking for a late, greasy meal had gone home, and it was early for the breakfast crowd. At 4:00am, the twenty-four-hour diner was sparsely occupied. He quickly spotted Ozzy tucked into a booth near the rear, his back to the door.

Nessman walked the length of the diner, a row of counter stools on his right and banquettes on the left. As he passed the counter, he caught the attention of the lone waitress, mimed drinking a cup of coffee, and pointed to Ozzy. She smiled and nodded.

He arrived, and stood at the end of the table. Ozzy looked up, smiled genuinely, and offered his hand. Nessman took it, and the former officer gestured toward the booth across from him. Nessman slid in.

"Coffee? Something else?" he asked just as the waitress delivered a steaming cup and offered to refill Ozzy's. He put his hands in his lap and leaned back in assent.

"Something to eat, boys?"

Both men shook their heads in unison.

"Let me know if you change your minds."

"You know what?" Ozzy decided. "How about a muffin, cut open and grilled?"

"Sure, sweetheart." She looked at Nessman with raised eyebrows. When he remained silent, she turned on her heel and walked off.

"Thanks for coming, Paul."

Nessman nodded and sipped his coffee.

"How's it going? How's business?"

Nessman didn't want small talk. He set his mug down carefully and looked up at Ozzy.

"What do you need?" he asked coldly.

"Let's wait for my muffin, shall we?"

Nessman huffed and sipped the scalding drink again. His gaze fell out the window to the parking lot. An MPD cruiser drove down Lowell Street.

The oversized muffin, split, buttered, and grilled arrived with more butter on the side. Their coffee was warmed up, and the waitress left.

"I'm worried about Brass," Ozzy began.

"Mm-Hmm."

Ozzy looked at him curiously. "You're not, Paul?"

"What're you worried about?"

"Jail. Prison. He's looking at a lot of time."

"Yeah, I guess he is," said Nessman.

"That doesn't worry you?"

"He's a big boy. He'll be alright."

Ozzy cocked his head, silently asking a question. Nessman ignored it and asked his own.

"Why am I here?"

"Would you agree, Paul, that we want the same thing out of this?"

"I don't follow."

"That we both want Brass to do the least amount of time he can, and come out of this whole mess as quickly as possible?"

"He'll be fine, Oz."

"He's looking at a solid bit."

"It's not the first time he's been jammed up. He can stand up to a few lumps in the joint."

"This is a little different." Ozzy prodded. When Nessman didn't respond, he continued. "He's not looking at a nickel for extortion. This is real time. They linked him to guns and bodies. At least they think they did."

Brass Malone had spent five years in the Souza-Baranowski supermax facility in Shirley, Massachusetts for extortion and assault. He had been in his late twenties.

"And?"

"And he's no spring chicken anymore, Paul."

"He can do the time," Nessman said, confidently.

Ozzy Ostrowski sipped his coffee and fought the urge to roll his eyes at the man's posturing. It was ludicrous that Nessman was going to make him ask about the murder for hire out loud.

"We had some things in the works to help him out that didn't come through. An arrangement, you could say, with the court," Ozzy started cautiously.

Nessman looked straight at him and spoke in a slow, measured tone. "So I heard."

"And?" Ozzy prodded.

"And what, Oz?"

"And... now you have something else in the works, correct? Another option?"

At that, Nessman lowered his hand until the mug it held clunked down at an awkward angle, spilling coffee. He eyed the door, then the parking lot, scanning back and forth. He reached into a coat pocket and withdrew a small black device, the size of a pack of cigarettes. Lifting a cover on its side, he manipulated a switch.

The Protech 1207i was not the latest radio-frequency detection device on the market, but it worked exceptionally well. Paul Nessman found it unlikely that

Ozzy was wearing a wire, but if he was, the twelve-hundred-dollar device would inform him.

He could have checked with it in his pocket, but he wanted Ozzy, who would recognize it, to see.

"Is that really necessary, Paul?"

Nessman had the device set to stealth mode, which meant it would vibrate, but the indicator lights and tones would not activate. It remained still.

"Take your phone out, Ozzy."

"Jesus Christ, Paul. Really?"

Nessman just stared at him.

Ozzy knew what Nessman was doing. The obvious effort was to ensure he wasn't wearing a wire or transmitting with a phone app. More importantly he was posturing, and Ozzy decided to let him. Nessman would never rise above the position of enforcer because he still thought authority came from broken bones and bullet holes. Ozzy knew true power came with the stroke of a pen, the tap of a keyboard, and the proper distribution of corrupt funds. The judicious application of violence best served as an occasional exclamation point, not common vernacular.

Taking his phone out, Ozzy unlocked it and swiped up, displaying the open applications. He turned it so it faced Nessman, who looked at the phone, not possibly identifying everything on the screen. The enforcer grunted his approval.

"You were saying?" Ozzy continued.

"I wasn't saying anything," replied Nessman.

You fatuous bastard. Why can't we just act like two professionals with a common goal, and talk this through? Why the tough-guy act every damn time?

"Okay, *I* was saying that we both have some goals

in common, here."

"Do we?"

"Related to Brass. Yes, we do. Neither one of us benefits if he spends much time in jail."

"Okay," said Nessman.

Ozzy smiled in appreciation that perhaps progress was finally being made.

"So, this new project you're working on for him. That has to be handled just right."

"I've got it, Ozzy. We're good."

"What do you know about this guy out of Boston?" asked Ozzy.

Nessman was swallowing coffee, and visibly fought to avoid choking on his own surprise.

"What do you know about Boston?" he asked.

"Paul, you need to get used to the fact that you and I both work for Malone, but that we satisfy two distinctly different needs. Going forward, it would be in your best interest to operate under the assumption that I know more about what is going on than you do. You occupy a space that I cannot fill, I'll grant you that. But know that my particular skill set, and the services it allows me to provide, are unique. Yours, on the other hand, are not. There are a lot of men out there who are good at breaking things. Only a rare few can put them back together again."

Nessman looked to interrupt, but Ozzy silenced him with a pointedly erect finger, held up between them.

"You'd be wise to remember that."

Nessman remained quiet as the upbraiding sat on the table between them. Ozzy broke off a large chunk of muffin and stuffed it into his mouth. He chewed slowly, sipped some coffee, and extended a piece to Nessman, who ignored it. Ozzy shrugged and crammed in that piece as well.

"Now," Ozzy began again, as if the tension-filled exchange never happened. "Tell me about Boston."

Nessman's right eye twitched, and he pursed his lips. It was evident he was thinking. Ozzy gave him the time he needed.

"You should know some of this, maybe, in case the cops get involved," Nessman offered.

Ozzy hoped his condescension didn't show. Of course the police would be involved in the murder of a judge. Investigative step-number-one would be to look at every defendant on his docket. Sometimes Ozzy was amazed that Brass Malone hadn't been arrested sooner with people like Nessman on his payroll.

"Sure. That makes sense," Ozzy said.

"I talked to a guy in Southie. The guy who's helping us out did some work down there. He's legit."

"How do you know that?" Ozzy asked.

"It was a big-time story down there. He killed some banker's wife."

"Did you talk to the banker?"

"No. I'm not talking to some stuffed shirt who had his wife killed. I talked to our people, this guy from Southie."

The condescension was thick, and the reference to a stuffed-shirt-banker-type a clear reference to Ozzy and his 'kind'.

"Where'd you get the Southie guy's name? How did you hook up with him?" Ozzy asked.

Nessman was taking a sip of coffee when he realized he'd been taken. He had done exactly what he promised himself he wouldn't do. Ozzy was smarter, and he'd been talked out of his shoes.

"I think we've gotten just about deep enough into this," said Nessman.

Ozzy pressed on.

"You're a hundred percent on this? Boston PD just locked up three of their own for bribery and racketeering. They are cleaning house, and I don't have much of a hook down there to clean this up if things get messy."

Within the parts of Ozzy's statement, the former was true, the latter a lie, but keeping Nessman on his toes was a good idea.

"Yeah. I'm a hundred percent. We've got research and surveillance on the guy who's helping, the banker, and the hooker."

Ozzy raised an eyebrow. "What hooker?"

Nessman tried and failed to hide his frustration at mentioning the girl.

"Forget the hooker," Nessman sputtered. "We're good."

"Okay," Ozzy said, allowing Nessman's slip-up to pass but making a mental note. "Did you run checks on the guy from Southie, too?"

"Of course," Nessman lied. "He's legit."

"Last thing. You have a picture?" Ozzy asked.

"Of the guy from Boston? Oh yeah, sure. He submitted it with his job application."

"Don't be an asshole. I know even you would be smart enough to take a stealth photo of the guy," Ozzy said, hoping his assumption was correct.

Nessman shook his head and took out his cell phone. He scrolled through his 'recents' until a photo of Jimmy Brennan appeared, out of focus and sideways. He held it up to Ozzy.

"You want me to text it to you?"

"And have our phones linked? No thanks," Ozzy said. He took his phone out and snapped a picture of the picture.

Ozzy set the heavy mug down and leaned far to the left. He pulled a small wallet from his right pocket, peeled off a twenty, and tossed it to the center of the table. He stood, and after putting his phone away peered down at Nessman.

"Look hard at these people, Paul. No screw ups. I'm going to have to clean up whatever goes sideways."

"Relax. It's under control."

"All angles?"

"Every one."

"Alright," Ozzy said extending his hand.

Nessman took it and heard himself say, "thanks for the coffee." Ozzy smiled but didn't reply. He turned and walked to the door. A clamoring bell told Nessman he had left.

The now doubt-filled criminal sat in the booth five more minutes, going over how many ways he might have screwed this up.

CHAPTER 29

Ozzy Ostrowski was not terribly surprised that Detective Don Mollie was late to their meeting. The New England Patriots had played at one o'clock that afternoon and had covered the point spread. It was now seven, dusk, and Mollie was probably half in the bag from celebrating.

While Ozzy was not part of that side of the business, he did keep track of the gambling habits of Mollie, if for no other reason than to use the information as leverage against him. Mollie hadn't just bet on the game. He had bet on the point total for each quarter, on which team would score first, and on whether the opposing New York Jets would pass or run on their first offensive play of the second half. He had lost two of the side bets, won the rest, and came out nine-thousand dollars ahead.

As Ozzy was reviewing different strategies to deflect what would likely be an arrogantly confident Don Mollie, the detective pulled into the lot. Ozzy could see the smug look on his face even before he rolled down the window.

"You bring my money?" Mollie asked.

Ozzy assumed the most disinterested look he could muster.

"Number one, I don't take bets, and I don't pay them out. Two, I have no doubt that a degenerate and undisciplined speculator such as yourself is just going to roll it over."

Perhaps indicative of the depth of his illness, Mollie didn't seem to notice the derisive comment, let alone contest it.

"The Bruins are hosting the Red Wings this week," he said. "Maybe I'll leave it in the bank."

Ozzy shook his head at the man's obliviousness. There was no more hopelessly optimistic human than a gambler deep in the red who recently placed a winning bet. The juxtaposition of reality versus perception was stunning. Mollie had won nine-thousand dollars, reducing his life-threatening debt to organized crime from eighty to seventy-one thousand dollars. And he was ecstatic about it.

"Can we get on with it?" Ozzy asked.

"Whatever," Mollie shrugged. "So, you've got a problem. Malone's shit-head brother is completely out of fucking control."

"We've been over this," Ozzy said. "We know about Vincent Underwood."

"Yeah, well, there've been some developments."

"What kind of developments?"

"I'm wondering if maybe this is above your pay grade, Oz. How about I meet with Malone directly."

"Malone's in jail." Ozzy said plainly.

"So, he'd have time to meet, then, wouldn't he?"

Ozzy remained silent, staring at Mollie. After ten seconds he spoke, noticeably softer.

"Why?"

"To make sure he gets the right information. That

he appreciates the risks I'm taking to get it to him."

Ozzy briefly considered flattery or reason as a polemic against Mollie's logic. Ultimately, he reverted to the tried and true methods of controlling a bettor. Intimidation and shame.

"The risk for you is in *not* giving me the information. And make no mistake, *Detective*, potential employment consequences should be the least of your concern. Do you have any idea what actually happens to people that are high five-figures in the hole to our organization? Have you thought about that?"

Mollie's silence and slack-jawed face indicated he had not given sufficient consideration to the facts about to be laid before him.

"I joked about the dislocated fingers at our last meeting, but that's just the beginning of the pain you'll feel. And lest you decide you're a tough guy who can handle it, you need to recognize that we know everything about you."

Mollie recovered and attempted to regain control.

"I'm not worried about..."

Ozzy ignored the man and read from a file he had brought up on his phone. He interrupted.

"Mrs. Siobhan Mollie, widowed, of 62 Grenier Boulevard, would be devastated to hear that something had happened to her youngest son. As you know, debts don't disappear just because the debtor does, so Mrs. Mollie would get a visit from associates of ours who would convince her it was in her best interest to share with us, let's say half, of the," Ozzy scanned the phone screen, "twenty-three-hundred dollars and eighty-six cents of social security payments she gets every month."

"You motherfu..."

"Life would also become much harder for Mom when we took custody of the," he looked at the phone a final time, "2020 Honda Civic you so generously bought for her. How would dear Mrs. Mollie get to her doctor appointments, or bingo, or to the Wednesday free lunch at the senior center?

"All she would have left would be the memory of her brave son, who died serving her beloved City of Manchester. But then the truth about that would emerge in the papers as well. The world would learn that the only reason Mrs. Mollie's scum-bag son could afford her Honda Civic was because he had abused his job as a police detective and agreed to help the sales manager at Grappone Honda hide the quarter-million dollars he had embezzled from the dealership. Then, of course, questions would be asked about where the money had gone, and the gambling would come to light. Poor Mrs. Mollie would become a pariah. I doubt they'd even let her in the door at Saint Anthony's."

Ozzy allowed Mollie to sit in stunned silence. The man had no idea how deep he truly was into the Malone organization. Finally, Ozzy provided relief.

"Thankfully, none of that is going to be necessary, because you're going to do the right thing and continue answering every question I ask of you. Now, can we get on with it?"

"They made him for a murder," Mollie said, defeated.

"Who?"

"Underwood. He choked out a whore and dumped her behind some car repair shop. The arrest warrant's going to come out tomorrow."

"Any link to Malone?" Ozzy asked.

"No, nothing past the brother connection. And as far as I know they haven't dived too deeply into that. They've had other leads to find him. They're chasing those down and haven't spent much time pulling the thread that connects Underwood and Malone."

"What kind of leads," Ozzy asked.

"The mom, Lorraine. She bought bus tickets they thought were for Underwood. We set up on the bus terminal but he never showed."

"Did the mom show?"

"Yeah, we were on her at the bus station, figuring she'd either bring Underwood there or meet him. It got dicey, so we had to clear out."

"Dicey how?" Ozzy asked.

"Believe it or not Diaz showed up."

"Who is Diaz?"

"The bitch trooper that Underwood tuned up in the alley."

"Jesus, I figured she'd still be on crutches and laying low at home."

"Yeah, well, she still had her ankle in a cast and arm in a sling. Dumb fucking broad," Mollie said.

Ozzy ignored the insults.

"Does her job know she was out there?"

"No, she showed on her own. No one knew she was tailing the mother."

Ozzy punched information into his phone, then looked back up at Mollie.

"What's this girl's name again?"

"Betsy Diaz. She's a detective trooper out of headquarters."

"I don't have a Betsy Diaz in here," Ozzy offered

absentmindedly as he scrolled through his phone.

"Jesus, do you have a list with every damn cop in the state on that thing?" Mollie asked. Ozzy stared at him with a look that indicated he thought anything less would be professionally irresponsible.

"How about Betsaida Diaz? Could that be her?" he asked.

"Yeah, sure. I don't fucking know. She looks Puerto Rican so she could have some kind of name like that," Mollie said.

"Not very politically correct of you," Ozzy said piously.

"You have something for me?" Mollie asked, anxious to move the meeting along.

The scales began to teeter in Ozzy's risk-calculating brain. He had come to the meeting prepared to give Mollie five-thousand dollars to smuggle to Underwood, but now he had killed a prostitute. The last thing they needed was a dirty cop who worked for them making moves on the street with someone wanted for murder. Underwood was too hot.

And Diaz was a new wildcard. A trooper that would pass up a tax-free vacation from the state worker's compensation fund so she could hit the street and hunt down the guy that nearly killed her was someone he needed to pay attention to. And she had done it off the books, without help from her department. Diaz sounded like a dog after a bone, and if she had nearly tracked down Underwood on her own, it stood to reason she'd eventually stumble onto a link to Malone.

It violated Malone's instructions, but the exposure was too great. Ozzy would hold on to the money for now.

"Two more things," Ozzy said. "First, next time we meet I want more on this Diaz woman. Married, kids, bad habits? You know the drill."

"Sure. What else?" Mollie asked.

Ozzy punched up a photo on his phone and held it out the window. It was the image Paul Nessman had given him of the man he was hiring to kill the judge in Brass Malone's case.

"Do you know this guy?"

Mollie leaned over and looked at the screen.

"Yeah, that's Jimmy Brennan. He's been helping us work this Vincent Underwood case. He and Charlie Wilcox go back a ways, I guess."

"Helping how?" Ozzy asked, his stomach sinking.

"I don't know," Mollie said, frustrated. "Doing some background, helping with surveillance. He was there the other night when Diaz showed up at the bus station surveillance. He's a pretty sharp cop, actually."

Ozzy fought not to let the concern show on his face. Mollie was crooked and dirty, but he was still a cop, and he detected the change in affect.

"Why do you ask? What do you have that photo for?" Mollie asked.

"Part of the Underwood thing, that's all," Ozzy said, recovering quickly. "I just wanted to confirm he's one of the cops on that case."

Mollie looked at him skeptically, but remained silent.

"Anything else?"

"No, we're good."

CHAPTER 30

Detective Rey Johnston was perched on the top of the Mall of New Hampshire, three stories above Macy's main entrance. Lying uncomfortably next to him on the gravel-topped roof was his partner, Jimmy Brennan.

"Is Patterson coming?" Johnston asked.

"Nah," Brennan said. "He wanted to, but I talked him out of it. He's too close to the whole thing."

"I don't know about that. I know if someone was smacking around my daughter, I'd want to be here to watch him take a fall."

"Exactly. We set up this three-ring circus to jam up his daughter's boyfriend. He's got a personal interest, and if it doesn't work out and we don't snag the guy, or if it goes south, Patterson would try to step in."

"You think?"

"Wouldn't you?"

"Good point," Johnston said, focusing his attention back on the task at hand.

Johnston held a twenty-four-inch wide plastic bowl with a microphone mounted in the center. Attached to the top of the item was a spotting scope, not unlike those mounted atop sniper rifles. A thick cable ran from the back of each to an open Pelican briefcase, which itself had wires leading to a set of headphones.

The Klover MiK 26 Parabolic Collector could detect conversational tones up to two-hundred yards
away. With only a low frequency response due to the
portable size, high-fidelity reception was not possible.
But Johnston could hear conversation, and that was all
he needed today.

"It this going to happen or what?" Brennan asked
impatiently.

"Sounds like it. No one bugged out yet."

"What're they saying? Where are we at?"

Johnston slipped the noise-cancelling headphones off his temples and handed them to Brennan.

"Listen for yourself."

Brennan adjusted the headset for size and swept
the wire around his shoulder. After putting the soft
rubber around his ears, he pressed them inward and
squinted to help focus on the conversation occurring between Frank Doran and Mike Thompson in the
pickup truck far across the lot.

"You see, this is the fucking problem dealing with
Puerto Ricans. They have no respect for other people's
time," Doran offered. He was sitting in the driver's seat
of his truck, drumming frustrated fingers on the steering wheel. Thompson sat to his right.

"Traffic's a bitch, Frank. *We* didn't even get here
on time," Thompson responded reasonably. "This Rodriguez guy is probably stuck on the highway."

Doran shot him a disapproving look. "What do
you want to do, go in the mall and do some shopping
while we wait?"

"Shut up, asshole."

Doran had met Jason Rodriguez in a Concord bar

six months earlier. He had bought a gram of cocaine from him, hoping, ultimately without success, to use it to convince one of the NH Tech girls playing pool to party with him in his truck. Two weeks later Mike Thompson had introduced Doran to his cousin, Alan McBride, who complained about how difficult it was to find soft coke in the city these days. It seemed all anybody wanted to do was smoke crack. Doran had seen the opportunity and told McBride he knew a guy in Concord and could score coke for him.

McBride liked cocaine, and had taken a chance when he fronted Doran a hundred-eighty dollars for a couple of grams. He had laid himself fifty-fifty odds he'd never see the money again, but was pleasantly surprised when the package was delivered three days later. For his part, Frank Doran had decided to deal with Rodriguez regularly, despite his misgivings related to the man's ethnicity.

Usually, the deals had happened in the same bar. If it was earlier in the day, Rodriguez preferred one of the commercial parking lots off Storrs Street in Concord. Doran didn't much care where it happened, and he didn't mind the fifteen-minute drive between cities. Sometimes it was nice to get out of town.

Two nights ago, McBride had texted Doran and ordered up an ounce. A pang of anxiety had gripped Doran's stomach after they'd set up the deal. He had sold McBride grams three times, and it was getting regular, but an ounce was a big jump. His brief apprehension had been ameliorated by delusions of grandeur. Doran was going to sell an ounce to McBride, and there was no way the meth dealer was going to blow that much cocaine up his nose partying with his girlfriend. That meant he intended to chop it up and sell it himself, which in some small way made McBride an employee of Doran's.

But first, Doran had to get the ounce from his supplier. Rodriguez had wanted to do the deal in Manchester, not Concord. "The mall," he had texted. "Macy's lot. Four-thirty."

And Johnston and Brennan, thanks to a search warrant granting them access to Frank Doran's text messages, had known just when to set up.

Doran had agreed to the new location. After all, he was a business man now, and his business was growing by leaps and bounds. To his frustration, his friend Mike Thompson had not been suitably awed by his self-appointed status as a burgeoning drug king-pin.

"Makes sense, right?" Doran had said to Thompson after explaining this logic.

"I don't know, Frank. You're just selling the guy an ounce. Don't get ahead of yourself."

"Yeah, an ounce today, maybe another next week. Then he bumps up again, or sends someone else my way. That's how this shit works, you know? I'm building something here," Doran said proudly.

"How the hell do you know how it works, Frank? You've never done this before. Don't let it go to your head. Let's just get this done and get out of here." Thompson's voice betrayed his worry.

"Speak for yourself, lightweight. I'm ready," Doran said. With that, he lifted his shirt, revealing a revolver tucked into his waistband.

"Jesus, Frank. Where the fuck did you get that?"

"It was my father's."

"You're just as likely to shoot your dick off with it

sitting in your belt like that. You got a holster or something?"

"Shut up, Mike."

"Hey, there he is," Thompson said, pointing through the windshield toward the left.

Because he wanted to see who came and went, Doran had backed into a space facing the parking lot's exit. That time of day, during busy afternoon shopping, had made finding just the right spot problematic.

Doran's gaze followed Thompson's pointed finger and saw the gray Audi A4 crawling through the lot. It paused in front of Doran's truck and Rodriguez, the only visible occupant, nodded once. He drove past, turned into the next row, and parked.

Doran's phone vibrated and made the synthesized sound of a gunshot. He looked down and saw a dollar sign and question mark, sent by Rodriguez. He responded with a thumbs-up emoji. Thirty seconds passed. Then a minute. The noise signifying a text message came again.

'Wait.'

"That's Rodriguez, in the Audi," Johnston said on the roof.

Two subpoenas to Verizon and one to Sprint, combined with a few hours' surveillance, had told the detectives everything they needed to know about twenty-four-year-old Jason Rodriguez of Concord, New Hampshire.

"You sure?"

Johnston tossed a sarcastic look at Brennan. "No jackass, I'm guessing."

Brennan extended his middle finger, then picked

up a portable radio. He ensured he was on the proper tactical channel and not the main citywide frequency, and said "Both players are on set. Stand by."

Looking through binoculars, Brennan saw Rodriguez exit his sedan and lock it. He first walked away from Doran's truck, looking all around. After moving down two rows of cars he turned and walked back. Instead of stopping at the truck, he walked right by. Proceeding to the end of that row, he leaned on the cement foundation of a light pole and lit a cigarette. He took a deep drag and looked around.

"Decent countersurveillance," Brennan said approvingly. Johnston nodded.

When he was half done the menthol, Rodriguez dropped it onto the pavement and left it smoldering. He walked back to his car, unlocked it when he was in range, and sat inside. He emerged two minutes later, carrying a McDonald's takeout bag. This time he walked directly to the truck, slid up from behind, and dropped it in the bed. He walked to Doran's open window.

Brennan, still peering through binoculars, spoke quickly. "Okay he dropped it in the bed. Give me the audio."

Rey Johnston began to repeat each phrase he monitored over the parabolic microphone, as a narrative.

"That it? Ya, buddy. You good? Square. You want it here? Yeah. Here you go. Twelve? You bet, man. Twelve."

"That's good enough," Brennan decided. He picked up the portable radio, pressed the transmit button, and clearly articulated "Green at Macy's. Green at Macy's."

###

As soon as Doran handed Rodriguez the envelope of money, the seller backed away and disappeared between two parked cars.

"Go grab it," Doran said smiling as he turned to his passenger and gestured toward the bed of the truck. Mike Thompson complied, opening his door and stepping out. Doran refocused his gaze out the window and saw a Manchester police cruiser crawling toward them between rows of parked cars. His stomach dropped.

"Get in the truck, Mike."

"Hang on. Let me grab it."

Doran looked behind him and saw that Thompson could not reach across the bed to where Rodriguez had dropped the package. He was now walking around the back of the vehicle.

"Get in the fucking truck, Mike!" he hollered.

Then the cruiser's blue lights came on, and it accelerated. Doran made a decision.

His pickup had been running, so all Doran had to do was slap the column shifter down into 'drive' and stomp on the gas. The accelerator engaged before the transmission, and the engine raced. When gears finally meshed, the truck lurched forward, too quickly for Doran to control. The front right fender raked across the bumpers of two parked cars across from him.

With the engine screaming, Doran regained control and swerved down the line of cars. As he spotted the cruiser behind him in the mirror, his mind immediately went to Rodriguez.

"Fucking rat!" he yelled.

Looking toward the row end, Doran saw another cruiser enter the line of cars. He slammed on the brakes and simultaneously lifted the shifter into reverse, then buried the gas pedal again. The transmission groaned in complaint as the rear wheels began spinning backward before the truck ceased its forward motion.

Doran twisted to the right and threw his arm across the back of the bench seat. He steered with his left hand atop the wheel and aimed directly for the cruiser closing in behind him. The panicked mind of a fleeing felon remained stuck on the binary decision of stopping or ramming through. The distance between the two vehicles shrank rapidly, and time ran short.

Doran's focus on the approaching cruiser prevented him from noticing his terror-stricken friend darting between cars, running for freedom. Two uniformed officers chased Mike Thompson on foot, one with a K-9 on a long lead.

As he dashed from behind a parked minivan into the travel lane, Thompson found himself in the travel path of Doran's pickup. The steel bumper struck him mid-thigh, snapping his femur. His body folded over to the left as his torso absorbed the brake light assembly. Thompson's whiplashed head struck the tailgate. Then, he was airborne.

It was near the apex of Thompson's flight that Doran realized what had happened and crushed the brake pedal. He watched his friend's body descend and career off the rear quarter panel of a black jeep, landing in a crumpled heap.

"Jesus Christ!" Doran cried out.

Adrenaline drove Doran's mind into the black. His hearing was reduced to a series of muffled warbles and tunnel vision blocked everything from view save his friend. He opened the creaky truck door, stepped out in a daze, and ran three steps toward Mike Thompson's broken body. Twenty feet shy of his friend, the back of Doran's thigh was squeezed in the vice-like jaws of a Belgian Malinois named Buster. The energy of the dog's run-up and attack-leap threw his prey to the ground.

Brennan and Johnston, mouths agape, stared in awe at the unfolding scene below. Johnston was the first to speak.

"You want to go down now, or wait for a boss to show up?"

Deep in thought, Brennan's eyebrows bent, then straightened. His lips alternatively pursed and flexed. Johnston set to packing up his equipment rather than interrupting his partner's thinking. Two minutes later he was finished cleaning up the gear, and a decision had to be made.

"Jimmy?"

"Okay. Yup, okay," Brennan whispered, nodding to himself. But he didn't get up. Another twenty seconds passed. Johnston saw that now his gaze was skyward, alternating left to right. More nodding. Brennan was writing a narrative that would fit what had happened.

"Are we going down?" Johnston asked.

Brennan's head snapped to his partner, surprise on his face. The look melted into one of resignation.

"I got it. I think we're good," he told his partner.

"You think? Christ, Jimmy. The shit show we just witnessed was not part of the plan. You're sure you've got this covered?"

Brennan stood up and retrieved the portable radio, clattering with voices. He mentally selected the right smile and showed it to his partner.

"I'm sure," said Brennan. "I think I can explain

this whole thing so no one gets jammed up. Let's get down there and sort it out."

CHAPTER 31

"I have to say, Jimmy. This was not your finest fucking hour."

For twenty minutes, Jimmy Brennan had been sitting in the outer office of Deputy Chief Lewis Fawcett of the Manchester Police Department. He sat in one of three chairs pressed against the wall, across from Fawcett's secretary's desk. Captain Edward Soffit occupied another.

Soffit had been in Fawcett's office when Brennan arrived, ten minutes early, for his eleven o'clock briefing with the chief. He had just come out, eased into the chair, and was in the process of rubbing stress from his temples when he offered Brennan his succinct assessment of the situation.

"You want me to..."

"Save it for the chief, Jimmy. He wants someone's ass for this, and right now the only one I've got to offer him is yours. I don't know what the hell happened Sunday at that mall, but you better be ready to explain it."

"You worry too much, Ed," Brennan said. Soffit cocked an eyebrow at the use of his given name.

"I don't much appreciate your cavalier attitude, Brennan. This isn't just some lost buy-money or bad PR that might serve to besmirch the reputation of the ever popular 'Jimmy Brennan'. You better have your shit together in there. A kid is dead."

Brennan stopped smiling and looked away.

Captain Soffit placed his hands onto his thighs and pushed himself up to standing. Brennan followed suit, and the two men walked toward the closed door of Deputy Chief Lewis Fawcett's office. Soffit knocked once, then opened it before there was an answer.

A barrel-chested man of fifty-eight, with tightly cut silver hair and wearing the white uniform shirt of the Manchester police department command staff, rose to his feet from behind an enormous mahogany desk. He extended his hand and Brennan stepped forward to take it. The greetings were curt.

"'Morning, Sir."

"Detective."

Deputy Chief Fawcett gestured to the two upholstered chairs before his desk. As they settled in, Brennan sized him up. He cut an imposing figure, with a chest and arms that more than filled his taut uniform blouse. Each epaulet bore a single star, identifying him as one of three deputy chiefs in the department. Only the chief of police, upon whose shoulders sat two stars, outranked him.

"Detective Brennan, I'm going to cut right to the chase. I need the name of the informant who turned you on to that coke deal Sunday afternoon at the mall," said Fawcett.

Brennan had known the question would come, but did not expect it straightaway. His brief hesitation gave him away. Fawcett had already decided he would not tolerate that.

"Do you know what my career path has been here

at MPD?" The question surprised Brennan further. He backpedaled.

"Yes, Sir. Sure. A few years in patrol, then some work in narcotics, then major crimes and now here." Brennan tried to gesture grandly toward Fawcett's desk upon saying the word 'here'.

"No, Brennan. Not 'some work' in narcotics. Twelve years in narcotics. First as a detective, then a supervisor, then as a lieutenant running the whole thing. Then I had his job," Fawcett pointed to Captain Soffit, "and now I'm here." He gestured just as grandly, the physical sarcasm thick, as he said the word 'here'.

Not knowing what to say, Brennan remained silent.

"During my time working dope, way back in the dark ages, we had shitty cell phones, weak internet, and no Google-fucking-maps or GPS to track dealers. We had one body wire for the entire unit, and it was the size of a suitcase."

"I understand, Sir," Brennan offered. "In this case we..."

Fawcett held up an enormous hand, blunting the interruption.

"There is a point to me walking you down memory lane like this, Detective. If anyone knows how to fabricate surveillance logs and create fictitious informants, it is me. And if anyone knows how to detect when another officer is fabricating surveillance logs and creating fictitious informants, that is also me."

Brennan shifted uncomfortably in his chair and stole a glance at Captain Soffit, who was unabashedly staring back at him. Deputy Chief Fawcett, controlling the room, let his comments hang in the air before continuing.

"Son, I have a meeting with the chief of this department at noon to explain to him the circumstances that led us to have the entire fucking south side of the mall shut down all night, a dead twenty-eight-year-old kid, two low-end drug dealers in custody, and a measly ounce of cocaine to show for it.

"So, I am going to ask you again, and I better get either the truth or a rock-solid and unbreakable bullshit story. Who turned you on to that deal last night?"

Brennan had already thought of how he would play it. He'd tossed it back and forth all night, and on balance the answer was obvious. He either had to A – tell the truth to Soffit and Fawcett and betray the confidentiality he had promised Alan McBride or B – lie to his bosses. Captain Soffit and Chief Fawcett were lifelong, respected police officers. McBride was a mid-level meth dealer. The answer should have been clear. But as Brennan had come to know, it seldom was.

If Brennan brought up McBride's name, homicide detectives working Mike Thompson's death would be at his home within the hour. McBride would not hold up under that kind of questioning, and in short order he would tell them about Brennan and Ross Patterson's late-night visit. It was that visit in which Brennan and Patterson had coerced McBride to set up Frank Doran. It was the best, fastest way they had thought of to help Patterson's daughter, Bridget, break away from her abuser.

If McBride revealed what had happened, the consequences would be enormous, if not career-ending, for both of them. He couldn't do that to Patterson. He couldn't do it to his family, either. He was going to have to lie.

Brennan tried to reason how he had gotten into this situation. Why had he cooked up such a convoluted plan to make a case against Frank Doran? It had been the best he could come up with at the time, and he had done it for Patterson. The man would have done the same for him. Regardless, there was no turning back now.

Brennan shifted his weight, sat erect in preparation, and cleared his throat.

"Chief, this case was the result of an anonymous tip."

Fawcett had thought Brennan might stretch the truth, but the idea of an anonymous tip was absurd. He lost his temper.

"Jesus Christ, Brennan! An anonymous fucking tip? Are you..." he looked away from Brennan and pointed a sharp finger at Captain Soffit. "Is he fucking kidding me?"

"Sir," Brennan ventured. "If I can just explain."

"Explain? Oh, shit. This I've got to hear." Fawcett slumped back into his chair, arms crossed over his massive chest. "Yes, Detective, please. Beguile us with the tale of how an anonymous tip from some pissed off ex-girlfriend or some other bullshit source turned into a goddamned vehicle rodeo that damaged two police cars and killed a twenty-eight-year-old with nothing but a shoplifting arrest on his record."

Brennan looked at Soffit, but saw that he, too, had put a wall up by crossing his arms. His face said *you dug this hole.* Brennan was on his own.

"Sir, six days ago I received a call on the anonymous tip line regarding a drug dealer by the name of Frank Doran. The caller, a woman, said she knew Doran and had been buying coke from him for several months. She said he was ramping up his business and has started carrying a gun. She wanted him arrested before he hurt someone."

"*You* received a call on the A-line?" interrupted Fawcett. "Since when does the most prolific undercover we have sit around the office waiting for the tip line to ring?"

"I was in writing up my notes for the Nessman case, Sir. That murder for hire? I happened to be sitting by the phone when it rang. May I continue, Sir?"

"I assume the A-line phone log shows this incoming call?" Fawcett pressed.

"Yes, Sir. I'm sure it does. It's likely in the file somewhere."

There was a ten second pause before Chief Fawcett gestured for Brennan to continue.

"Thank you, Sir. So, I ran this guy..."

"Doran?"

"Yes, Sir. Frank Doran. I ran him and saw that he has some drug arrests and a domestic charge as well. He had a heroin bust that was dismissed, which means he probably worked it off as an informant. I checked into that and sure enough, three years ago he worked for the state police NIU buying heroin off some kid from Lowell. Anyway, I figured if we could put a case on him, maybe I could recruit Doran and give him to one of the new detectives to work as a CI."

Brennan looked back and forth between Soffit and Fawcett but saw no change in expression. He took it as permission to continue.

"I had a free afternoon and did a four-hour surveillance on Doran and identified a running buddy of his, Mike Thompson. He's the kid that got run over."

"Yes, Detective, thank you. I'm aware he's the kid that got run over," Fawcett repeated sarcastically.

"Sorry, Sir."

"You had a free afternoon to do this? Are we not giving you enough to do?"

Brennan took a chance and ignored the comment.

"Anyway, I decided that if I was going to make a case against Doran, I needed a CI to get into him, an informant. The person I ended up recruiting wouldn't wear a wire, but did let me monitor a few phone calls. I heard him and Frank Doran talking about this coke deal a few days ago and decided to take him down."

"You have that call recorded?"

"No, Sir. He wouldn't let us."

Fawcett raised an eyebrow. "Convenient."

"Sir…" Brennan began to explain, but was interrupted when the chief waved to concede the point.

"That's pretty much it," said Brennan. "I borrowed ten uniforms from patrol, plus a dog, and we set up on the mall. You know what happened from there, Sir."

"Why so heavy on the uniforms?" asked Captain Soffit, adding voice to the question in Fawcett's mind.

"Because of the gun, Cap'. You recall the original tip said he was carrying a gun. He was, in fact, armed with a revolver when we arrested him."

Fawcett let out a deep sigh as he uncrossed his arms and rubbed his ruddy face with both hands.

"I assume you have all the paperwork supporting this fantastical story of good intentioned police work gone awry? Surveillance reports, CI contact logs, evidence?"

"Yes, Sir," Brennan answered. "It's all in the case file. I just need a few hours to wrap up my reports."

"Okay, then. Let's have it." Fawcett said.

"Have what, Sir?"

"Jesus, are we back to this? The name of the CI. Homicide is going to want to talk to him."

"The CI was Doran's buddy, Mike Thompson. When I recruited him, he told me he was worried about Doran and wanted them both out of it before someone got hurt."

Fawcett, now leaning forward with his elbows on his desk looked at Captain Soffit, stone faced.

"And now he's dead."

"Yes, Sir. That seems to be the case," Brennan replied.

Chief Fawcett looked back and forth between the two men seated before him. He refocused his gaze on Brennan, and an almost imperceptible smile tugged at the corner of his mouth.

"And thus, your tale of woe comes to a close. All tied up with a bow," Fawcett said contemptuously.

"To the extent I'm prepared to explain at this time, Sir, yes," Brennan replied. "There are some smaller details, I'm sure, that I can fill in after I..."

Fawcett raised an authoritative hand. The tugging at the corner of his mouth started to break into a smile. He had to rub his chin to disguise it.

"Get the hell out of my office."

"Yes, Sir. Thank you for your time."

Both Brennan and Soffit stood and walked to the door, in that order. Brennan made it out, but the deputy chief called out to Soffit, who turned to look back. Fawcett was pointing directly at him.

"Every goddamned 'i' and every goddamned 't', Edward. You understand me? The media is all over the chief on this, which means he's up my ass. Which means I'm up yours."

"Yes, Sir. Thank you, Sir."

CHAPTER 32

In his decades as a crime boss, Brass Malone had required one thing of people. Absolute loyalty. Mistakes happened. People were arrested. His people got robbed. Such was the way in their business. But his insistence on absolute fidelity was uncompromising.

Paul Nessman had learned this truism from afar. Ten years prior he was working with a high-end burglary crew in the Boston-metro area. At the time, a Boston police sergeant working in property crimes owed Malone money. A lot of money. The property crime unit, like every unit of a city police department, had fewer resources than it needed. They did not investigate every burglary. Rather, they focused on those with reasonably high solvability factors.

At a payoff rate of a thousand dollars per tip, the BPD sergeant advised one of Malone's associates what cases the burglary unit was working hard to solve and which ones they let slide. Malone's man then fed this information to burglary crews in the area. It was a loose affiliation, but a valuable one. Malone took half of anything the crews stole.

For their part, the break-in teams garnered significant benefit from the arrangement. First, the likelihood of getting pinched by the police was lessened.

Second, and more importantly, no one fucked with you if you were affiliated with Brass Malone. Crews like Nessman's robbed each other as much as they did commercial businesses, but if you were in bed with Malone, and stayed north of Providence and east of Springfield, no one touched you.

Nessman had a partner for a time named Jacob Weston. They had hit an antique dealer's warehouse and, expecting only cash, found a safe of uncut diamonds. Nessman had insisted that per the agreement they turn half over to Malone, but sharing his opinion earned him nothing but a bloody nose from Weston. Nessman had taken his cut of the cash but refused the diamonds.

"There's no way that two-bit wanna-be gangster Malone has any idea we scored diamonds," Weston had insisted.

"Suit yourself," Nessman had replied. "But I ain't taking shit."

Neither man knew the antique dealer had himself stolen the diamonds two weeks earlier, and was sitting on them while things cooled off. Word of the burglary spread when the jewel dealer put money out on the street for anyone who identified the sons-of-bitches who had stolen from him. That word had spread to Malone.

That was the last job Nessman ever did with Weston. Not because he stopped, but because Weston never showed up again. The diamonds had turned out to be worth sixty-thousand dollars and Brass Malone had arbitrarily decided a finger was worth fifteen grand. Weston stopped showing up because it was hard to commit high end burglaries with only six fingers.

Now, years later and two days after Ozzy found out that "Jimmy" was a goddamned cop, Nessman sat in silence at a bolted-to-the-floor table across from Brass Malone. Knowing Malone's monolithic rule on loyalty, he had come to confess.

"It took you two days to come to me with this? Who else knows?" Malone asked.

"This is the earliest I could get in to see you, Boss. Yesterday was lawyers only."

"You say Ozzy gave this information to you? Where did he get it?"

"I don't know," Nessman answered. "Ozzy said he found out from someone he knows. I'm guessing he showed a cop the picture I gave him of Jimmy."

"You're showing pictures of our associates around now? To cops?"

"No. I mean, yes." Confused panic was apparent in Nessman's voice. "I showed Ozzy a picture of the guy I was hiring for the judge thing. He had come to me worried I didn't have all the bases covered. Then a few days later he came back and told me the guy's a cop. Some detective named Jimmy Brennan."

"Who did Ozzy show the picture to?" Malone repeated.

"I have no idea, I swear. I told Ozzy he should come tell you but he said since it was my fuck-up I had to do it. He wouldn't tell me who the guy was. You know how Ozzy is. He keeps everything to himself. He compactizes it."

"He does what?" Malone asked, confused.

"You know, he compactizes everything, so no one knows what anyone else is doing."

Malone shook his head at his illiterate soldier.

"Compartmentalizes, Paul. Ozzy likes to compartmentalize information."

"Yeah, that's what I meant."

Malone's next words were spoken very slowly.

"In addition to making sure information doesn't leak, compartmentalizing also allows us to know who has been talking, in the rare case someone in our organization decides to run their mouth."

Malone stared the man down, and when Nessman's gaze fell, he reached over and touched his chin, raising it back to his own.

"Have you been running your mouth, Paul?"

The tender touch of Malone's calloused fingers on Nessman's scruffy face was juxtaposed against the threat inherent to the question. After a moment, he took his hand back.

"Tell me, Paul, how many times have you met with this man? Jimmy Brennan, you said?"

"Twice, and both times he was ice cold."

"And who did the surveillance of this man after each of your meets?" asked Malone.

There was no response, which did not surprise Malone, so he pressed on.

"I mention surveillance, Paul, to be certain you made an effort to ascertain whether, after your meeting, he traveled to the precinct to write a report or went somewhere to meet his handler, or perhaps any of a hundred other things he might have done that suggested to you his profession as a police officer."

Nessman shifted in his chair. The calm and rhythmic timbre of Malone's voice hardly concealed the rage boiling just under the surface. Nessman struggled past the fear, and remembered Malone's single, inflexible rule. Loyalty and honesty.

"No one did, Boss. There was no surveillance. We checked him out online, made some calls down to Boston. There was even a murder down there he'd been linked to. Some banker's wife."

There was another pause in the conversation. This one longer. Malone took a breath, clenched his jaw, and grasped the edge of the metal table, his forearms quaking. Nessman's mind was filled with an image of him tearing it from its bolts and beating him to death with it.

"Paul," Malone proceeded cautiously. "You hired a man to kill a judge and all you did was Google him?"

The sting of the question bit, and an image of Malone removing Jacob Weston's fingers with a band saw entered Nessman's mind.

"We called down to Boston, too. Some guy out of Southie vouched for him. I thought we were in the clear."

Malone stared at the man before him. Nessman had been exceptionally loyal for years, a rare trait worth holding on to given their vocation. Still, to have hired an undercover cop for what was conceivably the riskiest job Malone had ever put out was inexcusable. Nessman had never been that careless before, and there would be a price to pay. Malone didn't have the luxury of time to determine what it would be. There were more pressing matters.

"Any overt acts yet?"

"No boss, nothing," Nessman replied.

"But they know it's a judge, right?"

"No, just that it was a hit. We could still just chalk it up to planning and talk. I doubt there's enough to charge anyone."

Planning murder, even discussing one, was not in and of itself a crime. In order to advance a charge of conspiracy or solicitation, the prosecution generally needed to prove at least one of the people involved actually *did* something to further the plan, such as buying a weapon or paying money. Nessman was glad it had not yet come to that.

"When's your next meet with him?" asked Malone

"Tomorrow night."

Sitting in silence for an excruciating five minutes, Nessman watched as his employer visibly deliberated his fate. It was almost physically painful. In that time, Malone made two important decisions.

"Dump the cop. You take care of this, personally. Depending on how that goes we'll see what happens to you from there," Malone declared.

"You want *me* to do it?" Nessman asked. "The judge?"

Malone glared at him as if reconsidering his decision. "Are you going to make me repeat myself, Pauly?"

"No, we're good. I got it." After a brief pause, Nessman continued. "You want me to do anything with the cop?"

"You think this is a good time to go to war with the police? Keep your eye on the ball," Malone said.

Nessman raised his hands to chest level, signaling he had figured out he should stop asking questions. "You got it, Brass. I'm on it."

"A week, Pauly. Within one week I want to be reading about the death of that black-robed, self-righteous, greedy son-of-a-bitch."

Brass Malone leaned back, looked over his shoulder, and yelled to the guard that their meeting was over.

CHAPTER 33

After breaking the news about Jimmy Brennan to Malone, two thoughts crept into Paul Nessman's mind as he walked through the overcrowded visitor's waiting area of the Valley Street Jail. The first was gratitude that Malone had enough influence in the jail to hold private visits so Nessman did not have to negotiate the bleak scene. The rows of folding chairs filled with disappointed women and fatherless toddlers was too goddamned depressing.

The second thought revolved around the long, smooth legs attached to the tall, good-looking redhead sitting in the front row, and the lucky bastard in jail who had her waiting for him when he got out.

Bridget Patterson, against the reasonable advice of her parents, had insisted on visiting Frank Doran in jail. She asserted knowing nothing of his drug dealing and that the entire affair must have been a setup.

"No, Mom. I am not leaving him," she had said. Then she turned to her father. "Whatever happened in that parking lot is the fault of your crazy goddamned cops driving like lunatics, Dad. And I had better not find out you had anything to do with this!"

She had sounded like a petulant teenager and, storming out of the house, she knew it. She also knew that Frank Doran had killed his best friend, maybe not on purpose, but while doing something incredibly stupid and dangerous. If building a life with him was challenging before, she had no concept of how to proceed now.

"Patterson, Bridget," a voice rattled. Bridget considered waiting until they called the next name after hers, then quietly standing and stealing away unnoticed.

"Patterson. Bridget Patterson." After a moment the corrections officer at the front of the room pointed an inquiring finger at his clipboard, crossed something off, and lifted his head again.

"Jordan, Chanelle," he announced.

"Here," Bridget called out as she walked forward. "I'm here."

"You're Chanelle Jordan?" the guard challenged as he looked at the red-haired, pale-skinned woman before him.

"No, Sir. I'm Bridget Patterson, here to see Frank Doran."

The guard looked at the short skirt and snug sweater Bridget had worn and determined there was no set of circumstances under which he was going to search her. He pointed a silent finger to his left, her right. Bridget's gaze followed it to a heavy-set female guard bearing nitrile examination gloves and a metal-detecting wand.

The search was brief and demeaning. In a room of twenty-three strangers Bridget had her breasts fondled, her shoes removed, and her crotch scanned.

"Over there," the woman said curtly, pointing to a steel door cut into a wall of gray cement blocks.

Bridget walked to the door and stood there, alone. The harsh grinding noise of the door release caused her to flinch. Without thinking, she grabbed the handle and pulled. The heavy door opened an inch. She applied her other hand and forced it wide enough to get a hip around, then eased past. It slammed behind her.

It took Bridget two attempts to negotiate the baffled door system before she managed to reach the visiting area. After getting the second door open, she was met by an older, female corrections officer whose graying hair and soft features gave her a grandmotherly appearance.

The woman recognized the wide-eyed befuddlement inherent to first time visitors and adopted a gentle tack.

"Who are you here to see, Sweetheart?"

"Frank Doran, please, Ma'am."

CO Theresa Bravard appreciated the respectful appellation and smiled.

"Have a seat right over there," she said, gesturing toward an empty metal table, "and someone will bring him out."

Bridget summoned her dignity and walked to the table. After sitting in one of the chairs she tried to slide it forward, but found it immovably bolted to the floor. She perched on the metal edge until CO Bravard returned five minutes later.

"I'm sorry Bridget, but Frank is not 'low,'" she said.

Bridget looked up at her. "'Low?'"

"A 'low' is a low security prisoner, Honey. Frank is a medium security prisoner. 'Mediums' aren't allowed visitors in this area."

"So, I don't get to see him?" Bridget asked, feeling the ache of budding tears behind her eyes. "After all of...all that?" She gestured back through the door she had come through, her mind's eye recalling the guard's hands on her breasts.

"Well, not in here, at least," Bravard said. "Come with me."

She took Bridget's arm and led her to another steel gray door cut into the wall. To Bridget's relief, Bravard negotiated the baffle for her. When the final door opened, she stood before a bank of six metal booths, each built with thick Plexiglass windows. There was a steel-cabled telephone on the wall of each, and one on the other side of the glass.

"Sit at number two," Bravard said. Then she pointed to a thick roll of sanitizing wipes bolted to the wall. "Use those on the phone. The counter, too. When he comes out, you'll have about ten minutes."

Bridget grabbed two wipes and walked to the booth with an eighteen-inch red "2" emblazoned above it. She grasped the chair and pulled, and it scraped backward. Her head snapped back to Bravard, as if she had broken a rule.

"It's alright," the woman chuckled out of sympathy rather than spite. "The chairs move in here. No prisoners on this side."

"Of course," Bridget commented.

Bridget weighed the value of that in her mind as she wiped down the phone, then the counter. Upon further consideration she stood and wiped the chair as well. When she sat again, Frank Doran was across from her, the phone to his ear.

"Hey, Babe. I'm so glad to see you. God, I miss

you."

"Hi Frank," Bridget responded softly. "I miss you, too. How are you doing in here?"

"How am I doing? Jesus, Bridget. How do you think I'm doing? I'm in jail."

"I'm sorry, Frank. I didn't mean it like that. I mean how are you holding up. How are you feeling?"

Doran ignored the question. "My bail is twenty-five-thousand, Bridge. I know you have a thousand in the bank, and I talked to my mom. She can probably come up with a few more. You have any ideas?"

"I don't have any money, Frank. You know that."

"What about that college money? That fund your parents gave you. You haven't used that."

"That's not what that money is for, Frank. I can't just take it out for any reason."

"Any reason? I'm in jail for crying out loud. What better reason? Don't you want to help me?"

"Of course I do. I'm sorry. This is so hard. All of Mike's friends keep calling the house. They want to know what's going on. The news said you were in jail for killing him and they keep asking me about it. I don't know what to tell anyone. I'm really struggling."

"You are struggling?" Doran erupted. "I'm the one in fucking jail. Did you think about that? Stop being so goddamned selfish for a change."

"I'm sorry. I just meant..."

"Meant what, Bridget?" he barked as her eyes fell away. "Look at me," he continued, spreading his arms wide and gesturing at his surroundings. "I'm in jail. I have to get out of here. You have to get me out of here."

"I'm sorry, Frank. I don't know how."

Bridget nibbled the inside of her lip. She was trying to understand what kept compelling her to apologize.

"Just forget it, alright?" He put his head down and rubbed his forehead dramatically.

Bridget was not sure she was allowed to talk yet. She waited a few moments to make sure it was okay.

"Frank, I'm not sure what I should tell people."

"Don't tell them anything," he said, looking up. "Not a goddamned thing. Just get me out of here. We still have the four grand in the safe, right? In the closet floor? With your money in the bank, plus a few from my mom that brings us up to what, seven thousand? We can get the rest from the college money. Or maybe a bondsman."

"We don't have that anymore, Frank. The money in the safe. The cops took it."

"What do you mean, 'the cops took it?'"

"They came to the apartment and took it, a few hours after you got arrested. They had a search warrant and took a bunch of stuff. The safe, my computer, a bunch of notebooks."

"And you let them? You just let them come in and take my money?"

"They had a warrant, Frank," Bridget protested. "What was I going to do, fight with the police? I didn't give it to them. They took it."

"You stupid bitch!" Doran cried out. "Why didn't you move it? When you heard I got pinched you didn't move it? You had to know the cops were going to come search the place."

"You always tell me to stay out of your business and not touch any of your stuff. Never to talk about money, that it's all your money, anyway. I didn't think you'd want me to...I'm sorry...I didn't know what to do."

The tears came freely now, and Bridget was ashamed. Not of what had happened, but that she kept apologizing, and of what she had become with Frank Doran.

Doran stared at her through squinted eyes. Then he spoke in the angry hushed tone through gritted teeth that usually accompanied one of the bear hugs that made it hard to breathe. Even with a half-inch of glass between them, the rage-filled whisper suffocated her.

"Maybe you did move it," Doran hissed. "I bet you moved it and now you have it and you're keeping it from me. You have a new boyfriend? I've only been in jail two goddamned days and you already have a new boyfriend." His face was ice. "Or maybe you already had one, and this is your chance. Fucking slut."

"I'm not a slut, Frank."

Doran's face reddened and he lost control. "You bitch!" he yelled into the phone.

The volume attracted the attention of a guard on the other side who walked over to booth number two. He made eye contact with Bridget and raised his eyebrows in question. She looked back at Doran, who cocked his head menacingly. She peered up to the guard, feigned a smile, and silently mouthed 'I'm okay.' The guard laid a heavy hand on Doran's shoulder, then walked away.

Doran's tone changed.

"I'm sorry, Baby. You know how I get when I'm stressed like this. I wish I could just smoke a little. It mellows me out, right? Mellows us both out." He winked at Bridget. "You know I love you, right? I know you wouldn't leave me."

"I know," she acknowledged softly.

"It just upsets me when you make decisions like that, you know? But, it's okay. I forgive you for the money thing, alright?"

Bridget tried to think of what Doran was 'forgiving' her for.

"Yeah, okay," she said.

Doran changed the subject. "Have a lot of people been by the apartment looking for me? Asking what's up?"

"Not really. Maybe a few. I haven't actually been there all that much. I've been at my folks' house a lot. I spent the past few nights there."

Doran furrowed his brow. "Why? What's wrong with our place?"

"Nothing," Bridget replied as passively as she could. "I just needed some help these past few days. Like I said, it's been really hard."

"Yeah, tell me about it. I'm the one locked up, remember?"

"I know, Frank, but you're the one that broke the law. That's why you're here." she regretted saying it the moment it came out.

"Is that what they've been telling you? Your parents? Jesus, Bridget, you know they never liked me. They tell you that because they want me out of your life. They're pissed off I actually work for a living and am not some jackass college-boy they'd rather you end up with."

"That's not true, Frank."

"The hell it's not. You can't listen to them, Baby. It's just you and me now. We have to get through this together. Us against the world."

They sat in silence, and when Doran said "I love you" the silence continued.

"You love me, Bridget?"

"Yes, Frank. I love you."

"Sweetheart, you have to understand a lot of people are going to make up lies about me now. Especially your parents. You can't listen to them. Your friends either. They know I'm in here and can't defend myself so all the made-up stories are going to start to fly. That's why we have to stick together. You and me. No one else is going to help us."

"Okay, Frank. Okay," she said softly, not looking at him.

Doran eyed her suspiciously. "What is it? Are you keeping something from me?"

"I don't know. Maybe we should take a break for a while. Back off a little just until this blows over. Then you could focus on the charges and I could..."

"You could what? Find someone else? Are we back to that again?"

"No, Frank. Not that. I just need to take care of myself. I need time to..."

"Who told you that? Your dad? Your fucking cop dad? Of course he said that. He wants to see me rot in here."

"That's not true. He's just worried about me, that's all."

"Bridget," Frank started, his voice lower. "If you leave me, I'll kill myself in here. I swear to fucking God I will. I'll kill myself and it'll be completely your fault. You have to stay with me, please. I need you to help me get through this."

"Don't say that," Bridget said.

A surprising hand landed firmly on Doran's shoulder.

"Time's up, Doran."

The prisoner ignored the instruction.

"I'm going to call you every day at six o'clock, right after they feed us dinner. You have to be there to answer. At our apartment, I mean."

"Okay, Frank. I'll try. But tomorrow I'm supposed to go out to dinner with my folks. I'm meeting them at six."

"No way, Bridget," he said shaking his head defiantly. "You have to be there to answer. If you're not there I'll know it's because you're with someone else and aren't committed to this. I swear to God I'll kill myself."

"Frank," she pleaded in a whisper. The tears returned.

"You have to, Bridget. You have to be there."

As Doran said this, the guard took him by the upper arm and tugged him up and out of the chair.

"I love you, Baby. I do," he said.

The last words were slightly fainter as the short phone cord didn't follow Doran's head as he was yanked away.

Bridget sat still for a moment, then stood and turned around. She scanned the room left to right until she saw Bravard, and quickly walked to her.

"You okay, Honey?"

"Please, let me out of here."

CHAPTER 34

Following his jailhouse visit with Brass Malone, Paul Nessman had spent the rest of the morning contemplating how he was going to kill Judge G. Robert Christiansen, preferably without getting caught. Judges didn't have government protection, but they didn't walk the streets alone at night either, even a reprobate like Christiansen. It was going to take some planning.

But first, the hooker. Weeks earlier, when Nessman was looking for someone new to bring on to handle the hit on the judge, Tricky, one of his regulars, had given him Jimmy Brennan's number. She had also provided the reference in Boston to back him up. The woman obviously thought she had played Nessman for a fool. She needed to be schooled.

Tricky's real name was Patricia Leonard. In elementary school Patricia had naturally become Trisha, then Trish by eleventh grade, which she left incomplete. Alone, addicted, and homeless, the young woman was surviving by way of petty cons and more recently, prostitution. Tricky was the next logical appellation.

As much as admitting it pained him, Ozzy Ostrowski's concern as to how thoroughly Nessman had vetted Jimmy Brennan had been valid. After leaving Malone in jail he had texted Tricky, demanding to meet.

Hours of calls and texts failed to physically locate the woman. He'd finally run her to ground at the New Horizons homeless shelter. When Nessman pulled up to the curb next to Tricky, it was nine o'clock, one hour before the facility required guests to be in for the night.

"Get in Tricks," he said, leaning over the passenger seat to talk through the open window.

"I can't, Pauly. I've got a date."

"Work?"

The question was met with silence, which in effect answered it.

"Cancel. I'm taking you out. It'll be worth your while."

Tricky's radar went up. She'd known Nessman for a year, and benevolence was not in his nature.

"Sure," she replied, then turned her head and whistled, waving toward a girl halfway down the block. Another skin-and-bones teenager strolled up to her. Tricky leaned her heavily made-up face into Nessman's rolled-down passenger window and spoke in cigarette fumes.

"Jennifer's coming, too, 'kay?"

"Nah, no good. Just you Tricks. Let's go."

The younger woman ducked her head into the window, tight to Tricky's. "C'mon sweetheart. Two for the price of one." she cooed.

"No, it's not like that. Let's go," he said assertively, leaning across the seat and pressing the door open from the inside. The women eased their heads out and Tricky stepped away, then pulled her friend close.

"His name is Paul Nessman. Take a picture of the license plate when we pull away. If you don't hear from me by midnight, call the cops," she whispered.

"Baby," Jennifer sighed back to her. "Just stay. He's sketching me out. Let's go score. C'mon."

"Get in the fucking car, Tricky!" Nessman barked.

Tricky kissed Jennifer's check and patted her bottom, and they shared a strained smile.

"I'm sure it'll be fine."

She eased the door open, slid in, and pulled it shut. Nessman squealed away from the curb and was around the corner before Jennifer could get the camera on her phone activated.

Nessman turned the car hard onto Beech Street, headed south, and accelerated.

"Where are we going?" Tricky asked.

"Don't pull that shit again," Nessman said, ignoring the question. "When I tell you I'm picking you up, it means *you*. If I want company, I'll tell you."

"Kiss my ass, Pauly," she retorted, looking out the window. They rode in silence for a few blocks.

"Where are we going?"

"To talk."

"About what?"

Nessman didn't respond. He continued across the city, through downtown and past a sprawling middle-class neighborhood. Beech Street split that section of town like the vein of a leaf, with capillary streets growing off it and ending in tidy cul-de-sacs. He continued south to the intersection with Route 3A.

"We going to the airport?" Tricky asked.

"Sure," Nessman muttered.

It was an odd response, and the already tingling sixth-sense inherent to a young woman of the street began to sound alarms. Tricky needed more information before deciding what to do. She decided to use the oldest method of obtaining it.

"You taking me somewhere special, Pauly?" she asked softly, her voice a sweet octave higher. The question coincided with her hand on Nessman's upper thigh, headed inward. He shifted his weight, and brushed it away.

It was a disconcerting response from a man who had demanded oral satisfaction from her during every previous encounter. Something else was on Nessman's mind, and Tricky worried she knew what it was. She tried again. Leaning over, she put her open mouth to his ear. Her hand returned as well.

"Maybe I can suck the truth out of you, eh Pauly," she said, exchanging sweetness for smut.

Nessman smeared his hand onto her face and pushed hard, sliding her lanky body across the seat.

"Shut up and just sit there," he growled.

Tricky complied. They continued on Brown Avenue as the airport entrance approached and then passed. Her anxiety grew and she took her cell phone from her purse.

"Give me that," Nessman said, his hand extended.

"I have to cancel my date," she lied, furiously punching information into a text for Jennifer.

Nessman drew back his hand and extended it hard, cracking Tricky in the left eye and nose. She shrieked as her hands went to her face. Nessman took the phone and tossed it into the back seat.

"You need to learn to fucking listen," he said.

The rest of the trip was silent, and a few miles later Nessman turned onto Morgan Road, in the outskirts of the city. The only address holder was Litchfield Sand and Gravel. When Tricky saw the sign, panic set into her bones.

Her thoughts went to the small folding knife in her purse. Tricky gestured toward a red line oozing from her nostril and said "I need a tissue to clean this up." She reached toward the floor, where the small clutch had fallen.

Nessman palmed her shoulder and pushed her laterally, into the door. He reached for the purse and tossed it into the back seat with her phone.

"Jesus, Pauly. What the fuck?" There was no response.

The road opened into a wide expanse of sand. A series of trailers that served as offices extended to the left. Oversized earth movers and a belt-fed stone crusher were parked haphazardly about, as if when the workday ended, they were shut off and abandoned in place. Massive piles of sand and rock, some a hundred feet high, dotted the massive quarry. There was no sign of life.

Nessman turned hard, away from the trailers. He accelerated past two small mountains of aggregate and turned left, nestling the car between two piles. A third was in front of them. The three hills served as silent sentries. They were boxed in.

"What the fuck are we doing here?" Tricky asked, hoping to sound casually annoyed, but her cracking voice betrayed the fear. Nessman didn't respond. He got out of the car, marched purposefully to the other side, and tore open the passenger door. He grabbed Tricky by the hair and yanked her to her feet.

The girl cried out, and scratched at Nessman's neck, hard enough to tear skin. He slapped her, hard, and she bounced against the car then fell to one knee.

He grabbed her hair again and pulled her to her feet. His hand encircled her neck and she gasped. He put his face close to hers.

"Who is Jimmy Brennan?" he asked simply.

"I don't know. Is he the..."

Tricky's voice fell silent when Nessman squeezed, stealing her breath. Her hands instinctively went to his wrists and heaved downward like a child pulling an iron bar. She began to make silent popping noises, a fish out of water, opening and closing her mouth in a circle. She started scratching, which hurt him. Nessman released her throat with one hand while punching her, closed fist, with the other.

Tricky fell to the ground, semi-conscious and gasping.

"Don't lie to me. I asked you a question," he said.

Tricky heard only ringing. She lay on her side, knees coiled to chest, and coughed herself hoarse. Her desperate lungs spasmed in search of oxygen.

"Please, Pauly. I had to," she pleaded.

"Shit," Nessman said, kicking the woman's leg as he turned away. It wasn't a hard strike, more the way an abusive dog owner expresses displeasure with a contumacious puppy. He paced the length of the car. Now that she had admitted it, to being a rat, Nessman had a decision to make.

"Why, Tricks. Why did you *have to*?" he asked, mocking her desperation.

"I got picked up two months ago for dope, Pauly." She struggled to form sentences, still regaining her wind. "Some uniform grabbed me and said I was walking where a bunch of burglaries had been committed and he searched my purse. I keep my kit in there and he arrested me for it."

"Stupid bitch," Nessman railed. "What are you supposed to do when you get picked up?"

"I know. I've got the number. I was going to call."

"Did you?"

"I was scared, Pauly. And I was aching so bad. I hadn't scored since that morning. It hurt so bad. They took me to the station and this detective, some kid, walked in and told me if I gave them information, they would release me with a court citation and maybe drop the charges. If I didn't agree, they were going to lock me up."

"Jesus, Tricks. How long do you think they would have locked you up for a couple bags of heroin?"

"I don't know. Overnight, maybe?"

"Yeah, if that. You would have been out the next day."

"But I needed to get out *then*! I was so sick. I needed to score. You don't know what it's like!"

Nessman huffed his frustration as the anger grew again. He had no sympathy for addicts like Tricky Leonard. Their lack of loyalty was matched only by their predictability. When a decision had to be made, the shortest path to the next high always won out.

Taking out his phone and bringing up the picture of Brennan, Nessman walked back to Tricky, who was now sitting against the car, hugging her knees.

"Is this the guy who talked to you?"

"No," she said. "Not that night. After they signed me up, I bought dope for them a couple of times. Two weeks in they said I was doing a really good job, and introduced me to that guy. His name's Jimmy Brennan."

Nessman figured out on his own what had happened next. He had been drunk, and horny, and had picked up Tricky for satisfaction. He didn't remember telling her he was looking to take on some more people to help with a 'special project,' but the next day when Tricky brought it up he knew he must have said something to her.

Nessman had played it cool, not letting on that he had talked about something he shouldn't have. And it seemed to have worked out, because Tricky said she might know someone who could help him. Two days later Nessman had sat in a bar with Detective Jimmy Brennan.

"Shit," he said, as much to himself.

"I'm sorry."

"Are you fucking him?"

"No, it's not like that. He tries to play himself off as the big-brother type. Looking to help me out, gives me a little money, stuff like that."

"Oh, for fuck's sake! What are you an idiot?" yelled Nessman. "How many times has this cop helped you out? Has he taken you to rehab? Has he given you enough money to help you, or just enough so you can score dope? They want you out on the street using heroin and hooking johns so you stay up on what's happening and rat to them. Christ, they use you worse than I do."

Tricky looked up at her attacker through smeared mascara and asked, "Can I get up?"

Nessman waved at her dismissively as he turned his back again to pace. She held the side of the car and eased up to her knees, then feet. The one stiletto still on her foot penetrated the sand, making balance a challenge. She kicked it off.

Nessman turned to face her.

"Lay it out, then. How much have you told him?"

"Nothing, I swear. Brennan, said to give you his number, and he'd take care of the rest."

Wheels turned in Nessman's head. This was going in the wrong direction for Tricky. There was a lot of information she could testify about.

"What else?"

"Not a word."

Nessman covered the distance between them in two strides and grabbed the woman by two pieces of thin cloth on the front of her tank top. He jostled her hard, ripping one. Her breast fell out the side, and when she reached to cover it he slapped her across the face with an open hand.

"Pauly, please," she cried meekly, a hand to her stinging face. "I promise I didn't say anything else. About you or Malone."

The sound of his boss's name enraged him.

"I've never mentioned Brass Malone to you. Why'd you say that?"

A flare of panic dumped into Tricky's stomach, and her eyes widened.

"I don't know. Maybe Brennan asked about him or something. I don't even know who he is."

Bitter frustration with his own negligence blended with unabashed rage at the young woman's lies. Nessman lost control. He coiled his shoulder, rounded his hip, and drove an uppercut into Tricky's face. Her jaw dislocated, tearing some of the thick muscles that attached it to her head. The energy of the punch rocked her backward, smacking her skull against the roof of the car. Concussed and bleeding, Tricky's limp body collapsed and slid to the ground.

Nessman wasn't done. He reached down and grasped her hair, pulling upward as he coiled his arm to strike again. He noted Tricky's rolled-white eyes and now-distorted face. The left side of her mandible sat askew, a half-inch lower than the other where the bone remained attached to her skull. He changed his mind and tossed her head into the sand.

Nessman stood and stalked away from his victim. He yelled a vulgarity and ran aggressive fingers through his hair. He paced back and gnashed his teeth, hoping to grind away the frustration. He knew what he had to do.

Tricky Leonard represented a living witness that could connect him to Malone, the police, and a murder for hire. But he was not ready to execute the teenager that lay before him. If she talked, and it inevitably got back to Malone, it would be all over for him. She had to be silenced.

When his internal monologue stumbled to the name 'Malone,' Nessman found the answer. He was a soldier, not a planner. Malone was the boss, Ozzy the brains, he was the muscle. Nessman remembered the solitary and absolute demand of his employer – unyielding loyalty. Having found succor in admitting his own limits, the decision came more easily. If Malone wanted the girl dead, he would have told Nessman to do it.

Nessman walked to Tricky's broken body. He tapped her knee with his boot, and she stirred. He bent over her and placed his hand under her neck. Raising it gently, he turned her face toward his.

"Can you hear me."

There was no response.

"Shit," he muttered. Cupping her cheeks with

both hands, he lifted her head from the dirt. A bit of sand mixed with blood pouring from her mouth to form grainy red mud. It reminded Nessman of playdoh. He spoke in a hushed growl.

"Hey, Tricks. You hear me?"

A dull hissing sound, close enough to 'yes', emanated from her mouth.

"What's my name? You remember where you are?" he asked, trying to orient her.

A dull hiss came again, followed by either an 'mmm' or an 'nnn.' Nessman. She was conscious.

"If I ever hear of you so much as smiling at a cop I will snap your scrawny fucking neck. You hear me?"

Tricky let out a gentle humming noise and shifted her hips. An eye cracked open.

"You got it, Tricky? And you tell that friend of yours on the street that I fucked you then dropped you off downtown. Then you picked up another john. He's the one that did this to you, and you have no idea who he is. Got it?"

Her face nearly demolished, it hurt too much to nod. But she tried, and Nessman felt the subtle up-down movement of her neck in his hands.

"Good," he said, plopping her head back down as an exclamation point. He looked around to make sure he hadn't dropped anything, walked to the driver's door, opened it, and sat heavily into the leather seat. As he reached for the ignition his eyes were drawn to four clear red lines scraped horizontally across his forearms. His mind's eye went back to strangling Tricky and her desperately panicked attempts to get away.

"Dammit," he muttered as he climbed back out of the seat. He walked behind the vehicle and after popping the trunk, retrieved an unmarked plastic bottle and small scrub brush. Returning to Tricky, he knelt next to her.

Nessman spun the lid off the bottle and picked up the woman's hand as if it were an inanimate object. He poured bleach onto her fingers and forearm as well as the brush. The pungent sting of chlorine filled his nose as he scrubbed the girl's hand. Grasping each finger in turn, he washed deeply underneath the nails. When he was finished, he repeated the process with the other hand.

Having taken care of the main physical link between them, it was time to break the electronic connection. Detectives investigating the assault of Patricia "Tricky" Leonard would track where her cell phone had been for the previous 24 hours. If anyone mentioned his name, or the cameras at New Horizon Shelter had recorded his image, they would check his as well.

Fabricating the evidence related to their travel took two hours. Nessman drove downtown and hid Tricky's cell phone in an outdoor floral arrangement near the Bank of America. He went home and dropped off his own device. Additionally, he opened Netflix on his television and queued up The Godfather, a three-hour biopic. Then he drove back to the bank, retrieved Tricky's phone, and walked the typical streetwalker pattern for a half hour. Finally, he drove back to the scene of the crime and tossed Tricky's phone next to her as yet undiscovered, but fortunately still alive, body.

It was unlikely Nessman would ever be identified as a suspect. But if he was, the police would lay out the timeline of the hours preceding Tricky's violent assault. The cell phone evidence would show that after Nessman picked her up, they went to what he would claim was her favorite spot to do 'business.' He would explain that afterward, they drove back downtown and he dropped her off. He went home, got drunk, and passed out in front of a movie. Maybe Tricky went out, walked around, and picked up another customer, Nessman would say. She probably took him to the same favorite sex-spot. Then the son-of-bitch beat her senseless. Too bad, he would tell the cops. She's a nice girl.

There would be no DNA evidence, and both their cell phones would corroborate his story. A subpoena to Netflix for his usage records would do the same.

"You've got me," he would tell the cops. "I hired a whore for a blow job. Paid her fifty bucks. If I have to take a pinch for that, I guess that's the way it'll be."

Confident his tracks were adequately covered, Nessman went home, got drunk, and passed out in front of a movie.

CHAPTER 35

Jimmy Brennan peered into each of the soiled and dimly lit stalls in the men's room of Three Brother's Pub before speaking in a manner that, had anyone been there to hear him, would have colored him a crazy man mumbling incoherently to himself. He was, in fact, speaking to his partner parked in a van two blocks away.

"Rey, I don't think he's going to show. I've been sitting out there for an hour."

This had been Brennan's last scheduled meet with Paul Nessman. It was planned to identify the person to be killed, provide a profile, and deliver the first payment. Nessman was late.

Rey Johnston was in a familiar spot, sitting inside a cramped van with four tactically outfitted MPD SWAT officers. His ears were covered with noise cancelling headphones that allowed him to monitor the audio being routed through Brennan's body wire to a recording device on a small table in front of him. He could not, however, talk back.

Johnston's face contorted into a frown.

"Everything alright?" asked the officer in charge of the four-man tactical unit. Johnston held his hand up at eye level and shook his head as he touched one of the headphone cups with the other.

"Text me if the wire's still good," Brennan said. Fifteen seconds later his pocket vibrated.

Finishing up at the urinal, Brennan looked at himself in the stained mirror as he washed his hands with water. There was no soap. He made a decision.

"I don't like this, Rey. Doesn't feel right. I'm coming out."

Johnston wanted to wait longer. He had a text message saying as much half written when he thought better of it. The man on the inside always had the most up-to-date information, and surveillance never questioned their decisions.

Brennan left the bathroom and walked to the bar, where he laid down a twenty to cover the two drinks he'd had. It had started to rain, and Brennan jerked up his collar against the chill as he jogged the final steps to his car. He sat down, shook off the cold, and gave Siri an instruction. The call connected quickly.

"Nessman has been late before, Jimmy. What's got you spooked?" Johnston asked without any pleasantries.

"I don't know, Rey. I just don't like it. Has intelligence had a tail on him lately?"

Brennan started the car and waited for the call to transfer to Bluetooth. He dropped the phone into his jacket pocket and pulled into traffic.

"Let me check the log," Johnston answered. Brennan heard keystrokes. "Okay, yeah. They were on him four days ago. He visited Brass Malone in jail."

"Jesus, Rey, that would have been nice to know. Can we get anything off of that? We have anyone on the inside there?" asked Brennan.

"I'm sure intelligence has a few people in there,

but no one's going to spill on Malone. He probably has more guards on the take than we have inmates signed up as informants. He gets to use attorney rooms for all his visits, lawyer or not. There's no recording in there."

"Well, that's terrific. I feel like maybe these are things it might have been good to know before going into this meeting," said Brennan.

It was a subtle rebuke, but it stung. Brennan hung up the call and grabbed a different phone from his pocket. He dialed a number and put the device on speaker just as a monotone recorded voice informed him the number was no longer in service.

Tossing that phone onto the seat beside him, Brennan called Johnston again.

"I just called Nessman. It's discon. Check the ping logs. I want to know where he's been the past few days."

'Pinging' allowed police to bounce a signal off an individual cell phone from all the cellular service towers in a large area. By analyzing which towers the phone responded to, they could determine the general location of the phone. In urban areas, when multiple towers responded, the system was quite accurate. By tracking 'ping logs' over time, police could establish a pattern of travel and activity.

Recent supreme court decisions had ruled ping searches unconstitutional without a search warrant, and service providers such as Verizon and Sprint would no longer provide the information without court orders. As soon as this occurred, the organized criminal element began recruiting helpers in the phone companies. Employees making fifteen dollars an hour to monitor a phone network were easily susceptible to thousand-dollar monthly bribes to let gangsters know when a warrant was out on a phone. That made search warrants all but useless to police when investigating organized crime.

To fight this, some police departments had figured out how to do it themselves, without involving the phone company. A sixty-five-thousand-dollar equipment purchase and a few weeks of training allowed them to do just that. It wasn't admissible in court, but it provided valuable information.

"I'll check it and call you back," Johnston replied and hung up.

Brennan took a right on Silver Street and then another onto Maple. He wanted to get back downtown and try to figure out what was going on with Paul Nessman. His phone vibrated before the next turn.

"What have you got?"

"I don't like this, Jimmy. His phone completely dropped off the logs. He's gone."

"What do you mean, 'gone?' What the fuck does 'dropped off' mean. Doesn't everyone's phone have to hit a tower to function?" Brennan demanded.

"Hey, don't get pissed at me. I'm just as frustrated as you are. That's what intel just told me. We've been pinging him four times a day, six in the morning, noon, six at night, and midnight. We've had a good, solid pattern for weeks now. But four days ago, it stopped. No more tower hits."

"Well shit, Rey. What the fuck happened four days ago?" The answer struck them both at the same time.

Malone.

"What time did Nessman visit Malone at Valley Street?" asked Brennan.

"Hang on."

Ninety seconds later Johnston was back on the line. "Two in the afternoon."

"And let me guess. The last ping hit was at noon the same day, right?" Brennan asked, but he knew the answer. Johnston typed an inquiry.

"Shit. Yeah, noon exactly."

"So, what we have on Nessman is two righteous undercover meets, consistent ping logs, and then a few hours after meeting with Malone, he dumps his phone, and me."

"Yeah, it looks that way."

Brennan's thoughts raced. The case had been solid, and Nessman had shown no pattern of swapping phones or dumping lines, a common tactic. Brennan had earned his way in. There had been no reason for Nessman to suspect him. He had one final thought.

"Has Nessman been talking to anyone else on that particular phone line, or just us?"

It was not a frequently used tool, but some criminals utilized separate phones for separate accomplices, especially ones they did not trust. It helped compartmentalize information and throw off police investigations.

Johnston hesitated, then said "That's kind of pushing it. I don't mind running a few warrantless ping logs off the books, but to find that out I'd have to make some calls to people I know at Verizon. Calls that would leave a record."

"We have to find out if I've been burned or not."

"Jimmy, we could get into a lot..."

"Dammit, this is important! There's no other way we can know for sure."

The line lay silent for five seconds.

"I'll call you back."

Ten minutes later, when Brennan was just about at his wits end, the phone rang.

"How bad is it?" he asked.

"Pretty fucking bad. Yours was the only number ever dialed in or out of that line. That means Nessman kept it as a burner just for talking to you."

"Shit," Brennan muttered.

"There's more, Partner."

"What is it?"

"I got a call just now from Detective Ballister of violent crimes. He's out at Litchfield Sand and Gravel with Tricky Leonard. Your number was in her purse."

"Shit, don't tell me..."

"She's alive," Johnston interrupted. "But it's bad. Broken jaw, bad head injury."

"That's pretty goddamned convenient."

"Yeah, it is. Paul Nessman meets with his boss, Brass Malone in jail. As soon as that happens, he dumps the phone he has been using to talk to us. A few days later he misses a meeting with you, and Tricky Leonard gets her ass kicked."

"You think she told them about me?" Brennan asked.

"She must have. Man, that sucks. Blows our case out of the water."

"Nice, Johnston. How about having a little compassion for the poor kid that got her head caved in for helping us out?"

"She knew what she was doing when she signed on. No one forced her to do it."

"That's pretty fucking heartless, isn't it?"

Johnston let the comment slide.

"Detective Ballister said the scene had been cleaned."

"Cleaned how? It's a friggin' sand pit." Brennan asked.

"Bleached her hands and scrubbed them."

"Smart. That means whoever did it probably accounted for surveillance cameras and phone logs, too."

"Yeah, Ballister has his work cut out for him. And he said Tricky's not saying shit."

"So, the question is do we give him Nessman as a suspect?"

"I don't see any reason not to. This investigation is blown. There's no case integrity to protect."

"Okay, I'll call him back and explain it all," Brennan said, and hung up without another word.

CHAPTER 36

Officer Randy Richardson's thoughts were not at all focused on guarding the homicide scene to which he had been assigned. His wife was going to be damn bitter when he called and told her he would not be off duty in time to take the kids to school. A gruff voice pulled him back.

"Richardson, are the marshals here yet?" a bleary eyed, impatient overnight shift sergeant asked.

Richardson was standing on the third of five granite steps leading to the front entrance of a forty-two-hundred square foot brick home.

"Sarge," he responded. "Would I still be standing here if the goddamned U.S. Marshals were here yet?"

"Just let me know when they show up."

Sergeant Donald Cobb of the Goffstown, New Hampshire police department turned on his heel and walked across the neatly landscaped walkway to his cruiser. Any murder in the suburban town west of the Manchester was bound to give the community fits, but the execution of Judge G. Robert Christiansen was likely to keep him awake and on overtime all day feeding oxygen to his nervous bosses.

After popping open the cruiser door, he stepped inside and prepared to sit when two shiny black Chevrolet Tahoes pulled in behind him. Cobb stood back up and eased the door closed.

Two tall men, identically dressed, exited the rear vehicle and walked directly to the house without a word. From the closer SUV, a man and woman emerged and walked to Cobb.

I'm Special Agent Davis, FBI," the man said as he extended his hand. Cobb looked at him for a brief but detectable moment, then shook it.

"Sergeant Cobb, Goffstown PD."

Davis jerked his thumb sideways toward the woman next to him. "This is Special Agent McDonough."

Cobb and McDonough shook hands.

"Where are they going?" Cobb asked, pointing at the front of the house.

"That's Foster and Collins with the marshal's service. They're going to assist on this. They'll take over security, relieve your man at the door, that sort of thing," Davis said.

Sergeant Cobb looked back and forth between the two agents, as if analyzing whether or not they were telling the truth. Then he shrugged.

"You need anything from us?"

"We've got a crime scene unit coming out of Concord, and a half dozen more agents on the way up from Boston. We should be good for now. I'd appreciate it if you'd run what you've got so far for us. Your dispatcher said it came in as a 911 call. Was that from the victim?"

"No, it came in off a neighbor who reported hearing loud popping noises inside the house. We were here in about four minutes. It's a nice neighborhood, so that sort of thing gets a pretty quick response from us. Actual taxpayers here, not our usual clientele. You know how it is."

Cobb smiled and paused his explanation for the expected chuckles. There were none.

"Anyway, there was no answer at the door, but when you go up there you'll see there's a lot of blood visible from the side windows. We entered through the back and found him. Multiple gunshot wounds. Very clearly dead. We didn't bother calling EMS."

This caught McDonough's attention and she looked up from her notebook.

"Why not?"

Sergeant Cobb furrowed his brow.

"Why not, what?"

"Why no EMS, Sergeant? Is that protocol?"

Cobb looked at Davis skeptically, then back at his partner.

"Have you seen a lot of dead bodies on the job, Agent McDonough?"

"Special Agent McDonough was with Atlanta, Georgia PD for five years before coming on with the Bureau," Davis answered for her.

"Good for her," Cobb retorted, his eyes still on McDonough. "Can Agent McDonough talk? What did you do for Atlanta, *Special* Agent McDonough?"

"Vice, mostly."

"And now, what do you do for the FBI, *mostly.*"

"White collar. Embezzlement, high-end extortion," she answered.

"Explain to me exactly how that qualifies you to give me shit about not calling EMS for a bled-out murder victim with half his head blown off?"

"Alright, listen. Let's start over," Davis said, holding up his hands between them. "Sergeant Cobb, please just run the case for us."

Cobb smirked sarcastically. "Sure. Like I said, we came in the back. The body's in the living room, but there's blood all over the place. You're either looking at a pissed off lover or a really shitty professional job. We cleared the house for more victims, then backed out and secured it."

He paused, so McDonough's notes could catch up. It was an olive branch.

"Your crime scene guys are going to have a hell of a time in there. Overlapping blood spatters, multiple rooms, footprints everywhere. Messy."

"Looks like a struggle, you think? He fought the killer off?" asked Davis.

"Yeah, I'd say so. Your victim moved around a lot after the first shot, that's for sure. One in the leg and at least one or more in the torso. Then a head-shot to end it," Cobb added.

"You mentioned footprints in the blood. Enough for there to have been two shooters?" McDonough asked without looking up from her notes.

"No, I'd say just one shooter. Lots of footprints but I only saw one pattern in the blood. Victim is in his slippers, and they're slick-bottomed. Only one caliber of shell casings, too. Nine-millimeter, I think."

"You didn't pick them up..." Davis said unnecessarily.

"Oh, sure, Davis. Right after we flushed the toilet and used the phone."

"Sorry."

McDonough finished her notes, then looked at Davis. "Okay, I'm good. You have anything?"

"Nope, we're good. Thanks for your help, Sarge. I assume a couple of days for the reports from the first responding officers?"

"I'd give it a week to be sure," said Cobb. He shook both agents' hands and turned to walk up to the house. Halfway there, Davis, who had jogged to catch up to him, touched his shoulder.

"Listen," he began. "I know it can be a pain in the ass when we come in like thieves in the night and steal away a case like this, but the murder of a judge automatically goes to the FBI. Your state attorney general and the US Attorney in Concord have it set up that way."

"No worries, Davis. I get it," Cobb said, meaning it.

"Between you and me," Davis added. "Judge G. Robert Christiansen was on our radar already."

This caused Cobb's eyebrows to rise. "He dirty or something?"

"You know I can't answer that. Suffice it to say when I got the call that a judge had been killed, I wasn't particularly surprised to hear it was him."

"Fair enough," Cobb said, extending his hand again. "Let me know if we can do anything else."

Sergeant Cobb didn't wait for a response from Davis before turning to face the house. He cupped his hands over his mouth for amplification.

"Richardson, is Smith still out back?"

"Yeah, Sarge. You need him?"

"Get him on the radio. We're done here."

CHAPTER 37

Two days after Judge Christiansen's murder, Don Mollie pulled up in front of a classic center-stair colonial on Haywood Road in Londonderry, a sleepy bedroom community southeast of Manchester. There were no cars on the street at eleven in the evening. Garage doors were down, kids in bed, and the neighborhood prepared to tuck in for the night.

Judge Preston Shelbourne's fifty-five hundred square foot behemoth, painted Yarmouth Grey with an Eggplant door, was no exception. The driveway was empty, and barn-style garage doors concealed his brand-new Audi A8 as well as Mrs. Shelbourne's BMW SUV. She had hated buying such an ostentatious vehicle, but had found it necessary to tote around a thirteen-year-old girl and twin nine-year-old boys.

Shelbourne was in his library with the lights dimmed. He wore simple cotton pajamas, a silk robe, and sat in a deeply red, butter soft, leather armchair. His feet, clad in four-hundred-dollar chinchilla lined slippers rested on a low footstool. His iPad, the one his wife did not know about, lay in his lap. As he tapped messages into the chatroom with one hand, he held a glass of Glenlivet in the other.

An assertive knock at the front door rattled his

thoughts. As if answering the internal question of whether he heard properly, it came again five seconds later. Shelbourne, a short, balding, bespectacled French-Canadian, set the tablet down on his desk. He placed the drink next to it and walked into the hallway and through the foyer to the door.

Peering through the thickly waved glass on either side, Shelbourne could make out the image of a man in a suit. The way he stood in his unbuttoned blazer made him look like a police detective. In the course of his work day, Shelbourne saw a lot of detectives. He decided to step to an adjacent window in hopes of a better view. As soon as he moved, the knock came again, startling him.

"Oh, Jesus Christ," he muttered. "He's going to wake the entire house."

Shelbourne stalked back to the door, defeated the deadbolt, and yanked it open.

"May I help you?"

The man held a badge to the judge's face, an uncomfortable six inches away.

"Hi there, Preston!" he said. "I'm Detective Mollie. Mind if I come in?"

With that, Mollie shouldered past Shelbourne and into the foyer. He looked around with wide eyes and feigned interest.

"Wow, this is really nice."

"Excuse me, Detective. Can I help you?"

"Sure, Judge. But first, let's get a drink, eh?" Mollie walked toward the kitchen. "Here?" he asked, pointing.

Shelbourne looked on, confused. He nervously adjusted the waist of his robe and re-tied the sash.

"Are you here to get a search warrant signed or something? The protocol requires you to call the court first, who in turn notifies me."

Mollie ignored the comment. Looking past the foyer and down the wide hall, he saw a glow emanating from the small library.

"Oh, you must have been down here. You keep the booze in there?" As he spoke, Mollie brushed past the judge and headed into the room. Shelbourne scurried to catch up.

"Excuse me, you can't just..."

"This is *really* nice!" Mollie said with renewed admiration. By the time Shelbourne entered the room behind him, he had already uncorked the scotch and was pouring it into a stout glass. Satisfied, he tipped the bottle toward the judge, silently asking if he wanted a taste. Shelbourne looked over at the desk and his half-filled glass. Mollie's gaze followed.

"Ah, I see you've got a head start."

Mollie walked casually to the armchair, fiddling with a nameplate on the desk, and slumped down with a heavy sigh. He allowed the momentum of the movement to lift his feet off the ground and they landed, crossed at the ankles, on the footstool.

Shelbourne, dumbfounded, stared at the cartoon character that had invaded his home. Mollie gestured to a nearby loveseat. When the judge didn't move, his face turned cold.

"Sit down, judge. We've got a lot to talk about."

Shelbourne sat gingerly on the edge of the sofa, knees touching, hands clasped in his lap. Mollie took a deep sip of his drink, smiled at the glass, and set it down. He reached into a breast pocket to retrieve an iPhone. In doing so his jacket fell open, revealing the pistol on his hip. Shelbourne's heart jumped. Mollie manipulated the device until the proper image came up.

"Detective...Mollie, did you say? This is highly irregular. Might I have the name of your supervisor?"

"Oh no, Judge Shelbourne. *This* is highly irregular."

Mollie tossed the phone at him, bouncing it off his hip. It landed face up, and the man looked down at an image of the front entrance of the Lotus Flower Salon in Hartford, Connecticut. Careful not to touch the phone, he bent a bit lower and squinted. He could just make out the image of himself, walking out of the massage parlor.

"Is this supposed to mean something to me?" Shelbourne asked. "Do you intend it to have some bearing on our conversation?"

"Why, yes, Your Honor," Mollie said, mocking the judge's formal intonation. "If you would be so kind as to pick up the phone and peruse the adjacent images, it might serve to elucidate the purpose of my visit."

Shelbourne scowled, but complied. Three photos into the examination, each showing him in various states of undressed congress with a Korean teenager, he dropped the phone. Standing assertively, he moved to the desk and slugged down the remaining scotch. He walked around to face the desk and opened a drawer. Mollie's hand went to his pistol.

"Relax," the judge said, holding up a marijuana cigarette. "Takes the edge off." He touched a button on the wall, and a silent fan in the ceiling began to exhaust the room. He lit the joint, took a heavy drag, then extended it toward Mollie.

"Well aren't you full of surprises," Mollie said, taking the offered cigarette. He took a drag and held it. The smoke was smooth, almost velvety in his lungs, and the high hit immediately. He exhaled upward, creating a swirl that spun into the ceiling.

"Nice," he said.

"It better be, at four-hundred an ounce."

"Jesus, is it fertilized with unicorn shit or something?"

Shelbourne ignored the comment. "Now that we've established both of us as aficionados of fine scotch and dank nugs, is there a more specific purpose to your visit?"

"You're going to have a series of new cases assigned to you next week. There seems to be a shortage of judges." Mollie said. He smiled, then chuckled at his own little joke.

"I hardly think the circumstances of Judge Christiansen's passing are a laughing matter."

"Yeah, well, maybe you didn't know him very well," Mollie offered.

"You were saying?" Shelbourne prompted.

"You will be assigned part of Christiansen's backlogged docket. Some of these cases are of interest to me. One, actually, in particular." Mollie passed the joint back to the judge. "You've heard of Brass Malone?"

"The name has some familiarity."

"Jesus, can't you just say 'yes'?"

Shelbourne scowled at his intruder. "Yes."

"The Malone case will be reassigned to you. He is due for sentencing, and you're going to give him two years."

"My understanding is Mr. Malone intends to plead guilty to charges related to the larceny of firearms that were subsequently used in the commission of felonies."

"Yeah, Judge. They say he lifted some guns that

ended up with bodies on them. Or at least that someone in his organization did."

"I don't know if I can sentence him to two years, just to facilitate the return of those photographs," Shelbourne said, gesturing toward the iPhone.

"That's why we're going to sweeten the pot with fifty-thousand dollars."

Shelbourne considered that as he poured himself another drink.

"And if I refuse?"

"And give up all this?" Mollie asked, gesturing broadly across the room. "I doubt the lodgings you'll find yourself in after the wife takes you to the cleaners in a divorce will be quite as august."

The judge stood in silence, then looked up at the ceiling as he did some back-of-the-napkin math in his head. He leveled his gaze to Mollie's and spoke in an even tone.

"Make it a hundred-thousand, and I'll even let the gentleman out on bail. I can't imagine he is satisfied with his current...*lodgings.*"

Mollie smiled and finished his drink. He stood and walked to the oak bureau that held the bottle of scotch, examined the label, then held it up toward Shelbourne. There was a question in his eyes.

"Please, Detective Mollie, by all means. Consider it a symbol of the consummation of our accord."

Mollie smiled. "Decide how you want the money. Cash, wired, whatever. Someone will be in touch."

Judge Shelbourne heard Mollie's wingtips in the hallway, then the front door open and close.

CHAPTER 38

When laid out plainly and examined with the benefit of hindsight, Bridget Patterson should have seen Frank Doran coming a mile away. If he had simply begun beating her, she would have left the same day. Instead, he had seduced her, lied to her, manipulated her, and abused her.

Eighteen months into the relationship, Frank Doran was regularly stalking, threatening, and assaulting Bridget Patterson. But now, in the week following his arrest, she had spent most of her time in the bosom of home, surrounded by family. She was trying to reconnect with friends, who tentatively allowed her to re-approach after Doran had forced them apart. It had been easy to dodge Doran's calls. He was in jail. She was safe.

And then Bridget learned he had been let out on bail, and it began again.

It was a crisp, cold, autumn afternoon in New England, and Bridget was feeling both grateful and apprehensive. She was thankful for Stacy, who despite nearly a year of radio silence had welcomed her best friend back with open arms. Stacy had agreed to help Bridget move out of Doran's apartment, but she was anxious that they might not complete the project before Doran showed up.

Bridget had made the decision to move back in with her parents three days earlier, with the intention of making several trips over as many days to get the job done. But that morning a victim advocate from the county prosecutor's office had called and told her that Frank Doran was getting bailed out of jail – today.

"How did you get this number? Why are you calling me? He wasn't arrested for anything related to me," Bridget had asked.

"Let's just say family is important, and sometimes we try to look out for our friends. Tell your dad I said hello."

Bridget had panicked. She had growing confidence in her regained identity, but was also possessed of enough self-doubt that a little pressure from Doran would snap her back. The symbolic move of vacating Doran's apartment would consummate her decision. It would serve as a symbol she could grasp for strength in resisting him. If she could do it in time.

They were almost done, and all Bridget's belongings were packed into boxes. Stacy was making a trip down to the car, leaving her alone in the apartment. She heard a noise in the doorway behind her and made an assumption.

"Stace, I'm not going to box up the lamps. We can just carry them out," Bridget said.

"Hey, Babe," a deeper voice replied. "What are you doing?"

Bridget's feet almost left the ground as she spun. Her eyes met the soft gaze of Frank Doran. He was dressed in khakis and a button-down shirt, sized too large. He was clean-shaven and looked rested.

"Hey, Frank," she replied, looking past him to the

doorway. Stacy would be back soon.

"Are we going somewhere?" he asked.

"How did you get out? When, I mean. I thought it wasn't until later today."

"Yesterday the judge reduced my bail to personal recognizance instead of cash because I'm not a flight risk," Doran said. "They let me out early this morning."

He smoothed up next to her and held his arms open for a hug. She hesitated, and his smile faded. She recognized the look and moved into his arms. They embraced.

"I asked if we're going somewhere," he repeated. When there was no answer, the embrace tightened uncomfortably. Bridget gasped.

Stacy's voice echoed up the hallway as she approached the open apartment door. "You definitely have too much shit in this apartment, Bridge."

When she rounded into the room, she pulled up short. "What is *he* doing here?" she asked.

Doran released Bridget and turned to face Stacy, a plastic smile on his face.

"Hi Stacy."

The woman ignored him and walked around a coffee table to Bridget, who had unconsciously taken a step back. Stacy gently touched her friend's upper arm and asked "You okay?"

"She's fine," Doran answered.

"Let's go," Stacy continued softly. "I just brought down the last box of clothes. We can replace the rest of this stuff. Let him keep it."

"What's going on here?" Doran asked.

Stacy looked over her shoulder at him, then shuffled around sideways, keeping her back to him and guiding Bridget toward the door while staying between them. It was an awkward dance.

"Hey, I asked a question. I think I have a right to know what the hell is going on!"

"She's moving out," Stacy said.

"I'd like to hear that from her."

"We're leaving, Frank," Stacy repeated.

Bridget's stomach churned, and her fingers and face felt numb. Doran ventured an arm around to touch Bridget's shoulder. When Stacy moved her hand to block it, he brushed it away. Stacy spun full around.

"Back off, Frank!" she hollered, a hard finger inches from his chest. "Don't you ever fucking touch me!"

Doran put both his hands up at shoulder level, palms out. He looked past Stacy.

"Look, I just want a minute to talk to you, Sweetheart. That's all."

Bridget saw the remorse on his face. He had been in jail for days, and they say jail can change a man. He had a right to talk to her, maybe even try to talk her out of it, depending on what he had to say. She felt the pull.

"It's okay, Stace. Let me talk to him for a minute."

Stacy looked at her friend with concern, then lowered her finger and backed away to the couch and sat.

"Alone, please," Doran asked.

"No," Stacy replied.

He turned his attention to Bridget. "Can we *please* just talk privately for a minute? Don't I get a say in all this?" he pleaded.

"It's okay. I'm okay," Bridget said to Stacy. "You can wait outside for a bit."

"Yeah, I know you're okay," Stacy said. "You're okay because I'm here. And I'm okay because you are here. Together, we're okay, even with this dickhead in the room. Apart, we're not."

"What the fuck does that mean?" Doran demanded, some of his smothered anger leaking out of a crack.

"It means exactly what I just said, Frank. You want to talk, then talk."

With that, Stacy picked up her cell phone and began absentmindedly scrolling through her feed. Resigned this was the best chance he'd get, Doran focused on Bridget, and lowered his voice.

"Can we please just go somewhere to talk? I've got so many things I want to say to you. So much I'm sorry for. Please?"

"I don't know Frank," Bridget said, looking at her shoes. "Maybe just let us finish here, then I can call you tomorrow."

"No, Baby. That won't work. It's gotta be now. I just got out of jail. Look at me. I look good, right?" he stepped back, arms wide, and gestured toward himself with a self-deprecating smile.

He did look good, the best she had seen him in a while. He was clean-shaven, sober, and sweet. Doran noted Bridget's shy smile and softening posture and took advantage. He eased into her for a hug, and she didn't flinch away. He put his mouth close to her ear and whispered.

"Why don't we go get some food and talk. I'm going to visit my grandmother at the center tomorrow. You can come with me. We can play cribbage and feed her Oreos, like old times."

Bridget smiled at the memory, and relaxed further. She let his mouth move to hers, and he kissed her chastely. She smiled.

Bridget took his hand in hers, and they turned to face Stacy, still seated on the couch.

"Hey, Stace," she started. "I think we're good for now. We can leave that stuff in my car and I'll call you later."

Stacy glowered at both of them. She looked back at her phone, swiped a few times, then stood and walked to her friend. She stuffed the phone into Bridget's face.

"Recognize this?" she asked.

"Stacy, please..."

"No, no, Bridge," Stacy said, full of frustrated sarcasm. "If you're going to do this, do it with your eyes open."

She shouldered around parallel to her friend so they could both see the screen and scrolled through the pictures.

"This one, with the finger marks on your arms, was supposedly from when you slipped on ice and he grabbed you hard to catch you. This other one was from the door hitting you in the face. Actually, both of these were. And this last one was from rough sex. That was the easiest one for me to know you were lying, since I've never heard of anyone getting cigarette burns from rough sex. You remember letting me take these, after you admitted what he had done to you?"

"It's not like that anymore, Stacy. Maybe he's changed," Bridget said lamely.

"In five days? C'mon Bridget. Listen to yourself," Stacy said.

"Bitch," Doran muttered.

"Yes, that's right, Frank. I am a bitch. But I'm her bitch," Stacy said, gesturing toward Bridget. "Now if you two want to go somewhere and talk, have at it. Frank can preach on and on about how he's a changed man and things are going to be different."

"Thank you," Doran said lamely.

"I wasn't done," Stacy interrupted. "If you plan all that, then neither of you should have any problem with me tagging along. If you're such a good man you should want to show it off. You should be proud of what you're going to say, not try to hide it."

She turned a pointed finger at her friend. "And you should too, Bridget. No secrets. No privacy. I'm here and I love you and I'm staying."

With that, she backed away and stood by the couch with her arms crossed. Bridget, tears in her eyes, looked at Doran. Ten painful seconds ticked past.

"Call me tomorrow, Frank."

She released his hand and walked to Stacy. Frank started to follow, and Bridget turned squarely around to him. As it happened, her shoulder lined up with Stacy's, and they stood side by side facing him.

"Let's go," Stacy said, and they turned and walked out.

CHAPTER 39

To placate a small but growing progressive constituency, the City of Manchester had partially funded efforts to increase energy efficiency in municipal buildings. At the police department, that meant replacing wasteful fluorescent lighting with efficient LED's. Funding had allowed for completion of half the project, and the dividing line between old and new lay in the center of the office of the violent crimes unit.

The effect, as Jimmy Brennan walked into the room, was disorienting. Bright, buzzing light assaulted his senses from the left, while a warm, soothing glow welcomed him on the right. If old-style office lighting was detrimental to one's vision and focus, this new arrangement was visually schizophrenic.

As Brennan entered the broad room crowded with desks, he found the man he was looking for seated near the center. It was late, well after midnight, and the ocular invasion of lights had not been sufficient to prevent Charlie Wilcox from falling asleep. His feet occupied their usual space on an open drawer. A thick file rested on his chest, supported by the ample belly beneath it. Empty coffee cups were littered about, and with his chin buried into his chest, there was nothing to obstruct a deep, vibrato snore.

Brennan decided not to seize the opportunity to jovially rattle his friend. There was a time for jokes, and a time for compassion. Wilcox was working eighteen-hour days hunting Vincent Underwood while still working his other cases. He didn't need another reason to be frustrated.

Sitting at Mollie's desk, Brennan logged into his own profile and checked his email. He typed loudly and mixed in a throat clearing to ensure Wilcox woke up on his own terms. After half a minute, the man stirred.

"Good morning," Brennan offered.

"I apologize. I didn't hear you come in," Wilcox said, putting down his feet and removing the file from his chest. He winced as razor blades rocketed up from his ankle, then rubbed his calf to massage blood back into it.

"Don't worry about it. You've been busting your ass on this case."

Brennan peered around the computer screen and saw Wilcox had pulled down his necktie. There was a notable coffee stain on his otherwise stark white shirt. Wilcox saw him looking.

"Not my usual sartorial splendor, is it?" he said.

"I'm fairly certain most detectives banging their heads against a desk at midnight take their neckties off completely, assuming they even wore one. You're fine," said Brennan.

"Still, it's not the image I like to project, sleeping on the job in a rumpled suit."

Brennan realized he was not going to convince his old friend, and decided to move on.

"Where are you at with it?"

"As you so eloquently put it, we're banging our

heads against the desk."

"You and Mollie?"

"No," Wilcox said, absentmindedly pulling up his tie. "Diaz and me."

"No shit. Good for her."

"Yes, she's been quite helpful, actually. A very capable detective."

Wilcox stood, stretched, and walked to the Keurig on the far side of the room. He put in a pod, slapped down the lever, and activated it. Then, realizing he had not put a cup under the spout, scrambled to find one and tossed it beneath. He took another and waved it toward Brennan.

"Yeah, sure. Thanks."

Wilcox poured an entirely unreasonable amount of sugar into his cup then carried them both to his desk.

"What has Diaz been doing for you?" asked Brennan.

"Research, mostly. She's been my liaison to the finance people, looking for any connection between Brass Malone or Lorraine Underwood and Vincent."

"Any luck?"

"Not in that regard, but we have learned a hell of a lot about Malone's finances and money laundering. He's got real estate in Boston, Colorado, and Florida. We know he's got some in New Hampshire as well, but strangely we're having a hell of a time finding it. He's very good at hiding his money. He's got a private construction company that he runs a lot of cash through."

"Construction? Do they actually build anything?"

"In a manner of speaking, yes. Twice now they have bought run-down old apartment buildings, fixed them up, then sold them to the local housing authority at a discount. Sometimes they build houses then leave them vacant."

"Why?"

"Because it makes for slushy money. The more money you've got moving around, the easier it is to lose track of it and hide it. For example, the company buys a ten-unit apartment building for half a million, spends several hundred thousand improving it, then sells it for the original purchase price. They'll claim some of the money was from investors, some theirs, and some from loans. No one really knows where it comes from. They do the improvements themselves, paying four hundred dollars for every eight-foot-long two-by-four and compensate the painters at three-hundred per hour. There's a lot of money moving around."

Brennan picked up the narrative. "And I bet it's a private company, so they don't have to share a lot of their books. No one looks too hard anyway because it's a feel-good story where a decent building is sold at a cut rate to the housing authority. Who would do that if they were trying to launder money and hide illegal profits?"

"Exactly," Wilcox said. "They sell the building for the same price they bought it for, which washes that money and doesn't raise eyebrows. They can funnel in additional funds from 'investors,' which is really just more dirty money, as cash that gets overpaid for materials and labor when they do the improvements. Some of it pays for the actual work to be done, the rest is laundered profits."

"Where does he do this, locally?" asked Brennan.

"No. The company is out of Millville, New Jersey."

"Where the hell is that?"

"I suspect that's the point. Keep your dirty money

far from where you're earning it. Diaz had the sheriff's office down there check out the address listed for the business. It's a tiny storefront with a desk and phone, but no one there."

"You said Diaz worked that out? From the office?"

"Yes, through public records and a few subpoenas. She's a very capable investigator. Underutilized by the state police working in her current capacity."

"Something tells me she's not satisfied just doing that. Let me ask you, Charlie, how many times have you caught her stepping out?"

"Interesting you would ask," Wilcox said, smiling. "She went to get take-out lunch for us yesterday afternoon and took three hours. She wouldn't answer her phone. I found out she was doing surveillance at a job site she suspected was involved in this scheme."

"With her arm in a sling and the cast on her ankle, right? And on the odd chance Underwood would randomly show up? That seems pretty unlikely."

"Very unlikely, but she wants to work the case and attacks every lead. She did something similar two days ago when she braced a loan officer at TD Bank about a line of credit they had given Malone. She obtained a fair amount of information, but as you said, is not supposed to be doing field work in her condition."

"Like a dog after a bone."

"It would seem," Wilcox said. With that, he stood and began tidying his desk.

Brennan sipped his coffee and watched the detective work. He moved with surprising grace for a man of his size. Wilcox began to speak again as he moved files into a stack.

"I'm sure you didn't come all the way out here in

the middle of the night just to share a cup of coffee."

"Right," Brennan said. "I got a call this evening from a buddy of mine at Hartford PD. He works internal affairs down there."

"*You* are friends with someone that works for internal affairs?" Wilcox said provokingly.

"No offense taken, thank you very much," Brennan smiled. He continued, "They just wrapped up an investigation where a couple of their patrolmen were getting the 'happy ending' service at a massage parlor down there. On duty, apparently."

"Fascinating," Wilcox said flatly.

"Don't be an ass, Charles," Brennan said, handing him his iPhone. Wilcox scrolled, examining pictures. He pinched into one, squinted, then handed it back.

"That's Shelbourne, isn't it?" Wilcox asked.

Brennan nodded.

"That's certainly unexpected. Are there any decent judges in this county?" asked Wilcox.

"It would seem not. According to my friend in Hartford, Shelbourne's been visiting pretty regularly."

"So, here is my question, Jimmy. I could not care less what Judge Shelbourne does with his free time, save the fact that he's contributing to the significant problem of the human trafficking of teenaged girls. Hartford's IA unit finding these photos would ordinarily result in them conducting a criminal investigation into His Honor, or perhaps making a referral to the New Hampshire Bar. The fact that your 'friend' gave you this information tends to imply it bears on an investigation you have an interest in. And the fact that you now share it with me, that it bears on one of mine."

"Are you done, professor?"

"Drop the other shoe, please, James."

"Two shoes, actually. When the Hartford vice unit executed a search warrant on the massage parlor, they found some evidence that Malone is involved with running the girls there."

Wilcox narrowed his eyes. "Okay, and the other?"

"You heard about Christiansen getting murdered, out in Goffstown?"

"Of course," Wilcox said. "Tragic."

"But perhaps not surprising," Brennan added. Wilcox didn't bite the prompt, so he continued. "Christiansen was the presiding judge on Malone's current prosecution. It was recently set for trial after a plea deal fell through when Christiansen wouldn't accept it."

Wilcox began to understand. "You're kidding me. This is the part where you inform me that Malone's case was reassigned to Shelbourne, isn't it? Log into the court's online docket and confirm that, would you?"

"Already done. It did go to Judge Shelbourne."

"That's rather convenient, isn't it?" Wilcox added, completing the circle in his mind. "Let's run it through. Assume Malone's people knew Christiansen's cases would be reassigned to Shelbourne. Is that fair to say?"

Brennan twisted his face and wobbled his head, weighing facts. "Yeah, most likely. Both of their dockets are a public record, and with a few well-placed phone calls one could find out the case assignment order for all the judges."

"Then perhaps that is the connection," Wilcox said. "Malone's people, who obviously would have cameras all over this massage parlor, keep a dossier on Judge Shelbourne. When they gather sufficient evidence of his moral turpitude, they check and confirm that he's next in line to take on Malone's case if Christiansen becomes unavailable. Then they kill Christiansen."

Brennan sat with his arms crossed, eyes cast downward in thought. Ten seconds passed.

"You don't approve of the theory?" Wilcox asked.

"It's a bit tidy. And killing a sitting judge? That's pretty bold, even for Malone," Brennan said.

"Perhaps that's why they were going to hire you to do it."

"Holy shit! How did I miss that connection?" Brennan said, picking up the narrative. "Then Tricky rats me out and gets beat up..."

"Which you are assuming," Wilcox interrupted.

"Okay, which I am assuming, but the facts certainly point that way. Once I got burned, Malone's people drop me and farm it out to someone else, who gets the job done. Then they confront Shelbourne with these photos, and whatever else they have on him, and get him to lay a softball prison sentence on Malone once he pleads guilty."

By this time, Wilcox was back in his chair, awake and alert. Brennan, too, was exhilarated. This kind of detective work, weighing facts, considering evidence, and inferring theories was the stuff of major crime investigations. While working undercover, tying up suspects with lies, subterfuge, and transactions, Brennan had missed the inductive reasoning and scientific method involved in complex casework. And he missed the camaraderie.

Both men sat in silence, but each knew what the other was doing. Going through the mental machinations of building a strong case. They were identifying gaps, playing the role of defense attorney in an effort to poke holes in their own working hypothesis. They chewed through facts, laying out evidence that would be needed, required interviews, possible search warrants. Then, Wilcox came to a realization.

"It seems we have come up with a plausible and working theory for a series of crimes, none of which have been committed in our jurisdiction."

"I suppose that's true," Brennan said. "But we can certainly pass it on to Hartford PD and the FBI."

Wilcox nodded approvingly. "Returning to the proverbial square one, how does any of this get us closer to locating Vincent Underwood."

"I think that's obvious," Brennan said. "We've got Malone on the ropes. I doubt he has much love or loyalty for his brother. Maybe we should confront him with what we know and threaten to blow the whole thing open unless he gives up Underwood."

"You might be surprised. Familial connection is important to these people," said Wilcox.

"Okay, fine. But let's try it anyway. What does it hurt if we get together with him? We lay out the facts as we know them, let Malone know he's fucked, then lean on him to give up his shit-bag brother."

"Eloquently put," Wilcox said with a chuckle.

Brennan began to type again. "While I'm logged into the court database I'll check and see who Malone's attorney is. We'll have to go through him to set up a meeting."

"I've got a better idea," Wilcox said. "Have you heard of a gentleman named Ozzy Ostrowski?"

"No, should I?"

"Not if he's doing his job right. He's an old timer off the job in Concord. He is now in the employ of Brass

Malone."

"How'd he manage that? Going from working for the cops to schlepping for the likes of Malone."

"Well, he hardly schlepps for him. Ozzy's a bit of a fixer, sort of a Michael Cohen to Malone's Donald Trump, minus the embarrassing sex-scandals and shallow, self-loathing narcissism."

"Cute, Charlie."

"Anyway, Ozzy's fall from grace and eventual resurrection is a story for another time. Just know that if you want a sit-down with Malone, you go through Ozzy."

"You got it, Boss. How do we reach this Ozzy character?" Brennan asked.

Wilcox wasn't paying attention as he scrolled through the contacts in his phone. He raised a finger to pause Brennan, found the number, and tapped it. He pressed the phone to his ear.

"Jesus, you've got this guy's number in your contacts? Now *that's* a story I want to hear."

"Perhaps another time," Wilcox repeated, then focused on the message he was about to leave.

CHAPTER 40

Justine Malone bent over the leather chair in which her husband sat and kissed him softly on the lips. In doing so, she provided an ample view of her heavily restrained and augmented breasts, which stood firm beneath a sheer blouse. She touched his face, and he felt both the warmth of her fingers and the coolness of the diamonds dripping from them.

"I'm going up, Sweetheart. Don't be too long," she said.

Turning, she laid a hand on the shoulder of Ozzy Ostrowski, who sat in an identical chair across a low-slung table.

"Thanks for bringing him home, Oz."

"My pleasure," Ozzy said.

Both men watched as the woman, fifteen years their junior, gracefully moved across the study and up the stairs.

"You're a lucky man, Brass."

"And you're the only person who can get away with staring at my wife's ass like that," Malone said. It was a compliment, strangely worded to an outside observer, that acknowledged the unflappable loyalty between them.

Ozzy reached forward and took a bottle of Macallan thirty-four-year-old scotch from the table. He peeled the seal, uncorked it, and poured on inch into squat crystal glasses. The two men held them forward, eye level.

"To the good things we have," Ozzy said.

"And the better things we'll take," Malone followed.

They clinked glasses and slugged them down appreciatively. Malone put his back on the table and Ozzy filled them again.

"That's nice. You get it from Delaknore?" Malone asked.

"Of course. He sent it over as soon as he heard you were getting out. I'm guessing after gifting you a thirteen-hundred-dollar bottle of single-malt, he'll probably be reaching out for a favor in the not-too-distant future."

"I'm sure," Malone said, reaching for his glass and sipping this time. There was no discernable burn in the butter-smooth liquid.

Anticipating Judge Shelbourne's assignment to the case, Malone's attorney had requested a new bail hearing the week before. As a gesture of good faith toward his part in the plea-deal scandal, Judge Shelbourne had set the defendant's bail at a manageable hundred-thousand-dollars. Ozzy had posted it, and a limousine picked up Malone that morning when he walked out of the Valley Street Jail.

Justine Malone, clad in an eleven-thousand-dollar Chinchilla coat and nothing else, had been in the back seat with a bottle of champagne to welcome him home.

Safely ensconced in a summer home overlooking Lake Winnipesaukee, Malone could now finally put up his feet and relax. He stood and walked to a cedar lined humidor set into the sideboard. After retrieving two Arturo Fuente Churchills he cut the ends with a guillotine. Cigars were the one vice in which Malone enjoyed quality, but did not splurge to the extravagant. He had smoked two-hundred-dollar Cubans and found little difference between them and a simple hand-rolled Nicaraguan leaf he could pick up for eight bucks.

Malone lit his stick, then handed the box of wooden matches to Ozzy and eased into the chair. Once his was lit, Ozzy took a broad puff, then picked an errant piece of tobacco from his tongue.

"To coin a phrase, how was the joint?" Ozzy asked.

"Same as it ever was," Malone replied. Then, remembering, he continued. "Although I did meet an interesting kid this past week."

"Just this week? You've been in a couple months."

"This guy just recently came in. He got jammed up on a vehicular manslaughter charge. Someone ratted on him during a coke deal and when he ran from the cops, an accomplice of his got run over and killed."

"Was this at the mall?" Ozzy asked. "I read something about that."

"I don't know. What I *do* know is the kid didn't say shit when they picked him up. He didn't name the seller, even though the police arrested him at the same time. He wouldn't admit the drugs they found in his truck were his. He wouldn't even confirm the identity of his dead friend."

There was admiration in Malone's voice.

"Well, what *did* he tell them?"

"To fuck off, I think," Malone chuckled. "Then last Friday there was a pretty brutal fight in the mess hall.

The kid was sitting at the same table where it broke out. He didn't lift his head once. Didn't want to see a thing. When the bulls came around asking for witnesses, they questioned him pretty hard and he didn't give up shit. He said the meatloaf was too good to be distracted from."

"Sounds like he knows how to keep his mouth shut. How old is this kid? Has he done time before?"

"No, that's just it. I think this was his first real pinch, and he handled it like a pro. He was maybe twenty-two, twenty-three years old."

Ozzy read into his boss's words and made a few assumptions.

"You want me to look into him? See what kind of exposure he would give us if you took him on?" Ozzy asked.

"Do that. Bring him around, too. I'd like to see how he does with our people, if he holds his tongue or asks a lot of questions. His name is Frank Doran. He was released over the weekend. I chatted him up a bit and got his number. I'll get it to you later. As an added bonus he might have some kind of a connection to the cops?"

"Oh?" Ozzy said, his interest piqued.

"His girlfriend's brother or dad or something is on the job. We didn't get very deep into it, but make sure you check that out as well. It might be nice to have another angle into the cops."

"Indeed. Did you get the girlfriend's name?"

"Must I do everything, Oz?" Malone asked, not serious, then added, "No, I don't know it."

"No problem," Ozzy said, tapping notes into his phone. "I'll chase it down."

Malone finished his drink, and reached forward

to fill it again. Ozzy beat him and topped them both up.

"Do you remember a detective named Charlie Wilcox?" Ozzy asked, changing the subject.

"Not particularly, why?"

"The Treetop Trading fire? Does that ring a bell?"

Treetop Trading was a construction materials distributor that Malone had used as a shell company through which he funneled dirty money. He had spent years paying a thousand-dollars for a box of nails and two-hundred for a paintbrush. After the company served its purpose it was time to clear the records, so the office of Treetop Trading, Inc had suffered a catastrophic fire. Thankfully, there were no injuries, but the building, including all of the company's records, had been a total loss.

"Sure," Malone said. "What about it."

"Detective Wilcox was working white collar crime then. He went at that fire pretty hard, thinking it had been insurance fraud. He managed to link the insurance payment to Switzerland, and we had routed it through two domestic banks and one in Germany before it landed there. Fortunately, the trail died after that. If he had made that final connection, there wouldn't have been many more steps before it landed at our doorway."

Malone noted the admiration in Ozzy's voice and raised a skeptical eyebrow at his longtime friend.

"Why do I get the impression there's more between you and this Wilcox character than you're letting on?"

"We came on the job around the same time," said Ozzy. "Me in Concord and him in Manchester."

"The two cities are not so far apart, are they?"

Malone prodded.

"No, they certainly are not. Especially when you both work the overnight shift and are driving police cruisers."

They paused for puffs of their cigars, topped off by a sip of scotch. Malone realized Ozzy did not intend to explain that any further.

"Wilcox reached out to me this morning. He wants to meet," Ozzy said.

"About what?"

"He's the detective assigned to your brother's case. I'm guessing it's about that."

"You're guessing? I don't pay you to guess."

"What else could it be? They want Underwood badly, and he refuses to go off into that good night. They're looking at him for a pros-murder now."

"Jesus, he killed a whore?"

"Apparently. The warrant came out the other day. It's a solid case. Wilcox caught that one, too."

"Well, now that Vincent's got the cash you gave him maybe he'll be smart and get the hell out of Dodge."

Ozzy slugged down the rest of his drink. He hoped its warmth would give him the courage to explain disobeying Malone's instruction to give Underwood the money.

"I didn't give it to him," Ozzy said plainly.

Malone caught Ozzy's eyes and held them. He puffed at his cigar, squinted, then finally looked away to set it into an ashtray.

"Why not?"

"I had to call an audible, Brass. It's too hot out there. Underwood's wanted for murder now, and the cop I was going to use to funnel it to him is starting to come unraveled."

"That's Mollie? Out of violent crimes?" Malone confirmed.

Ozzy was surprised his boss knew the name. While Malone knew Ozzy had a cop on the take, he had not shared his name.

"Yes, that's him. We might have to cut him loose soon."

Malone nodded, in effect approving Ozzy to take whatever steps he felt necessary with Don Mollie.

"What do you want to do about Wilcox?" Malone asked.

Ozzy leaned back and took a series of puffs from his cigar. His shoulders came down as cortisol diluted from his blood. He had talked through both the issue with Mollie and his own disobedience of Malone's instructions. He felt better.

"I think we should meet with him. It can't hurt."

"Lawyer or no lawyer?" Malone asked.

Ozzy toddled his head back and forth a few times as he looked upward. "I'd say no lawyer. Portman is smart, but he's got regulations he has to follow, disclosure requirements, that sort of thing."

"Ethics, you mean?" Malone offered.

"Yeah," Ozzy smiled. "Ethics."

Malone picked his cigar up, relit it, and leaned back in the chair.

"Go ahead and set it up."

CHAPTER 41

As usual, Monday's schedule had been relentless, and Vanessa Washington was exhausted. The day included four classes, a lab, and an afternoon shift at the tutoring center. Washington, an athletic, five-foot-four woman aged twenty, trudged along the well-worn path between the Dana Center for the Humanities and her dorm, Baroody House.

Autumn on the campus of Saint Anselm College, just outside the western limits of Manchester, was captivating. Icy air, classic New England architecture, and the crunched rustle of leaves filled Vanessa with appreciation for her good fortune. Not many girls from her Queens neighborhood left the city at all, let alone to obtain an education in a place so beautiful.

As a biochemistry major, Vanessa's academic schedule was dominated by massive lecture hall instruction and scientific lab analysis. Believing a well-rounded education necessary for success in life, the school's academic standards committee also maintained certain general course requirements. Vanessa had loaded up on two such classes this semester.

Stooped under the yoke of an overstuffed backpack, Vanessa began to regret signing up for *Intro to Greek Philosophy,* held every Monday evening from six-fifteen to nine. It was this class that had her walking home so late.

It was dark, and the school's safety lights, installed at fifty-foot intervals, cast downward circles that created a path of illuminated Venn diagrams. Vanessa stuck to their middle, comfortable enough with the brief walk to have forgone the campus escort program. Making that call would have been safer, but usually resulted in a twenty-minute wait. The walk itself was half that.

As she passed Davison Dining Hall, movement caught her eye. She looked in that direction and saw two co-eds walking east, away from her. They were too far to hear, and only the occasional chortle of laughter proved loud enough to penetrate the scraping of leaves at her feet.

Vanessa's dorm room was on the back side of Baroody House, near the tree line. It was significantly more convenient to walk around the outside of the building to the rear entrance than to enter the front, negotiate the lobby doors, and make her way down the hall. She deked toward the ice arena, then just before it came into view turned right into the woods. A well-worn if unsanctioned path led from there to the back of the dorm.

While the path had been worn smooth by years of shuffling Birkenstocks, adjacent trees and underbrush along its length had not. Dense shrubbery came right up to the edge, providing a wall of impenetrable green.

A chill crept into Vanessa's spine, as it always did when she chose the shortcut. Even with the path's exit visible shortly after she entered, the overgrown brush and dark canopy created a haunted house tunnel that proved terrifying for the uninitiated. Vanessa had travelled it dozens of times unmolested, save the one occasion she had met a garter snake on a sunny afternoon jog.

As she came to the trail's terminus, Vanessa made out the rough outlines of a figure near her dorm. The person was pressed against the brick façade, clad in dark clothing and wearing a hood. She squinted to confirm her light starved eyes weren't playing tricks on her when the subject moved, removing all doubt.

Vanessa stepped out of the woods and took a few steps closer. It became apparent the figure was a man, his gaze focused through a window. His hands were in front of him, out of sight at waist level. A grotesquely guttural breath escaped his lips, betraying the silence he worked so hard to maintain.

Vincent Underwood's face flushed with arousal. He leaned in, sucking away the radiated coolness of the glass window before him. The young woman in the room lay on her bed, facing away. The glow of a laptop provided the only light, but it was sufficient to illuminate her nubile body, clad scantily in dorm-room leisurewear. The subtle interior illumination served to mirror the glass and secrete his presence.

"What are you doing?" Vanessa called out.

Underwood whipped his body around, struggling to tuck himself away. His eyes met Vanessa's and he instinctively stepped toward her. She stepped back.

"What are you doing back here?" she demanded again. There was no response.

Underwood's mind shifted from observer to actor. Fortune had taken him from self-satisfaction to an opportunity to perform. He quickly sized up

Vanessa's appearance. Young, spoiled, weak. His eyes darted to the darkened path from which she had emerged. His hasty plan established, he lunged forward.

Vanessa's stomach churned as adrenaline dumped into her blood, dilating her pupils and recalibrating insulin to jack-up her sugar level. Certain pain receptors switched off and clotting chemicals increased in her bloodstream. By the time Underwood arrived to her, her body, if not her mind, was ready to fight.

Underwood drove a fist into her stomach, doubling her over. Lowering his hips, he dropped an elbow squarely between her shoulder blades. The move served to stun Vanessa and drove her to her knees. Her hands slapped onto the ground to brace her fall, nose inches from the dirt. She looked a foot in front of her at Underwood's shoes.

Vanessa's ponytail had flopped forward, and Underwood bent down to grasp it and drag his victim to the wood line. Instead, he saw the girl's arms flash forward. Her hands curled behind his ankles, and she yanked back with the force of Athena. Underwood's knees locked and his feet left the ground. His tailbone struck the turf unsupported, and the man cried out in pain.

"Fucking bitch," he bellowed, kicking his heels into the dirt in an attempt to scurry back and create distance.

Vanessa used the momentum of her pull to draw further up onto her knees, toes, and then to stand. As she did, she dipped a shoulder and eased out of the backpack. She grasped the padded straps and, using the momentum of the falling bag, swung it overhead like a splitting maul. Sweeping down in an arc, the twenty-pound sack of philosophy smashed into Underwood's torso, crushing the wind out of him.

Releasing the bag, Vanessa ran to the rear entrance of Baroody, broke the plastic over a fire alarm, and tore the lever down. A piercing whistle accompanied white strobes. There was stirring in the dorm, and the back door opened. Vanessa looked behind her at the vacant clearing in time to see Underwood scurry into the trees like a rat. She sat, leaned against the cool brick building, and closed her eyes.

CHAPTER 42

Branches scraped the leathery face of Vincent Underwood as he fled through the dense thicket. Saplings slapped his arms and roots reached out to trip him as he bushwhacked through the underbrush. Three hundred yards in, he stopped. Glass tore at the base of his lungs as his diaphragm continued to catch up. After Vanessa's devastating assault to his torso, his body had wanted nothing more than to rest and recover, but his mind had forced it to take flight.

Underwood pressed inward against the bottom three ribs on each side. There was pain, but not to the degree present had one been fractured. He took a moment to orient himself. There were sirens in the distance, undiscernible as police responding to him or fire engines tending the alarm. Both events would result in people milling about the area, and the police would collapse onto the scene. Underwood altered his path north, and headed deeper into the campus.

Moments after Vanessa Washington sat against the building, she had pulled her cell phone from a pocket and dialed 911. She was brief, but laconic.

"My name is Vanessa Washington. My cell number is 718-528-0681. I have been attacked by a man behind Baroody House. I just pulled the fire alarm there, but it was because he attacked me. There is no fire. He ran into the woods. He was wearing jeans and a hoodie, with white shoes."

Just before flipping Underwood over, Vanessa had stared at the shoes. They would haunt her dreams.

Underwood reached the edge of the woods and peered down Eaton Road. A car drove by, and when its lights faded there was no follower. His wind had returned. Underwood considered discarding the hoodie to alter his description, but a middle-aged man walking in a t-shirt would attract attention, and he needed to blend. He stepped out, quickly covered the six feet of grass to the sidewalk, then casually strode east.

Academic buildings passed on both sides, and he reached another intersection. Across from it lay a baseball field, then more woods. Beyond that was the chaotic refuge of the city. As Underwood crossed the street, he saw the approach of a bicycle mounted police officer. He decided to continue walking and as the officer pedaled by, even took a moment to smile and nod, as anyone else on campus would.

Twenty-three-year-old Rob Shine, having graduated from the New Hampshire Criminal Justice Center's part-time officer course three weeks earlier, was proud to be the newest member of the Saint Anselm's College security team. He had been paying attention to his radio and the emergency broadcast about an attack at Baroody House. The person that just walked past him wore jeans and a hooded sweatshirt. He looked over his shoulder to confirm the white shoes, but it was too dark.

Shine stopped and put a foot down. He turned the handlebars, straightened them again, then looked over his shoulder. Finally, he committed.

As he completed the U-turn, the officer called out to Underwood.

"Sir. Hey, Sir. Stop for a moment, please. I need to talk to you."

Underwood slowed his pace to a shuffle, but didn't stop. Shine rode around the front of him, dismounted, and gently pushed the kickstand down with the toe of his shoe. The mechanism was just short of locked open when Vincent Underwood sprang forward and drove his fist into Officer Shine's windpipe, cracking the fragile bones.

The young man gagged as both hands went to his throat. Underwood struck again, smashing his elbow into the defenseless officer's nose. He staggered back as his attacker reached down and removed the expandable baton from his belt with both hands. Grasping the extended end, Underwood swung and crushed it into Shine's temple.

A two second examination permitted Underwood to identify the now-crumpled officer's holster as a Safariland level three device. He quickly pressed the hood out of the way, activated the hidden release, and pulled the weapon free. It was a Glock, no safety to defeat, and he pointed it at Shine's torso. Underwood looked closer and saw the outline of a ballistic vest pressing through the uniform shirt. It would stop the bullet. He raised the muzzle to Shine's head, and took up the trigger slack. He hesitated. The officer lay motionless, blood pouring from a gaping wound just above his ear. Breathing came in labored gurgles. Underwood left him.

Two steps into his escape, Underwood stopped

and returned to the side of his victim. He grasped the leather duty belt and lifted hard, rolling the man to his side. He detached the radio clip and grabbed the extended microphone from his lapel. There was a brief mental struggle, trying to remember if Kimball Road was north or west of his position. He decided it didn't matter.

Underwood pressed the microphone transmit button and said, "Foot pursuit, westbound on Kimball. Suspect is in a light blue jacket."

Underwood walked east, aware that the downed officer lay only meters behind him. When he reached the next intersection, he keyed the radio mic again and said, "Shots fired. Officer shot! I've been shot!"

When he passed the baseball field, Underwood quickened his pace but did not break into a run. Two police cruisers, lights blazing, tore past. After they faded from view, he broke into a jog and ducked down a path that led away from campus. Underwood heard additional sirens, all driving away from him. He dropped the radio into a trashcan.

Five minutes later, emerging from the path, he turned toward a Cumberland Farm's convenience store. A man pumping gas left his car unattended and went into the store. There was a red jacket in the backseat. Underwood swiped it quickly, slid it on, and continued walking.

A few blocks to his left, Underwood saw the overhead sign for Queen City Lanes. It struck his fancy that he had been kicking around the same fifteen city blocks, with the exception of a failed attempt at a bus ride in Concord arranged by Lorraine, and the cops had gotten no closer to him. Their incompetence made him smile.

The levity gave him energy and carried him, fleet of foot, as he disappeared again into the west side of Manchester.

CHAPTER 43

Charlie Wilcox swung the Chevrolet Tahoe off Boylston Street, out of the evening Boston traffic, and into the porte-cochere of the Four Seasons Hotel. It had hardly stopped moving when an attentive young valet popped open the passenger door, then stepped aside. Another attendant approached.

"Good evening, Sir," the doorman said to Jimmy Brennan as he stepped out of the dark SUV. He was a tall, elegant man in his early fifties, dressed in a knee-length overcoat and cap. "Will you be checking in?"

"Sadly, no," Brennan replied. "My colleague will likely have a better idea where we're going."

"Of course," the man said, walking around the driver's side. There, he found Charlie Wilcox engaged in a debate with the valet.

"I'm sorry, Sir," the young man insisted. "But there is simply no parking available in the chute. I would be happy to take it for you, and return it at a moment's notice."

"That won't do, young man. Perhaps I could have a word with your doorman," Charlie offered.

"How can I help," the elegant man said as he came around the front of the vehicle.

Wilcox presented his badge, which the doorman

examined carefully.

"What brings you to Boston, Detective?"

"Business, unfortunately. This is a city vehicle, and I can't have it driven by a civilian."

"I understand, of course." The doorman turned to the valet and issued a series of orders. The boy scurried off in search of the driver of a live-parked limousine in order to have it moved.

"That will take just a few moments. Please secure your vehicle right here and join us inside. Once we have this sorted out you can return and park properly. Could I get you a cup of coffee? Something stronger?"

"That would be very nice, thank you."

With that he led them toward the hotel entrance. Once inside, he raised his hand and snapped loudly. A bellhop scurried over.

"Notify the bell captain that these detectives are my special guests, then show them to the bar," the doorman said. The teenager nodded and gestured Wilcox and Brennan along. As they walked away, Brennan turned to see the doorman jotting something down in a small notebook.

Both men denied a drink but accepted coffee. Ten minutes later a bellhop fetched them, and Brennan waited in the main lobby as Wilcox parked the Tahoe. When he returned, the bell captain walked up to them, a bellhop on his heels.

"Mr. Malone extends his compliments, and hopes your trip down from Manchester was uneventful. He'd like you to join him in the Royal Suite, if that would be convenient."

Brennan smiled at Wilcox, who shrugged.

"Yes, thank you," Brennan said. "That would be

fine."

"Very good," said the captain. "Joshua here will show you the way."

The bellhop led them across the foyer to a bank of elevators. One opened and they entered the marble-floored car, its brass walls polished to mirrors.

Joshua was not used to guests that acknowledged his existence, let alone engaged in conversation. He was at first taken aback, then flattered, by the chatty detectives.

"After BU, what's your plan?" Brennan asked part way through the ride.

"I am applying to law school, Sir. My hope is Northeastern or Harvard. Either would keep me in the city, and I could stay on here part-time."

"Both are respected institutions," Wilcox said. "Good luck to you."

A pleasant bong sounded, indicating their arrival at the sixth floor. Joshua exited first, then led them to the end of the hall. A set of double doors stood ten feet tall, each adorned with the likeness of a heavy, brass crown. Joshua prepared to knock, but Brennan stayed his hand.

"We've got it from here, thank you," he said, pressing a ten-dollar bill into the young man's hand.

"Certainly, Sir. Enjoy your stay." Joshua gave a shallow bow, then turned on his heel and walked away. When he was out of sight, Brennan spoke again.

"If you want, I'll just take the door, then you dump Malone, handcuff him, and I'll call Boston PD to drag him out."

"Now is hardly the time for jokes," said Wilcox.

"You think this is going to work?" Brennan asked.

"To be frank, no. But there is often value in looking into a man's eyes, regardless of the final outcome."

"I just don't like the idea of meeting with Malone like this. The man's a lifelong criminal. He belongs in prison."

"That may very well be," said Wilcox. "But, not today. Try not to agitate him, would you? We are here to ask for his assistance."

"Who, me?" teased Brennan. "Why would *I* ever agitate someone?"

Wilcox raised a skeptical eyebrow, then gestured toward the door. Brennan raised his fist and knocked twice. It was opened immediately.

"Good afternoon, detectives. Welcome," said Ozzy. He was dressed in wide-wale corduroy pants and a cashmere sweater. Ozzy extended his arm sideward and bowed them into the room. "To your left please. Mr. Malone is in the living room."

Wilcox and Brennan entered, in that order. From the foyer, to the right lay a dining room and the residence. To the left, the living room, and both men walked in.

A baby-grand sat in the corner, its glistening black lid resting on a half-prop. Two Marie Antoinette armchairs flanked one of the six floor-to-ceiling windows overlooking Boston Common. Across a low-slung coffee table was Brass Malone, seated on the far end of a Louis XIV style rolled arm sofa.

Malone, dressed in khaki pants, button-down shirt, and tweed blazer, rose to greet them. He shook both men's hands, but held Brennan's a moment longer than appropriate. Their eyes locked, then released.

"You both know Ozzy?" he asked.

"No," Brennan said, extending his hand. Ozzy shook it, then looked at Wilcox.

"How have you been, Charlie?"

"It's been a long time, hasn't it?" said Wilcox.

"Indeed. You can't have much time left, do you?" Ozzy asked, referencing Wilcox's pension.

"I'm eligible next year, but I'll stay on a few more to build the multiplier."

"There are always other employment options," Ozzy said. He looked around the room, then at Malone.

"It's not for me, I suspect," Wilcox offered.

"Maybe for your partner then," Malone interjected. He was seated again, holding a cup of coffee. "I am led to believe Detective Brennan isn't afflicted by the same moral code you are."

"Excuse me?" Brennan said.

"You heard me. It seems lying, cheating, and manipulating are solidly within your skill set," said Malone.

Brennan's face soured.

"The difference of course being that I *pretend* to be a cowering, low-life, scum-sucker, as opposed to truly living like one."

Wilcox touched Brennan's arm and tried, but failed, to catch his eye.

"Does it appear to you that I am living the *low*-life, as you so eloquently put it?" Malone asked, gesturing around the room. "You are a visitor here, and arrived in a Chevy. When Ozzy called the hotel manager yesterday to set this up, they greeted him by name, and sent a Cadillac limousine to be at our disposal."

"And notified Boston PD of your pending arrival, no doubt," said Brennan. "You're marked, known, and far from untouchable. Especially given your most recent address on Valley Street."

"Of course they notified Boston PD, after which two detectives and a lieutenant there called Ozzy, to make sure we knew there was a rat in the Four Seasons. Not much happens down here without my knowledge, you understand."

"So, you're the puppet master," Brennan said full of condescension. "How long do you think that will last? You're old, and tired, and now that you're afraid to get your hands messy, it's only a matter of time before an up-and-comer decides they aren't afraid of getting a little dirty pushing you off the throne."

With that, Malone stood. "Who the fuck do you think you're talking to? How many phone calls do you think I'd have to make to your beloved city to have you writing parking tickets on the overnight shift?"

Wilcox leaned into Brennan and spoke softly. "What happened to not agitating him?"

"There you go again with the string pulling," Brennan pressed. "I call you out as a coward and the best you can do is threaten to make a few phone calls? God forbid you dirty your loafers. Pretty fucking weak, Brass. What would daddy think?"

Ozzy saw the ice in his boss's eyes as the man started around the table. Malone's hand went to the small of his back. Ozzy intercepted him, placed a heavy hand on his shoulder, and held his bicep with the other. His mouth went to Malone's ear and whispered. Then he stepped away. Malone continued to glare at Brennan.

There were six guns in the room, distributed between the hips, waistbands, and ankles of the four men. They all knew the consequences if tempers got the best of one of them.

Malone broke the gaze, and spoke as if the previous two minutes had not transpired.

"Sit please, gentlemen," he said, gesturing to the arm chairs. Ozzy joined Malone on the couch. "My esteemed assistant here has reminded me that you requested this meeting, and that I am being impolite. Please, what can we do for the Manchester police department?"

"We want your brother," Brennan said simply. Ozzy's eyebrows went up, and he looked at Wilcox but remained silent.

"Yes, I know you do. I've seen the news," Malone replied.

Brennan shook his head. "You know what we're asking."

"Yes, I believe I do," Malone said. "But I have no idea where Vincent is, and if I did, I would not tell you. He's family."

"You're shitting me, right? You're going to hang your hat on that? He's an animal," Brennan said.

"Perhaps he is. The two are not mutually exclusive," said Malone.

"Gentlemen, why would Mr. Malone even consider helping you with your problem? There is no benefit to him," asked Ozzy.

"Perhaps to get a 'brag' at the next Rotary Club meeting?" Brennan said. Malone's back stiffened.

"Before we go down another unpleasant conversational path, allow me to simply lay it out for you," Wilcox said. "You are not the only organization with friends in the Hartford, Connecticut police department."

"Meaning what?"

"Meaning Judge Preston Shelbourne's proclivities toward young Asian women who have not yet attained the legal age of maturity is not as well-kept a secret as you had likely hoped."

Malone's eyes flashed to Ozzy, then back to Wilcox. Both detectives caught it.

"That's right, Brass," Brennan said. "You see where we're going with this now? Blackmail leverage is somewhat dependent on the blackmailer being the only one with access to the dirty information."

"And you expect us to believe that if I give up Vincent to you, you'll let our little arrangement with the judge proceed unmolested?" Malone asked.

"Brass," Ozzy said, putting a cautionary hand on Malone's leg. "Maybe we should talk privately for a moment."

"Why bother," Malone said. "We're all honest men here, right Brennan?" He eyed the detective sarcastically. "So, answer me that. You get Vincent and then you'll back off and leave Shelbourne to me?"

"Not exactly," Wilcox explained. "Shelbourne's going to be implicated regardless. The unanswered question is whether that happens before or after you get sentenced to your sweetheart deal."

"Sure," Malone said, frustrated. "Then once the entire scandal comes out, they revoke my sentence and throw the book at me."

"Not if you've been sentenced already, Brass," Ozzy said softly. "Double jeopardy will have attached, so once you're convicted, it's over. There is no 'mysterious scandal' exception to the double jeopardy rule. They would not be able to go after you again."

Malone picked up his mug of coffee and took a sip. He held it in his lap with two hands and looked down at the table, staring into it. After a minute he set the mug down and looked at both men in turn.

"Gents, I think we've got a deal. Just try not to kill the miserable sonofabitch when you bring him in."

"That will largely be up to him," Brennan said.

"Right," Malone said, bile in his voice. "Because we all know the cops *never* set up illegal shootings then set the scene to make it look legit, right?"

At that moment, a young man, dressed in blue jeans and a sweatshirt, walked into the room from the foyer. He carried a tray with a small humidor, cutter, and wooden matches.

"Is now a good time, Mr. Malone?"

"Sure, Frank. C'mon in and meet these gentlemen."

Frank Doran set the tray down on the table, then turned to Wilcox and Brennan. "Good to meet you both."

"Take a good look at the one on the left, Frankie. You'll want to remember his face," Malone said. "Sometimes he tries to pass himself off as a regular hardworking citizen, as opposed to a government hack."

Frank Doran smiled at the men, then walked back through the foyer to a back room. When he was out of earshot, Malone spoke.

"Small world, isn't it, Brennan. We met in jail. Decent kid."

"He killed his best friend trying to buy an ounce of cocaine," Brennan recited lamely.

"And from the time of his arrest to now, he has told you cops exactly jack-shit. Tight lips are a valuable asset. I'm just showing him the ropes, see if there's a place he can fit in."

"Wonderful. An apprenticeship program for the underbelly of the city."

Malone ignored the comment. "I tell you what. I've got another offer for you, since we're all in such an agreeable mood."

He took a cigar from the humidor and rolled it between the thumb and index finger of one hand while reaching for the guillotine with the other.

"For this, you two will get my sentence reduced to time-already-served and a few years' probation. And get the county attorney to reduce the charges on young Mr. Doran as well."

Brennan scoffed. "First of all, you'd have to give up the second gunman on the grassy knoll at the Kennedy assassination to get a deal like that. Second, even if you did, we can't authorize that kind of deal. You know that."

"Then I suggest you make some calls to someone who can. Because I'm about to give you one of your own."

Malone stood up and Ozzy, stunned at the unexpected announcement, did as well.

"Oz and I will excuse ourselves while you make a call."

Wilcox, surprised by the disclosure, exchanged glances with Brennan before addressing Malone.

"If I'm going to call the prosecutor about a deal, we're going to need something more than a vague promise about 'one of our own.'"

Ozzy interrupted the exchange. "Are you sure, Boss? There's value in keeping him."

Malone waved him off dismissively.

"He's run his course. Besides, gamblers by nature take too many chances. And as you said the other day, he's getting sloppy."

Malone turned his attention back to Wilcox.

"I tell you what. You get the prosecutor on the phone and tell him if I get my deal, I'll give you a cop so dirty he has to scrub under his nails after every shift. He might even have something to do with how you got burned, Brennan, and how that sweet little whore of yours got her ass kicked at the gravel pit."

Brennan took a step forward without thinking, then felt Wilcox's hand on his arm. Malone bit down on his unlit cigar, and spoke around it.

"Make your calls, Detective. We'll give you some privacy. Order up some food, if you'd like. The oysters are amazing.

With that, Ozzy and Malone left the room.

CHAPTER 44

By its very nature, trust between partners ran uncommonly deep, and Wilcox and Mollie had been no exception. When there was a betrayal, the shame was just as onerous. Brennan and Wilcox shared few words during the ride back to Manchester.

By the time they pulled into the Brennan family driveway, they had completed the litany of phone calls required by the circumstance in which they found themselves. More notifications would follow, but it was enough for tonight.

After hearing what Ozzy had to say, they had sat, shamed and embarrassed, for an additional forty-five minutes, forced to hammer out a deal with Ozzy and Malone as if they were professional colleagues. The new arrangement would result in both Mollie and Underwood in handcuffs, and Malone walking away with a sentence of time served.

Back in the Tahoe and headed north, Brennan had first called his wife.

"Maybe you and Maggie can go to your mom's for the night," he had said. "Charlie and I need a place to hash a few things out, and we can't do it at the office."

Sarah had been a cop's wife for a long time. She recognized her husband's tone, and had asked only two questions.

"Is anyone hurt?" followed by "Do you still have a job when this gets sorted out."

The answers had been no, and yes, respectively. With that, Sarah packed up Maggie and left for the night. Before departing, she had left a bottle of scotch on the counter and a note that said 'I love you. Be safe.'

Wilcox's phone calls had been less pleasant, and concluded with one to Deputy Chief Lewis Fawcett.

"You've been partnered with this kid eight goddamned months and you had no fucking clue what he was up to? You're one of my best goddamned detectives, Charles. Jesus fucking Christ!"

After the initial shock wore off, Wilcox had answered the DC's questions. Then they had talked logistics. The chief's temper flared a few more times, but Fawcett had come back down to earth and been reasonable. Yes, they were certain it was true. No, Mollie did not know they were on to him. Yes, they have records of Mollie's debt. And finally, no, as far as they knew no one had been killed as a result of Mollie's deception.

"I'm going to let you two run this operation," Fawcett had said. "But you're going to review everything with Lieutenant Pederson in IA. Internal affairs will be part of this, and once Mollie's in custody we'll turn the whole thing over to the state police to investigate."

"Would it be wise, Sir, to have NHSP handle Mollie entirely going forward?" Wilcox had asked, hoping to get far away from the facts and his own guilted doubt.

"How are you sure Malone doesn't have someone in their shop on the take, too?" Fawcett had asked reasonably. "No. You run it, keep IA in the loop, and don't fuck this up. We clean up our own dirty laundry, you hear me?"

There had been a pause as another call rang into Fawcett's cell phone.

"That's the chief. I've got to figure out how to give this to him without him running to the goddamned mayor as soon as we're off the phone. Keep me updated, Wilcox." The deputy chief had hung up before Wilcox could accede.

Despite a vacant house equipped with a comfortably appointed living room and pleasant rec-room in the basement, the two men had not made it past the breakfast bar stools in the kitchen. Each held a stubby, thick-bottomed glass, dark with scotch. Brennan had removed the foil from the fresh bottle when they arrived, and it was now half empty. They had been at it for an hour.

"You're going to have to let that part of this go, Charlie."

"Why is that?" Wilcox asked. "Do I not bear some responsibility?"

"No, you don't. If you wanted to always have your radar up for bad cops, you would have joined IA."

"Unless you took a different oath than I did, we are required to detect, investigate, and make arrests for violations of all statutes, not just the ones conveniently delineated to whichever unit we are currently assigned."

Brennan had been taking a sip of his drink as Wilcox spoke. He felt frustration grow and set the glass down hard, sloshing out a few drops.

"See, that right there is your problem," he muttered. Wilcox looked at him strangely.

"What, pray tell, is my problem?" he asked.

"Christ, Charlie. *That!* Maybe if you didn't think so academically all the time, speak with such deliberate articulation, you could get some of this shit off your chest before it built up on you."

"Just because I don't swear like a sailor and share intimate relations with half the secretarial staff in the city does not mean I don't vent my frustrations other ways. I happen to think it's important to bring a level of sophistication to this job. There is enough dirt circulating and trying to pull us down without willingly inviting it into the house."

Wilcox had gestured toward Brennan at his last comment. The detective, unshaven and dressed in jeans and Timberland boots contrasted sharply with Wilcox's Brooks Brothers ensemble.

"What the hell is that supposed to mean?" Brennan protested.

"Forget it," Wilcox said, waving dismissively.

"Oh, so now we're junior high girls, is that it? You want to have Johnston hand me a note at recess tomorrow explaining why you're upset."

"I'm not certain you're interested in hearing what I meant."

"Try me," Brennan said. It was both a request and a challenge.

"Corruption exists on a scale, Jimmy. It's not all about right and wrong."

"What the hell are you talking about?"

"Have you ever lost sight of a suspect for a few minutes during a surveillance, only to later testify that you had not because you knew it didn't really matter? Perhaps said you saw a hand-to-hand deal that you know for certain happened, but that you actually missed? Or, maybe a little closer to home, have you done a favor for an old friend's daughter and got a young man killed in the process?"

"Listen, don't put your guilt about this Mollie thing on me. You missed it, I didn't. He's not my partner," said Brennan.

"And you don't lie?" Wilcox challenged. "Are you telling me there was any veracity to your explanation to DC Fawcett and Captain Soffit about how that Doran case at the mall unfolded? You came out of that smelling like a rose."

"You can't honestly tell me that's anything like what Mollie has done," Brennan flared. "He sold me out and got Tricky beaten nearly to death. I was doing a favor for a friend."

"Yes, and Mollie kept it all to himself, much like you did with the Frank Doran case," Wilcox said.

"For Christ's sake, Charlie. If you had asked me, I would have told you what happened."

"That is precisely my point. We don't ask. Cops don't ask questions of other cops. We trust each other, especially partners. Our loyalty and forgiveness for things that would otherwise raise eyebrows is broad and generous. When a person places their life into the hands of another, it must be."

"That's a bit dramatic, isn't it?" Brennan asked.

"Perhaps, but you take my point."

There was a pause as both men drank, then Brennan decided to press again.

"Are you going to tell me why you and Ozzy Ostrowski are so chummy?"

"Were you not paying attention to me just now? I said sometimes it's best that we don't ask questions of each other," Wilcox said.

"Yeah, I heard you say that. I also heard you talk about trust."

"Have you any reason to question my integrity now, as we sit here today?" Wilcox asked.

"Of course not."

"Then leave it alone."

"Then again," Brennan said. "After Diaz showed up at the bus station surveillance last week and jacked up Lorraine Underwood, you came up with a bullshit story for us to sell to the bosses pretty quickly in order to cover for her. Is that the kind of 'integrity' you're talking about?"

Wilcox banged his drink down onto the counter. The scotch had warmed him, and his depth perception was off enough to clank the glass hard. He stood and paced.

"Do that again," Wilcox demanded, gesturing toward his near empty glass. Brennan poured an inch-and-a-half into it for the fifth time.

"Have you a cigar in this house?" Wilcox asked.

"Sure," Brennan answered, surprised by the unexpected request. "You want to go out on the deck?"

"No. I want to smoke it here, and you being forced to explain that barbaric decision to your wife will be your penance for hurting my feelings."

Thirty minutes and another drink later, Wilcox leaned forward to tap the ash of his Davidoff Maduro onto one of Sarah Brennan's china teacup saucers.

"In for a penny, in for a pound," Brennan said when he saw Wilcox question the wisdom of his choice of ashtrays. "I'll have it all washed up..."

"...and hopefully ventilated..."

"Yes, and hopefully ventilated, before they get home tomorrow."

"I believe I will retain the services of an Uber," Wilcox said, stumbling a bit on the words.

Brennan laughed out loud. Then, mocking his friend, said, "Shit man. I'm gooned. Better call a taxi."

"Are you implying I am not a proper drunk, and am incapable of sufficiently inarticulate cop-speak?" asked Wilcox.

"Nah, just that you're a classy one. It's probably good for the rest of us. Dresses us up a bit."

"Indeed. And you, perhaps, keep me grounded in the unfortunate reality of our shared vocation."

"I have come to believe that you, in fact, become more snobbish the drunker you get," Brennan said.

"Touché, my friend."

Wilcox finished summoning the Uber in his phone and set it down.

"So, what have we settled tonight, besides that you stock good scotch and fresh cigars, both of which I am pleased to have learned?" Wilcox asked thickly.

"I think we have established that the scales of justice, at least on the street, are in fact that. Scales. And they are fluid rather than binary. We just hope one side is heavier, and use that to resolve our ethical dilemmas."

"You sound downright academic, Detective Brennan."

"Thanks. So, where does that leave us?"

"Unethical and dirty cops are perhaps like obscenity then," said Wilcox. "You can't define it, but you know it when you see it."

"Indeed," Brennan said, smiling. He raised his drink to Wilcox and the men clanked glasses.

CHAPTER 45

Two days later Charlie Wilcox walked into the Manchester police major crime unit in a superbly tailored Burberry glen plaid suit, complete to pocket square. Mirror polished Toga Virilis wingtips grounded the costume, which he had selected in a deliberate attempt to counteract the mushy collection of cobwebs in his brain. He had been up until five o'clock that morning working a surveillance detail he knew was a farce. And he was exhausted.

Brennan sat at Don Mollie's desk where for the previous half hour he had been reviewing a surveillance plan for the next day's operation. The arrangement to arrest Vincent Underwood and Donovan Mollie was actually quite simple. That said, it involved multiple police agencies and an abundance of resources. A litany of bosses was monitoring closely, and it was turning into a circus.

Wilcox obtained a cup of coffee, sweetened it, and walked to his desk.

"How was last night?" Brennan asked.

"As you would suspect. Sitting in a car, feigning niceties with a corrupt felon still wearing a badge, wears on one's psyche," said Wilcox.

"So, it sucked. Is that what you're saying?"

Wilcox managed a smile. "In so many words, yes. It sucked. Where are we?" he asked, gesturing toward the ream of paper in front of Brennan.

"I think we're just about there. We can review it in a moment, but first I need to debrief you on last night. Are you certain Mollie has no idea? You know both his unwitting participation and his ignorance that we're on to him are essential for this operation to succeed."

"The integrity of the plan is secure in that regard," Wilcox said. "To coin a phrase you might appreciate, the arrogant bastard is fucking clueless."

In the days following the revelation of Mollie's corruption, it had become apparent that the most effective way to incriminate him would be to capture him and Underwood simultaneously. The idea had actually been Ozzy's, and it made perfect sense. Malone's organization would arrange for Mollie to deliver twenty thousand dollars to Underwood to aid in his escape. The police would arrest them at the exchange, or shortly thereafter. The evidence against Underwood was already overwhelming. His possession of twenty-thousand in marked bills that had been given to Mollie would add icing to the cake of the growing case against the detective. It would serve to kill two birds with one stone.

Unfortunately for Wilcox, the plan required maintaining the fiction that Mollie and he were still partners, and actively working the case against Underwood. The previous night, the two detectives had conducted surveillance at the bus station, in Manchester this time, based on a fabricated tip that Underwood may appear. It was necessary counterintelligence, fake propaganda aimed at convincing Mollie he was still a trusted member of the team.

After the unsuccessful overnight operation, Mollie had gone home to sleep for the day. Wilcox had napped for two hours, then rose, dressed, and went to work.

Wilcox sat down, squared up to his desk with a steno pad and sharpened pencil, and gestured for Brennan to proceed.

"At twenty-one-hundred hours tomorrow night, all units will be on station. You and I are mobile surveillance. The FBI is sending two teams up from Boston, also both mobile. And IA will have a car out. The state police wanted to contribute a ground team as well but I got Lieutenant Dawson to nix it."

"Why?" Wilcox asked.

"Because, why broaden the circle? I want to make sure we have enough people, but am not really interested in running into any more 'Don Mollie's' that might be out there."

Wilcox nodded, then gestured for him to continue.

"Ozzy set it up for him to meet Mollie in the parking garage at the Bedford Medical Center, just off South River Street. They are meeting at twenty-one-thirty. Ozzy said their meet-ups are usually pretty brief. He'll give Mollie the car with the money in the trunk, then walk out."

Ozzy, under the guise that an unfamiliar vehicle would spook Underwood, had told Mollie he had to use one of the vehicles operated by Malone's crew. Mollie had not questioned the demand. Conveniently, doing so would allow the police to install electronics directly into the vehicle their suspect would be driving.

"Is Bedford PD involved?" Wilcox asked.

"No. Our duty shift commander is going to notify them that we're doing a routine surveillance in their city about a half-hour before it goes down. No details."

"Good."

"Once Mollie has the car, we'll go mobile. I'm guessing he won't have far to travel. We know Underwood is around the city."

"I'm not a big fan of guessing, Jimmy."

"Me neither. But that's where the facts point us. It would have been nice to set it up so that Ozzy brings Underwood directly to us, but then we wouldn't be able to rope Mollie into it. I also don't think Ozzy or Malone would have gone for that. It's a bit too close to home."

"Fair enough," said Wilcox.

"From there it should be routine. We tail Mollie to Underwood, then take them both down after the money exchange."

"Air assets?" asked Wilcox.

"Yes. NHSP will have their helicopter up. The only thing we've told the pilots is that they'll be doing a surveillance of multiple targets, and that there's a tracker in one of the vehicles. They are part of the assets to be on station at the medical center at twenty-one-hundred."

"Tell me more about that," Wilcox said. "The tracker, I mean. We're set for electronics?"

"We should be. Rey Johnston is wiring it up, three different components. First is the tracker. It's the same kind of device pilots use for no-visual instrument flying, except instead of homing in on a stationary airport, they follow a moving object."

Wilcox nodded understanding, but did not interrupt.

"The second piece is a GPS. All the ground surveillance units will have the app on phones so we can see the little blue dot on a map overlay. And it is satellite based, not cell signal, so even if they leave a coverage area, we'll still have them. Third is audio. There will be a microphone in the front seat, back, and one in the trunk, just in case."

"Video?"

"No. The transmittal bandwidth will be too high. There will be a pinhole camera in the rearview mirror recording, but not transmitting. We won't be able to monitor it live, just watch when it's all over."

"Excellent work. You said Johnston is setting up the car?"

"Yeah, he should be done by noon today. We're going to run some tests on it this afternoon before dropping it off to Ozzy."

"How much does he know about the overall case?" Wilcox asked.

"Johnston?"

"Yeah."

"As far as Mollie's involvement? Nothing. I actually wanted to talk to you about that. Rey is sharp as a tack on surveillance. He blends like vanilla flavored water. No one ever sees him. We could really use him on this. And he knows how to keep his mouth shut. I've got him setting up this car, obviously for a surveillance of significant importance, and he hasn't asked me a single question about it."

"You're one-hundred percent on him?"

"Absolutely."

"I heard he's going through a messy divorce," Wilcox said.

Brennan's face hardened as Wilcox's question triggered loyalty to Johnston, his partner. "And?"

"And, that often leads to financial problems, does it not? Significant ones, in many cases. Are there children involved?"

"Wilcox, if every time an officer got divorced he was suspected of corruption, three-quarters of the cops in the country would be out of a job."

"That's a fair point. You've been partnered with him a long time? Have you been to his house? Know his financials?" Wilcox asked.

"Listen to yourself, Charlie. What do you want me to do, subpoena Johnston's bank records before I take him along on a surveillance? Look, I get it. You're still torn up about Mollie and missing the signs, assuming there even were any. But you've got to get past that."

"This is not a play we can afford to foul up," said Wilcox.

"I know. But understand, having Johnston on board reduces the chances of that happening. He's an asset, I'm telling you."

Wilcox leaned back in his chair and crossed his arms. Ten seconds passed as he decided.

"Okay, bring him in,"

"Excellent. I'll fill him in when we do the vehicle test this afternoon."

Brennan shuffled through several pages of the surveillance plan until he reached the tactical support section. There would be eighteen SWAT officers, split between three blacked-out SUV's. Each arrest team consisted of five officers and a sergeant. There was also a mobile sniper element available in a separate car. One

SUV would try to lead the surveillance, setting up at whatever destination seemed likely given the route. The second would follow on, a half mile behind the ground surveillance units. Finally, the third vehicle would stand as ready reserve, prepared to back up any of the teams involved.

That afternoon, while Brennan tested the target car with Johnston, Wilcox walked the document through a litany of required approvals. He reviewed it with the heads of IA, SWAT, major crime, and eventually command. The final step was easiest. Deputy Chief Fawcett was worn ragged after days of engaging in the political machinations that followed the discovery of a dirty cop. He had quickly granted his approval.

"It seems we've dotted the i's and crossed the t's," Wilcox offered.

"All but one," Brennan said. Wilcox looked at him curiously. "Are you going to bring in Diaz?"

"I had considered that, but decided against it. If she knows, she's likely to try and show up. I did see her yesterday, though," said Wilcox.

"And how is our Puerto Rican firebrand?"

"For one, she is probably not a fan of being called our 'Puerto Rican firebrand.'" Wilcox replied.

"Sorry."

"She seemed well, actually. The cast is off her foot, and her arm is freed from restraint as well."

"Good for her. Still on light duty?" asked Brennan.

"Yes, but if there's one thing you can say about Betsy Diaz, she is certainly an effective advocate for herself. She told me the biweekly physical therapy is insufficient to support the rate of recovery she is aiming for. For example, they still will not let her run, and pushups are prohibited."

"Didn't the cast and sling just come off? It's only been what, five weeks since the attack? She's lucky to be alive."

"Yes, about that long. Anyway, I informed her of our plans to arrest Underwood soon."

"You didn't tell her about Mollie, I hope."

"Obviously not," Wilcox said. "I told her there had been developments, and that Underwood's arrest was imminent, nothing more."

"Well, God willing, tomorrow night you can let her know they're both in custody."

CHAPTER 46

Don Mollie was upset. Ozzy Ostrowski was supposed to have met him at nine o'clock that evening at the Bedford Mall, but the man had called at five after and said things didn't look right. He was changing the meet location. It was now going to be at the east end of the top level of the parking garage at the Bedford Medical Center. They'd meet at nine-thirty.

The ruse had been a last-minute alteration to the plan suggested by Rey Johnston. It would serve to keep Mollie back on his heels. Further, if Mollie had clandestine plans of his own, the change would, at best, short circuit his efforts. At worst, he would cancel. Either way, it would prevent Mollie from taking control as the night unfolded.

Lieutenant Frederick Dawson of the major crime unit was in overall command of the operation. He rode in an SUV driven by his sergeant, and would monitor radios that covered four surveillance teams, three tactical trucks, and an ambulance. He would also spend a fair amount of time fending off cell phone calls from bosses demanding up-to-the-minute status reports. In the end he would take credit for the success of the operation, or suffer the consequences of its failure.

Dawson sat calmly in the front passenger seat

of an extended Chevrolet Tahoe. It was unmarked, but festooned with antennae, both three-foot analog whips and four-inch digital spikes. To a keen eye, it was unmistakably a police vehicle. Sergeant Daniel Vallejo, Dawson's second in command, sat in the driver's seat, sipping a Red Bull.

"Danny, get me Wilcox, would you?"

Vallejo silently set down his beverage and manipulated a dial on one of four radio devices mounted in the center console, then picked up the microphone.

"Command-one to Delta-one," he said conversationally.

"Go for one," came the almost instantaneous response. Vallejo looked over to Dawson with a question mark on his face.

"See if he's got an update."

"L-T," Vallejo said to his boss. "Wilcox will tell us when there's anything new to report. We just have to wait."

"Alright, Sarge," Dawson said reasonably. "Then when the deputy chief calls me in five minutes and demands to know when I last asked Wilcox for an update, you can explain that to him."

Vallejo shrugged and pressed the transmit button on his radio mic. "Delta-one, can we get a status update?"

"No, Command. I have no update," came the curt response.

Vallejo set down the microphone and looked at Dawson with a 'told-you-so' expression. The lieutenant's phone rang, and after looking at it, he held it up to his assistant.

"Big fucking shocker. It's the DC," he said.

On the west side of the top level of the parking garage, Wilcox and Brennan sat in a 2015 Subaru Outback.

"For God's sake. Why do bosses do shit like that. He knows we'll tell him when something happens," Brennan said.

"Because everyone has a boss, and you know as well as I do that as we speak the chief is calling the DC for an update, and he's calling Dawson, who will then call us. Until this thing gets rolling, that will continue to happen."

A moment later, Johnston's voice came over the radio. He occupied a one-man surveillance vehicle on the bottom floor. No one knew what he was driving, because he had not told anyone. That was how he liked it.

"Delta-six to all units. I have a visual on Mollie. He's on foot, climbing the stairs."

"Copy that," Brennan said into the radio, sitting erect. Thirty seconds later, peering through binoculars, he watched Don Mollie walk to the vehicle occupied by Ozzy and get in the passenger side.

"The wire is good," Johnston said. "I hear them. Stand by."

Then, sixty seconds later, Johnston transmitted again, "They are talking about the money. It's a good, recorded signal." Then, ten seconds later, "Okay. They're making the vehicle switch. Surveillance units get ready to move."

At the same time as Johnston's transmission, both Ozzy and Mollie emerged from the sedan. The detective walked around and slid into the driver's seat. Ozzy walked off toward the stairwell. Brennan started their car.

"Don't get anxious," Wilcox warned. "We've got the GPS and the air unit. There's no reason to get close and risk blowing this."

Brennan nodded. Mollie pulled out and turned down the ramp. Brennan waited a full minute before he turned to follow. The air unit called out that they were tracking the target both via GPS and visually from five-thousand feet.

"We've got him," they announced confidently. "He's southbound on South River Road."

Brennan coiled down the parking garage ramp to the bottom level. Just before he exited, a non-descript bicyclist pedaled by. Ignoring him, Brennan checked traffic then began to pull out. The cyclist turned and swerved in front of him.

"Hey! Watch it, jackass!" complained Johnston as he smiled from under his bike helmet. The detectives squinted to ensure the identification, then laughed out loud. They had no idea Johnston had been on a bicycle rather than in a car. Wilcox rolled down his window.

"Offer you a ride, Sir?"

"Nah, I'll manage," Johnston said as he pedaled off. Wilcox hit the up button.

"You think he'll catch up?"

"I wouldn't be surprised if he was the first unit on scene wherever we end up," said Brennan, squealing the tires as he turned south.

The New Hampshire state police helicopter, having the most consistent and advantageous visual position, took over calling out the surveillance. It was clear to all the teams when Air-one transmitted due to the muffled thunder of rotor blades spinning in the background.

"Air-one has it," announced the co-pilot, confirming they had a definitive location of the suspect vehicle. "Continuing south. He's got a red ball."

'Red ball' was the vernacular used to indicate a red traffic light. Thirty seconds later the co-pilot spoke again.

"Green ball."

Brennan had turned out of the medical complex and just started trailing the surveillance set when a dark blue Honda Pilot, accelerating hard, overtook him on the left. The vehicle pulled directly in front of him, then braked unexpectedly. Brennan swore as he decelerated. There wasn't space to avoid a collision, so he veered hard to the right, stopping just before the front tires struck the curb. The Honda angled to the right and blocked him in. Brennan's hand went to his gun, then relaxed.

"Oh, you've got to be fucking kidding me," he said once the vehicle's only occupant emerged.

"I can't say I'm particularly surprised," said Wilcox. He lowered his window as Betsy Diaz walked back to them and up onto the curb.

"Hey, fellas. Unlock the back, would you?"

"You're not coming with us," Brennan announced.

"Sure I am," she said smiling. "And the longer you take to agree to that, the further behind you're falling in the surveillance."

"Maybe I just pull away and leave your ass standing here," Brennan said.

"You could do that, but then I'll have to jump back in my car and follow the set visually, without the benefit of radios and the air unit. That means I'll have to get close, and will probably blow your entire plan."

Wilcox turned to Brennan and spoke with a measured voice. "Let her in, Jimmy."

"No way! She's not even cleared for full duty yet, and you want to take her out on this?"

"If she's with us, at least we know what she is up to and can maybe control her. Out there, we have no idea what she's doing. This is the less-bad of several options facing us," Wilcox said.

Brennan shook his head and punched a finger against the unlock button. Diaz yanked the handle and slid into the back seat. She was thrown forward as Brennan spun the tires in reverse to get out from behind Diaz's vehicle, then back again as he accelerated around her car.

"I suppose we'll just leave her car dumped haphazardly on the side of the road like that." Wilcox said.

"She's the fool that parked it that way, and I don't want to lose the set."

Mobile surveillance was one of the most challenging aspects of clandestine police investigations, particularly if the final destination was unknown. They knew Mollie was meeting with Underwood, because that is what Ozzy told him to do. But they had no idea where or under what circumstances. Wilcox had wanted Ozzy to direct that aspect of the meeting as well, but he had refused. If Ozzy had told Mollie where and when to meet Underwood, he would have become suspicious. In the end, Wilcox had agreed, and they decided to do an open-ended mobile surveillance, the hardest kind.

It was likely the meeting would take place in the Manchester area, and that it would happen tonight.

Mollie would not want to drive around in a borrowed car with twenty-thousand dollars in the trunk any longer than necessary. But the fact was he and Underwood could have set the meeting for anywhere in northern New England. The surveillance and arrest plan were tight, but they had to be ready for any contingency.

The agenda called for the air unit to monitor the suspect vehicle directly. The several ground surveillance units would run parallels, following on side streets or highways. They would also leapfrog, taking turns passing the suspect vehicle then turning off or taking highway exits, after which they would catch back up. The strategy was resource intensive, but allowed police to weave a net that would track the suspect while allowing him some freedom of movement within it.

The entire system, once assembled, was referred to as a set. It was tight enough to maintain some semblance of control, but nimble enough to adapt to unpredictable actions by the suspect. At least in theory.

"Dare I ask, Betsy, how it is you knew where we were tonight?" asked Wilcox.

"I don't think you want to know," Diaz said.

"Try me," he said.

Diaz paused in consideration, then said, "To go no further than the three of us?"

"Of course," Wilcox said, then turned to Brennan. "Jimmy?"

"Sure," he muttered, still frustrated with the woman.

"Probably the two professions that talk about their jobs most in an effort to seduce women are cops and pilots. Now, if you find someone that fills both those roles..."

"Jesus Christ," said Brennan. "I think you better stop talking before someone loses their job."

"He merely told me he had a surveillance mission tonight, and that the starting point was the Bedford Medical Park. The fact that I have not been able to get either of you, Johnston, or Mollie to return my texts for the past two days led me to suspect it was related to Underwood. Putting one and one together, I landed here."

Both men spoke in worried unison upon hearing the reference to Don Mollie.

"What did you say to Mollie?" they asked.

"Not much," she said. "That prick doesn't like me anyway. I only texted him after you guys wouldn't respond, and then only once."

Wilcox turned fully and pushed his left shoulder into the seat, so he was facing Diaz.

"Betsaida, I need to know exactly what you texted to him. Can you bring it up on your phone?" The serious measure of his voice was not lost on her.

"Sure, hang on." Diaz scrolled through her phone, then found the text. "Here it is. 'Any movement on Underwood? Wilcox won't call me back,'" she read. "I sent it at ten forty-six PM two days ago. That's all."

Wilcox looked over at Brennan. "That's when Mollie and I were on the false surveillance. It would make sense to Mollie that we would both ignore her. We're probably alright."

Brennan nodded, but kept his eyes on the road.

"What the hell is a false surveillance?" Diaz asked. "Will someone tell me what's going on?"

Brennan nodded again, then Wilcox spoke. He

took five minutes to explain that Don Mollie was a corrupt gambling addict into the mob for almost a hundred-thousand dollars. Tonight, he was delivering twenty-thousand to Underwood, and both would be arrested.

Diaz didn't have time to react before the surveillance went hot again.

"Air-one to all units, he's getting on the highway...293 south...headed around the south end of the city."

Sporadic radio transmissions followed as the ground surveillance teams adjusted their positions to modify the net. The forward tactical team announced they were relocating to a large parking lot between the airport and nearby mall.

"Air-one to all units, he took the very next exit. He's jumping right back off the interstate. Looks like an SDR."

Lt. Dawson's voice commanded the frequency. "All units hold until we get a better idea what he's doing." Brennan pulled off the road into a nearby gas station.

"What's going on," asked Diaz. "SDR?"

"He's doing countersurveillance," Brennan said. "It's probably a surveillance detection route. He'll double back and try to see any repeat cars. He'll look for people making U-turns, an out of place sedan parked in the corner of a lot, that sort of thing."

"And the air unit can tell that just by the way he's driving?" she asked.

Brennan and Wilcox exchanged a worried glance. Diaz caught it, then realized the problem.

"Shit, do you guys think I fucked this up by cutting you off? By getting involved?" she asked.

"You think Mollie saw it?" Brennan asked Wilcox.

"No, but if he's got someone else stationed somewhere and watching for a tail, Underwood maybe, then we might be cooked."

"Dammit guys. I didn't mean to..." Diaz was silenced by Wilcox's raised hand. There was no further comment, and Diaz was forced to sit in her discomfort.

"Air-one to all units, the target has exited the highway and is headed directly for Delta-one at that gas station. I recommend you hold in that parking lot."

"Dammit," Wilcox mumbled. Beginning when Mollie had started his SDR, they had been parked in the corner of the gas station lot. To a citizen, they were indistinguishable from any other family sedan. To the practiced eye of a police detective, the three adults sitting alone in a parked car would appear highly suspicious. They needed to move.

Brennan pulled forward to the pumps. He yanked his hoodie over his head and tugged down the front. He grabbed a nozzle and stuffed it into the side of the car. Wilcox tuned to a country radio station. When Diaz leaned forward to see what he was doing, she was met with a rare, harsh rebuke.

"Sit back, Diaz! Play with your phone or something," he barked.

She obeyed. Five minutes passed, and Brennan got back into the car. If they had been spotted by Mollie, it would already have happened.

"Air-one to all units, the target drove right past Delta-one and turned around again. He's at a red ball, in the turn lane to get back on the highway. Stand by." Then thirty seconds later. "Air-one you can confirm my last. He's on 293, same direction of travel as previous."

"Shall we go for a drive?" Wilcox asked with a smirk. Brennan turned onto the road and accelerated.

"I hope I didn't blow this for you guys," Diaz said. "I just can't sit on my ass at home, knowing people are out here risking their lives to bring Underwood in."

"Shut up, Diaz," Brennan said. "You wanted in on this so you took a chance and risked fucking up our operation. But you're here now and you're on the team, so quit whining and start thinking how you can contribute."

Diaz paused at what first seemed like an insult. As the brief lecture settled over her, she realized it more resembled a family argument, a partner giving another grief, then welcoming her back into the fold.

"Thanks," she said.

"Happy to have you, Diaz," Wilcox added. "But this is the second time you've acted unilaterally on this case, without consideration for how it could result in Underwood escaping. And now with the involvement of Mollie's corruption, the stakes are even higher."

"I get it. I'm sorry."

"But as my esteemed colleague here said, you are now on the team, so stop apologizing and come up with a way to help?"

"You got it."

The surveillance teams monitored Mollie as he traveled south on 293, then took the Brown Avenue exit. The route led directly to the airport and a multitude of industrial parks. Save for a few factories, it was a ghost town at night. A mile down the road, Mollie approached the intersection of Airport Road. His route had been direct and appeared intentional. The detective appeared satisfied with his first and only countersurveillance route.

When Mollie turned onto Airport Road, Lieutenant Dawson began giving commands over the radio.

"Forward tactical unit, post up somewhere near the airport. Team two, stay near the city in case this goes mobile again." Both teams clicked back their acknowledgement.

Brennan broke the silence in their vehicle.

"Looks like it's going to happen at the airport."

"Patience, my friend," cautioned Wilcox.

"Air-one to all units, the target has turned off Airport Road onto Commerce Avenue. He is slowing. Stand by."

Thirty seconds later the helicopter reported that the suspect vehicle had pulled into the public parking lot of the aircraft loading terminal for FedEx shipping. Then, it got worse.

"Security down there has unlocked the access gate for him, and he drove around the aircraft side of the building. We're static now. We have no visual."

As the co-pilot said this, the helicopter flared back into a six-thousand-foot hover. Doing so had momentarily amplified the rotor noise, and the detectives hoped they had misheard what he said. Lieutenant Dawson beat them to the request.

"Command-one to Air-one. Please repeat your last."

"Air-one reporting we are static on station and have no visual. Your target vehicle was last seen headed to the aircraft side of the FedEx hangar."

Sergeant Vallejo leaned over to look at his boss. "L-T, static means they can't move any further. They can't fly over a commercial airport. We're lucky they got as close as they did. They're only about two thousand feet away from the terminal. FCC will be on the phone with the colonel in an hour if they get any closer."

"Shit!" Dawson said needlessly. Then he rattled through each of the surveillance teams and confirmed that no one had visual contact with Mollie or his vehicle. They did, however, still have GPS, and it showed the vehicle had not moved.

"Do we have audio?" Dawson asked.

"Negative," Johnston replied. "We've got a solid signal. There's just nothing being transmitted."

Brennan smiled at Wilcox and said, "I told you Johnston would show up on time to monitor."

Wilcox was listening to Dawson losing his patience on the radio and ignored Brennan. Then, his iPhone rang. When he examined the screen, it was his boss calling directly.

"Yes, Sir?" Wilcox answered. There were no pleasantries.

"Wilcox, am I to understand that we know Mollie is behind FedEx because of the GPS, but we have no audio and we cannot see him? Is that accurate?" Dawson asked in frustration.

"That's nearly correct, Sir. We know the *car* is behind FedEx. The GPS is on the car, not Mollie. We can't confirm *his* location. Other than that, you are correct."

"Jesus, Wilcox. You didn't account for this possibility? Didn't you think he might come to the airport?"

Wilcox had nothing to say, and remained silent.

"Let me get this straight," Dawson railed. "The suspect car has been sitting there stationary for," he glanced at his watch. "four minutes now and we have no fucking clue if Mollie is even in it, or if he took the money and transferred it to another car, or went for a walk, or even got on a goddamned airplane. Meanwhile, I've got thirty cops on overtime sitting around waiting to arrest this asshole, and a frigging helicopter costing the city two-thousand dollars an hour to count shooting stars, since it can't fly over the airport. And we have no way to confirm where Mollie or Underwood actually are. Is that about it?"

"Yes, Sir. That about sums it up," Wilcox said.

"Goddammit!"

CHAPTER 47

The quiet police radio frequency at Manchester Airport did not reflect the chaos that was occurring inside the vehicles of Command-one and Delta-one. The deputy chief was on the phone demanding an update, Dawson wanted options and next steps from Wilcox, and Brennan was trying to get ahold of Johnston to determine if there was activity on the audio transmitter.

None of these efforts was successful.

"On a surveillance like this, how long do you usually wait before doing something?" Diaz asked.

Neither Wilcox nor Brennan answered. Diaz's frustration grew.

"So, we just sit here? It's going on ten minutes. Why don't we just have someone walk in and see what's going on. Put them in a FedEx uniform or something," she said.

The detectives, caught by the simplicity of the suggestion, exchanged a glance. The complex, technology laden surveillance they had laid on had resulted in losing sight of the obvious, and Diaz had brought them back to earth. Brennan picked up his phone and dialed Johnston's number, then put it on speaker.

"Where you at, Rey?" he asked.

"On the bike, between Harvey Road and the

southern runway."

"You're on the airfield? How the hell did you get in there? There's a fifteen-foot fence with razor wire."

"Does that really matter?" Johnston said reasonably. "What do you need, Jimmy?"

"You have any kind of visual?"

"No, but I saw him pull around the back of the building. After that he turned into one of the loading docks. I can't see him anymore. I'm trying to work my way around to a better view but I don't think I'll be able to without crossing the flight line. If I do the tower will see me and this'll get blown."

"Shit," Brennan muttered, then, "Okay. Keep us updated."

"Of course," Johnston said, then hung up.

Wilcox was jotting notes furiously, devising a tentative foot surveillance plan when Johnston came over the main surveillance radio frequency.

"Delta-six to all units, I've got some audio coming out of the vehicle. Stand by."

A few seconds later he continued.

"No voices, but I can hear the sound of doors opening and closing. Three times. Possibly two doors and the trunk. I have no idea if the money was removed or not."

"You think he picked up Underwood?" Diaz asked.

Ignoring her, Brennan looked over at Wilcox, who had stopped writing.

"We probably should have put a separate GPS with the money."

"Indeed," Wilcox said stoically. Things were breaking down fast. He picked up his phone to call Dawson and propose Diaz's foot surveillance plan. As he did the phone's GPS tracking app blinked on. Mollie was moving.

"Air-one to all units, the target vehicle is moving."

"Command-one," Dawson called out. "Is the suspect in the vehicle?"

"This is Delta-six," Johnston answered. "That is unknown at this time. I can't see."

"Command one, is Underwood with him? What is our status?" The frustration in Dawson's voice bled heavily into his radio transmission.

"Air-one has it," the pilot announced, clearing the frequency and demanding air priority. "The suspect vehicle is moving back onto Commerce Avenue, headed west. We have no visual inside the car."

"Who can see?" Dawson demanded, breaking protocol by not identifying himself on the frequency. There was no response.

"Someone has to be able to see inside that fucking car," he said to Sergeant Vallejo.

"Probably not, Sir," Vallejo said. "My guess is they all took up posts around the area in preparation for an arrest, and no one was ready to go mobile. They're all behind the set now."

"Dammit," said Dawson. He keyed the radio mic and called the helicopter.

"Air-one, can you get far enough away to shoot an angle and identify the driver?"

"Negative, Command. We would have to get down around a thousand feet, and I can't do that within a mile of the airport."

"Shit!"

"The suspect vehicle is headed north now on Perimeter Road," said Air-one.

Brennan was steering furiously through an inter-section in an effort to parallel up to the suspect vehicle and get a look at the driver.

"You think he's headed for the highway?" Wilcox asked.

"I would."

Wilcox called Dawson on the phone. It didn't even ring on his end before it was answered.

"What's the plan here, Charlie?"

"I think we should arrest them now, Sir. We have to assume there was some kind of a meeting behind FedEx, and that he was not just doing more countersur-veillance."

"What if it's just Mollie in the car with the money. We're no closer to arresting Underwood, and all we've got Mollie on is some gambling charges. And we will have blown our case."

"That is all true, Sir," Wilcox agreed. "But the facts support the likelihood that some sort of meeting or ex-change occurred, and that Underwood is probably with him in the car. It's worth the risk. Underwood is too dangerous for us to just keep following, and if we don't do it soon this could turn into a pursuit on the high-way."

Dawson quickly weighed the risks, benefits, and possible outcomes, then made a decision. He hung up on Wilcox and keyed his radio microphone.

"Tac-one, coordinate with Air-one for a vehicle assault. Take them now."

"Tac-one copies," came the response from the lead SWAT SUV, followed by "Air-one copies. Your sus-pect is now on Brown Avenue, headed north. What is your time to intercept?"

The sergeant leading tactical element-one looked at the blinking blue dot on his phone overlay, and compared it to his current location. He made a quick plan for a vehicle assault and relayed it to the group.

"Three minutes. We are on a parallel side street and will come up behind him. Tac-two, you come off of Greenleaf Street and run the front unit."

"Tac-two copy."

Tense minutes passed as the two SUV's full of SWAT officers maneuvered into position. Air-one then reported the status of the takedown.

"Air-one to all units. I have Tac-two headed north, suspect vehicle directly behind, and Tac-one behind him. You are approaching Raymond Street."

"Tac-one copy," the SWAT sergeant said into his radio. Then he announced, "We will take him at Raymond Street. This will be a standard rear-side vehicle assault."

The next events unfolded with surprising speed.

At the intersection of Raymond Street, the Tac-two SUV slowed gradually for a yellow light, then the driver slammed on the brakes. The suspect vehicle, which had been following too closely, braked hard and barely avoided a collision.

The driver of Tac-two put his vehicle in reverse and backed up quickly, bumping the front of the suspect vehicle. At the same time, the Tac-one SUV drove up from behind and struck the target with its bumper, hard enough to cause all three vehicles to shake. The suspect car was boxed in.

Immediately, six SWAT officers poured from each vehicle. The first two threw flashbangs onto the roof of the suspect vehicle. The second emerged with a forty-millimeter launcher and fired foam batons into the rear window, shattering it. This occurred at the same time the flashbangs ignited in quick succession, shuddering the car and creating enough concussive energy to disorient any occupants.

Four team members approached the car, two on either side. The first officer slammed a window punch tool into the glass of the front driver window. It shattered into tiny cubes of glass that cascaded down the inside of the door. He reached in, cut the seatbelt with a razor, and yanked open the door. Finally, the officer grabbed a handful of the suspect's hair, tearing them from the vehicle and sending them sprawling across the pavement. Throughout, the second officer on that side kept overwatch with an M4 assault rifle pointed at the suspect.

The exact procedure was repeated on the passenger side, but there was no one there to remove. The back seat was unoccupied. A check of the trunk revealed no additional suspects.

The entire arrest operation lasted just under twenty seconds. The handcuffed suspect was quickly searched for identification, then the lead SWAT supervisor walked calmly to his vehicle and keyed the radio mic.

"Tac-one to Command-one, we have one subject in custody, please advise."

"Give me a name," Dawson ordered.

"Driver's license says Lorraine Underwood, and the photo matches."

"Oh, my God," Dawson said to himself. He keyed the mic again as his heart sank.

"And the money?"

"Not here, Sir."

CHAPTER 48

"Does anyone have any idea where the hell these people are?" asked Dawson.

The question was met with awkward silence. Dawson had summoned all the surveillance units to the UPS distribution center on Pettengill Road, just south of the airport. A variety of family wagons, late model pickup trucks, and innocuous sedans littered the otherwise vacant parking lot. Two SWAT SUV's idled in the corner, waiting to be activated. The third was still at the arrest scene, waiting for a patrol car to take custody of Lorraine Underwood so they could rejoin the others.

Most of the officers, detectives, and troopers involved in the operation stood in small groups near their cars. Dawson had assembled the relevant parties around his command SUV, and he was trying to orchestrate next steps.

"The deputy chief is going to call me any minute to find out what our contingency plan is, and I don't want to have to tell him we don't have one. I need ideas, now. Nothing is off the table."

"Could they have boarded a plane?" Brennan asked.

"With what ticket?" Vallejo said. "All the airlines have been flagged with both names. We would have been notified."

"Snuck on one maybe?" Brennan added, then said, "No way, forget it. Not these days."

"Called a cab maybe? Or an Uber?" a nearby trooper said.

"And we missed that? A cab picking him up?" Wilcox challenged.

"Sure. I mean, maybe they took off on foot, then met someone."

"With six surveillance teams and a goddamned helicopter watching them? Jesus Christ, we're grasping at straws here!" said Dawson.

Diaz was standing next to Brennan. She didn't want to risk getting him and Wilcox in trouble for allowing her to stay, so she touched Brennan's arm before speaking. He looked over, and she asked the question with her eyes.

"Yeah, sure. Anything might help," he said quietly, gesturing to the center of the group.

"Excuse me, Lieutenant?" she began.

"What," Dawson said more harshly than he intended. He shook that off. "Yeah, what is it?"

"Bars, Sir. He runs to bars."

"Okay, sure. Sometimes people run to bars. We'll check those eventually," Dawson said dismissively.

But then Wilcox picked up on Diaz's line of thinking and spoke up.

"L-T, she's got a point. When he first ran from Diaz and Guthman, he ran to Slice of Life Pizza. Despite the name, that place is as much a dive bar as any in the city. And Diaz, if I remember correctly you said in your original statement that Underwood seemed to be running directly there, not just following his feet."

"That's true," Diaz said. "And the bowling alley, too. He went straight to Tully's Bar on Roosevelt after shooting at you guys. That's where he stabbed Shattuck."

"Yeah, and Underwood knew the bartender there, Dave Ester." The comment came from an internal affairs investigator who had been part of the surveillance team and was eavesdropping on them. "I interviewed him as part of the investigation into your shooting. He knew Underwood."

"Okay, good. So let's talk bars," Dawson said, convinced. "Get me some cops here that are assigned to the airport patrol sector. They'll know what is in the area."

"There's no time for that," Wilcox said. "My guess is Underwood and Mollie have already planned their out and are going to be in the wind soon. Worse still, if they saw us take down the mother, then they're on to us and will be running further."

"So, what, Wilcox, we check every friggin' bar in the airport, plus any within a few miles? Walk in, look around, ask questions? That'll take forever, especially on a Friday night."

At that moment, Rey Johnston pedaled into the lot on his bicycle. He waved cheerfully at the SWAT operators in the corner as he rolled past, then stopped at the ring of investigators.

"Hey, guys. How's it going?" he asked with a smile. Brennan fought to suppress a chuckle. Dawson ignored him.

"Wilcox, you and Brennan get a list of the bars within two miles. Vallejo, go coordinate with SWAT. We're going to need them to help on this."

Johnston interrupted and said, "You guys want to

see something cool on my phone?"

"What?" Dawson said in frustration.

"Check this out," Johnston said, holding out the device. He tapped the screen and a poorly lit video appeared. It showed the fuzzy outline of a man walking from behind a building to a nearby car. He appeared to speak to the driver, then walk to the trunk and retrieve something. Then the driver got out and both men walked to a box-truck with FedEx emblazoned on the sides. They got in.

"That looks like Mollie," said Dawson.

"Oh, wait, L-T. There's more," Johnston said as he scrolled to the next clip. Lorraine Underwood appeared on the screen, got into the driver's seat of the sedan, and drove off. Johnston skipped the video forward, and two minutes later, the FedEx truck departed.

"Where did you get that?" Dawson asked.

"Security at FedEx. It's from the surveillance cameras in their back parking lot. They're very accommodating."

"That's fantastic! Tell me they've got a GPS in that truck," the boss demanded.

"Nah, but I got the license plate. New Hampshire 2074531."

"Perfect," Dawson said. "Vallejo, BOL that plate with an armed and dangerous alert. Make sure to put it into the state's LPR database as well. I know not many departments have license plate readers, but we might get lucky. Give it to the toll booth systems as well."

"Yes, Sir."

"Brennan, I still need that list of bars from you two," Dawson continued. Brennan was on the phone and didn't hear him, but Dawson could overhear his end of the conversation. He was speaking with a patrol lieutenant, requesting all uniformed officers in the area look for the FedEx truck, with a special effort near bars. When he got off the phone, he looked at Dawson for instructions.

"Never mind. It sounds like you've got a handle on it. I'm going to stay here with SWAT and keep running the operation. All the surveillance units go help check the bars for that truck."

Wilcox, Brennan, and Diaz walked to their car. Dawson called after them.

"Trooper Diaz. Since you are not actually 'here' right now, maybe you should stay at the command post."

"That's okay, Sir. I'll just go with Brennan and Wilcox. They can drop me off at my apartment while they're checking bars," Diaz said.

"You live nearby?"

Diaz smiled and got into the back seat without responding.

"Don't you live in Concord?" Brennan asked once the doors were closed.

"Yes, I do. If we happen up there while we search, you can drop me off."

Brennan smiled as he popped the car into drive and spun around and out of the parking lot.

Thirty minutes and two bar checks later, they were driving on North Wentworth Avenue when Diaz pointed hard toward the left.

"There it is," she said. All eyes snapped to the side and saw a FedEx truck backed up to one of six loading docks behind EasyGo Warehouse. A UPS truck and a larger eighteen-wheeler were adjacent to it.

"Smart," Brennan said. "Makes it look like they're just making a delivery. Let me swing around to check the plate."

He did, and they confirmed it.

"You want to call it in and get some help to start a ground search?" Brennan asked. "Maybe get some dogs?"

"Before you do that, check the map to see what we've got for bars nearby," Wilcox said.

"Right here," Diaz said, already into the map on her phone. "Pipe Dreams Brew Pub. It's one street over."

Brennan was skeptical. "Charlie, do you think they would stay so close? We're only a few miles from the airport."

"I would if I were them. Better to lay low for a few hours and let the trail grow cold before making an escape. I wouldn't want to be driving around in a stolen FedEx truck with the whole city out looking for it."

"Okay. Let's check it out," Brennan agreed. He drove around the block and pulled into the parking lot of the bar. It was packed with Friday night revelers. The muffled sounds of a live band bled out of the building.

"There are going to be a lot of people in there. Maybe we should call for some help looking," Brennan said.

As they pulled into a parking space, Diaz's eyes widened when she saw Don Mollie standing next to a small group of smokers by the front door. He took a final drag off his butt, stepped on it, then walked back inside.

"Jesus, that was Mollie, with the smokers," she said.

"Are you certain?" asked Wilcox.

"Positive."

The threesome hatched a hasty plan. Wilcox called Lieutenant Dawson directly and informed him of the development. The surveillance teams were scattered and would take time to arrive. SWAT had been redeployed to a domestic dispute with a hostage on the north end of the city. One patrol officer was in the area to respond, and more were on the way.

Wilcox told Dawson that he and Brennan would go inside to monitor until other units arrived. The lieutenant reluctantly agreed.

"Diaz, you're going to have to stay here," Brennan said.

"Are you shitting me? If you think I'm going to sit back while someone else collars this asshole, you're out of your mind."

"Betsy, this is not your call to make," Wilcox said. "You're still recovering from your injuries. No one is questioning your abilities. You got us here. No one's going to forget that."

Diaz sat back and crossed her arms. Both men exited the car.

The smell of perfumed and sweaty millennials washed over the two detectives as they entered the club. The band covered a classic rock song, entertaining several dozen dancers in front of the small stage. A bar stretched to the left, and nearly every one of the twenty stools were occupied. Two waitresses mingled among fifteen tables, trying to keep up.

Vincent Underwood, seated at the far end of the bar, had been monitoring the door. Brennan was an unknown, but he recognized Wilcox immediately. He averted his eyes in an effort to blend, sipped his beer, then set it down and slipped off the stool. He glanced at the door again just as Brennan's scan landed on him. Their eyes met for an instant, then Underwood turned toward the back and walked away.

"Is that him?" Brennan asked, jutting his chin toward the man he had seen. "Gray hoodie with the shaved head."

By that point, the man's back was fully to them, and they couldn't see his face.

"I don't know," Wilcox said. "Height and build look right. And the gait, I'd say. Did you see his face?"

Underwood had mingled into the edge of the dance floor, and they were losing sight of him. Both detectives knew there was likely a door in the back, and that Underwood was about to escape again. Alternatively, it could simply be another patron headed for the bathroom.

"I saw the eyes. I think maybe it's him," Brennan said. Then, decisive action overtook measured consideration. "Fuck it, Charlie. We have to know for sure. Keep your eye on him."

With that, Brennan picked up the half empty beer in front of a man seated at the bar. He held it over his head and yelled an obscenity, just before slamming it down hard onto the floor. It smashed loudly, and every head in the room turned toward him. Every head save one. That man started to run, and both Wilcox and Brennan knew.

CHAPTER 49

As Vincent Underwood bolted for the skinny hall-way that led to the bathrooms at the back of the bar, he drew the Glock from the small of his back and fired reck-lessly behind him. Bargoers scattered for cover as two bullets smashed the mirrored wall behind the bar and a third lodged into the ceiling.

His lack of accuracy was of no consequence as the reckless firing did its job. The mob panicked further, which Underwood knew would clog his pursuers in a throng of rushing bodies and flailing limbs.

Brennan had not ducked at the gunfire. He had seen enough unaimed shooting, both overseas and at home, to know that it rarely hit its intended target. Instead, he ran directly toward Underwood. The suspect was easy to spot now, the only shark swimming straight among a school of twitching minnows.

Wilcox fled the bar through the front door, his intention to run around the back. As he did, he radioed to backup units that Underwood was fleeing out the back.

Underwood reached the back hall and was greeted by a glut of customers cowering by the bathrooms. He stomped, pushed, and leapt his way past, eyeing the overhead emergency exit sign at the end of the hallway. It pointed right. As soon as he rounded the corner, he met a black painted steel door. He kicked the center retention bar and it swung open.

Fresh air met Underwood's lungs as he inhaled deeply. A dull, buzzing sodium light illuminated the back of the business enough to see, but not so much as to blind him. His head swiveled left, then right. He was too slow.

Diaz swung her expandable baton with a two-handed grip, striking Underwood squarely in the chest. He stumbled backward as she stepped into him and delivered another blow, this time to his thigh. Underwood fell to one knee, and his pistol clattered to the pavement. Diaz coiled for a downward strike to his ribs. She rotated hard from the hips, slowing the movement but adding significant force. Underwood raised his left arm and took the blow at his torso. In doing so he wrapped his arm around the baton. He pulled it toward him, taking advantage of Diaz's forward momentum and up-ending her balance. He partially stood and drove a fist toward her jaw, landing a glancing blow that caused her to drop the baton.

Underwood's hand swept the ground behind him for the Glock. He found it, secured a grip, then spun up to where Diaz had been standing. Simultaneously, she had backed away while drawing her own Smith and Wesson .45. Fifteen feet from each other, both combatants fired.

Diaz's first two bullets struck the dirt just in front of Underwood's feet. The third round struck the outside of his thigh, passing all the way through and burrowing a half-inch thick groove through the flesh. After firing, she took two steps to the right and leapt for a stack of empty beer kegs. All four of Underwood's bullets missed, one striking the dirt and three clanking though the metallic barrels.

Wilcox came round the back of the building at the moment Brennan exited the same door Underwood had. Neither had time to assess the unfolding events before Underwood began firing at them. This time his bullets found their mark, and Wilcox went down on both knees, then sat back. Underwood fled around the corner and out of sight.

Brennan ran to his downed partner. Wilcox was conscious and breathing, but did not speak. His eyes were open, if somewhat glazed. Brennan began to paw all over him, trying to find a wound. Diaz came to his side.

"Where's he hit?" she asked.

"I don't know. Help me get his jacket off."

The two struggled to remove Wilcox's dark coat, revealing a gray button-down shirt. The dark colors prevented the detection of red, so Brennan ran his fingers all over the man's torso, feeling for dampness. He found it at the shoulder. Frustrated, he grabbed Wilcox's shirt at both sides of the button placket and tore sideward. The shirt came open revealing a ballistic vest.

"Oh, thank God," Brennan said. "You wore it." He was aware that detectives, out of patrol and accustomed to no longer wearing a ballistic vest on a daily basis, rarely went back to it.

Brennan continued to search for the source of the dampness. He located the place on the vest where two bullets had struck and stopped. Even though they did not penetrate, they had likely broken ribs and caused other trauma sufficient to stop the man.

"Where are you hit," Brennan asked.

"Shoulder," Wilcox said, answering for the first time. Brennan pressed his hand there, and Wilcox winced.

"I'm going after him," Diaz said, standing abruptly.

"No, you're not," yelled Brennan. "Backup's coming."

"He'll slip away by then," she said, frustrated. "I'm not waiting."

With that, she stood and ran toward the corner after Underwood.

Just before Diaz rounded the building, she heard two more gunshots. As she cleared the edge, a uniformed body lay twenty feet away. She ran to it and saw a Manchester patrol officer. A startled look was imprinted on his face, his eyes frozen open. An entrance wound on his left cheek seeped blood, and the back of his head from the ear to the crown was missing.

The officer had been armed with a shotgun. Diaz looked up and saw Underwood loping across a small connector road, his gait slowed by the wound she had given him. She picked up the shotgun and took aim at the fleeing felon, but he disappeared into the darkness before she could fire.

Keeping the gun, a Remington pump-action 870, Diaz ran after him. Her own stride was heavily restricted by residual pain in her ankle. It was the first time she had sprinted hard since surgery, and she felt the screws pulling against bone in her joint. After twenty yards, she was reduced to a hop-skip running style.

Diaz reached the other side of the street, and the gate to a landscaping supply company. There was a dirt driveway, bracketed on one side by three porta-potties and row upon row of palleted paving stones on the other. At the end was a housing trailer set up as an office space, with dump trucks and earth-movers parked adjacent to it.

Diaz looked behind her and heard the distant cries of fear and panic from the bar. There was yelling, and the occasional command that resembled the tenor of a police officer. But there were no blue lights. No sirens. She was unable to determine a likely arrival time for backup, and Underwood was either fleeing further or burrowing deeper with each passing moment.

The action of an 870 could be opened by pressing a small slide release, and Diaz executed that function in order to ensure that a shell was in the chamber and ready to fire. There were six additional buckshot shells on a carrier screwed to the side of the weapon. She tried to push another shell into the magazine tube but couldn't. The gun was fully loaded.

Underwood's unusual stride had left obvious marks in the loose dirt of the driveway, but thirty feet in they were lost in the mix of tire treads and work boots. The massive stacks of stones on the right would provide the best cover, and Underwood would likely hide there. Diaz shouldered the weapon, and stalked cautiously toward the first row. She moved wide to increase the angle of her vision around the pile.

As she approached the first pallet, the sound of gunshots erupted behind her. A bullet struck a stone at eye level, blasting off a chunk of rock that tore into her face. It penetrated skin and fat but did no real damage. A second round missed high, and the third struck the meaty front of her thigh, lodging in the muscle. Heavy doses of adrenaline rushed through Diaz's body and she did not register the pain of the leg wound.

Diaz spun quickly, driving the stock of the shotgun into her shoulder. The front sight landed on a dark figure by the port-a-potties and she fired. Cycling the pump action, a shell ejected, and Diaz fired again, and again. The weapon hammered against her shoulder and threw foot-long flames into night. This pain she felt as the stock pressured her still-healing joint.

The first round of shotgun pellets tore through Underwood's calf, pulling muscle from bone. He half-jumped, half-fell to the right, heaving his body behind a plastic toilet. The next two blasts punched holes into the corner of the small structure exactly where Underwood had fled. Diaz was certain she had hit him.

Fumbling with fingers made fat by adrenaline, Diaz pulled additional shells from the side mounted carrier on the 870. Reloading fast, she stuffed them into the magazine tube, then planted the weapon into her shoulder again. The choices were to wait behind cover for Underwood to come for her, or advance.

She had been chasing the man long enough. Diaz decided to take the fight to him.

Underwood crouched behind the center of three toilets. He looked at the weapon in his hand and ejected the magazine. It was empty. He pulled the slide back an inch and angled it to look into the chamber. There was one round. He would have to make it count.

Underwood could hear the woman's shuffle-steps as she crossed the open area on her injured legs. He decided to wait until she rounded the edge of the small structures. He would have to time it perfectly.

Diaz advanced, shotgun at the ready. Blood

throbbed through her temples, forcing her eyes to squint. The muzzle of her weapon rose and fell with each step. She arrived at the row, and began to ease around the first corner.

Gunfire erupted two feet to her left, blinding her. Underwood had come around the opposite side of the plastic structures and stood a mere four feet away. His bullet tore through her ear but missed her skull. Diaz's shotgun was pointed the wrong direction so she swung it as a club, striking the man's arm. He grasped the barrel and pointed the weapon downward. It discharged, and sent dirt and rocks across the lot.

Diaz released the shotgun and drew her pistol, but before she could bring it to bear, Underwood drove a fist toward her throat. Diaz knew that in any fight, protecting the neck was paramount and she lowered her chin. His fist struck her jaw, setting it back painfully and knocking out a tooth. He followed the move with a hard kick to the chest, and Diaz sailed backward, dropping her handgun. She sprawled onto her back.

Diaz swept her arm wildly in search of any weapon. Her hand found a fist-sized rock. Underwood moved to kneel on her chest and she swung upward, smashing the stone against his head. He stood and staggered back.

Diaz found the shotgun by her leg and picked it up. She aimed blindly and pulled the trigger, but it did not fire. The weapon's action had not been cycled after the last shell was fired into the dirt. Underwood regained his composure and stomped forward, crushing Diaz's already injured ankle under his boot.

The pain was tremendous as the steel plate in Diaz's ankle was torn from the bone. She yanked the shotgun slide rearward, then slammed it home, chambering a shell. She pressed the trigger and the weapon boomed. Unsupported by anything behind the stock, it tried to tear itself from her hands. She held on. Cycling the action again and again she fired until the weapon was empty.

The flashes of gunfire temporarily blinded her, and Diaz didn't know if her shots had found their mark. Her eyes adjusted slowly as she limped up onto one foot. The other ankle was unable to support any weight on shattered bone and torn muscle. She stuffed more shells into the shotgun magazine, and scuffed herself forward.

Diaz saw a figure slumped against a wall of plastic. Its torso was leaning awkwardly, the chest violently torn open. The left side of the head was destroyed, but the right side held the unmistakably evil eye of Vincent Underwood.

CHAPTER 50

"I don't think you should get it fixed. It's a good look for you, kind of bad-ass," teased Brennan.

Betsy Diaz was sitting in a chair at Don Mollie's former desk, absentmindedly fiddling with the gap Underwood had given her by knocking out a tooth. The adjacent one had been chipped.

"Thanks a bunch," she said, lowering her hand. She reached for a coffee mug on the desk and caught the eye of Charlie Wilcox, seated at his desk across from her.

The strap of a sling dug into his shoulder, and Wilcox tugged on it awkwardly as he adjusted his arm. Underwood's bullet had penetrated the upper part of his chest on the far-right side, damaging muscle and breaking his collar bone but missing anything vital. The rounds that struck his ballistic vest had been stopped, but nevertheless transferred their energy to his body. Two ribs had been cracked, and his liver was bruised.

"So, what happens now?" she asked, looking at Wilcox. "You just work your next case and he goes back to being a street hoodlum?" Diaz jerked her thumb sideways toward Brennan, who sat on a nearby stool.

"Actually, starting next week I'll be a respectable, well dressed detective again, much like you two esteemed investigators," Brennan said.

"You sound just like him," said Johnston as he walked into the room and pointed at Wilcox. "Before we know it, you'll be eating with silverware and peeing indoors."

"Oh, I don't think I'd go that far," said Wilcox.

"How was court?" Diaz asked.

"They held Mollie on a half-million cash bail," said Johnston. "The judge said if even half the charges he is facing are true, he's looking at a couple decades in prison. The fact that we found ten of the twenty-thousand on him and the other half on Underwood's body didn't help his case much."

"Today was just the arraignment, right? When is his next court date?" Brennan asked.

"I don't know. Our internal affairs unit and the state police still have a lot of work to do, but the case is rock solid. He gave the whole thing up during his interrogation."

"Really?" Diaz asked.

"Yeah," Johnston continued. "After they found him hiding in a bathroom stall at Pipe Dreams Brewery he wouldn't shut up. Between his confession and the data linking his phone to the one Underwood was using, there is more than enough evidence. I don't even think they'll need to use the material Brass Malone and Ozzy gave you guys."

"What happens to him, then. Malone just gets a walk?" asked Diaz.

"Pretty much, yeah," Brennan piped in. "That was the deal. We had to make a judgement call. Or the prosecutor did, rather. Underwood was on the run, hurting people and terrorizing the city. He had to go down, even if it meant letting Malone slide."

"The Feds have been after Malone for years. They must have been pissed he skated on those gun charges," said Diaz.

"They'll get another opportunity," said Wilcox. "I doubt his newfound cooperative relationship with Manchester PD has set him on the straight and narrow."

"Not likely," said Brennan.

"Rey, are you going to join your partner here and return to the world of reputable policing?" asked Wilcox.

"Nah, someone's got to keep a finger on the pulse of society's underbelly."

"Rey likes to keep his dirty little secrets," Brennan said as if the man weren't in the room. "He doesn't like people to know too much about what he's up to."

"Yeah, like during the surveillance," added Diaz. "How the hell did you travel four miles from the parking garage to the airport on a bicycle faster than we all did in cars?"

Johnston smiled and bit his lips together, then twisted his fingers in front of them and tossed sideward, as if securing a lock and tossing the key.

"And last but not least, the intrepid, if somewhat impulsive, Detective Trooper Betsaida Diaz. What are your plans, young lady?" asked Wilcox.

"Yeah, Bets, how about it. You looking for a new job?" Brennan added, gesturing around the office.

"I don't think so, fellas. If I came on the job with Manchester PD, I'd have to spend five years in the patrol division pushing a cruiser around the city before I was even eligible to apply as a detective. No thanks."

"Oh, c'mon," said Johnston. "I'm sure there's some way around that."

"Well," Diaz said. "If I've learned anything during my time riding with you three, there are not many rules for which you haven't found a workaround."

ABOUT THE AUTHOR

Mark Carignan

Mark has been a police officer since 1996, working as a street cop, undercover detective, and supervisor. Early mornings he can be found hiking with his dog Charlie while planning his next novel. Mark is a strong advocate for first responder resiliency and wellness, and donates a portion of his profits to post-trauma recovery programs.

Follow on Instagram and Twitter @MarkCBooks. Send feedback or drop a line to say hello MarkCBooks@gmail.com

Made in the USA
Middletown, DE
31 December 2021